BY THE BALLS: THE COMPLETE COLLECTION

BY THE BALLS

THE COMPLETE COLLECTION

JIM PASCOE & TOM FASSBENDER

ILLUSTRATIONS BY PAUL POPE

AKASHIC BOOKS

Published by Akashic Books
Text ©2013 Jim Pascoe & Tom Fassbender
Illustrations ©2013 Paul Pope, except pages 256, 258–260, art ©2013 Paul Lee (originally published by Dark Horse Comics in *Dark Horse Extra*)

ISBN-13: 978-1-61775-159-2
Library of Congress Control Number: 2012954509

Printed in Canada

Akashic Books
PO Box 1456
New York, NY 10009
info@akashicbooks.com
www.akashicbooks.com

TABLE OF CONTENTS

THE TRUE HISTORY OF
BY THE BALLS
AND THE BIRTH OF
UGLYTOWN

an introduction

It all started with an idea, a bold idea, a youthful punk rock idea that we believed with all our might. The idea that we were right and everyone else was wrong.

Let's back up a bit.

We met each other at the beginning of the 1990s while attending various comic book conventions and trade shows. At the end of these events, it always seemed that we were the last two standing, long after last call came and went. Fueled by adrenaline and a few drinks, we would talk about what was wrong with comics, what was wrong with books and publishing, and how everything would be better—at least a little bit better—if only someone would listen to us. We had the answers. We knew it. Not a single doubt in our minds.

What we needed was a plan, a path of action. Once you've identified your solution as "if only someone would listen to us," the next step is clear: find someone who will listen, preferably someone with money.

Around this same time, a new entertainment conglomerate sprung up. Its name: DreamWorks SKG, formed by the power trio of Steven Spielberg, Jeffrey Katzenberg, and David Geffen.

We began assembling a proposal. We crunched numbers, put

together spreadsheets, did competitive analyses on existing content producers. When we were happy with the results, we printed three copies and FedEx'd them individually to Spielberg, Katzenberg, and Geffen along with a cover letter that said essentially: *Enclosed is confidential material. For the eyes of the recipient only.*

Then we waited. One week. Two weeks.

No response. Time to follow up. We picked up the phone, dialed Universal Studios, and asked to speak with Steven Spielberg. We did that two more times. Two of the three calls we made were pretty unsuccessful. But the call to Jeffrey Katzenberg got us talking to his lovely assistant. She said she had received our proposal, but Mr. Katzenberg hadn't had time to review it. Could we call back?

You bet.

We called back every few weeks to check in. Mr. Katzenberg was a very busy man. Eventually a letter arrived to our attention.

Dear Mr. Fassbender and Mr. Pascoe, thank you for your proposal. We are not interested at this time.

Something like that. We forget exactly. We threw it away.

We called back immediately. "Hello. We have received your letter. We would be happy to schedule that meeting at your earliest convenience."

"Um, the letter we sent you was a rejection letter."

"We realize that. And we look forward to discussing your feedback in a face-to-face meeting. That way when you are ready to go ahead with what we are proposing, we will have adjusted the plan to your liking and you will have two partners ready to execute."

Two months later we had a meeting at DreamWorks.

The content of that proposal was something we had been thinking about for a while. It started with what we thought was a simple, self-evident truth: all great entertainment successes are based on great stories. Hopefully you're nodding your head right now. A no-brainer, you might be thinking. But it's sad how our experience showed that the industry did not think like you.

A few years prior, when we had first started working together, we were pitching ourselves as storytellers. We had decided to spend the money to go to the Toronto Film Festival because there was a film production trade show attached to it and we had somehow managed to acquire VIP passes. The registration form that we were gleefully filling out asked for a company name.

We could have put down anything. But we took this seriously. We took everything very seriously. We needed something that would get people's attention, something like . . . UglyTown. We laughed. We started a list. Every name we came up with got measured against UglyTown. None felt as right.

When we arrived in Toronto, with our suits and slicked-back hair, we picked up badges that said: *UglyTown Productions, Hollywood.*

Let's just say that the combination of UglyTown + production + Hollywood + suits made us the most popular guys in the room. It was unreal. We had folks stop their conversations mid-sentence just to lean over and introduce themselves to us. They invited us to after-parties. When they asked us for business cards, we told them we already ran out. "It's been a great show so far."

Then they asked us what we did.

"We're storytellers. Anything that needs a story, we can write."

Huh?

The responses fell into two categories: 1. Screenwriters can't write TV. And vice versa. You have to pick a specialty and stick to it; 2. What have you done? And more importantly, what have you done that I've already seen and liked?

Ultimately we left the show disappointed. We also left with a plan: If people wanted to see what we'd done, we would show them. We would create a multimedia property that showcased our ability to write for film, for the web, for print.

That project was called *The Red Hat.* It was the story of Dashiell Loveless.

The meeting at DreamWorks was not with Jeffrey Katzenberg (or the other two big wigs for that matter). We met with a room full of executives from the just-launched animation studio. It took place on one of the top floors of the Texaco building in Universal City. It felt magnificent.

We pitched them a fourth division of the company. Joining the film, music, and animation teams would be a print division, run by the two of us. We asked for enormous salaries; although, in retrospect, while it was probably three times what we were making at the time, it was probably a third of what a position like that should have demanded. The centerpiece of the proposal was the creation of a magazine, modeled after *Disney Adventures*, which would promote new stories while leveraging the characters the other divisions were creating. The magazine would be called *UglyTown*.

They asked a lot of questions. We answered confidently. We pulled no punches.

And at the end of the meeting, they said the most amazing thing.

While they had no intention of starting a print division, as they had stated in their original rejection letter, they liked us, liked what we had to say. Plus, though still early in the process, they were looking for a publishing partner.

This was their offer: if you two can build a team and secure an established publishing/distribution partner, we will give you the DreamWorks license to create comics and stories using our characters.

Perhaps what we should have done was taken this tentative commitment, redrafted our proposal, sought out investment money, and then headed off to do a dog-and-pony tour of New York in search of an existing publishing company to partner with. But we were young—young men of action. Starting a publishing venture meant *doing* something. Something exciting.

We still had this idea for *The Red Hat* kicking around. The story we had come up with involved a hapless pulp writer named Dashiell Loveless who wrote a surprise best seller titled *By the Balls: A Bowling Alley Murder Mystery*. Taken aback by its success, poor Dashiell faced the dreaded sophomore slump and had no idea how to follow up his first novel. He was out of ideas. Then an article about a murder in the *Los Angeles Times* got him thinking: *If I start investigating this murder myself and find some answers, I can use this as the plot for my next book.*

This led our man into the dark, downward spiral of a noir world. Once in, he couldn't pull himself out.

We liked this idea, but as young writers, we couldn't figure out how to pull *ourselves* out or how to break this story. We couldn't figure out who Dashiell Loveless *was*.

Then came the idea that would change our lives forever: Let's write Dashiell Loveless's first book, *By the Balls*. It would serve as a character study for the fictional Loveless. We could get our up-and-coming cartoonist friend Paul Pope to illustrate it. Which meant that we could print it and sell it to his fans. During this process we would be able to figure out all of the ins and outs of publishing, which meant that we could go back to DreamWorks with a publishing company established, distribution partners attached, and a physical product to show. We would win. Easy.

We thought of it as a big business card. It would prove that we could do it, whatever *it* was.

We announced *By the Balls* in February of 1998 as an online web serial. We wrote it in the spirit of old pulp writers—often drunk and pounding the keys, struggling to make our weekly deadlines. We made it up as we went along. We tried to outdo each other. Our goal wasn't to write something good . . . it was to write something *fun*. And fast. And it set us free.

We thought we knew everything. We knew nothing. We worked around the clock. We figured things out as best we could.

In July of that same year, in time for Comic-Con in San Diego, we published *By the Balls*. We got cartoonist Don Simpson to hand draw the title treatment. We worked with cartoonist Jay Stephens to design the UglyTown logo. And just like that, UglyTown was real. We printed five thousand copies of that book. Sold them for the ridiculously low price of $5.95.

We had our detractors, of course. The old guard. The tired, stale, do-business-as-it's-always-been-done types. Those who sneered, saying patronizing things. "Oh, cute. A trade paperback in mass market format . . . interesting choice." Whatever. We ignored them. Get on board or get left behind.

The distributor orders came in. We sold just 338 of them.

We didn't care. We made a book. A book! It was intoxicating, addictive. We were ready for the next step.

We flew to New York, eager to talk up a possible deal with DreamWorks now that we were real publishers. But no one cared about some flighty DreamWorks thing. Everyone wanted to talk about *By the Balls*.

During lunch with Calvin Reid, a reporter from *Publishers Weekly*, the next step started to come to focus. He'd read the book, and wanted to write an article for *PW*. We were ready for the hard questions. All except for one: "When does the next book come out?"

The next book? What next book? Dashiell Loveless only wrote one book!

You can have all the plans in the world, but once you've experienced the ecstasy of having someone read what you've written and then ask for more, well, there is no turning back.

We came up with *Five Shots and a Funeral*—the title and a loose outline of the five short stories that would make up the book—on the plane ride back to Los Angeles. We made it a prequel consisting of shorts because that made the most sense within the mythology of Dashiell Loveless we had created—even though *no one* knew anything about him or his story.

UglyTown grew a lot over the next decade. Other people started to move in. Talented newcomers like Sean Doolittle, Victor Gischler, Curt Colbert, and Brett Battles looking for a break. Established veterans like Gary Phillips, Nathan Walpow, and Eddie Muller looking for something new.

Other industry types noticed us and liked what we were doing. We got serious distribution. We got publishing cred. We got imitated.

As we strove to publish four books a year (that was the goal at least), we got offered the chance to write comics based on *Buffy the Vampire Slayer*. That gig came our way after an editor took a liking to *By the Balls*. So it turned out that the big business card worked.

All of that meant less and less time for Ben Drake, the hardboiled PI we created for those first books. We wrote a few stories for some small magazines, but even by the early 2000s the perfect partnership of Fassbender/Pascoe was starting to strain under the pressure and the work.

Then our distributor filed Chapter 11. We got another one. They filed Chapter 7.

Despite our seemingly tremendous success, losing tens of thousands of dollars sucked.

So we did one final rock star move. We disappeared.

We tried to take care of as many people as possible. Truth is, some people got hurt. A lot of people didn't get paid. Maybe we could have sold UglyTown to a larger publisher. But we had long ago realized that UglyTown owned by DreamWorks wasn't really a good idea. A lot of folks would have loved an UglyTown imprint at a major New York company. Just not us. We did our thing, we did it our way. We were done. Better to burn out than fade away.

Although . . . some things don't die. They won't stay down. Through the years, we remained humbled by the love people continued to express about all that we achieved during those crazy UglyTown days.

At some point we looked up and realized that 2013 would mean fifteen years had passed since we launched *By the Balls* on an unsuspecting public.

And we thought, you know, publishing needs a good kick in the balls now.

With the help of a true rock star, Johnny Temple, and his amazing team at Akashic, we have collected all of the writing of the fictional Dashiell Loveless. We have arranged the stories in their narrative chronological order, along with new opening and closing stories, which represent the first Pascoe and Fassbender writing collaboration in over ten years.

Who knows how long we'll stay this time? For now, it's good to be back.

Jim Pascoe and Tom Fassbender
Los Angeles
January 2013

FIREPROOF

(2013)

I smelled like smoke and sweat, like I usually did after a fire. My wife was used to it—as much as anyone could be—but this morning was different. She knew there was something else hanging over me. The stench of death.

She kissed me. "Mm. Good morning."

I could have kept kissing her, just standing there, despite how exhausted I felt. But I knew I stunk something bad. A shower would probably be best for both of us.

"You're up early," I said as I unbuttoned my shirt, got my arms out of it, then pulled the stained ribbed T-shirt over my head.

"Insomnia again. Must be the heat." She sat down at the table where she had set her coffee cup. "Thought I would get up and read a bit while I waited for you."

My body slumped against the bathroom doorjamb, partially because I didn't want to walk away from my wife while she was talking, but mostly because my muscles were ready to give up.

"It was a tough one, yeah?" she asked.

I exhaled the tension as it all came back to me. "We found a body. Man in his thirties, probably. Hard to tell. He was charcoal. Well, mostly, anyway."

She let that hang in the air a bit. She was a firefighter's wife, well familiar with the horror stories I brought home. She didn't like 'em.

And even though I'd developed a stomach for them, I didn't like them either.

"Found him in a bathtub. I had been following the burn, trying to contain it. Forgot the plan: evacuate, isolate, terminate. I should have found that guy sooner. There might have been a chance. At least Kenny Shrubb wasn't handling the sweep. Boy is so gung-ho about fighting fire, he can't see the details. That body would probably still be in the tub."

She came over to me to rub my back, rough with ash. "You were doing your job. I'm sure you did everything you could."

"My job is to put out fires, and I put it out. That won't make me sleep any easier. Plus I had a bad run-in with the police, these two detectives who said the most ridiculous . . ." I pinched the bridge of my nose with my hand like I was trying to deflate a giant beach ball. "You know, never mind. I've laid too much of the job on you. Get back to your book and your coffee. I'm going to let a bunch of water pour over me."

"Wash away the sadness and stress of Testacy City. Think about Los Angeles."

I smiled. "Was it really only last week? Christ, it feels like forever ago already."

"Don't let it get away. It could be ours, Benny. A new city, a new life." She looked down and pulled a strand of hair behind her ear. "A new everything."

The energy came to me to go over and kiss her on her beautiful forehead. I stumbled back into the bathroom and twisted the shower handle. The hot water came down.

But I couldn't wash out the memory of those two cops.

"Hey, soldier, get over here!" Sweat beaded up on the forehead of the meaty cop with the crewcut. It was still hot in there, even though the fire was out.

I took my helmet off, went over to the plainclothes. His partner was playing the silent type, hanging back, smoking a cigarette. I addressed the loud one: "I'm not a soldier. If there's a problem, I'd be happy to help you boys."

"Want to talk to you about this body you found. Heard you were talking to your buddies about some foul play. Why don't you give me a little bit of your story time?"

I remember thinking that these guys were early on the scene. The inspector hadn't even arrived yet.

"Sorry if you think I'm telling tales out of school. I know I'm not the one who gets to make the call, but that guy I found in the bathtub looked suspicious to me."

"Okay, soldier, let me stop you right there." He pulled a slim wallet out of the inside pocket of his coat and flashed a badge my way, like I didn't know he was a cop. "Name's Brockman. Detective Brockman. That good-looking guy behind me, that's Detective Weisnecki. Hey, when I say 'good-looking,' that's just a choice of words, nothing weird. Mark's not my type, are you, Mark?"

Brockman stuffed the wallet back into his coat, barely pausing to give Weisnecki a chance to respond. Which was fine. Weisnecki had nothing to say.

"Anywho, let's cut to the chase. What we're looking at here is an accident. Smoke inhalation. Nasty way to die. But maybe that's a good reason not to be in a damn bathtub when your building's on fire. Ha!"

"Look, detective, I know it's hard to tell with the condition the body's in, but I've seen more than a few like that, and I gotta say, what isn't burned looks . . . beaten. As in, severely beaten."

Brockman crumpled his face in something that was probably meant to be a smile. It wasn't.

"That's pretty observant. What's your name?"

"Ben Drake."

"Drake, you a fire inspector?"

"No."

"You a medical examiner?"

"No."

"Then you don't know a damn thing. Repeat after me: smoke inhalation. Now get the hell out of my crime scene."

I had to laugh. "If this fire and this death are all one big accident, what makes this a crime scene?"

"Soldier, this whole town is a crime scene."

I woke up in the late afternoon. Even though I had taken a shower right before I passed out, I took another. The heat wasn't being particularly kind, and while the night would bring a temporary chill to the air, I had to rid myself of the sweltering grip of the desert.

Testacy City was always hot, but this was the time of year when the heat really settled in. Fires started easily and fought back hard when we tried to put them out. The jokers on the nightly news called it "fire season." None of us at the station liked that.

I put on a fresh-pressed shirt and a dark gray suit. I straightened my tie in the round mirror by the door and grabbed my hat on the way out. If you asked my wife, she would tell you I dressed like a slob when she met me. Actually, she wouldn't be so blunt, but that's the truth of it. I wore whatever I could find from the pile on the floor. Though the worst of it were my shoes. A true embarrassment. But in a way, I owe my marriage to those bad shoes.

I had been drinking at this joint off of Cherry Boulevard. I saw her the moment she waltzed in and couldn't stop eyeing her. She looked like a movie star who'd walked right off the silver screen. She wasn't overly glitzy, wasn't wearing anything super fancy. Nevertheless, wherever she moved, the lights moved with her.

She moved over to me.

We talked a bit, the standard flirty back-and-forth. I thought I had been doing pretty well, at least holding my own with her smart, dry wit. I made her guess what I did for a living. She got firefighter on her second try. I went round and round before she had to tell me that she was a graduate student studying epistemology. I told her I was impressed. She laughed at me.

I was building up the nerve to ask her out, when she fidgeted, ready to return to her friends. I stammered out a few words, sounding no better than a car with a bad carburetor.

She reached for my shoulder. It instantly calmed me, though my heart was in my throat.

"Benny—I can call you Benny, yeah?"

I couldn't speak.

"Benny, you're mighty handsome. And I dare say you're built better than most men in this sad, sleazy town. But if you're going to see me again, you can't wear those shoes."

I looked down to the beat-up tennis shoes I had on. I had never even played tennis.

She went on: "I could tell you something like 'good shoes always class up a bad outfit,' but I think you're ready to hear the real truth."

Somehow I managed to take a breath. "Go on."

"All of our actions define us. Everything we choose. Everything we choose not to choose. We all like to think we can make the correct choice between right and wrong when faced with something big. But what really defines us is our ability to make the right choice on all the small things."

My mouth was dry; my head, in a fog. I knew right then I was in love.

A week later I saw her again in the same bar. I was wearing polished oxfords. She gave me her number that night. And all this time later, she'd never again mentioned my shoes.

If only I could keep warm thoughts of my lovely wife in my head instead of images of a burned-up body. That's what haunted my mind when I walked into the H.M.S. Pandora. The first person I saw was my friend Harper "Pappy" Meriwether, seated in his regular spot at the far corner of the bar. He chose this seat so he could keep an eye on all the action. The second thing I saw was a drink on the bar in front of the empty stool next to him. He was a good friend.

"What's wrong, my boy?" Pappy sipped at his gin.

I dropped onto the stool next to him and picked up my drink. The Pandora's air conditioner was on the fritz, and a single, tiny ice cube floated in the glass, fighting the heat. Fighting, and losing. "Nothing. Had a long shift yesterday, but I slept it all off. Nothing to worry about."

"Listen, Ben. You can't lie to a detective." He tapped his long, narrow nose. "This thing can smell a lie a mile away, and you started stinking up the place the moment you walked through that door. Now level with me."

I inhaled a deep breath and blew it out of my nostrils. Pappy was good, better than a shrink. "All right. This fire I worked last night? It's been eating at me. I found a body, and I'm second-guessing myself. I hate losing someone. I always feel like I could have done more."

"You should stop thinking like that, Ben. That road will only lead to disappointment. I know you, and I am certain you did everything you could have done."

"But there's more to it than that. Something about the whole thing isn't right. I just can't figure it out. It's like looking at an unfinished puzzle made with pieces from two different boxes. You hear anything about this case?"

I felt a little silly asking, because I knew he'd have an answer. In addition to working at the Always Reddy Detective Agency, Pappy made a habit of picking whatever gossip he could off the grapevine. There wasn't much that went on in this town Pappy didn't know about.

"It so happens I do know something about the case. I know the gentleman you found went by the name of Moshi Scavone. Business owner, married, no kids."

The fact that he was married made me wince, thinking of my own wife. What if she found my body burned beyond recognition? I didn't want to imagine her pain. I tried my best to ignore it.

"Drake! You're here!" A loud voice from the other side of the bar helped me push the bad thoughts from my mind. Barton Bourke, the nosy loudmouth who worked the joint, stumbled out from the back room holding a six-pack of Old Style in each puffy fist.

I sighed. "You know me, Barton. Never miss a night out with the boys."

Bourke pulled a can off its plastic ring and jammed the rest under the bar. He popped the top on his beer, tipped it back, guzzled it down. The whole thing sounded like an asthmatic elephant at a watering hole. Beer trickled down his stubbly chin. He wiped it away with the back of his hand, smacked his lips, and leaned across the bar toward me. "So, hot enough for ya?"

My patience for Barton was minimal on the best of nights, and this wasn't the best of nights. "Look, Barton—"

Pappy knew I was about to lose my cool, so he cut me off. "Barton, old friend, we're in the middle of a rather frank discussion. Can you give us a few minutes of isolation?"

"Oh, right, right. Talking up a big case, are ya?" Bourke winked at Pappy. "Sure, sure. I get it. You let me know if you need anything, now."

I shook my head as Bourke wandered off to the other side of the bar and started wiping it down with a rag. "What a clown."

"Now, now, Ben. You should try to give Barton a little bit of a break. I know he gets under your skin, but he means well. He just lacks the grace of social interaction."

"Yeah, I know. Just sometimes . . . I have to be in the mood."

"You've got a dark cloud hanging over you today, my boy. So what else is eating you? What's the situation at home?"

Pappy really knew how to read me. Or maybe I was just that easy to read. "The wife. She's got plans. Wants to move, wants kids."

"Kids, eh? That's great news, my boy. Being a father keeps a man honest."

I chuckled. "Maybe. But I don't know."

"I ever tell you about my kids, Ben?"

I nodded. "You've mentioned them."

"They're all grown up now, so I don't see them much anymore. But I think about them—even dream about them—all the time. And here's something odd: in my dreams, they're never adults. They're always kids, young, like ten. Strangest thing ever . . ."

Pappy's voice drifted off. I glanced over at him, saw a slight smile on his lips and a distant twinkle in his eyes. I let him have a moment with his thoughts.

Kids. A big step, and one I felt like I wanted to take. But a call like the one last night, it made me think. What if, one of these times, I didn't make it out? And that made me think about the burned-up body in the bathtub all over again.

"Say, Pappy, you said Moshi was into business. What sort of business?"

"If I may continue your simile of the unfinished puzzle: detective work is often more about figuring out how many different boxes you have than simply putting the pieces together. One of these boxes has a picture that looks like this—Moshi is a well-known gambler. Said to frequent a certain bookie by the name of Tyrone Tyrell. The boys call Tyrell 'Bones' on account of his affinity with games involving dice."

"Damn. So this guy's into Bones for a lot of cash?"

"Exactly the opposite, my dear boy. Moshi wins. He wins often, and he wins big."

A cold shiver wriggled around in my guts. "All right then, here's something that might be something. You know I've seen more than a few bodies, and I got a good look at this one. I think our man Moshi took a pretty good beating before he got caught in that fire." I paused, giving Pappy an opening to tell me what he knew. He didn't take it. I kept going: "So get this. Then a couple of cops showed up, almost before the fire was out, and started shoving their weight around."

"Ah, sounds like Bob Brockman and Mark Weisnecki, the finest of Testacy City's finest."

"Yeah, that's them," I said. "This Brockman character got in my face and started telling me what I saw—and it wasn't what I really saw. Makes me wonder what his deal is."

"He's an old jarhead who's had his gene for compassion replaced with the one for vengeance. An unpleasant fellow."

Images of Brockman jabbed at my mind. "What aren't you telling me, Pappy?"

"Just steer clear of this guy, Ben. He's not the kind of man you want to go up against. If he wants you to back off, then back off. Just do your job, go home, and take care of your wife. That's the wise course of action here. Trust me."

He sipped some more gin, shooting me an admonishing glance over the edge of his glass. I tried to shrug it off, downed the rest of my whiskey. The ice cube had long since given up. Maybe I needed to do the same.

"All right. It's just that I'm really concerned the cops are playing the accidental death angle too hard."

"Accident? What in heavens are you talking about, my boy? They arrested Kane McInnis, a small timer, on multiple counts, including arson and the murder of good ol' Moshi Scavone."

I hadn't planned to spend so much time at the Pandora with Pappy, the time just got away from me. When I got home, my wife was cleaning up after dinner. My plate was in the oven.

I grabbed some silverware, put the plate on the counter, started eating standing up. "How was your day?" I asked.

"Fine."

The chicken was dry, but that was my own damn fault.

"You should sit," she said, drying her hands on a dish towel. "Just because I ate doesn't mean we can't have dinner together."

I sat down at the small Formica table in the area off the kitchen. She joined me with her glass of white wine. I looked at the opened bottle on the counter and it made me feel like I'd missed something. Maybe I had.

"You get some rest?" She traced the circle of the wine glass edge with her finger.

"A little, yeah. Wanted to get more, especially with what's on my mind."

"Still the body in the fire?"

"Yeah."

She drank some more. "You know, I got some news today."

I put my fork down. "Are you okay?"

She smiled. "Yeah, I'm okay. It was a call from UCLA."

"Los Angeles."

"Yes, silly, University of California Los Angeles. They have a job. Their Kant expert is retiring. They want me in the department. It's a huge opportunity. For us."

I got up and splashed some of the white wine into a water glass, drank a gulp. "That's great."

The excitement she had tried to contain was now bubbling up. "It's really perfect. Everything we've been planning for. Now we can leave this city, start fresh, start making babies." She winked at me.

"Maybe we should wait on the kids . . . you know, until you get tenure."

My wife cocked her head. She had an insightful streak wider than the 15 freeway that cut through town. "Benny, are you . . . scared? I thought we were on the same page about all this."

I paused, only for a second, but it was a second too long.

"Jesus, Benny. I didn't know."

"Hey, come on. I want kids. I do."

"Don't say it like that, like you have to justify yourself."

"I'm not. Not at all." I took a big breath. Then I grasped her hand. "This is great. You are great. I love you, love you with all my heart. Okay, am I scared? Maybe a little. Maybe a lot. Doesn't mean this isn't what I want."

We kissed madly. I had half a mind to sweep the plate, silverware, and glasses off the table and start this baby-making business right then and there. I hesitated again, just enough for her to notice. It's the small things that matter, that determine what kind of man you are.

She pulled away and smiled, put her hand on my cheek.

I said, "We should celebrate. A night out. Dinner."

"That sounds lovely."

We kissed again, like young lovers.

It was the last time I would ever kiss my wife.

I had to switch my shift so this dinner would be possible. With my wife working down at the public library, I had a few hours of free time. I hadn't planned on using it to get into trouble, but I could feel the tug of a current more powerful than my self-control. So here I was, walking up the steps of the Testacy City Jail.

I had never been to a jail before, and I was surprised how easy it was to get through the door. All I had to do was tell a bored police officer my name and that I was here to visit Kane McInnis. I signed a log, and just like that, the guy led me to a small room with a high ceiling. A large piece of Plexiglas divided the space, complete with a pink fiberglass chair and a beige phone bolted to the desk on both sides.

I sat down, waiting for McInnis to show, and started to wonder what the hell I was doing.

I'd woken up that morning with renewed vigor, and while finishing up a plate of eggs with thick-cut toast, I'd run across a write-up of the arrest of Kane McInnis in the *Testacy City Herald-Tribune*. No real detail on the lead-up to his takedown, just a bunch of baloney about "forensic evidence" and the like. No motive, though the papers weren't likely to speculate on that anyway. They did mention he was in the lockup downtown awaiting a bail hearing.

So I thought, if I had some questions about this fire, maybe I'd just go straight to the source.

McInnis shuffled into the other side of the room and lowered himself into the chair across from me. He rubbed at a bruise under his eye and picked up the phone. I did the same.

The first words out of his mouth surprised me. "Who sent you?"

"Who do you think sent me?"

"So you ain't my lawyer?"

"No."

"Some kind of doctor?"

"Do you need a doctor?"

"Some kind of news hound?"

"No, look, I . . ."

He glowered at me with thin eyes. "I ain't liking this game you're playing."

"What? I'm not playing a game! I came here to talk. You're the one who started in with the twenty questions."

He grabbed the phone tighter. His bottom jaw stuck out with an underbite that made him look like a werewolf. "You came here to talk? Do I look like the talking type?"

I'm not sure what I expected to get here, but this sure wasn't it. "All right, listen. Let's start over. I'm Ben Drake, with the fire department. I found the body—"

"Then you know!"

"Hold on . . . know what?"

"A setup! A big, stinking setup. Nothing ain't what it seems."

"So why don't you tell me about it?"

"You're kidding me, right? You say you ain't playing a game, but you're playing all right. You just don't know it. What you want, man?"

"I just want to know about Moshi. And the fire. Did you beat him up before you started the fire? Or . . ." I sighed and pushed my fedora back on my head, then rubbed my eyes. "Hell, I don't even know. I just need some answers. I don't like things that are unresolved."

Kane's eyes darted around the empty room, searching. Then he looked back at me, hard, cold, sizing me up. When he finally spoke, his voice was a raw whisper. "Answers, huh? Maybe I got something to say about all that, but I ain't saying it here. Ain't safe. He's got people, and this place gots ears."

My stomach started doing flip-flops. I didn't know who he was talking about, but I could guess. I leaned in closer to the glass. "So what do you want me to do?"

"Get me out of here."

"Are you insane? I wouldn't even know where to start—"

"What are you, a moron? Post my bail. You do that, and we'll have plenty to talk about."

* * *

I drove past three bail bond places before I shook my head and talked myself out of it. What would my wife say? She would remind me that this guy was a criminal, a killer.

I didn't think mentioning bail was a good idea when I called her, especially after I dug myself into a hole by suggesting a slight re-schedule. The logistics of the evening had started worrying me. So I told her that maybe we should meet at the restaurant.

Not very romantic, she'd said. I had been too buzzed up after meeting Kane to think straight. I'd forced the plan, had come off too brusque. She'd said fine and hung up.

It was going to be quite the celebration if I didn't pull it around. Maybe I'd have time to stop and get her flowers.

All that meant I was late getting to the station. The captain wasn't happy. When he wasn't happy, he made me wash and wax the truck.

A clean fire truck didn't put out fires any more than a dirty one. But firemen spend a lot of time waiting for the alarm to sound, and waiting is always a little better with something to do. So we wash that truck over and over. Didn't bother me. It was a fine way to kill a shift.

By the time I got to buffing the wax, I was spending more time checking my watch than rubbing the rag over the chrome. When I heard my name called, I assumed it was the captain telling me to finish her up.

It wasn't the captain. It was Detective Brockman and his partner Weisnecki.

"You oughta get some coeds to clean that truck for you. Get 'em all soaped up and charge people to watch." Brockman let out a wolf whistle. "Ha. That's what I call a fundraiser."

I tossed the polish rag on my shoulder, wiped my hands on my work pants. "Detectives. What can I do for you?"

Weisnecki twitched his square mustache. "Ben, we know you went to visit Kane McInnis. You want to tell us why?"

Brockman barely let him finish his question. "More importantly, soldier, how about you tell us what he had to say."

"You're going to be disappointed, fellas. He didn't say anything."

"He didn't?" Brockman growled. "Seems unlikely. Did you two

get together to do some yoga? I bet not. What did you talk about? What did he say?"

"It's like this," I rubbed my forehead, "I have a friend who is a private detective—"

"You hear that, Mark?" Brockman put his hands on his knees and pretended to laugh. "A private detective. Man oh man."

"Anyway, my friend told me that Moshi was connected to a bookie named Bones. I'm sure you guys know that. I just wanted to hear McInnis tell his side of the story. But he wasn't talking."

Weisnecki laughed out loud. He wasn't pretending.

Brockman, however, lost all humor in his face. "What, are you looking for some big payday? Think you're going to find a stash of Moshi's winnings? That what you're after?"

"No, I didn't even think—"

"That's right you didn't think. That's the problem with amateur detectives and punk wannabes who stick their noses where they don't belong. No thinking. And no thinking means people get hurt."

"Come on, I didn't do anything wrong. I wasn't trying to mess with your investigation."

"Oh, there's no more investigation, soldier. Case closed. McInnis killed himself in his cell about an hour ago. And wouldn't you know, you were the last person he talked to."

"What?" Kane's words came back at me. He knew he wasn't safe. He knew he was a target. This felt wrong.

Weisnecki cracked his knuckles. "Why don't we start over? Let's try to remember this conversation you had, word for word."

I didn't have a chance to answer. Both detectives flinched at the sudden scream of the fire alarm. They tried to shout something at me, but I couldn't hear them. Instinct kicked in and I ran to put on my gear.

As I threw on my heavy coat, I watched them slink away like hungry cats.

Minutes later we were at the blaze. Black smoke from the two-story stucco rose up into the blue of the twilight sky. I had come to hate fires, big fires. My stomach got a bit queasy, not so much from nerves, just the raw adrenaline and anxiety of facing a relentless beast. Maybe some people thought that fighting a fire was as easy as holding a hose on a bunch of flames until they fizzled out. The truth was different. It was an athletic activity. Grueling, demanding, draining, and never ever easy.

Fire is alive. It doesn't want to die. It searches out any path it can find to keep itself living. Like a wild animal, if you force it into a corner, it will attack. Well, let me tell you, I'm the guy who attacks back.

I grabbed my axe and ran inside.

The plan was always the same: evacuate, isolate, terminate. More than putting out the fire, the primary goal is always to make sure no one dies. In a building this size that means a quick and thorough scan to see who's there and get them the hell out.

I heard feet stomping up the staircase so I grabbed the guys next to me and surged forward. The dense smoke blocked our way. I peeled off Petey Ivers, told him to take the rooms to our left. Made Kenny Shrubb take the ones to the right.

Kenny was always a little too eager to work the hose, didn't want to spend the time figuring the fire out. "Come on, man, let's just take care of it!"

"Search the rooms, Shrubb! We'll get all hands on soon enough!"

The heat was getting to me. I instinctively flipped my left wrist up to check the time, though I couldn't see my watch through all the gear. Tried to do the math in my head. Putting out a burner like this, forty-five minutes tops. Back to the station, clean myself up. I'd be late for sure, but my wife was patient . . .

"Drake!" The shout from upstairs jarred me. I knew I needed more focus. I growled at myself, turned back to the front.

Kenny Shrubb stood at the base of the stairs. He looked confused, shell-shocked. He always did.

The voice called down again: "We clear down there?"

I looked at Shrubb. He said, "Ivers already went up. Nobody down here. Side bedroom freaked me out. Burned up *Ouija* board sitting in a puddle of wax near the window."

I grabbed him by the shoulder and pushed him up the stairs. He continued, "Burn pattern looks like it jumped up the curtains and took over the ceiling. I gotta tell you, man, I looked at it a long time. I could swear I saw the smoke forming a pentagram . . . that's the sign of the devil!"

"Don't be an idiot, Shrubb." My tolerance for mumbo-jumbo was always low, but even more so now. I pushed Shrubb again, a little harder than I had to.

At the top, the heat formed a wall that allowed no passage and no mercy. Ivers looked over at me. "Bad up here, Drake. Whoever owned this place stuffed the rooms with furniture and racks of clothes. A real pack rat. Too much fuel."

He shouted to be heard over the roar of the flames. I shouted back: "No way to vent the roof?"

He shook his head while gripping the large hose. "No way. Can't risk getting the ladders up here. No stability. Briggs and Hurley are hitting the exterior on the east side with the master stream."

Long minutes passed. Another team came up to replace us. Ivers signaled me down the stairs, but I couldn't move. I had to get this fire out. I waved him off, stayed on the line. It was unreasonable of me, but the heat and the stress . . .

I fell to one knee, my eyes tearing from the smoke. I couldn't blink out the sting fast enough. Someone lifted me up by the armpits. "Get out of here!"

I relented, anger eating away at my stomach.

My hand found the railing as I inched down the stairs. Thought I was taking it slow enough, but my brain was full of too much fuzz. Don't know if I missed that last step or if I slipped on the water from the hose. But I was down. Twisted my damn ankle.

They dragged me out of there. Gasping for air, I slumped on the ground near the truck.

The building was a goner. The job had switched to containment. I shook my head; this was going to take awhile.

I muttered, "I'm sorry." But no one could hear me, especially not my wife.

Events replayed over and over. I know I was distracted, but something else was bugging me. Something wasn't right.

A wailing woman broke my concentration. I searched her out, found her ringing her hands over by the deputy chief. She had more jewelry on than I thought possible. It weighed her down, but not any more than the grief all over her face.

"My baby! Where's my baby?"

The deputy chief tried calming her down. Not an easy task. "We evacuated the building, ma'am. There was no baby."

The something that was bugging me kicked into overdrive.

"She's not a baby, she's almost ten . . . she's a big girl. I was only going to be gone an hour, maybe two . . ."

I was on my feet. I found Kenny Shrubb.

"Kenny, the room with the candles and the witch board. You searched the whole room, right? Under the bed . . . the closets?"

He didn't answer. He didn't have to. His eyes went wide, his face went sallow.

That's when I ran back inside.

It wasn't much of a run with my ankle screaming up at me. I grit my teeth and pushed through a wall of flame.

I pulled the girl out of the closet and ran her out through the flames. She was in pretty bad shape. The EMTs said she would make it, though maybe they were lying to me. They could see it in my face that I needed her to live.

The boys said I was a hero, but I didn't feel like a hero. Tomorrow I would let them all clap me on the back. I might even puff out my chest for them. But tonight, tonight I just wanted to be gone.

It was the longest fire I'd ever worked, and in the end we lost the structure. My anger and resentment made me think it was probably for the better.

I went straight to the restaurant without showering. I would have been horrible dinner company, but since I was almost two hours late, I knew she wouldn't be there. Guy at the host counter said she had waited a long time. He put a lot of nasal sound into the words *long time*. He also looked at me like I was a maniac. He wasn't far from wrong.

I stopped at the grocery store on the way home, bought a dozen wilted roses. She was going to be furious, but she would understand. She always did.

I pulled into my spot and immediately noticed her car wasn't there. I thought about turning right around and trying to find her. But where would I go? Where could she be?

At my front door, two uniformed policemen stood patiently.

I didn't say anything to them, just eyed them both up and down.

"Excuse me, sir, are you Benjamin Drake?"

I didn't answer them, and they didn't continue. We stood there. I hid my hand, the one not holding the flowers, in my pocket. It was shaking.

"Give it to me." My fist clenched the flowers.

"Why don't we—"

"Give it to me!"

The cop exhaled. He gave it to me all right, more tactfully than I would have been able to. Some auto accident.

Inside I howled, a long hollow howl. She was gone. Everything was gone. Everything.

I looked at the two men. They couldn't hear my howl. No one could have. And no one ever will.

The younger cop wouldn't meet my gaze, but the other one looked right back at me. "You got somewhere to go? Someone you can be with?"

The flowers fell from my grasp, spilling onto the steps in front of the door. "Yeah."

It only took five drinks to get me kicked out of the first bar. My judgment was probably already starting to get impaired, but I think the bartender was overreacting. I snapped at a young couple necking at the bar. I told them to get a booth or better yet a cheap room at the Purple Knights Motel. Don Juan wanted to plant a five-finger kiss on my face. The bartender threw a fit and showed me the door. The night was early.

I hadn't been so drunk since I was a kid. I can remember being at parties, wanting to get wasted. Back then, did I have any idea what that meant? Wasted. That's where I was headed now. I was going to lay waste to my body, my thoughts, everyone and everything around me. I was pretty sure I didn't want to come back.

I left the second bar on my own because it was too quiet. I wanted noise.

I fought not to think about my wife, and without really trying, I thought about Moshi instead.

Kane McInnis was dead. They said suicide, but I wasn't buying it. The whole thing was too neat, too suspicious, and it made Moshi's death seem like a targeted kill. Even if Kane weren't a professional, professionals were definitely involved.

I remembered telling Pappy that I thought I should have been able to save Moshi. Now it was hard to figure out why I would possibly imagine that. I was thinking too much, because my mind jumped to the idea that maybe if I hadn't gone back into that fire tonight to save that little girl, then maybe I could have made it to dinner on time. If I would have let that young girl die, maybe I could have saved my wife. She had been at the wrong place at the wrong time. It was an accident. She should have been with me. Celebrating.

Despite all the drink, I knew it was ridiculous. But slowly, with every new drink, it became the truth.

The third bar eighty-sixed me at two drinks. It was really only one. I'd spilled the second.

Everything in the world was wrong. Nothing made sense. Could I find a way to fix it? Tomorrow? The day after tomorrow?

The answer wouldn't have to wait. I was already beginning to black out.

I lost count of the bars. Before long I couldn't find one that would serve me at all. Apparently the foreigner working the Junior Captain Jr. Mart had lower standards. I gave him some cash and walked out with a bottle.

I blinked my eyes open. I was behind the wheel of my car. Going too fast, I saw the lights flash past my windows.

My eyelids felt heavy, so heavy. I gripped the steering wheel hard. My neck started to get soft.

My wife looked at me with that smile of hers. She held out her arms to hold me. She was more beautiful than ever, the most beautiful thing I had ever seen. She was made of light.

A quick intake of breath. My head snapped back. I slammed on the brakes. I couldn't see the road. My car spun hard, smoke and cinders coming up from the tires.

The car came to a stop but I was still moving, moving down a dark spiral going who knows where.

I kept gulping up air, my body in spasms from the hyperventilation. It was hard to see with all the dust I'd kicked up. It looked like I was in an alley.

My breathing slowed. It was dark outside, but I knew exactly where I was. I was outside the remains of Moshi Scavone's burned building.

Blackness took me.

The sharp sound of broken glass brought me around. I opened my eyes; it was still dark. I looked at my watch. It didn't make sense. Where was the sun? How long had I been there? My stomach groaned and my head ached. My eyes searched out what had made the sound.

A small light bounced around inside Moshi's shell of a house. Then it hit me—an intruder.

I tried to get out of the car, but I doubled over, grabbing my stomach. I looked around the car for any stray food, but the only thing there was a bottle of Old Grand-Dad. I twisted the cap off and took a swig. My stomach contracted in a fist; I almost threw it all up. Instead I choked down another swig.

I stalked over to the building on my twisted ankle. The pain helped me ignore my hunger. My left eye twitched.

Yellow police tape over the doors, the windows. A silly gesture since there were man-sized holes in the exterior wall.

I entered the building when I heard the heavy bang of metal on metal. I moved my way toward it slowly, checking each step for solid purchase, making sure the fire hadn't weakened the floorboards.

Another metallic bang. A grunt.

I didn't have a flashlight, but I knew where I was going. Now that I was inside, I had a feeling I knew who I'd find.

A string of profanities followed the next bang. I was close enough to hear heavy breathing.

I stood at the broken doorframe of Moshi's bathroom. The dirty bathtub he'd been found in reflected the light that was shining down from a cheap plastic camping lantern. The lantern light also lit up a hole in the wall, a hole big enough to hide a fireproof safe.

The big man stood there, obscured by shadows and leaning on a long-handled sledgehammer. When he saw me, he stepped forward into the light. His angular face was covered in sweat and dirt.

"Brockman, put down the hammer. Step away from the safe."

"Who . . . wait . . . Drake? What are you doing here?"

"I'm a concerned citizen. I heard a racket. This place isn't stable, you know."

"This place is a crime scene. Didn't you see the tape?"

"Yeah, I saw it."

"Then get out of here. This is none of your business."

"You made it my business—when you had McInnis kill Moshi Scavone."

He growled and ran toward me, sledgehammer held out to the side in a double-fisted grip, like he was going for a home run.

The whole world slowed down. It was like watching a movie fight scene, and all I could see on the screen was the business end of a giant hammer coming at my face.

I'd only been in one serious fight before in my life, way back in the seventh grade when Dale Van Holten's girlfriend decided I was her boyfriend. Van Holten took it hard and came at me in the locker room. It was over fast. I don't remember much about it, other than Van Holten helicoptering his arms at me in wild haymakers.

I ducked then, and I ducked now. The hammer whipped over my head and hit the wall behind me with a heavy crunch. Plaster, dust, and wood showered down around me.

I came up fast, burying a fist into Brockman's guts. I didn't really know how to throw a punch, but Brockman grunted and staggered back so I must have done something right. Then he slammed me behind the ear with his elbow. A firecracker went off inside my head. I went down, hitting the floor like a bag of rice.

I scrambled to get up, but my legs weren't cooperating. My ankle hurt like hell. I could hear Brockman's ragged breathing. I twisted, looked up. Brockman stood over me in a wide-legged stance, sledgehammer held high over his head.

He swung. I rolled.

The sledgehammer tore through the floor where I'd been lying. I heard—felt—a deep crack and the building shivered. The place definitely wasn't all that stable, and I feared that Brockman's blow splintered a floor joist.

I kicked out at his legs, caught him in the shin. He was off-balance after his swing, and he toppled over onto his back.

I managed to pull myself to my feet, tried to breathe. I held my hands out toward Brockman. "Look, let's talk this out . . ."

That's when he tackled me. We fell backward, a struggling mass of arms, legs, anger. Somehow he ended up on top, and somehow his fist found my jaw. Once, twice.

I could taste iron in my mouth, and a black hole started to close in around me. A small part of me was saying I should give up, dive in, lose myself, and go find my wife in the big upstairs. I told that part of me I wasn't the quitting type. I reached out, and frantic fingers closed around a chunk of something heavy—wood, I thought. I slammed it into Brockman's temple.

He toppled off me. I scrambled away from him as he slowly rose to his feet. He wiped at the blood pouring from the cut I'd opened above his eye. "You're a dead man, Drake. Dead as McInnis."

He ran at me. I struggled to get up again, but couldn't. I thrust my legs straight out in front of me.

Piledriver.

Brockman didn't see it coming. He ran straight into me, taking my heels on his chin. He bounced off, staggering backward, arms flailing, off-balance, slipping, falling. He hit the floor with a heavy thud, then a crack as the floor gave way beneath him.

He disappeared from my sight, letting loose with a garbled cry of surprise cut short when he hit the cement floor of the basement below.

I crawled over to the crater and peered down. There was just enough light to see Brockman lying there, motionless. It looked like he'd landed headfirst. Hollow eyes stared out from a rainbow of blood and brains.

I threw up.

When I got home I found the flowers where I had dropped them by the front door. The desert heat had reclaimed them, draining them of color and all moisture. I kicked them to the side. They turned to dust.

I opened the door. The house had a warm, sweet smell. The air conditioner had been turned off for a couple days, leaving everything inside with a radiant heat that filled the thin air.

I cranked the thermostat, heard the fans kick in. Went to the refrigerator to look for something cold to drink. All I found was her stuff.

I closed the fridge. Sat at the kitchen table and let my eyes get wet.

I needed to make so many damn calls. I needed to call the station and tell the chief I quit. I needed to call Pappy, tell him my plan for a new career, ask for his help. Needed to call the funeral home and make all kinds of arrangements. Christ. I needed to call Weisnecki, tell him his partner was dead, littering a crime scene that included a safe full of cash.

I stood, went over to the wall, picked up the phone. I held the receiver at my waist, but I could still hear it. The dial tone wailing its relentless cry for a connection, any connection.

PARTNERS

(2002)

Tires squealed as the end of the big Dodge Monaco swung around the corner, followed by the sharp sound of blaring horns. The big cop switched his big foot to the gas pedal and spun the wheel back to the right; the car fishtailed, then straightened out, before it managed to catch some air off a poorly patched manhole. Duke Wellington took his eyes off the road for just a second to glare at his nonplussed partner sitting next to him.

"Sweet Jesus! I need a little notice before I gotta turn!" he shouted. "Next time give me some notice, would ya?"

Mark Weisnecki slouched down in the passenger seat and shrugged. "It's like I told you—it makes more sense for me to take the wheel until you learn your way around the city."

"An' it's like I told *you*—Duke Wellington always drives. I'll get the layout of this crazy town mapped out in my head as I go, but I *always* drive."

"Hey, I'm not one of these guys who's going to tussle over who gets to be wheelman. But I ain't used to riding shotgun, so you're gonna have to put up with the occasional last-second navigation, at least till we get all the bugs worked outta this arrangement."

Duke Wellington grunted in response and stared straight ahead as the car screamed down Cherry Boulevard.

Weisnecki had never driven this fast to a murder scene in his near fifteen years on the force. Sure, he ignored speed limits often enough, mostly on his way to shootouts, heists, or bachelor parties—anything that had a little action and opportunity.

But the guy they were visiting was dead. No need to rush. The afternoon sun's reflection swam in the storefront windows they raced past.

Weisnecki grinned a little through his square mustache. "So, what'd you think of breakfast?" he asked, digging between his teeth with a mint-flavored toothpick. "Pretty good grub, eh?"

"It was all right," Duke Wellington said with a wave of his large black hand.

"All right? Man, you don't like anything, do you?"

"I'll tell you what I don't like." DW gestured wildly with his index finger, wagging it about like a cat toy. "I don't like that cook."

"You mean Papademos? You didn't like him?"

"That's right. Not one bit. And that made my breakfast taste foul."

"What's not to like? He's a damn good cook."

"He had no right to hassle those boys at the counter like he did. No right at all."

Weisnecki turned slightly toward his new partner, arching an eyebrow. "You mean the couple of bums stinkin' up the joint?"

Duke Wellington tilted his head forward and lowered his voice an octave. "Just 'cause they're down and out don't mean he's gotta resort to racial slurs."

"What are you talking about? Man's got a right to clear his restaurant of . . . undesirables." Weisnecki dislodged a chunk of breakfast stuck between his back molars, then turned and spat it out the window.

More horns blared as the unmarked cop car sailed through a long yellow light.

Weisnecki let out a sigh that could have been a chuckle. "You're gonna have to learn to calm down. I mean, you're not even on the job three days. You've still got a helluva lot to learn about Testacy City, that's for sure."

"And Testacy City's got a lot to learn about me."

"Partner, this ain't the kind of town where a button-down lawman can come strollin' in and clean the place up overnight. This might be the West, but those cowboy days are long gone."

"We'll see, Weisnecki. We'll see."

Weisnecki shook his head and pointed down the road with his now-frayed toothpick. "Turn right, up here on Carter."

The brown Dodge rolled right behind the patrol car that rested in front of a ramshackle cottage. Duke Wellington jammed the car into park, wishing the thing had a manual transmission, then stepped from the car.

Weisnecki pulled himself out of the passenger seat. "Welcome to Testacy City's glorious south side, home of the finest dirtbags in the Southwest. Today's special smell is . . ." he sucked in a big breath of air, "garbage." He took a second to light up a cigarette before he plodded up the cracked cement walkway to the house.

The ripe smell settled on the back of Duke Wellington's tongue. He spat onto the dusty street, but he could still taste the air. He scowled and pushed his Panama hat far back on his forehead. A quick scan of the neighborhood, packed with beat-up cars parked in front of claptrap buildings, didn't improve his mood much. So far everything he'd come across in this city made his head hurt, a throbbing right behind his eyes.

"Hey! You coming?" Weisnecki's shout shocked Duke Wellington out of his thoughts and back to the job at hand. He lumbered up the walk to where his partner stood chatting it up with a young uniform cop. DW stole a glance at the kid's shiny brass name badge: *Coffman*.

"Hey, Billy," Weisnecki said, "let me introduce you to the new man on the job. Duke Wellington, Billy Coffman. Billy here is a real career man. You need something special done, he'll be glad to take care of you, if you get my drift."

"Good to meet you, detective," Billy said, blushing at the attention. "They say you worked Atlanta?"

"On the job there ten years, and I gotta say—"

"Speaking of partners," Weisnecki interrupted, "where's Chuck?"

"Inside. Tidying things up," Coffman said, jerking a thumb at the front door.

"Tidying up? What's this about tidying up? This Chuck better not be messin' up my crime scene," Duke Wellington said, poking a thick finger in Billy's face. "I don't like it when beat cops go messin' up my crime scene."

Coffman started to stammer, caught by surprise. Standing out in the desert sun always made a man in uniform sweat; there was no real escape from the heat.

The tension broke when Weisnecki let loose with a big laugh and said, "You sure got a way with folks. Come on, let's check this out." He clapped Duke Wellington on the back and started walking him toward the front door.

The two detectives stepped into a hot, muggy living room. Thick orange shag carpet ran wall-to-wall, accentuated by dirty, lemon-yellow wallpaper highlighted with some sort of swirly, carrot-inspired design. Duke Wellington squinted his eyes as the pain in his head throbbed on.

Immediately inside the door, a big red stain discolored the already ill-colored carpet, and in that stain lay the massive frame of a man wearing a grubby undershirt, white cotton boxer shorts, and too-thin black dress socks. His thick arms were spread wide, as if waiting for an embrace that would never come, and his big legs formed a macabre figure four. Blood covered his body.

A nervous-looking uniform cop in his late forties stood on the other side of the body, next to a bank of steel filing cabinets, the tall kind with four drawers. One of the drawers stood suspiciously open. The cop relaxed when he saw Weisnecki walk in.

"Oh, hiya, Mark. Mighty fine mess we got ourselves."

"A mess is good goddamn right. What's the situation here ..." Duke Wellington moved around the body and peered in close to get the cop's name, "Raffety?"

"Relax, big fella," Weisnecki said. "Chuck here's one of the good ones. Ain't that right, Chuck?"

"One hundred percent grade-A."

"This is Duke Wellington, new boy in town. Now, he ain't used to how we do things around here, so do me a favor and break him in gentle, won't ya?"

"Gentle it is." Raffety threw Weisnecki a sly wink, then turned to Duke Wellington. "Good to have you on the job, detective. You need anything, you know who to call." Raffety threw his wink at Wellington.

"All right, all right. Now that we're all friendly an' such, what do we got?" Wellington gestured at the body. Blood continued to slowly trickle out and pool on the floor.

"What we got is, someone finally caught up with old Bones," Weisnecki said. "Was bound to happen eventually."

"Bones? This guy's name was Bones?" Duke Wellington took a step back and sized up the body. "Looks like he must've weighed 350."

"Yeah, well, he ain't called Bones on account of his figure, you can be sure of that," Weisnecki said. "Chuck, give DW the skinny on our man."

Raffety stepped up with the facts. "Tyrone 'Bones' Tyrell. They called him Bones 'cause of his magic touch with the dice. Didn't matter what game he played or where he played it. The man had a gift for getting the dice to do what he wanted."

Duke Wellington made a brief survey of the room as Raffety prattled on. On the left side of the room, a well-worn easy chair extended to its full length waited patiently for someone to recline. Within a short arm's reach of the right side of the chair stood a low, narrow table with a bank of phones, six in all, each with its receiver off the hook. Four of them were black, cradle-style jobs. One was an off-green color. Duke Wellington remembered that Sears used to call it "avocado." The last phone was a pink princess model. A girlie calendar hung slightly off-center over the whole arrangement. A small table—stocked with plenty of pens, pencils, and pads of paper, as well as a simple off-yellow ceramic table lamp—sat just to the left of the recliner. Some kind of cartoon played on the large color television a few feet in front of the easy chair.

"This guy a bookie?" Duke Wellington asked as he bent over to pick up a crumpled sheet of notepaper.

"Not just a bookie, my man. *The* bookie. Biggest in Testacy City— and I'm not talking about weight. I mean, them phones were ringin' so bad when I got in here, I had to take 'em off the hook just so's I could think."

Weisnecki squatted in front of the huge body. "Three shots," he muttered, pointing at each wound with his smoldering cigarette as he talked. "One in the belly—like that did anything to him—one in the chest, and one in the face. That'll be the one that did him in."

"We got suspects lined up?"

"That's the hard part. Way I see it, every two-bit gambler in the city has a motive for whacking this guy."

"Yeah, a lot of people are, or were, in deep with him," Raffety said.

Duke Wellington flattened out the notepaper he'd picked up. It contained two columns of numbers: on the left were dates, about a week apart; on the right, dollar amounts, all under five hundred. "I hope this isn't what you're calling deep. In Atlanta, this is more like a grocery bill than a racketeer's profit margin."

"This ain't Atlanta." Raffety plucked the note from the detective's fingers.

Duke Wellington's eyes narrowed. He pointed at the open filing cabinet. "That why you're digging through those files?"

"What time is it?" Weisnecki asked.

His partner glanced down at his wrist. "Almost quarter past one. Ain't you got your own watch?"

"All right, then," Weisnecki said as he stood up and dusted his hands on his rumpled suit. His cigarette stuck out at a weird angle from the corner of his mouth. "Time for us to get going."

"Go? Hold on a second, we gotta wait for the scientists, and I want to do a walk-through of this whole place . . ."

"Do you wanna solve this murder or not?"

"What the hell kind of question is that?"

"It's like I said earlier—you've got a lot to learn about this town. Until then, follow my lead. Chuck and Bobby will wait here for forensics, won't you, Chuck?"

"You know it. We'll get everything wrapped up here, no trouble. Do up a nice report on it, even."

Duke Wellington looked at Raffety and back to Weisnecki. He didn't like leaving a crime scene before he was done with it. He sure didn't like leaving Raffety and Coffman behind to keep an eye on it. But Weisnecki hadn't steered him wrong yet, as much as he hated to admit it.

"All right, Weisnecki. I'll play this your way, for now. So where we goin'?"

"We've got a date at the Glass Slipper."

Weisnecki described the Glass Slipper as a dirty little secret right in the heart of Testacy City's downtown industrial district. Hidden down a narrow alley, spitting distance from the Testacy City police station, the seedy strip club sat clandestinely behind a tall fence topped off with razor wire. To any casual observer, the place looked like the beat-up back entrance to one of the many warehouses that lined the alley, the sort of door a blue-collar Joe would slip out of to grab a quick smoke. The only thing giving away its veiled existence was the small, inelegant plastic sign that read: *No Minors.*

Duke Wellington squared his shoulders and reached for the bent handle of the door, but Weisnecki clamped a firm hand down on his partner's bicep.

"Hold up there a sec. Let's lay a few ground rules before we hit the playing field."

Duke Wellington crossed his arms and shot a cockeyed glance at Weisnecki. He'd never been the type to follow someone else's lead. But he had to admit that this town seemed to operate with a whole different set of odds, and Weisnecki seemed to know the rules of the game.

"I'm listenin'."

Weisnecki combed several fingers through his mustache and said, "It's like this—the boys we're meeting here, you ain't gonna like 'em. I'll tell you that straight out. They're hard-core vice, and sometimes they get a little touchy about that. The way you've been charming your fellow cops today won't get us very far with them, so let me do the talking."

Duke Wellington nodded, then pulled open the door and stepped off to the side. "After you."

Weisnecki spotted Brad Makoff and Leo Nolan right where he knew they'd be: in the center booth at the back of the room, a seat that gave them a clear view of the stage, the bar, and anyone who walked through the front door. Makoff, an apelike guy with the forehead and nose of a turtle, had his hands full. He had one chubby fist wrapped tightly around what remained of a pastrami sandwich; the other hand stroked the long hair of the worn-out blonde curled up against his thigh. Next to Makoff, Nolan, a sloppy cop with a bad haircut and a heartless face, entertained a redhead with too-slim limbs who lounged on his lap. She kept sliding the sloppy knot of his tie up and down in a slow, rhythmic fashion.

Makoff noticed Wellington and Weisnecki strolling through the club just as the blonde ran a wet tongue up the side of his neck. He shoved her away roughly and took a big bite of his lunch, wiping his free hand across the front of his navy-blue windbreaker. He chewed slowly, not swallowing until Wellington and Weisnecki stood in front of the table.

"Hey, Makoff, how's the wife?" Weisnecki asked.

Makoff's tiny eyes turned to a glare. "Now, why you gotta be that way, Weisnecki—always ridin' me like that? I don't need this when I'm eatin' lunch." As he spoke, tiny bits of pastrami sprayed out of his mouth and danced through the air.

Nolan looked up from the girl on his lap. "Yeah, we got enough problems without you mouthin' off alla time."

Weisnecki smirked at the brutish cop and said, "Nolan! Look at you—all dressed up. Almost didn't recognize you in the tie."

"We got court."

At this, the redhead on Nolan's lap giggled and jerked sharply on his tie, pulling the cop's head down, then playfully bit him on the end of his nose.

"Hey!" Nolan moved fast, smacking her across the face with the back of his hand. "I'm in the middle of some business here."

A line of blood welled up on the girl's cheek where Nolan's over-sized class ring cut across her flesh. She dabbed at the wound with her fingers as tears welled up in her red-rimmed eyes. "I . . . I'm sorry . . . I was just—"

"You just sit still when we're doin' business." Nolan shoved her off his lap, and she tumbled out of the booth and floundered to the floor. "Shut your mouth an' get outta here."

Duke Wellington watched open-mouthed as the skinny girl picked herself up and skulked toward an open doorway at the back of the room covered with a ratty red curtain.

Makoff gave the blonde next to him a hard nudge with his elbow. After she took the hint and quickly followed the other girl, he waved his sandwich at Duke Wellington. "So, this the new guy?"

"Yeah, Duke Wellington. My new partner."

Nolan chuckled and gave Wellington a once-over. "Sucker."

Makoff set his sandwich down on a piece of wax paper, then smoothed back his thinning hair. "So why'd you drag yourselves down here to bother us? . . . Wait, let me guess. You guys caught the Bones killing, and now you need Makoff and Nolan to dig up the prime dirt."

"Now that's detective work in action, DW. We can take lessons from this guy."

Makoff's eyes narrowed and he paused a moment before he said, "You know, we've been working an angle on Bones for . . . how long, Nolan?"

"A long time."

"That's right. A long time. And now you're just gonna stroll in, interrupt our lunch, and expect us to hand over everything we know? Sorry, but that ain't how things work here in vice."

"Look, Makoff, we don't care about whatever it is you have on Bones. Whatever you're running on him, that's your business—and it can stay your business. We don't care." Weisnecki turned and looked at Duke Wellington, dropping his voice an octave. "Do we?"

Wellington thought for a moment. Weisnecki had been right, he didn't like these two at all. He jingled the keys in his pocket as he thought, then answered: "Not one bit. What's your business stays your business. We don't care one bit about that."

Weisnecki sighed in relief as he held his hands out in front of him. "See? All we need is a short list of folks who'd have liked to put a few holes in old Bones."

Makoff sat with a hand wrapped around his chin as he drummed his fingers on the table for a few moments. Then he looked over at his partner. "What do you think, Nolan?"

Nolan shrugged his shoulders and grabbed a handful of Beer Nuts from the bowl on the table, then crammed them into his maw.

"All right. We can give you a guy. Likely suspect."

Duke Wellington's eyes opened wide. "Only one?"

"Hey, greenhorn, this ain't the Salvation Army," Nolan said.

"What the . . . ? That's—"

"Fine. It's fine. We'll take what we can get," Weisnecki said.

Makoff looked around at the others. "Okay, then. Now that we've got this understanding, why don't you check out Arthur Wells. He's in deep to . . . ah . . . Bones."

"I heard of him," Weisnecki said.

"Yeah, gambling addict, because of which he's also a perpetual petty crook. He's been busted something like a hundred times. Devious little guy. Don't let him out of your sight."

Nolan leaned in near Makoff and whispered a little too loudly, "What do you want to tell Knicke?"

Makoff's face went white, and his head snapped around fast and pinned Nolan with hot eyes. "What the hell is wrong with you?"

"Well, hey, thanks for the help, boys. Me and DW got a murder to solve." Weisnecki rapped his knuckles on the table. "See you 'round."

When they got outside, Weisnecki started laughing as he lit a cigarette. He blew a long smoke plume straight up and said, "What a couple of clowns."

"So, that's your idea of smooth talkin'?"

"I never said anything about talking smooth. That was my idea of speaking the right language. It's like this—Nolan ain't that bright, and Makoff ain't that good at poker. Between all that, I figured they'd let something slip. And they did."

The big Dodge pulled away from the curb and roared off into the sparse traffic. "So, whaddya think? We goin' after this Knicke?" Duke Wellington asked.

"Let's hold off on that. If he's hooked up with Makoff and Nolan somehow, I'd rather know more about him so we don't walk into some kind of setup. Would rather see what kind of stink they're trying to spray on this Wells fellow."

Weisnecki made a quick call on the radio and found out that the last known address for one "Wells, Arthur Lee" was on Laramie Drive.

"Take a left at the next light. His place'll be on a side street a few blocks down."

As Duke Wellington eased the big car around the corner, Weisnecki flipped what was left of his cigarette out the window and slipped on a pair of gold-rimmed aviator sunglasses. "I gotta admit, partner, you handle this beast pretty well." He patted the dashboard.

Moments later, they stood on the front porch of a cracker-box house that looked just like the ones on either side of it. Duke Wellington knocked on the front door and it swung open with a long, slow creak.

Weisnecki shot his partner a hard look that said not to ask any questions, then he walked through the doorway.

"But—" Wellington interrupted himself with a shrug of his shoulders. Instead of saying anything else, he brushed his fingers across the gun on his hip—a nervous habit—and, with a deep sigh, followed his partner.

On the other side of the door, a worn maroon sofa took up most of the space in a tiny living room. A small television stand was crammed against the wall in front of the sofa, complete with an oversized television blasting out some daytime talk show. A narrow walkway behind the couch led toward the back of the building, ending at a closed wooden door. A matching door stood open in the right wall, leading to a smallish bedroom. Off to the left, an archway opened into what looked to be a kitchen.

Weisnecki stood guard, sweeping his eyes back and forth between the archway, the bedroom, and the back door. Duke Wellington strolled over to the blaring television and cranked down the volume just as a short, balding guy waddled out from the kitchen.

He jumped when he saw the two cops in the living room.

"Holy..." he stammered. His soft white skin made him look as if he were made out of raw bread dough.

Duke Wellington's pulse quickened. He spun around, fumbling for the pistol he should have had drawn before he walked in, feeling stupid at being caught in such a silly situation.

Weisnecki flipped back his jacket so the little man could see him put his hand on the butt of his gun, and said, "That's far enough, Wells. Hands in the air."

"Wh... wha... what's going on? Wh... who are you guys?" he asked, his hands held high above his head.

Wellington moved his jacket so the guy could see the badge he wore on his belt. "I'm Duke Wellington. That's my partner, Mark Weisnecki. We're Homicide, here on an investigation."

"Homicide? Oh, man. I didn't do nothin'."

"Then you won't mind having a little chat with us, will ya?"

"Chat? Sure, sure. No problem. You guys want some coffee? Hold on, make yourselves comfortable, I've gotta make a fresh pot." With that, Wells dropped his hands and disappeared into the kitchen.

Wellington drew his gun and held it pointed down at the floor, aimed about two feet in front of him, and cautiously inched his way through the arch into the kitchen. He could feel Weisnecki covering him from behind.

The kitchen was little bigger than an alcove. A counter ran along the back wall, complete with a sink on the left and four grease-caked cupboards above. Tucked along the right wall, a metal bread box sat forgotten next to a well-used hotplate and a disassembled, dented percolator. A refrigerator hummed loudly on the left wall next to the sink, and a small metal-and-Formica table with two mismatched chairs had been shoved up against the right wall.

Wells hurriedly filled the percolator with cold tap water. Then he fitted the stem and basket inside before he began an anxiety-filled rooting through the kitchen.

"You fellas don't need those pistols. I don't keep no guns around here," he said as he frantically opened a cupboard door, peered inside, then quickly slammed it shut. He continued his search at a frenetic pace, banging one cupboard door shut as he pulled another one open. There seemed to be no pattern to his searching; several times he'd open a cabinet he'd already investigated before continuing on.

"How about we skip the coffee," Duke Wellington said after a few minutes of watching Wells play hide-and-seek with nothing in particular.

"Ah, that's where I put them," Wells said, ignoring the detective's comment as he stretched his arm up to the top shelf of one of the cabinets. He angled up on the tips of his toes so he could reach inside. Even then, he could barely make it, but managed to pull out three plain white coffee mugs, the kind they use in diners, and set them on the counter. With the cups in place, he quickly spun and opened the freezer, rolling his head around on his stubby neck as he looked inside. Just as quickly, he pushed the freezer door shut and scanned the small kitchen.

He smiled and snapped his fingers, then walked over to another cabinet and pulled a can of Chock full o'Nuts off the bottom shelf. He peeled off the plastic lid and began filling the percolator's basket with coffee. He jammed the top of the percolator in place carelessly and plugged it in. A low hiss leaked into the room as the water started to heat up. Wells plopped down on one of the two cheap chairs and sighed.

"Now that you're done playin' around here, you ready to answer some questions?" Weisnecki said.

"Sure, sure," Wells replied, waving his hand toward his face in a "bring on the questions" motion.

"All right," Duke Wellington said. "Where were you—"

Without warning, Wells jumped to his feet. "Hey, before we get started, gotta hit the head. You guys wait right here. Be right back."

Before either of the cops could say anything, the man scurried out of the kitchen, across the living room, behind the sofa, and through the wooden door. The cops got a glimpse of the room beyond—a bathroom all right.

"You think he's got a gun in there?" Weisnecki asked as he slipped his own heater into its holster.

"No, but I think he's gonna run. This guy is as loony as a minister sippin' too much communion sauce."

"Can't argue with you there. You stay here and watch that door. I'm goin' outside."

"Me watch the door? Why don't you watch the door an' I go outside? Why do I gotta watch the door?"

"I see it like this," Weisnecki said, "you're the one does the driving, so you're the one gets to lean up there against that wall and watch that door. I got to grab a smoke." He slipped a Lucky between his stained teeth.

After Weisnecki left, Duke Wellington leaned against the archway between the kitchen and the living room. He checked his gun, making sure he had a round in the chamber, then he stared at the bathroom door, listening to Wells clunk around inside.

Duke Wellington turned his head and peered into the kitchen.

He stood there thinking about what a bundle of nerves this Wells was. Funny how some people got when talking to cops. They weren't even in an interview and this guy flipped out, like he had something to hide.

Then it hit him. He glanced back at the bathroom door. Still closed tight, but he could hear the toilet running. He didn't have much time. He clicked on the safety of his gun and put the piece back on his hip, then walked over to the bread box. His mind replayed Wells's frantic search of the kitchen; the guy had looked everywhere. Everywhere, that is, but the bread box. He pulled the handle, and the door flopped open with a small magnetic sound. Inside, tucked behind a loaf of Wonder bread, was a gun.

He pulled the handkerchief out of his breast pocket and gingerly picked up the cheap .38. He held it up to his nose and sniffed. Recently fired. He slipped the gun into his pocket and smiled.

When he heard footsteps behind him, Duke Wellington turned around. "Well, well. Looks like we're gonna have a few words about what's in your bread box . . ." he said, trailing off as his smile faded to a dumbfounded grimace. He stood looking at a slim black man in a shabby suit and tie carrying a bag of groceries.

The man didn't look happy. "Hey! What the hell is going on here? Who are you?"

"Who am I? Who am I? I might ask you the same question," Duke Wellington said, once again flashing his badge.

"Cop, huh? Well, who I am is the guy what lives here, and I sure don't appreciate you guys bustin' in and diggin' through my lunch fixin's."

"Don't worry about nothin', friend. We're here talking to your roommate."

"Nothin' 'cept I ain't got no roommate," the man said.

"No roommate . . . hold it. What's your name?"

"Don't you guys know whose house it is you go bustin' into? I'm Arthur Wells."

A wolf's grin broke across Duke Wellington's face, and he pointed over the guy's shoulder. "So if you're Wells, who's that?"

Wells spun around and saw Weisnecki standing there next to the short, nervous guy who had disappeared into the bathroom. The guy's face sported a few new bruises, and he winced in pain when Weisnecki cranked his arm deeper into a wrestler's arm lock.

"Knicke! What are you doin' here?"

Duke Wellington looked at Weisnecki and said, "Knicke? *Our* Knicke?"

"I'd say so," Weisnecki replied.

"Shut up, Wells, you squealer," Knicke said.

"So this is Wells, then," Weisnecki said.

"Well, now, if this ain't interesting. You boys know each other, huh? That's damn interesting," Duke Wellington said.

"Sure is." Weisnecki moved into the kitchen and shoved Knicke into the same chair he'd sat in earlier. "Why don't we start at the beginning. Tell us about Bones."

Knicke looked up at Weisnecki, an innocent mask spread across his face, and said, "Bones?"

Weisnecki backhanded Knicke across the face, then took off his jacket, draped it over the other chair, and loosened his tie. Duke Wellington watched his partner, hoping this wasn't going to go where it looked like it was going. This wasn't his style. Not his style at all.

"You talkin' about the bookie?" Wells asked, finally walking up to the counter to set down his bag of groceries.

"You know any other Bones?" Duke Wellington asked, turning so he could keep Weisnecki in the corner of his eye as he grilled Wells.

"Yeah, I do . . . but he's in prison."

"Knock it off. You know we mean the bookie," Weisnecki said.

"All right, so I know him, but only to place bets with. He treats me good. Gives me credit when I need it, and I always pay him, even if I can't cover the vig," Wells said, suddenly embarrassed. "I ain't exactly what people call a winner."

"That's for sure," Knicke said.

Duke Wellington shot a penetrating glance over to Knicke and said, "For sure, huh? What do you know about it?"

"Nothin'. He just looks like a loser."

"Don't give us that crap," Weisnecki snapped, aiming his hand at Knicke's face. Knicke flinched, and Weisnecki laughed, crossing his arms in front of his chest.

"Man, I'm tired of your mouth, Knicke," Wells said. "You got some nerve."

Knicke glared at Wells with malice as he rubbed his elbow and said, "Watch yourself, Wells."

"Comin' here every week, takin' my money—"

Knicke jumped to his feet. "I said shut up!"

Weisnecki shoved the diminutive thug backward, forcing him down into his chair.

Wellington looked from Knicke, who was starting to sweat, to Wells and said, "This guy takes your money?"

"Yeah, every week. He came by and collected yesterday."

"Collected for what?"

"You gotta be kiddin' me. You mean to tell me you guys don't know? He's an errand boy for Bones."

"I'm no errand boy!"

"Then what are you doing here?" Weisnecki asked.

Knicke crossed his arms and looked up at Weisnecki with a defiant smirk. Weisnecki unfolded his arms and took a threatening step forward.

Duke Wellington wiped his mouth with the back of his hand, afraid that Weisnecki would lose control and clean Knicke's clock, right there on the dirty linoleum. So he quickly shifted gears and changed his approach, turning to Wells and asking him, "Where were you last night?"

"The drunk tank."

Wellington pulled the gun he'd found in the bread box out of his pocket and held it by the trigger guard in front of Wells's nose. "This yours?"

Wells took a step back, hands open and up in front of him. "No sir. I haven't owned a gun since . . . before my last stretch."

Knicke laughed, and said, "You gonna believe that line, man? That's so old . . ."

Duke Wellington looked over at his partner and knew they were thinking the same thing. Weisnecki grimaced, like he'd just swallowed something bad, and nodded. Wellington nodded back. Yeah, they were thinking the same thing all right. What a mess.

Weisnecki kicked one of the legs of the chair Knicke sat on.

"Stand up and turn around," he said, pulling out a pair of handcuffs.

"You too, Wells. Let's see those hands," Wellington said, putting a big hand on the gambler's shoulder.

"What the hell's going on here? I got rights, you know," Knicke said as Weisnecki clicked the cuffs shut. The little thug yelped and tried to squirm out of the cop's grip.

"We know all about your rights, but it's like this," Weisnecki said, tightening the cuffs around Knicke's chubby little wrists. "Things are getting a little sticky here, so we're gonna continue this downtown."

"Downtown? Give me a break, man, I'm just tryin' to keep my nose clean," Wells said.

"If you're keeping clean you ain't got a thing to worry about, Wells. Not a thing," Duke Wellington said, giving Wells a gentle shove as they headed out of the kitchen, then out the front door of the house.

Once they got to the station, it only took a quick conversation with the desk sergeant to verify that Wells had spent the previous night and a good chunk of that morning in a cell with a few other hard drinkers. He didn't get out until after ten, too late for him to have gotten halfway across Testacy City to throw a few pills into Bones.

"No way Wells could've done this, no way at all. We gotta cut him loose," Duke Wellington said as he and Weisnecki walked down the dirty hallway that led to the interrogation rooms.

"What do you think of Knicke?" Weisnecki asked.

"What do I think of guy with the first name of Charles but prefers to go by Chip?" He flipped through the thin manila folder he held in his big hands. "Somethin' sure ain't right with that, that's what I think."

Weisnecki laughed. "Nervous little guy, ain't he?"

"Nervous as they come," Duke Wellington said, stopping outside the door to the interrogation room where Knicke was being held. "Tell you what, let me run this thing. I got an idea."

"Okay."

Duke Wellington opened the door and stepped inside. An anxious Chip Knicke sat hunched over the metal table with his hands in his lap. Sweat dotted his balding head, and he fidgeted as the two cops walked in, closing the door behind them.

Weisnecki leaned back against the wall and watched as Duke Wellington offered Knicke a cup of coffee. Knicke said yes, so Weisnecki stepped out and walked back down the hall to the coin-operated machine in the lobby. When he got back to the room, Knicke was sucking down a cigarette—one of Weisnecki's Luckys. By the end of the smoke, Knicke had relaxed a little, and that's when Duke Wellington got to work. He moved slowly, slipping into the role of Knicke's buddy, prodding him about what kind of living he made off collections, how he liked working for Bones, and what he'd done that day before they caught up with him at Wells's place. He even slipped Makoff's and Nolan's names into the mix at one point, and that got Knicke's full, wide-eyed attention.

Wellington kept hammering Knicke with the same questions, phrasing them slightly differently each time he asked, then stopping Knicke when he contradicted himself to let the guy dig himself in deeper. The hard thing about lying is that you have to remember to separate what really happened from what you're making up and then store them in different parts of your brain where they can't get all mixed up. Knicke couldn't do that very well.

It took a long time, but after a few cups of coffee, and a lot of cigarettes, Duke Wellington just stopped talking.

After an awkward moment, Knicke started looking all around the room. "What's going on? Are you letting me go now?"

"Are we lettin' you go? Mark, check out this funny guy. No, we're not lettin' you go. Not now that we know you did it."

"You . . . you know I did it?"

"A few months ago, you start skimmin' off the top of the take, nothin' bigger than five notes, like you don't think the big man's gonna know."

Knicke averted his eyes.

"But then, before you can make your nut, Bones tumbles to your skim, and BAM, it's showtime. Ain't that right?"

Knicke kept his mouth shut.

"How 'bout this then: where's the gun?"

"You already got the gun," Knicke snapped.

Duke Wellington leaned back in his chair. "Not your gun, bozo. You know we got that. I'm talkin' 'bout the gun that Bones pulled on you."

Weisnecki coughed. He didn't like interrogation; he really wasn't any good at it, and he knew it. But he did know a good interview when he saw one, and Duke Wellington ran one fine interview.

Knicke dropped his head, his whole body went slack, like all his muscles just stopped working, and he said, "Okay, okay. I killed him, okay? I didn't want to . . . but . . . but I had no choice. I was real careful with covering my tracks, but yeah, he figured it out. Damned if I know how. Hell, I was gonna pay him back too, but he just got mad and started coming after me."

"Coming after you with a gun," Wellington said with a smile. "Man, I can read you like the Bible. So you shot him."

"Well, yeah . . . he's waving his piece around and yelling like he did. But he's big, moves slow, you know. So I pulled out my heater and . . ." Knicke made a gun with his hand and pointed at his own reflection in the mirror on the wall. He dropped his thumb and said, "Blammo."

"Where's this gun that Bones used?" Weisnecki asked.

"I took it when I left and dumped it."

"That's a damn shame. We find that gun, you might get by with self-defense," Wellington said.

"Some vacant lot on Fifth—right by where the tracks come through."

"Why frame Wells?" Weisnecki asked.

"I don't know. I just never liked him 'cause he's a loser, I guess."

"Well that, Chip my man, is a feeling you got to get used to."

After they had Knicke tucked into a holding cell, Duke Wellington and Mark Weisnecki walked out into the cool night air and stopped on the front steps of the station house. Wellington took off his hat and stared up at the night sky, marveling at all the stars. He didn't remember ever seeing stars like that in Atlanta. Weisnecki, tweed coat folded over a forearm, chased away the darkness for a moment when he lit a cigarette with his butane lighter.

Wellington slipped his hat back on his head. "You think Knicke's hooked up with Makoff and Nolan somehow, don't you?"

"I know it."

"You know? As in you know for a fact?"

"Nope. I just know," Weisnecki said.

His partner laughed. "Intuition, huh? We gonna do anything about it?"

"Nope. Ain't worth it. Not right now, anyway."

Wellington shook his head and walked down the steps. He'd figure this town out sooner or later, and then he'd show everyone some real law enforcement. At the bottom of the steps, he turned back toward Weisnecki. "This a typical day in this town?"

Weisnecki shrugged. "Sometimes they're better. Usually they're a lot worse." He shook his pack of Luckys and offered one to his partner.

"Don't smoke."

Weisnecki chuckled for a moment. "Workin' this town? You will. You drink though, don't you?"

"Drink? Hell yes, I drink."

"Then why don't we grab a beer and talk, partner-to-partner? And I'll introduce you around to some of the guys."

Duke Wellington smiled, despite himself. "Best offer I've had all day. Lead the way."

"Forget that, pal," Weisnecki said. "You're driving."

"5 shots + A Funeral"
Paul Pope 2:15:99

FIVE SHOTS
AND A FUNERAL

(1999)

Case One
The Silent Ventriloquist

"Oh, Ben Drake, come in, come in," she said, taking my hand in both of hers, holding it up like she was going to kiss it. Thankfully, she didn't.

She led me into a modest one-bedroom apartment. A sheen of middle-class splendor covered the room. Cheap gold accents on picture frames, lamps, and fixtures made the room glow, an earnest attempt at looking rich. The place seemed more like a display than a living room, and something gave it a distinctly unwelcome feel.

My foot caught the edge of an upturned imitation Oriental rug. The short, showy hostess spun around on her toes. Her hand flicked long, dark, curly locks over her shoulder. She looked around, waiting for something, as if *she* were the one new to the room.

I stared straight at her. "Mrs. Summers, as I said on the phone—"

"Please. No need for formalities. It's Misty Summers, darling."

"Right." A chill hit my brainpan at the thought of being her darling. "Look, I thought we covered your concerns on the phone."

Misty tilted her head, and the way she held her arms to her hips made her chest thrust forward. Her height (I guessed her at not much over five feet) made the gestures even more pronounced.

"Don't you want to check out the crime scene?" she asked.

"I would if there actually *were* a crime scene. As it stands, I don't know what the crime is."

"Why, don't be silly, Ben Drake! The Sensational Stan Summers has gone missing!" She threw an upturned hand to her forehead, feigning the beginning of a faint. "Oh, it's all too much."

I stood in silence, rolling my eyes and trying not to sigh too loudly. I had come over here mostly because I had time to kill, and I wanted to put an end to the nonstop "missing persons" calls that had been coming to the office from this broad for the past two days.

"Can't you dust for clues?" she suggested. "Or ask me questions that might lead to the safe return of my husband? Please, Ben Drake, do something for me!"

"Okay," I said begrudgingly. "Let me ask you a few questions. When was the last time you saw Stan?"

"Stan Summers, my husband, who normally performed his act at a small community theater—it's a fabulous act, darling, simply fabulous. Have you seen it?"

"No. You mentioned earlier he is a ventriloquist, right?"

"Yes, yes. A ventriloquist." She clasped her hands to her chest. "Oh, I like the way that sounds, that word: ventriloquist. That's the sound of good-quality family entertainment."

The inhabitants of Testacy City liked their entertainment in the form of dice, cards, ponies, liquor, and loose women. Rarely did entertainment involve a man with a talking mannequin.

"He makes people laugh, Stan does." She smiled as she floated her eyes to the ceiling. "I have to ask you, isn't that what people really want?"

People wanted to forget about hardship and misfortune; about unfulfilled dreams and missed opportunities; about the crime, murder, and mayhem that so often filled the streets of Testacy City. Sure, they wanted to laugh.

I nodded in agreement.

"Stan and I moved here a couple of years ago." Misty stepped away from me and started aimlessly rearranging the knickknacks that littered her territory. "We wanted to be stars. I mean . . . we still want to be stars."

More and more people like these two were showing up here, hoping the glitz and glamour of '50s-era Las Vegas could be recaptured in this sister city a hundred miles to the north. But Testacy City wasn't ready for glitz. It wasn't ready for glamour. It certainly wasn't ready for a ventriloquist.

"Ah, you were telling me about the last time you saw your husband . . ."

"Yes . . . yes, I was. The last time I saw my darling Stan in the flesh was Monday night."

"What time would you say?"

"I think about nine . . . yes, nine p.m.—right before he left to do his . . . dreadful act."

"I thought you said his act was fabulous."

"Oh, it is, it is." She pooh-poohed the air with a tiny paw. "But he has another act, a simply terrible, dreadful act."

"What sort of dreadful act?"

"I honestly don't know. I'm even a little nervous just talking about it. But I know it has something to do with the occult."

"And what makes you think—"

"Stan lost his father when he was a young boy, and over the years he's tried a lot of different things to contact him: séances, *Ouija* boards, and all sorts of other weird ceremonies. He's just obsessed with the supernatural."

"And you think this obsession of his has something to do with his disappearance?"

"I most certainly do!"

"How so?"

"I have no idea, I just know. He hasn't called or even sent a note, and that's totally unlike him."

Her little round face pleaded with me.

"Oh, Ben Drake, I didn't want him to do the show, but I agreed, hoping that if I let him, he'd finally come to his senses and abandon all that silliness."

Her chest heaved as tears welled up in her eyes and ran down her cheeks, leaving streaks like scars in her heavy makeup.

"But deep down I knew he'd never stop," she whimpered. "He's just too superstitious."

I was going to have to sit. Something about this room made me feel uneasy. I only realized then that it wasn't the décor. It wasn't the clutter of useless objects; it was that there was nowhere to sit. No chairs, no sofa, no hospitable love seat. Not even a cold, impersonal bench.

An odd-shaped steamer trunk looked like as good a place as any to land my posterior. I made my way over to it to give my legs a break.

"So where did he go to do this show?" I asked.

I was half-seated when Misty cried out: "Oh please, don't! Don't sit there!" She rushed over with her arms extended, offering me help back up. I didn't need any.

"I'm sorry, Misty. I just assumed it would be strong enough for my weight."

"No, no, it's just . . . it's just, this is where Stan keeps his assistant."

"His assistant? You mean—"

She cut me off again; she was a regular pro at that. "Yes, Ben Drake, that's right. I mean his little person."

I couldn't hold back the laughter on that one, so I tried to cover it with a quick follow-up: "Where was this other show that Stan put on?"

"I don't know. I didn't want to know anything about it."

This was getting me no closer to tasting the bacon. I suspected there might be some meat in the trunk. "Can I take a look in here?"

"Why, of course you can. I'd be more than happy to open it up for you."

She put her hand on my shoulder, a token gesture to give herself a little space. I took the hint and took a few steps back. For the moment or so she was preoccupied with the trunk, I looked around the apartment.

Throw pillows of gaudy embroidered colors rested on the floor. Apparently this was the part of the clutter you were supposed to use for sitting. Between these seats, all kinds of tables held even more junk. My eye caught an old-fashioned metal lighter neatly arranged atop a battered book on one of the many tables.

"Well, here he is!"

Her voice broke my visual concentration. Perhaps because I wasn't paying attention to her, the line threw me for a second.

"Here who is?"

"Ta-da! The one . . . the only . . . the amazing assistant to the Sensational Stan Summers . . . Dandy Don!"

The trunk lid sprang open; I leaned over to peek in. Marble eyes stared back at me, along with a perpetual wooden smile, painted brown freckles, and molded blond hair, all dressed up in a tiny black suit, white shirt, and snappy red bow tie. This Don was dandy all right.

"Well, Ben Drake, darling, aren't you going to say something?"

"That's one nice dummy."

An annoying stream of laughter trickled from her painted mouth. Misty Summers was no spring chicken, but the more time I spent around her, the younger she seemed. I could picture her, over time, turning into a puppet herself.

"You may know a lot about detective work, Ben Drake, but you know very little about ventriloquism. This is called a vent figure."

"Right. I'll be sure to remember that."

"Dandy Don is Stan's favorite vent figure. He has this fabulous act worked up. I'll be honest; I did help him with it, only the littlest bit, I mean. Stan asks the kids in the audience—it's a kids act, did I mention that? Family entertainment, that's what pays the bills these days—Stan asks them jokes and then Dandy Don interrupts him with the punch line! There was this one time, it seems like just the other day, even though it had to be one, maybe two years . . ."

Misty was in her own world now, rattling off stories that were so candy-coated they gave me a bellyache. My eyes snapped back to the old-style lighter. Something about it got my senses buzzing, and I'd learned early in this business to trust my senses.

". . . the kids laughed and laughed. I kept telling Stan, 'They're laughing at your act, not at you, darling Stan.' But you know how performers are, right, Ben Drake?"

"Yeah, sure." I paused for a moment so she didn't think I was ignoring her as much as I actually was. "What exactly do you do for a living, Misty?"

"I'm a voice actress. Why, Ben Drake, don't tell me you don't recognize my voice."

"Misty, yours is a voice I wouldn't be quick to forget." I tipped my hat to her. It was the nicest backhanded compliment I could think of.

"Well, I guess after all it *was* a children's program." She stood up straight and said proudly, "I was the star of *Karl Kiwi's Outback Hour.* I performed the voice of Wanda Wombat. Would you like to hear a little bit, darling?"

Before I could say no, she raised her already high-pitched voice a couple of octaves: "Ooooo! Help me, Ben Drake! Help meeee! I'm all aloooone in the outback!"

That about did it for me. If I didn't think I was wasting my time before, I certainly did now. Even if this woman's husband really was missing, she seemed more concerned about herself than anything else.

"You know, Misty, I really got to be going," I said, making the perfunctory wristwatch glance, even tapping the face of it for effect. "I'm supposed to meet a friend . . ."

Though she kept smiling, she couldn't hide the disappointment that flashed in her eyes. "Please stay for one more moment longer. There's something else . . . something that might help you locate Stan."

She waited for me to bite. When I didn't, she kept trying to reel me in anyway.

Her voice dropped to a whisper: "A small matter of this other vent figure that went missing with him." She must have thought that hooked me, because she wasted no time switching back to full volume: "But first—my, my, my, I don't know where my manners are that I haven't done this already—may I offer you a drink?"

A drink was probably the only thing that could keep me from leaving, and the offer may have been the best thing I'd heard come out of Misty Summer's mouth yet. That funny feeling about the lighter came back to me, and I realized I'd better check it out now rather than risk having to come back to this place.

"Okay," I relented, "I'll stay for one drink."

She was already gone to the kitchen. I immediately went to the lighter. It rested on a thin, laminated hardback with a title that made me roll my eyes: *Old Jokes for Young Folks*. I picked up the Ronson lighter and examined the strange logo painted on its side. It read: *Independent Order of Foresters*. The flip side had emblazoned on it: *Dedicated to Family Security*. I set it aside and opened the book.

On the title page a short inscription, scratched out in a childlike scrawl, read:

Dear Stan: Keep 'em laughing!
—Rudy

I'm no expert on comedy, but neither was Rudy; the jokes in this book wouldn't make a hyena laugh.

"Here we are!"

I quickly closed the book. Her hips knocked back and forth as she entered the room, carrying a tall glass in each hand. "Two fresh, crisp ice waters, garnished with slices of lemon!"

I sighed. It was my turn to fail at concealing my disappointment.

"Is something wrong, Ben Drake, darling?"

"Well, I was hoping for something a little stronger, but I guess this will—"

"You mean alcohol?" Her eyes turned so bright I thought they could be headlights. Their beams burned holes right through me. "Oh my, oh my. I don't know why I didn't see it sooner. You must be a drinker. And how long have you known about this problem?"

"Problem? What are you talking about?"

"Do you keep alcohol in your apartment, Mr. Drake?"

"Sure, I have a bottle of—"

She wagged a scolding finger at me. "That's a sign, you know. Do your fellow detective friends have alcohol in their apartments?"

"Come on. Everyone I know has something to drink in their place."

"I suppose you drink alone?"

"I've got plenty of company, sister," I growled.

Misty flopped down onto one of the pillows, sat her water glass on the floor, crossed her arms, and pouted.

"All right, all right, I'm sorry."

"I'll have you know that Stan's father was an alcoholic—that's what killed him so young. Stan's very touchy about that, and so am I."

I cringed at the awkwardness of the situation; it was time for me to go. And yet this little confrontation shook the performance right out of Misty Summers, leaving behind a frightened, vulnerable woman. And I've always been a sucker for a woman in distress.

"You mentioned something about another puppet . . ." I said.

"Vent figure, yes. It scares the life out of me—I don't understand it, and I don't like it. Stan uses it in his sinister performances. It's the vent figure he took with him."

"This one got a name?" I braced myself for the alliteration.

"I don't know . . . I mean, I think he calls it Black Jack. I keep

telling you I don't know anything about this. I just want him back
... my husband ..." She had the girl tears turned off, but the way she
chewed her lower lip told me all I needed to know. "Oh, Ben Drake,
I'm really worried about him, I think something bad has happened.
I need you to find him. Please!"

"I tell you what, Misty. I'll do my best." I swallowed my water,
handed her the empty glass, and got out of there.

The door to the bar swung closed behind me with a soft whump. I
hopped down the three short steps and found myself inside the dark,
smoky, welcome atmosphere of the H.M.S. Pandora.

I loved this bar, and for all the right reasons. The bartenders poured
generous drinks. The jukebox featured the best of the best jazz. The
bar's soft, dark wood was fitted with classy brass accents and sported
an edge that made for comfortable leaning. The ceilings were high, and
management kept the lights low. In short: the Pandora had character.

Admittedly, on weekends the place got to be a bit crowded; local
kids eager to chew on anything nostalgic filled the place up. But on
weeknights it was just us regulars.

Barton Bourke stood behind the bar. Even though he was the
most irritating bartender who worked at the place, Barton could
pour drinks like the devil, so I put up with him. Besides, he knew
what I liked. Three fingers of bourbon sat on the bar waiting for me.
Next to it sat a drink that belonged to my friend Pappy.

Pappy was the nickname of Harper Meriwether, the oldest detective working for the Always Reddy Detective Agency. He was
also the best. You could tell that by the way he sat there—confident,
humble, sure. And he had style; you could tell that by the way he held
a glass of gin to his thin lips.

"Good evening, Ben, my boy," Pappy said as I placed myself on a
stool next to him. "You got a case that's running you down? It's not
like you to show up for one of our get-togethers so late."

"You know me, Pappy. I got it in my head that I'd stop and see
a client before coming here. Man, what a birdbrain she turned out
to be. She tried doing a whole song-and-dance for me, but she just
couldn't carry the tune."

His dry, raspy laugh imitated a dirty old man's evil snicker. It wasn't all that dirty—Pappy didn't have an evil bone in his body.

"That's because women find good-looking detectives irresistible. Believe me, I know."

"Come on," I said, giving him a nudge.

He laughed even harder. "Seriously, Benjamin, your forehead's got more lines than a road map. Not even your hat brim can hide it. What kind of case is doing this to you?"

"It's barely a case at all," I replied. "Some guy doesn't come home to his wife the other night. She calls us, all hysterical, claiming he disappeared. Well, I just spent some time with her, and believe me, Pappy, if I was standing in his shoes, I'd have wanted to disappear myself. Besides, she's not giving me the full story."

The old man just smiled at me. He knew when to talk and when to listen. I continued.

"Oh, and let me tell you the funny part: the guy's a ventriloquist."

"A ventriloquist?" He let loose with a low whistle. "There are not many things creepier than a puppet man, my boy, let me tell you."

"Maybe so, but this guy sounds like a babe in the woods."

Just then a slurred voice ripped through the cozy barroom: "Shay, can I getsh a refill here, Barton?"

One of the Pandora's regular lushes waved a draft glass in the air.

"Go ahead and pour it yourself, Eddie." Barton gestured toward the taps, then slid his bulk down the bar to where Pappy and I sat. He leaned in close to me and let fly with a whisper: "Trouble with a case, Drake?" His thick eyebrows jumped up and down over his eyes like a pair of drunken caterpillars. "Or trouble with the dames?"

"Nothing I can't handle, Bourke," I snapped.

Bourke loved a good crime story. He read all the old classic pulp authors: from Boucher to Hammett to Stout, and everyone in between. He fancied himself an intellectual problem solver, always attempting to match wits with me and the other ops who came here to unwind after a long day. He usually fared poorly, but that didn't stop him from thinking of himself as a latter-day Nero Wolfe.

"Come on, try me!"

"Christ, Barton, there's nothing to tell."

"Let him take a crack at it, Ben." Pappy smiled knowingly. "After all, you never know."

Pappy certainly had more patience for Bourke than I did, a fact I'd never understand.

I shrugged, then laid out what little of the story I had. When I got to the part about the lighter, an idea tickled my brain. Pappy had been a detective for something like fifty years, and he'd seen a lot in that time. Just maybe . . .

"Have you ever heard of the Independent Order of Foresters, Pappy? I saw a lighter with that logo on it at the house."

"Say, I've heard of them," Bourke drawled, rubbing his chin. "Aren't they some kind of secret society or something?"

"Thanks, Bourke, but I don't think so," I chided. "You're thinking of the Freemasons."

"No, no, I'm sure it's the Foresters."

Bourke squinted his eyes as if to squeeze the thoughts out of his brain. The man's inanities never failed to exasperate me.

"Come on, Bourke! Secret societies don't advertise on cigarette lighters!"

"Well, you don't gotta be like that, Drake. Jeez." Bourke, clearly dejected, shuffled back down the bar. I felt sort of bad about yelling at him.

Pappy shot me a look that let me feel his disappointment. "Anyway, yeah, I do know a little something about the Foresters," he said. "I think I may have even worked for them on a few occasions."

That last bit caught me off guard, and the sip of bourbon I'd just taken lodged itself in my throat. I coughed violently. "What?"

"Sure. They sell life insurance, and I don't have to tell you that in my many years I've dealt with a lot of life insurance scams."

"An insurance company . . ." I said, rubbing my jaw.

"That get you thinking about something, Ben?"

"Sure does, Pappy. Sure does."

It was late, but still about an hour too early to turn in. I've found that the best use of this particular hour is to make a quick stop at the office to check my messages. That way, anything left over from the day can simmer in the saucepan in my noggin. Come morning, I'd usually have something cooked up, even if it meant being a little late to the office.

On my way there, I couldn't resist the temptation to pick up a cup of the famous wonton soup from Cherry Boulevard Chinese. Take-out always tasted better in an unlit office. Or maybe it was just that I never felt like sitting alone in a bright red, green, and gold Chinese joint in the middle of the night.

Besides, ever since I'd left the Summers place, a strange little man in an oversized trench coat had been following me. When he wasn't behind me on foot, he tailed me in a tiny red car, almost cartoonlike in its size. I didn't know who he was, but I sure knew he wasn't a pro. Sitting in a public restaurant by myself just might give this gent enough courage to approach me. I'd rather keep him moving for now.

And so, soup in hand, I trotted up to the second floor of the William Kemmler Building, home of the Always Reddy Detective Agency's cluttered offices. As much time as I spent here, I've never felt at ease making my way through the dark, empty array of cubicles at night. I instinctively checked for my gun, a Smith & Wesson Model 637. The small frame allowed for only five shots, but I was more than willing to give up that one shot to gain the gun's easy-to-conceal size. If I couldn't bring down my target with five shots, that sixth wasn't going to be any good to me anyway.

At my desk I flicked on the banker's-style lamp; rays of soft light poured onto the floor and then rose up to create a halo around my space. On my desk sat a special file from the agency's receptionist, Rhoda Chang.

Rhoda was a secret asset to the agency. Nobody knew where she dug up her information—maybe she dated a policeman, or maybe she had an in-law working over at the records department. Then again, maybe she was a better detective than most of the ops gave her credit for. Regardless, she had a way of finding out the things detectives want found out.

The handwritten note from Rhoda on the front of the folder informed me that she had done some routine searches for the name *Stan Summers* and had found the enclosed news clippings.

I took a moment to remove my soup from its brown paper bag and speculate on what was going to be in those clippings. It could be standard fare: announcements of his act, perhaps a couple of reviews. It could be a wedding announcement; Misty struck me as the type who wouldn't pass up the opportunity to have her name in the papers.

I'd be lying if I said I wasn't hoping instead for something out of the crime blotter. I was willing to bet there were a few skeletons squirreled away in the Summers's closets along with the puppets. Maybe one of those skeletons was going to be kind enough to have made the front page.

I was in luck. After reading through the slim file, the whole sad situation made a lot more sense to me. I would have to ask Stan some questions before I could be sure of my hypothesis, and that would mean finding the missing ventriloquist.

Glancing at the small wristwatch I kept pinned by its strap to my cubicle wall, I knew finding Stan was tomorrow's task. Besides, Chinese always made me sleepy. And while it had been too early to go home when I got here, a stomach full of hot soup, along with a head boiling over with information, meant I was in no mood to read reports anymore—at least not unless I was lying down.

I took a quick peek out the front windows; my man was still hanging out in the shadows. I'd had enough company for one night, so I decided to slip out through the back alley. Keeping off the main streets, I'd have no problem losing this chump.

I'd parked a few blocks over on another street, partly to confuse my tail and partly for the exercise. As I hoofed it to my car, the wind fought my attempts to light one of the small cigars I liked to smoke. Frustrated and almost out of matches, I stepped into a phone booth to get my tobacco burning.

Just before I lit up, I thought I noticed a black shape duck behind a nearby telephone pole. A smoke would have to wait; I tucked my cigar away and slipped out of the booth. My eyes watered from both the wind and the fatigue of the day. I put a parked car between myself and where I thought I had seen something. That's when I noticed the shadow darting behind a mailbox. And that's when I pulled my gun.

I inched closer to the mailbox, my eyes scanning the whole area for any signs of movement. I got down close to the ground to see if that point of view would reveal my hiding man. Nothing.

Maybe I was seeing things; it was late, and I was exhausted. But just as I had almost convinced myself that my tired eyes made the whole thing up, I stopped dead in my tracks. I could feel a presence behind me.

I turned around slowly, my gun at my side.

A scream ripped through the night like the kind you hear in old monster movies. Only there weren't any giant spiders, big monkeys, fire-breathing lizards, robots, squids, blobs, or bogie men.

There was just me, my gun, and the guy doing the screaming.

He stood there clutching a battered paper bag to his chest. The fear running through his body made him look like a kid, though I guessed him to be in his early thirties. The numerous freckles dotting his face added to his youthful look, as did his uncombed light brown hair.

He was a tall, thin, frightened man. He looked taller than he really was because of the thick black-and-white vertical stripes on his pants and jacket. His pants must have been at least an inch too short, making him appear to have sprouted up like a weed. The high cuffs showed off his yellow and black polka-dot socks. In the low light, his loafer-style shoes looked as if they were made of dyed-red hair.

The only other red in his outfit was on the trim of the ruffles of his tuxedo shirt, which I could barely see peeking out from behind the bag he clung to.

His jaw bounced up and down, making his lips shake like he was in an earthquake, as he squeaked, "Oh my goodness, that's a gun! And I'm sure it's a real gun—you're a real detective, why wouldn't you be carrying a real gun? Only now that gun's pointed at me, and I can't help but think—"

"Cool it," I ordered. "Your name's Stan Summers, right? Now tell me how come the person I'm supposed to be finding is finding me."

He lowered the bag, still keeping it close to him, and leaned in to whisper: "You have to help me. I know you've been hired to find me, but you've got to save me from them."

"From who? Somebody's after you?"

"Of course! They're after me!" Again he brought his voice to a whisper. "I'm almost afraid to say their name out loud . . . You have to come with me, somewhere where it's safe."

When somebody was being chased in Testacy City, ten to one said it was a gambling debt. I tried to think of the sharks, numbers runners, and other underworld types who might have their hooks in this guy.

"Let me guess, Stan: It's either Small-Tooth Kelley, Manny 'the Rose' Flores, or Dan 'the Man' Neff. Or maybe Hermann the German."

He looked honestly confused by my list, though not as confused as I must have looked when he said, "No, no, not them, not any of them. Much worse, Mr. Detective, much worse . . ."

His voice trailed off, and he looked around frantically before he whispered his softest whisper yet: "It's The Brotherhood of Orpheus."

"What is that, some kind of entertainment fraternity?"

"Oh, you go ahead and laugh now, sir," he said.

I wasn't laughing.

"I wanted to laugh too, when they said they knew a way I could actually talk to my dead father, whom I love very much, thank you. Little did I know they could *torture the dead!*"

The ridiculousness of his statement certainly amused me, until I thought he might actually start to cry. He managed to continue: "That's why you have to help me. I didn't cooperate with them, so now they will defile my poor father's spirit by tormenting him forever!"

Misty had been right about one thing: superstition ran hot in this husband of hers. But just because I didn't believe this mumbo-jumbo didn't mean I couldn't see the harsh belief in his eyes. Someone or something had scared this guy bad—bad enough to give life to his own ghosts. He could tell I was skeptical, probably from the cock-eyed smirk I just couldn't wipe off my face.

He insisted: "I have proof! When you hear my story, you'll see."

"A story is hardly proof," I said, "but all right, let's hear the—"

"No! Not here. I can't stay in one place for too long or the Voice will find me—"

"The voice? What are you talking about?"

"We've got to go somewhere safe . . ." he pleaded.

"All right, let's get to my car. I'm parked right over here." I waved my hand, gesturing at a row of vehicles parked down the block.

"A car? That's no good, they'll—"

"It's good enough to get us somewhere else," I interrupted. "Now come on, unless you want to stay out here."

Stan gulped and nodded frantically.

"Then let's get going," I ordered, putting my gun back into its holster.

Anxious to get this business over with, I took off for the safety of my car with long, brisk strides. Stan wasted no time falling into step with me, managing to keep up and keep quiet.

"Windy tonight, isn't it?" Stan asked as I pulled my powder-blue Galaxie 500 away from the curb.

"Don't be a sap," I scolded, keeping one eye on the road in front of me and one eye on the rearview mirror.

Stan didn't respond; instead, he stared down at the rumpled paper bag, now resting between his feet.

"You've got better things to talk about than the weather," I growled, "so get yappin'."

"What do you want to know, Mr. Detective?"

"First, I want you to stop calling me Mr. Detective. It's unnerving. My name's Ben Drake."

"Okay, Mr. Drake. No problem."

"Good. Now give me all of it."

Stan took a deep breath, straightened his bow tie, cleared his throat, and began: "For you to really believe what I'm about to tell you—or at least for you to begin to understand—I have to start at the beginning. My father, Stan Summers Senior, never hurt anyone; he was an entertainer. He began teaching me sleight of hand before I could walk. I knew tricks that would amaze adults even when I was in kindergarten. But my real passion was my father's passion: ventriloquism." He slouched forward, his hands on his knees. "It was only me and my father growing up—"

Suddenly, he slid his body as far away from me as he could, pressing himself almost flat against the passenger door. "What are you doing!?"

I sat there dumbfounded. "I'm trying to light a cigar, what's it look like?"

"Smoking is a filthy habit, sir, absolutely filthy. And that's not to mention the devastating damage it does to your vocal cords. Just listen to what it has done to your voice—"

"Hey, I'm no singer." I slid the car's lighter back into its slot and dropped the cigar into the ashtray. I sighed. "There, no cigar for me. Now you keep talking."

"Thank you." He relaxed only slightly, smiling a smile meant to fade. It did. "My father was quite superstitious. He believed in the real power of ventriloquism. I didn't know what he meant by 'power' at the time, though I would one day find out. My hopes and dreams were very important to me when I was younger. And they were smashed to pieces the day my father died, penniless. He used alcohol to escape, you see, and in the end it took his life."

Stan sneered at me, I assumed, not because of anything to do with me personally. It was just the sneer of a man made bitter by having his family taken away. It made me wonder: how did a guy like this make it as an entertainer?

"Stan, are you just lying to me? Or are you lying to yourself too?"

Blank noncomprehension washed over his face.

"Don't play dumb. I did a little research this evening. Your father may have liked to booze it up, but that's not what killed him, and you know it."

His skin paled a few shades. "What do you mean by that?"

"Please. We both know you found your father dead, shot full of holes in his apartment! The police never solved the murder, but I've got a strong hunch I know what the killers were after."

The poor guy's lips trembled at my brutish behavior.

"Look, I realize I'm being harsh. Truth is, though, it's twenty-some years too late to help your father, but start giving me the real story and I'll help you out of this mess you're in tonight. How about it?"

I looked over at Stan. He stared straight ahead, arms folded angrily across his chest. His answer to me turned out to be a sullen pout.

We rode in silence for a few minutes. I craved a smoke something fierce but settled for listening to the soothing purr of my car's eight cylinders.

"Where are we going?" Stan asked.

"I'm taking you to my place. No one will bother us there."

"No! No! You'll get me killed!" Stan shouted, clawing at the handle of the door.

"Calm down, you crazy rabbit!" I shouted back. I reached over and grabbed a fistful of Stan's jacket, then slammed him back against the seat. "What's gotten into you?"

"They'll find me at your place . . . just keep moving . . . please."

I sighed again. "Fine, we'll keep moving."

I made a few turns and pointed the car back toward downtown, taking the occasional split-second corner. A pair of headlights kept my eyes pinned to the rearview. I steered us through a stretch of bright streetlights and noticed the headlights belonged to a tiny red car.

Looked like my trench-coated shadow had returned. I opted not to mention it to Stan; I didn't need him freaking out any more than he was already. I planned to just keep driving until he started talking again.

"My father wasn't dead yet, you know—when I found him, I mean. I'd like to think he held onto life's breath just long enough to tell me goodbye. I could see that he was trying to say something, but I could barely listen to him, I was so afraid and horrified. I was crying and screaming . . ." He paused to wipe the corners of his eyes. "But he kept telling me to be quiet and listen. 'Stanley,' he said. 'Go and get the brown performance case in the bedroom . . . the one that looks almost new.' After complaining that I didn't want to leave his side, I did what he asked."

"Let me guess: he gave you something special, right?"

"Very special." Summers reached down, gingerly lifted the paper bag, and set it on the seat between us. Nervously he reached in and slowly withdrew its contents.

Looking at what came out of the bag gave me a creepy, unbalanced feeling—a feeling I remembered getting from campfire ghost stories when I was young enough to believe in them.

He fiddled with the unfinished, handmade ventriloquist's puppet he held in his hands. The wooden smile—no, not a smile, a hinged slit—was the only feature on the blank face. No eyes, no ears, no nose. No molded hair, no painted freckles. Just a plain, oval, white-painted headlike shape.

Unlike Dandy Don and his snazzy suit, this figure wore an all-black jumpsuit. I wanted to reach out and touch it, simply because it looked so unreal. As Stan took it out of the bag, he sat it up in the crook of his left arm as delicately as if it were a flesh-and-blood baby.

"He gave you a puppet?" I asked.

"Yes, isn't it beautiful?"

"It doesn't look quite finished."

"My father had been working on it. When he gave it to me he said—and I'll never forget this as long as I'm on this good earth: 'I did some things that may not have been right, but I needed to do them for us . . . for you. Take this and make it your assistant. Let it be the gateway for all the voices you have in your head. It will protect you if you protect it. Never, ever let it out of your sight.'"

"What makes this figure so special?"

"It's filled with the *power*."

"What do you mean?"

"It took me a long time to figure it out, Mr. Drake. After my father left this world, I spent a lot of time alone. Most weekends I would go to his grave and read books on magic or practice my act. It was during this time, under the shade of cemetery trees, that I developed an interest in the occult. When I met my wife, Misty, this fascination of mine really made her feel uneasy. She thought I always went too far."

"What do you mean 'too far'?"

"Oh my God!" he shouted, and his eyes got real big. "Stop the car!"

Everything slipped into slow motion as I slammed on the brakes. My car's tires squealed on the dry pavement, and we came to a skidding halt. I'd been looking at Stan, and when my eyes snapped back to the road I expected to see another car, a person, or some sort of obstacle in the road. All I saw was air.

"Goddamnit, Summers! I've just about had it with your insanity!"

"This building," he murmured, indicating the boarded-up old theater we'd stopped in front of. "We'll be safe in here."

"What? How do you know that?" I glanced in my rearview mirror just in time to see a pair of headlights wink out.

"The Voice, it told me so!" At this bit of nonsense his face lit up, and he stuffed his prized puppet back into its bag. Before I could say anything he bolted out of the car.

Angrily, I spun the wheel and moved into a better parking position, then shut off the motor and followed Summers.

I found him trying to pull open the boarded-up front door.

"Didn't this voice tell you how to get into the joint?" I snickered.

"You should have more faith in the Voice, Mr. Drake," Summers scolded.

"I got plenty of faith right here," I grunted, pulling out my gun. "Come on, if you need to get in here so bad, let's try the back."

I wondered why I was playing out this charade as Stan led the way around the corner of the building. But this sort of puzzle is what I love about being a detective.

Before we slipped out of sight, I checked the street behind us; all seemed quiet. Still, I broke open my gun to make sure the cylinder held all five rounds.

In the narrow alley behind the derelict building we found a broken window that opened into the basement. We slipped through, landing inside a small, dark room.

I rubbed my jaw, doing my best to forget about that smoke I wanted, thinking instead it might be time to start taking pulls off the flask I had in my back pocket.

"Now what?" Stan asked.

I rolled my eyes, deciding I definitely needed to grab a drink. I pulled out my flask and took a satisfying swig.

Stan recoiled at the sight and shook his head. "Another bad habit—"

"Tough," I spat. "I'm putting up with your nonsense; you can put up with mine." I took another swallow of bourbon. "Now, how about we jump to the part about some brotherhood chasing you."

Instantly all the fear that had marked his features when I met him returned. His Adam's apple bobbed up and down as he struggled with his anxiety.

"Okay, yes, I can do that," he spluttered. "It was right after my performance on Monday night. You see, my friend, a circus clown named Rudy Romaine had put me in contact with a nightclub owner willing to let me perform my occult ventriloquism show. Only problem was, hardly anyone but Rudy and his friends showed up." Stan's fingers ran through his tousled head of hair. "Anyway, after the show, the club owner had a regular jolly time yelling at me, saying things like I was finished. I didn't need him to tell me that."

He scuffed his shoe against the ground.

"As I walked out from the back past the lonely chairs, Rudy stood near the exit, waiting for me. He told me he'd met some fellows—old carnies—who wanted to have a word with me. They said they had the ability to contact my father from beyond the grave."

Sure they did, I thought. I trickled a little more bourbon through my lips.

"Of course I wanted to find out more, so Rudy led the way to an apartment building on the south side of town. We all went up to the third floor, but before we went into the room, Rudy handed each of us a white, expressionless mask from a small box sitting outside the door and told me that during the ceremony everyone had to wear them."

A scratchy meow sounded from somewhere in the old theater. Stan jumped and almost lost his breath. I felt a chill run through my body. Standing in the small room suddenly made me very nervous.

"I could barely see with that mask on," Stan complained. "We went through the door into a big, open space, very dimly lit. It had tons of candles scattered all over the floor, but only a few of them were burning. They made the room smell like wax. An old strongbox rested on a table in the middle of the room."

"Say, Stan," I interjected, slipping my flask back into my pocket, "let's get a move on, okay?"

I pulled open the room's only door, not surprised to find a hallway on the other side.

"Uhhhh, where are we going?" Stan asked.

"You're the one who didn't think it was a good idea to stand around in one place too long. I'm starting to agree," I explained. "Let's look around. While we walk, why don't you tell me about the guys who ran this ceremony."

We moved our party into the cramped hallway, then toward what I guessed to be the front of the building.

"Oh, they were a motley group. The biggest one, a massive man, never spoke. There was another big guy; he was more like your build, except he had tattoos covering his arms. He didn't speak either. The last guy was named Phil. I could tell he used to be a carnival barker, and he did all the talking."

The hallway, which seemed to run the length of the building, held even less light than the room we'd left behind. I cautiously slinked forward, Stan Summers following closely behind me, now whispering.

"Rudy told me to put my vent figure into the strongbox. He said they would use it later as part of the ceremony. Well, I was willing to do a lot of crazy things to be able to talk to my father, but I didn't feel right letting go of Black Jack. Rudy started giving me some pleading explanation, when the little man cut him off with a sharp, booming voice. He asked me if I was familiar with . . . the *power* of ventriloquism. I remember he lathered his hands as he spoke."

I thought I heard the scrape of someone trying to be stealthy behind us. I paused in the hallway, wishing I'd had the foresight to get the pocket flashlight out of the trunk of my car before we began this adventure. Stan held his breath, face glowing with fear. After a moment, I nodded for him to continue.

"So I told him I knew a little bit. He laughed and said that it was good I came because I'd learn a lot more. But first he wanted me to put Black Jack in the box."

Ahead of us, I could just make out the end of the hallway and a set of rickety-looking iron steps that led up to the main floor.

"Rudy stood back and kept motioning at the table with his head. Then . . ."

I heard Stan scuffle to a halt, so I stopped and looked over my shoulder. He just stood in the hall and nervously chewed at his left pinky finger.

"Then what?" I whispered through clenched teeth.

"Then the two thugs lit some more of the candles as Phil explained to me that the only way for me to learn about the Voice was to be fully aware of a displaced source. He explained that he was no longer going to talk directly to me. He was going to have the Voice talk to me . . ."

Stan trailed off and went back to gnawing on his pinky.

"Phil motioned to the giant man, who then moved his huge body just behind me, on the left. The other silent man stepped into place to my right, boxing me in. This is when I really started to get scared. Phil told me not to look in his direction but to keep focused on the strongbox. I was to imagine that his voice was coming from it. This, Phil said, was what ventriloquism was all about—the Disassociated Voice."

Stan's fingers fanned out, and his voice took on a tone of mystery. It spooked me into thinking I'd heard something a few yards away. I strained against the darkness, looking down the hall, expecting whoever had followed us in the tiny red car to emerge. By now I knew who it was, and I was ready to make a stand. I just didn't want it to happen in this narrow hallway.

"Phil wasn't all that convincing; it was more a demonstration of the power of the Voice. But the more I listened, the more I knew that I was really hearing the Voice."

"So what'd it tell you?"

Stan began fidgeting more and more, tapping his foot nervously against the hard floor. I started up the iron steps and tried to coax him along with me.

"It told me that the tradition of ventriloquism is timeless." Stan rubbed his hand furiously over his brow, trying to flatten out the thick lines of anxiety. "And It gave me example after example. I didn't see how this applied to me, other than my being a ventriloquist. But then the Voice told me about Orpheus."

Another noise came from down the long, dark hallway.

"Orpheus had the greatest voice of any human being," Stan continued. "A voice so sweet it was said that it could charm wild animals, literally mesmerizing them. His bride was bit by a poisonous snake and taken away from him by cruel fate—like my father was cruelly taken from me. But unlike me, he vowed to do something about it."

Stan cursed and slammed a balled fist against his thigh.

"He journeyed into the Underworld, using his sweet singing voice for comfort and protection. When Hades, the lord of the dead, heard the songs of Orpheus, he agreed to let him take his true love back to the land of the living. But there was one condition."

I chimed in: "There's always one condition."

"I know, I know . . . All Orpheus had to do was walk out of the Underworld and not look back. But at the very last minute he did, and his love slipped from his fingers a second time. As if that wasn't enough punishment, his end was even more cruel."

I finished for him, pulling from the various books I'd read: "A band of witches ripped him to pieces. They scattered his dismembered body, throwing his head into the nearby river, where it floated downstream. And the damn thing kept singing. Well, Stan, you certainly made out better than that."

Summers just stared up at me on the stairs, thought etched across his face. "Orpheus. The disembodied voice; a ventriloquial voice."

He closed his eyes. I saw him shaking and felt the hairs on my arms standing straight up. I gazed down the hall, still seeing nothing. I wasn't going to wait all night.

"All right, time to get moving again," I ordered.

We marched to the top of the steps, arriving in another hallway much like the one below it but with a little more light. Without hesitating, Stan began hiking toward the back of the building. I followed, guessing the voice he talked about guided him.

"Stan . . ."

"Don't you get it, Mr. Drake? They were the Brotherhood of Orpheus! The legendary Voice of Orpheus taught them the secrets of the dead! That means they could reach my father. They offered to contact him for me . . . but, but they wanted something in exchange."

"Let me guess."

"They said they needed a sacrifice—a sacrifice to please Orpheus. Phil pointed at my father's vent figure and told me to give it to him!"

"What's Orpheus need with an unfinished puppet?" I asked.

"I don't know, and I never found out," Stan squealed. "I didn't want to hear any more! I grabbed Black Jack and ran out of there as fast as I could."

Sound carried much better on the main floor. I heard the low rumble of a big car outside. I thought I heard it drive by, but maybe I heard it idle for a moment, then stop. I couldn't tell for sure.

"As I ran out the door, I heard the ringleader's high-pitched shout: 'Think of your father, Stan! Orpheus will find you eventually, but it's your father who will suffer immediately!' That only made me run faster. I should have fled sooner, not that it would have helped. I wish I could just put the whole thing behind me."

I paused, cocking my head, trying to figure out if soft footprints echoed in my ears or if the puppet man's paranoia had me hearing things.

"We'll put it behind you soon enough," I assured. Probably sooner than Stan Summers would like. "Why'd you hide? Why didn't you just go home?"

"Home? I couldn't go home; they were watching me."

"Then call the cops," I grunted. "They take care of that sort of thing."

Stan took a deep, labored breath. "The cops couldn't do anything. The Brotherhood wasn't watching me like normal people watch people . . . they were using the magic of Orpheus."

"Come on! The magic of Orpheus?"

"Yes! Weren't you listening?" His lips quivered as the tears started.

"All right. So why didn't you call Misty? She's been worried about you."

"I know, I know," he cooed apologetically, "but I couldn't take the risk."

"Risk? Hell, man, use a pay phone! That's what they're for."

"No way could I call! Everyone knows the telephone itself is the ultimate Orphic invention! Alexander Graham Bell was a secret member of the Brotherhood of Orpheus, and he designed it to be a tool of the Disassociated Voice."

I frowned. I knew a woman from the county coroner's office who loved wacky conspiracies. I was going to score big points when I told her about Ma Bell and Orphism.

Stan Summers looked at me, wiping his eyes with his sleeve. "What could I do but run?" He pulled out a handkerchief and blew his nose. I noticed that it matched his socks. "And I've been hiding ever since."

Suddenly the sound of shattering glass echoed through the building. Stan Summers screamed.

I bolted to the nearest door and threw it open, then tossed the quivering mass of flesh that was Stan Summers through it. I followed, slamming the door shut behind me. The door had no lock, so I glanced quickly around, looking for something to block the door.

When I turned around I admit I felt a little shock run through me.

We stood on the old theater's stage.

Other than the two of us, nothing else filled the small scene. There weren't even any curtains. Beyond us—except for a dim light that glowed down from the broken skylights, illuminating the area in front of the stage—inky darkness consumed the empty theater.

Stan had curled into a ball, protecting his still-bagged puppet, right in the center of the stage.

"Oh my goodness!" he whimpered. "They've found me! I told you they could find me if I stayed in one place—"

"Calm down!" I snapped. "They can't see through the phone lines, Stan! They were lying to you. The only reason they knew you were here is because I was followed."

"You were followed?" Stan said.

"Yeah, ever since I left your place this evening I've had a tail. And not a very good one. There's a couple of other things you don't know . . ."

"What kind of things don't I know?"

"That whole bit about the Brotherhood and Orpheus . . . now, that's a great story, but it's nothing more than a story created by some people trying to pull a fast one on you."

I waited a couple of minutes, allowing the emptiness of the theater to sink in, then shouted out toward the dark: "Isn't that right, Misty?"

Stan pulled himself into a sitting position, a confused look on his face, just as Misty Summers stepped into the light, tears heavy on her cheeks. An unimposing figure wearing a trench coat waddled out beside her.

"I'm so sorry, Stan, darling," Misty choked out, "but I did it for us. I did it so we'd never have to worry about money again!"

"Yeah, Stan, I'm sorry too," her sidekick mumbled. "I thought I planned everything out."

Misty took a step toward her husband, who was still curled up clutching his puppet, then turned to me. "Ben Drake, how'd you figure out I had anything to do with it?"

"I'm a detective, lady. I get paid to figure things out. I told you in the beginning that I didn't know what the crime was. Once I nailed down the fact that this case was about money and not about a missing husband, I knew you were pulling the strings."

She stared at me like she didn't know what I was talking about. I made it simple for her: "Let's face it, Misty, you're no actress."

Stan sat there, slack-jawed, not knowing what to think. I helped him out.

"You see, Stan, I originally thought your wife was trying to pull some kind of insurance scam. Then I got my hands on the reports of your father's death. The killers were looking for something, something I bet they never found. What was it, Stan? Reports I saw said twenty years ago the talk on the street was that Stan Senior had some secret treasure he kept hidden." I rubbed the back of my neck. "Why don't you pick up the story from here, Rudy."

The clown in the trench coat stepped forward. Before he could start, Stan cried out: "That's just a myth! There's no secret treasure! I don't know how it all got started."

"It got started 'cause it was . . . 'cause it was true!" Rudy gasped.

"Shut up!" Stan yelled. He started rocking back and forth on the floor.

"Now, now, Stan," Misty said. "He's right. Tell him, Rudy."

"Ahh, it's kinda like, um, it's kinda like this: I was down on my luck, drinking in this old bar, and I talked to this guy, this . . . he was a retired clown. And, ah, he asked me if I knew anything about that killing, that ventriloquist that got killed years ago. Well, you know, I knew Stan Junior, so yeah, I knew about it. And he goes on and on about these diamonds that Stan's dad got somehow, maybe 'cause, well, Stan's dad did a little work for the Mexican Mafia."

"Stop it! Stop it!" Stan clutched his father's puppet even harder. His forehead looked like a compressed spring ready to pop. "That's not true!"

"Well, I wasn't ready to just go and believe this old guy, Stan," Rudy said with a bouncing lower lip. "But then he started telling all about all the, ah, criminals that came looking for it but couldn't find it. And then he said they weren't looking in the right places."

"They weren't looking in the unfinished puppet," I said.

"That's it exactly!" Rudy blurted out, throwing his hands into the air. "So I called, ah, Misty and tells her. But she goes into how the puppet never left Stan's side. And how Stan's father meant so much to him that she couldn't just *tell* him about the diamonds, 'cause he wouldn't go for it.

"So I thought of this whole, ah . . . ah, performance to get the puppet—you know, just like *borrow* it and then give it back later. That way we could all have a nice three-way split. I staged the whole thing, hiring these guys I used to know back in the circus, paying them five hundred dollars for a night's work. I just didn't, I couldn't know that Phil DeMarco musta heard the same story, and tried stealing the show from me."

"That ain't all we're going to steal, you clown!" a tough but chewy voice echoed out from the shadowy wings of the theater. "What you and the ventriloquist are gonna do now is hand over the puppet."

Three men moved into the light. The biggest of them stood un-armed, his mean knuckles prepared for doing damage. The tattooed fellow, an oily, big-boned brute, flicked open a long, thin switch-blade. The guy between them, the wild-eyed Phil DeMarco, held a gun. So did I.

"First of all," he squeaked, pointing at me with his gun, "would you be so kind as to put that nasty pistol away?"

"Do I have to? I'd rather keep it out so it can play nice with yours."

The Brotherhood of Orpheus stepped closer to me. They were on my right; Misty and Rudy were on my left.

Phil barked, "Now, how should I deal with this piece-of-meat detective? The choices are many and various indeed." He spoke to an imaginary audience in the empty seats. "Clearly, on the one hand, I could send Mugly, my strongman, to pound, pulverize, bash, and smash him with his massive fists. Of course, on the other hand, but also equally clearly, I could send Jacko, my nimble knife man, to slice, dice, and julienne him to bits. And then, very simply, I could just shoot him myself."

"Or I could, I could just shoot *you*!" Rudy's shaky hand pulled out his own gun. He shouted like a teakettle: "I've got a deal for you! I'll pay you the five hundred and get you a share of the diamonds . . ."

Phil laughed with smug stupidity. "And I've got a deal for *you*! You keep your lousy five and we get all the diamonds."

"Phil," I said, "the only deal you boys will be getting is a jail cell."

I kept my eyes bouncing between Rudy and the thugs. Thoughts sped around my brain: Could I take out Phil before he shot Rudy? Could I take out Rudy before he shot Phil? Or could I take out both of these guys before they shot me? My heart worked overtime, pumping blood through my body like cars around a racetrack.

Phil broke his tight frown long enough to complain: "Enough with this long-winded and entirely unnecessary discourse. We're going to grab the dingus, put the PI on ice, and vamoose on out of here."

"Don't be an idiot. Tougher guys than you have tried to cool me,"

I snarled. "You're better off dropping the pistol and letting me take you in."

"That's enough outta your mouth, you worthless piece of trash." Phil motioned over his shoulder to his giant associate who then stomped toward me. "Mugly, I want you to tear this detective apart limb by limb."

A low drone came out of Mugly's mouth: "I will hurt you now."

I had to take care of this thug—and fast. If I could drop the guy and push him in Phil's direction, I'd have a good chance to take control of this mess.

Suddenly the thunderous roar of a gunshot echoed through the room.

I immediately flattened myself on the stage.

A few more gunshots barked out in answer to the first.

I figured Rudy's trigger finger got a little itchy and that made Phil's itchy as well.

"You killed my father! You bastards killed my father!"

Oh, Christ. Stan Summers had a gun.

It was time for this caper to come to a close, but first I had to get behind something solid. I rolled off the stage and scampered behind the first row of theater seats, then peeked out just in time to see the knife man slump to the ground, clutching his belly.

"Jacko!" Mugly shouted, trudging over as fast as his thick legs would take him to help his fallen partner.

I looked over and saw Misty kneeling next to the bleeding Rudy Romaine. "No, no . . . please, don't let it end like this," she sobbed.

Phil's face burned as he took aim at Stan, who stood on stage as if in a trance, holding a smoking antique Colt service revolver.

"Stan, you stupid, stupid simpleton!" Phil screamed. "All you had to do was fork over the puppet. You weren't supposed to die, but now you've forced my hand and I have no recourse but to kill you!"

"No!" Misty screamed as she jumped in front of Phil's gun. "I won't let you hurt my Stan!"

"Jacko's dead!" Mugly bellowed, thudding his way over to the frightened Stan Summers, leaping up on the stage with ease.

"Mugly, grab the puppet and let's go!" Phil commanded.

But instead of grabbing the puppet, Mugly plucked the gun right out of the trembling ventriloquist's hand. Stan yelled like a girl, but went quiet when Mugly's fist connected with his jaw and sent him skating across the wooden floor of the stage.

The strongman picked up the puppet and headed for the door.

I flinched as the sound of another shot filled the theater. This one came from Phil's gun. Misty's body crumpled to the ground.

"Damn it, Phil," I cried from behind my hiding spot. "It's over! Drop the gun and—"

Bullets flew at me, ricocheting off the metal of the chairs in front of me.

I fired a couple back, but not in time. The two crooks had fled the scene. Only the echo of Phil's high-pitched laughter stayed behind.

I stood up and looked around. Rudy and Misty lay like a pair of dolls on a playroom floor. On the other side of the theater, Jacko had curled up, trying to hold his guts in. I could hear Stan sobbing up on the stage.

I walked over to Rudy Romaine. Half his face had been blown away. His one remaining eye stared straight at me. I shook my head and walked over to Misty.

The bullet had ripped through her shoulder. Blood soaked through most of her blouse. I checked for a pulse. She would live. Good thing Phil was a bad shot.

Jacko gurgled off to the side. He'd been hit squarely in the gut and blood trickled across his lips, but if he could hold out for the ambulance, he'd make it.

Stan pulled himself up to a sitting position and continued whimpering. His face was already starting to swell and bruise from the knuckles he took.

I wanted to tell him not to worry; his wife would live, and even Testacy City's police would be able to nab those two dummies soon enough, but I knew that would be no consolation for a man like Stan Summers.

"My father's dead . . . oh, God . . . my father's dead . . ." he said in a hoarse whisper.

I never knew my father, so I could only guess at how Stan felt. Even though his entire life had been spent in the shadow of his father's death, his real torment was only just now beginning.

But for this case, the curtains came down. The show was over.

Case Two
Death Plays a Foul Game

I spied Trout Mathers and his buddy Blackie Lawton chasing back tequila shots at the bar of the H.M.S. Pandora. It hadn't been my plan to spend Friday night watching two of Testacy City's most sought-after gangsters do the salt-slam-and-squeeze. I'd anticipated taking the night off, doing nothing but relaxing at my favorite hangout. But this particular Friday night found me pulling double duty as I lounged at the Pandora, a hand on a drink and an eye on these thugs.

Lawton's laughter ripped through the place like the growl of an angry dog. Mathers shot him an elbow to the ribs. The look he gave Lawton suggested they were there to lay low, not loudmouth their way into the spotlight.

I didn't know either of these heavies personally, but I sure knew their reputations. As a rule, Mathers pulled carefully calculated heists, the bigger the better. He was all spectacle and show. Even now at the bar he looked like a showman, with his tight pinstriped suit, his greased-back wavy hair, and his sharp mustache that resembled an upside-down V. Naturally, he caused quite a stir in the hot sheets, crime sheets, and bedsheets.

Lawton always got his share of attention too, though not because of his résumé. His loud mouth and violent habits, usually something to do with the drug trade, were what kept him in the spotlight. People dismissed him as stupid, but I sized him up as more careless than dumb. He'd been busted a lot but never spent too much time behind bars. Apparently, he knew the right people.

Another round of tequila kept my pals quiet for the moment, whispering back and forth to each other. When Trout Mathers spoke he flicked his index and middle fingers with his thumb, not at Lawton but randomly to the side. This motion somehow matched the devilish light in his burning eyes.

I could smell something foul brewing between the two of them. Yep, I could smell it all right, even though I sat all the way across the room in one of the Pandora's high-back leather booths.

Something else about Trout Mathers spelled certain trouble tonight: Last Tuesday he'd held a performance at a branch of the Second National Bank. Something happened and the whole thing went south. Typically, Mathers slipped through the cops' fingers; this time, not as typically, he did so empty-handed.

"Yo, buddy!" Lawton made an attempt to signal the bartender by snapping his fingers. The guy behind the bar, Barton Bourke, rarely went out of his way to rush serving me. Now he gave these guys the same treatment.

From all I'd heard and from what I was seeing, I knew Lawton to be the kind of gangster not used to waiting. He rubbed his nose back and forth with his hand like he was trying to paint his fingers with snot. When Bourke finally came over to him, Lawton roared about the service, threatening to take their drinking somewhere else.

Mathers coaxed Bourke into not turning his back on them. He spoke quickly but calmly. I couldn't make out most of it, but the look on the bartender's face slowly turned less sour. He even cracked a grin.

Mathers stepped back, smiled, adjusted the tie he wore with his crisp collar, and flicked fingers from Lawton to Bourke. Lawton shoved his fist into his pocket, pulled out a wad of bills, and slammed it on the bar counter.

Something fell from Lawton's pocket. I tried not to stare, so I began casually glancing around the place. When I threw my eyes back his way, I saw him pick up what looked like a dry, scaly chicken foot. He hastily repocketed it.

A voice from my immediate right distracted me. I leaned my head over to look in that direction, through the cigarette smoke turned gold by the yellow overhead lights. The voice came from a slippery college kid with too much gunk in his hair.

"Hey, don't I know you from somewhere?" he said, hovering over a girl with her back to me who was smoking a long thin cigarette. He held a drink in one hand; his other hand swam around in the pocket of his baggy trousers. A smile hung on his face, waiting for her to respond or even notice. She didn't do either.

"You know, I really think I know you from somewhere. Did you go to law school? Maybe that's where I recognize you from."

She gave him a quick but polite no, which is more than a chump like this guy deserved. If he had taken the hint and walked away, I wouldn't have thought twice about him or the girl and would have returned my attention to the gangsters at the bar.

But he didn't leave. He sat down next to her and leaned forward to look up at her downturned eyes.

"Wait a second. I've got it. You're from New York," he continued with a mock affluent wave of his hand. "You've totally got this East Coast thing going on."

I could only guess at her expression. She crossed her legs and flicked the ashes of her cigarette on the floor. A long, tight black dress with frills at the bottom exposed only her thin, milk-white ankles.

She breathed out, "Are *you* from New York?"

I smiled at her line. I'm not the kind to chase broads; that was Trout Mathers's bag. You could count on Mathers for a lot of things: he got the babes, he gave the bruises, he got the banks, he gave the slip to the cops. A regular old Mr. Smooth.

My eyes ran up the line of this girl's leg, and I thought again: I'm not the kind who chases broads. I'm the kind who chases crooks.

"Yes . . . well, New Jersey, actually," the boy stammered. "But I used to like to go into the city when I could. The club scene is really hot now . . . I, ah, really love to dance. You know, just let it all go. The energy, the lights, it all flows through you . . . Hey, can I buy you a drink?"

This was like watching a car accident. I shoveled a handful of nuts into my mouth.

Her hand reached down to rub a spot where the strap of her shoe wrapped around her ankle. She said, "I don't drink."

Lawton's laughter ripped through the place again. I looked to see if he was watching the same scene as me. He wasn't even facing this direction. Seems like Trout Mathers was entertaining him and Barton with some story or another. Barton would listen to anything as long as it meant he didn't have to move.

I licked my lips after taking another gulp of bourbon. I brought my eyes back to the girl.

"You don't drink?" He scratched the back of his head. "Yeah, I don't drink much either." He set his drink down on her table.

Another round of laughter rumbled through the joint. This time it came from me.

The girl turned and looked straight at me.

I tilted my head back as I tossed the last of my Old Grand-Dad down my throat. I couldn't keep my eyes off her. Short hair, black as wet ink, framed her porcelain face. Her straight bangs hung above her eyes like the blade of a razor. She wore her hair short in the back with the sides cut at an angle to match her cheekbones.

"You know," the kid kept going; she kept staring at me, "if you're not busy, we should take lunch together sometime."

Her heavily penciled eyes, fixed below sculpted eyebrows, looked bored and mischievous. A line of smoke rose from the cigarette in her upturned hand.

"Or maybe we could get some dinner . . . and a movie."

On her face, thin lips painted the deepest red formed a smile so sharp it could slice a weak man in two.

I'm not a weak man.

"How about I call you . . . ?" his voice trailed off.

She got up and walked over to my leather booth. It was hard to turn away from her, even for a moment, but I wanted to check on the two crooks; they were still busy with the bartender. I looked back, and before I could say anything, she sat next to me and asked, "What are you drinking?"

I spun the empty glass in front of me between my fingers. "Right now, I'm not drinking anything."

"Then we should get you a refill."

"Sure."

"Name your poison."

"Old Grand-Dad, three fingers."

She held my stare for a couple seconds, then flashed me some teeth through a sly smile. She waved over the old waitress and ordered: "Six fingers of Old Grand-Dad, three in one glass and three in another."

Before the waitress could acknowledge the order, a gaggle of drunk young folks sitting in the booth next to mine shouted for her attention.

"Hold on now, I'll be right with you," the barmaid called over to the rowdy group. The Pandora's weekend patrons, especially the kids with no sense of style or manners, always barked orders at her.

She turned back to the girl sitting next to me. "I'm sorry, dear, what was that you were saying about a bunch of fingers? Can I get you something to drink?"

The girl played it simple for her: "Two glasses of Old Grand-Dad, straight up." The waitress nodded and ambled off.

"I'd offer up a cheer for friends," she said, "but we must not be friends yet if I don't know your name."

"I'm Ben Drake—"

"Beth Hrubi. There's a silent h before the r . . . in case you want to write that down."

"I won't need to."

When we had full drinks in front of us, we clinked glasses and took our sips. Playing with her hair, she whispered, "Does this mean we're friends now, Benjamin?"

"You always this impatient, Elizabeth?"

"Don't call me that." Her acid attitude did nothing to stop the attraction that initially caught my eye.

"Call me Beth or Betty or even Liz. Only my mother calls me Elizabeth. You're not my mother, are you?" She sipped her bourbon without taking her eyes off me.

"Nope. I'm not."

"Good."

She reached out and smoothed her hand across the width of my broad shoulders. "Where're all your friends, Benjamin? A strong, good-looking man all alone on a Friday evening doesn't seem right."

"I'm not that good-looking, sister."

I pulled out a tin of smokes from my breast pocket. With the stroke of a wooden match, she and I got down to smoking.

"Normally, I'm a sit-at-the-bar kind of guy. But you see that oaf behind the counter?" I nodded my head in that direction. "That's my least favorite bartender, Barton Bourke. I can endure his enthusiasm for old pulp crime fiction and his constant inane yammering only when in the company of my regular drinking pals. Seeing as these pals of mine are all somewhere else tonight, I figured I'd relax in the secluded comfort of a booth. Not that I'm complaining about present company."

"And I was just about to get worried." She cocked her head in a way that made her teardrop earrings shake.

"I don't believe that for one moment."

We both laughed.

"So, Benjamin, what do you do for a living?"

Part of being a detective is knowing when to tell the truth about your job and when to conveniently come up with a new occupation. I thought I'd give this girl a chance with the straight skinny.

"I'm a detective."

"Really?" She shot me an impish grin. "Like a crook chaser?"

"Yeah, I've chased down a few crooks."

"What a coincidence. I just happen to *be* a crook."

My senses tingled like a kid caught looking at a girlie magazine.

"Very interesting," I said, sipping some more sauce. "Would I know your work?"

She laughed playfully. "I have the feeling that if you did, I'd be behind bars."

"True. In fact, that's something you can count on." More bourbon went past my lips. Booze seemed to go down better with Beth around. "But indulge me. What's your specialty?"

"I guess you could say . . . I cause trouble."

"Trouble, eh? What sort of trouble?"

"Usually the sort that someone else has to clean up."

"Someone like me?"

This was a cool game of cat-and-mouse we were playing. I just couldn't figure out which one of us was the mouse.

She purred, "I can't think of anyone I'd rather have cleaning up after me."

Before I could toss out my next verbal volley, I glanced up to find two guys standing in front of our booth: Trout Mathers and Blackie Lawton.

Lawton was the first to speak: "Yo, Beth. It's time to go. I don't want to be late."

Mathers held out his hand to silence his partner, then pointed my way. "Who is this guy?"

Beth spoke up for me: "This is Benjamin. He's a friend of mine."

Mathers gave me the tough-guy look. I gave it back to him. He said, "Yeah? Well, I don't trust a guy in a suit and tie. And guys in hats are even more cause for concern."

He fidgeted with his cat's-eye cuff links while he put this to me: "What's your deal?"

Again, Beth chirped up: "He's a salesman."

"Salesman?" Mathers needed convincing.

She tried to give it to him. "Yes. He sells vacuum cleaners, you know, door-to-door."

Now Lawton joined in. "You sell vacuum cleaners?"

I snapped back: "Yeah. You got a mess that needs cleaned up?"

The crooks laughed. All three of them.

Now, I'd be a fool to trust Beth Hrubi, and I was no fool. She was right in thinking I didn't want these joes knowing I was a detective, and I appreciated her covering for me. I decided to follow her lead a little while longer.

Lawton knocked his knuckles on our table. "Hello, people. Let's get going. I don't want to be late."

I had just set my drink down when Beth threw her spaghetti arms around me. She planted a wet one right on my cheek. Then I felt her hot breath tickle my earlobe.

She whispered, "Do you feel like getting into trouble tonight?"

Adrenaline surged through my system like high octane.

I said, "I'm always up for a little trouble. What's on the menu?"

She pulled away from me so she could look me in the eyes. Still whispering, she told me: "We're going to the hottest ticket in town. Where fortunes are made and lost. We're going to the Cockfight Club."

When we walked out of the Pandora, Beth took me by the hand and told me that Mathers insisted on driving us to the fights. The last thing I wanted to do was get myself stranded without means of getting out. But I had already committed to this masquerade, enough that it was best to go with the flow.

In Mathers's big, black touring sedan, we began heading south. Beth and I took the backseat. She curled up real nice next to me.

Nobody talked much on this ride, and I sure as hell wasn't going to start any conversation.

Some kind of dirty contemporary blues scratched out of the radio. Beth put her lips to my ears and sang right through me:

You can dream of drugs or dream of the deal
Don't mean a thing, don't mean a thing
You can put all your money on a guaranteed steal
Don't mean a thing, don't mean a thing
You can believe in love or believe in lies
Don't mean a thing, don't mean a thing
'Cause at the end of the day, we're all gonna die
Don't mean a thing, don't mean a thing
It's a fool's game, baby
Don't you make a sound
There's blood on the dirt
And dirt in the ground

Mathers's eyes haunted me from the rearview mirror. Once we had arrived at our destination—a collection of ramshackle huts on either side of an isolated road—we descended into the crowded basement of one of the abandoned buildings, and the four of us went our separate ways. Mathers and Lawton weren't the kind to keep me company, so their leaving me behind didn't seem out of place. But the way Beth left my side the moment we walked into this smoke-filled joint left me wondering. I tried not to wonder all that much; instead, my eyes took their turn haunting Mathers.

He strolled across the crowded room and took a moment to adjust the knot of his tie. Mathers made this gesture with the subtle flourish of a man in uncomfortable surroundings. This basement brouhaha obviously wasn't his territory, so why did he bring us here?

I kept my eyes on him and spent a good amount of time absorbing the atmosphere of the place. The stagnant air was hot and moist, and sweat started to seep slowly out from my pores. I expected the place to smell like a farm, but to my surprise it smelled more like a muddy high school football field.

On the other hand, the noise that filled the place *did* remind me of a farm. However, unlike the storybook sound of early country mornings, the endless cock-a-doodle-do's felt like nothing more than the screaming of roosters.

This was my first time at a cockfight.

A short man in a silver tie came up to Mathers. They exchanged a few friendly words that I couldn't hear. Mathers belched out a phony laugh, then tugged at the chain on his hip and pulled out a pocket watch. He quickly glanced at its face, while the short guy tried to light a cigarette with an empty lighter. Mathers was quick to hand him a bright purple pack of matches. He motioned for the guy to get lost, and the guy did.

The short man headed to the left of the entrance, where round tables lined a long wall. A small sampling of guys sat there with women in skimpy outfits—women with too much hairspray and sloppy lipstick, women with too many bracelets, women with a price tag.

Lawton had wasted no time in joining this group, though he didn't pay any attention to the short silver tie who sat elsewhere. Because of Lawton's reputation, I had a feeling I knew what the people dealt at these tables, and it wasn't cards. I could spot all kinds of dope exchanging hands—pot, pills, pharmaceuticals, you name it. In fact, he had already bent over to sample some speed.

To the right of all that sniffing, pinching, popping, and pushing, a large crowd gathered around what looked like, at this distance, an enclosed horseshoe pit; obviously, tonight's action happened here. A series of floodlamps hung from the beams of the ceiling, sending light as bright as the noon sun streaming into the pit.

I looked back at Mathers. A detective has to notice the little things that a person does, especially the kind of things they don't even realize they're doing—like the fact that a girl will play with her hair if she's interested in a guy she's talking to. Well, Mathers looked at that watch of his for the third time in about two minutes. And I'd bet that if somebody went up to him right then and asked him for the time, he'd have no idea what to say.

Naturally, I couldn't help checking my own watch. It was almost eleven thirty, still early for me. I hadn't forgotten about Miss Hrubi. Unlike Mathers, she blended into the crowd real nice.

The men who made up the audience could just as easily have made up a who's who list of crime. I didn't recognize all the faces, but I didn't need to. What really gave them away were the little details: the ostrich-skin boots, the gold-nugget pinky rings, the occasional flash of a holstered 9mm.

Mathers checked his watch yet again, shoved it back into a pocket, and crossed his arms. Despite being in the thick of the throng, he paid no attention to the action in the ring. He simply slinked ringside with the rest of the criminals, right where he belonged. Despite that, he stood out like a knife in a drawer full of forks.

Watching Mathers just stand there was like watching a ticking bomb. He could go off at any time, and if I just stared at him, I'd go mad. So I continued my surveillance of the room: A collection of cages, covered with blankets and stacked up to the ceiling, stood against the back wall behind the goon-encircled pit.

To my immediate right sat a small table set up with food and drinks. A few homely looking women served up some kind of sandwiches made with meat fresh from a Crock-Pot. I didn't know what looked worse, the processed supermarket buns or the mystery mash in the slow cooker, so I passed on the grub and grabbed myself some liquid refreshment.

With a paper cup of whiskey in hand, I glanced over at the tables; Lawton seemed content as could be, reclining in a chair with his head tilted back. Suddenly he sat up, grabbed the arm of a woman next to him, and checked her watch. He smiled and leaned back in his chair.

I wanted to talk with Beth and see what I could read between her coy lines. Maybe then I could figure this caper out before things flew out of control. I twisted my head around to find her; she had found someone else.

This guy checked in at about my height, about my same build; he even had a similar haircut as me. One big difference—he looked dumb, mean, and ready to prove it.

I saw her glance my way. The expression on her face puzzled me: a combination of playful indifference and joyous vindictiveness. Specifically, the way she latched onto this guy's huge arm and the way she leaned up to plant a kiss on his cheek suggested that she must be doing this mostly for my benefit. Whatever.

Trying my best to ignore her, I walked over to the pit. I couldn't deny that I was curious about what this cockfighting business was all about. Besides, it couldn't hurt to blend into the crowd a little better.

I guess I thought I'd see two roosters beating the feathers out of each other, real no-holds-barred action. Instead, what was most likely the end of the fight found these two fighters tired, barely able to stand, and only occasionally lunging in to peck at the other's head.

I had to struggle to see these birds, both because of the crowd in front of me and because of the three guys huddled in the pit with them. A guy crouched behind each cock, tending to it. The guy nursing the more-injured rooster lovingly stroked the bird's neck while trying to wipe the blood from the animal's eyes. He even stuck the rooster's head in his mouth; when he pulled it out, he spit the excess blood onto the dirt. Then it was ready to fight again.

Instead of watching the last throes of the fight, I found myself intrigued by the third man. Unlike the other two fellows, who wore dirty T-shirts and faded, muddy jeans, this one came decked out in a gray sharkskin suit, an open-collar tuxedo shirt, and a Mexican wrestling mask.

He looked like a dance hall demon, except this was no dance hall. He squatted down, knees pointing outward, and hovered over the men and their birds. He shook in a fit of ecstasy or hysteria— probably drug-induced—as he counted to ten. He drew two lines in the dirt with his index finger, then the men placed their roosters behind the lines. Wings outstretched, the cocks met in one last, tired embrace.

The end was quick: the one rooster fell beneath its stronger opponent. More blood had covered the losing cock's eyes—only this time, they were closed. The poor bird laid there like a wet towel, its feathers dark and slicked with blood. The winning cock walked around the loser. My eyes caught the reflection of the bloodied knife strapped to the shaft of its left leg.

I looked up at the crowd. For a moment, all the faces blended together. I shook off the hypnotic effect and focused my attention on finding Trout Mathers again. A couple glances back and forth, and I had his lean figure in sight. He just stood there, arms still crossed, with the thinnest smile cracked beneath his thin mustache. He checked his watch; I checked mine: eleven thirty-seven.

Beth was easier to spot. Blood and feathers didn't seem to faze her one bit. In fact, judging by the way she slobbered all over this new meathead of hers, I'd say the excitement of the fight had actually energized her.

The man in the wrestling mask collected and redistributed money from the losers to the winners, presumably keeping a little bit to line his own pockets. People didn't just bet against the house; plenty of money exchanged hands privately, discreetly. Good gangsters always act like they're being watched.

Lawton, though, looked more concerned about having a good time. He played around with one of the girls. She giggled as he fed her a drink from his cup.

I switched over and watched the guy who Beth had been kissing and hugging get a fistful of cash from the masked ringmaster. Beth kept picking at the wad of bills like she was trying to pluck a flower from a bouquet. Her new boyfriend just waved her off. With the hearty guffaws of a recent winner, he elbowed the guy next to him, a slightly overweight hooligan with a cheap-looking crewcut and the worst polyester suit I'd seen in a decade or two.

This guy had flabby skin that hung on his face, which was red and wet with sweat. Even from where I stood, I could hear his loud mouth: "The next fight my luck'll change! You'll see. I can feel it coming! I can feel it coming right to me! Tyler! Gimme the odds on the next round!"

Again Beth caught me staring. I turned and made my way back to the drink table, where I grabbed another cup of cheap whiskey.

My whole face wrinkled at the bite of the harsh alcohol, then from behind me came a voice.

"You look kinda confused there, like you're, I don't know . . . confused or something."

"I'm not confused," I turned and said to the scrawny, mouse-like man behind me. "I'm just a little bit—"

"Oh, I got it." He tapped the dimple in his chin with his index finger. "This is your first cockfight, right?"

"Right." I could bluff my way around a lot of things I only knew a little about, but this was one circus for which I could sure use a tour guide. Looked like this clown would do.

"So let me ask ya then," he continued. "What makes you interested in the chickens?"

His sparse mustache looked like animal whiskers. His mouth kept busy by chewing on a wooden match that danced from one side of his lips to the other. His eyes were less busy; they hung lazily in his head like two big sleeping pills.

"I suppose I'm just the curious type. How about I get you a drink, and you get me the highlights of all the interesting stuff going on here."

"No thanks." He pulled a cigarette from behind his ear and lit it with the chewed-up remains of the match. His first lungful of smoke came out of his mouth and nose like exhaust from an engine. "I don't drink. Bad for the health."

We both smiled. I offered him a hand to shake.

"Ben Drake, by the way."

"I'm Aubrey Barnes . . ." He grasped my hand, his words trailing into another puff of his cigarette. "So, lotta big names here tonight, huh?"

I looked around. "Yeah, I guess there's some real rooster star power here."

"No man, the G's in the crowd!" He gave me a friendly push to show he knew I was joking with him. "Look all around you. You don't have to work in a post office to see who's wanted around here. There's Nick 'Thin-Man' Reed, Small-Tooth Kelley, Tommy 'Two-Gun' Glanzer . . ."

Aubrey kept going with the list; some names I knew, some I

didn't. Two names I hadn't heard before, but just made my list of ones to remember: Stash Mulligan and Yo-Yo Harrington. Stash was the guy Beth had her arms around; Yo-Yo was the adrenaline-case next to him.

". . . Still, there's a couple of guys I never seen here before." Aubrey scratched the spotty stubble on his neck. "Like that guy over there."

My eyes went to the gent he singled out. With difficulty, I held back my smile as I uttered, "That's Trout Mathers, some big-time bank robber."

"There's another one, that guy there. See 'im? Hasn't said word one to nobody all night."

I saw him all right—a pasty youngish guy with long, slicked-back white hair, almost albino-like, dressed in a white, ribbed T-shirt and blue jean overalls.

"Don't know that one."

It occurred to me I should find out a bit more about my new friend. "Say, are *you* someone I should know?"

"Me?" Aubrey gasped in overreacting shock. "Naw, I'm here 'cause I grew up loving the sport. My daddy was a cocker just like his daddy before him."

You can grow up learning a lot of vices in Testacy City, but I didn't think you could grow up learning to fight roosters. I said as much.

"I wasn't raised here. This ain't my kind of town. In fact, I can't imagine why anyone would live here."

I'd run into this sort before. They lived in Testacy City but couldn't find a single damn good thing to say about it. I always felt that if they didn't like it, they could just ship out. This Barnes fellow was a little different, though, and that intrigued me.

"So what are you doing here then?" I asked.

"Well, I'm just waiting for the wife to get out of prison."

He spat out a stray bit of tobacco that sailed through the cloud of smoke hovering around his head and scuffed the toe of a well-worn work boot in the dirt floor.

"What did she do to get in there?"

"She was a bad girl," he slurred out of the side of his mouth.

I glanced at my watch: eleven forty-eight. I began to wander away from this guy, turning back toward Mathers. He'd gone over to talk to the man in the mask, and now the two of them stood away from the crowd.

Barnes clapped his hand on my shoulder.

"So . . . if you're new to cockfighting, then I bet there's somebody else you don't know. I bet . . . I bet you don't know Sven."

"Nope. He another gangster?"

"No man, he's the breeder, Sven Gali—everyone knows him as Sven the Hen. Come on, I'll introduce ya."

"So this guy knows what goes down here?"

"Oh yeah, he'll set ya straight for sure."

Aubrey cut a path through the crowd, steering me toward the cock cages in the corner. Maybe this Sven the Hen could set me straight on what Trout Mathers was after.

As we walked, I had a clear view of Mathers. He still talked to the dance hall demon, doing his best Mr. Smooth routine. The masked guy wasn't buying it. A lot of the assembled thugs clamored for his attention. He ignored them, shaking his head as the bank robber tapped a finger into his open palm. The masked man turned and began to walk away. Mathers grabbed him, spun him around, and pointed in his face. The ringmaster shrugged out of Mathers's grip and walked away. Mathers let him go.

Right after this exchange, we passed by Mathers. He surprised me by half-turning and slapping the back of his hand against my lapel.

"Hey, pal," he muttered to me while pointing across the room at Beth with a nod of his head, "looks like your new girlfriend is girl enough for everybody."

I didn't bother to answer; I just kept on walking with Aubrey. But as much as I wanted to resist, I couldn't help gazing over at Beth.

She had switched her amorous attentions from Stash Mulligan to the fat, hothead hooligan named Yo-Yo. Worse still, this simpleton side-of-beef pawed at her with no sense of decency or decorum.

And she looked like she loved every bit of it.

I asked Aubrey about Yo-Yo and what his deal was. Aubrey said he was your typical violent type—a sore loser always on a losing streak. Well, he may not be winning the fights, but tonight he apparently had marks in the win column for Beth.

"Come on! Come on! Come on! I ain't got time to wait!" Yo-Yo spat out into the center of the pit. He pulled up his jacket sleeve to get a look at his watch. Then, as if he knew I had my eyes on him, he lifted his head and stared right at me.

I held his stare. His beady eyes sized me up.

Beth grabbed his face and pulled it close to her. He thrust his nose into her neck and kissed her like he was a dog lapping up water. She winked at me.

Off to my side, a Mexican-looking gent in a blue baseball cap said, "Is she the little señorita that kissed you?"

"What are you talking about?" I tried not to act as flustered as I felt.

"I mean the little chickie, the one with Yo-Yo, she kissed you on the side of your face, eh?"

This guy sat there with his round, brown face smiling right at me. The tattered lawn chair that barely supported his frame kept him so low to the ground I almost tripped over him. His polished white teeth matched the brightness of his new all-white sneakers. He wore crisp, dark-blue jeans and a red-striped polo shirt. He was a man in his mid-to-late forties trying to look young and clean.

Aubrey jabbed me an elbow and muttered, "Mr. Sven probably noticed that lipstick smudged on your cheek."

"*This* is Sven Gali?" I said, rubbing the back of my hand against my cheek trying to remove what I could of Beth's kiss. "And you—" I shoved Aubrey, "how come you didn't tell me I had lip marks on my face?"

"You were not expecting a Mexican, eh, señor? Well, I tell you my full name is . . ." He tapped his rib cage loud enough for me to hear. "My full name is Sven Gali Chavez."

Aubrey gave a weak shove back. "This here is, ah, Ben Drake. It's his first time to a fight."

"I certainly didn't mean any offense," I said to Sven. "But you weren't wrong. That girl over there in the short hair and tight dress gave me a good smack on the cheek. What can you tell me about her?"

Sven rose to his feet. "Your first cockfight? You must be very excited, eh? You a friend of Tyler?"

I looked to Aubrey to give me some indication of how to answer, but his stone expression revealed nothing. So I fired straight off: "I don't know this Tyler."

Sven laughed in a way that made his jaw sink into his throat. I could smell the tequila rolling off him. "Of course you know this Tyler; everybody knows this Tyler. Funny man, you, this Tyler is the man in the mask. This is his club!"

The joker in the wrestling mask strutted in the center of the cockfighting pit. The crowd around him continued to make preparations for the next fight.

"Señor, look, right over there." Sven tugged at my elbow. He pointed to a couple of guys in suits who were now in the pit. One of them pulled out a long, thin wooden box.

"What d'you see?" he asked.

"Looks like that guy is about to offer up some choice cigars, judging from that box . . . except I've never seen a box of smokes that looked quite like that," I answered. Talking about smoking got my lips twitching. I pulled out a tin and lit up one of my own.

"Some choice cigars? Ha! You keep getting funnier, señor. No, no, they are no cigars. Look carefully."

I did what Sven said. The guy with the box went over to one of the two guys who seemed to be in charge of handling the birds when they fought in the pit, sort of like a boxer's coach. When the case opened up, I saw a series of inch-and-a-half-long blades with red, forked handles lined up against a bed of burgundy velvet.

"Very, very sharp, señor. You no want to smoke those, eh?"

In the pit, the two handlers in the dirt-spattered T-shirts selected their blades.

"Perhaps in some places, the owners fight their own birds. But here, we got Curtis and Jesse to tie and pit the cocks. It's easier, quicker, and a lot less dirty for well-dressed owners of prize game cocks, eh."

"Hey, Sven," Aubrey spoke up, "this looks like a good fight comin' up, pretty even match at that. Who's your favorite?"

"Well, I tell you, Señor Barnes. We got two hatch going to get pitted. Now, for fighting the short knife, I prefer a spangle hatch—you see how the yellow-leg has some markings in his hackle? It make me think maybe he got some spangle blood. Still, both these no match against my reds, I tell you that."

"Hatch is a breed of rooster," Aubrey whispered to me as if it were a secret.

"Yeah. I figured as much."

The chatter had already started to annoy me. I turned around to check on Mathers. He had his arm around the short man with the silver tie, who quivered, looking less friendly than before and plenty scared. He stared wide-eyed at Tyler, slipping the masked man a slow nod of his head. Mathers smiled and patted his gun beneath his jacket.

"You are wondering about how we keep the cocks, eh?" Sven crowed to me.

"Not really."

"All right then, I tell you." He grabbed the front of one of the larger cages that had a bar about five feet from the ground that looked like a swing from a trapeze act. "This is where we grow them up real powerful. They get their exercise, build their leg muscles nice and strong. On this swing here, they do the exercise, like the chicken push-ups, eh!" He laughed at his own joke.

"How do they get up there?"

"Do you know nothing about the chickens, señor? They may not be able to fly south in the winter, eh, but they got the wings that let them jump high off the ground. You see this?" He pointed to a feed dish and water supply. "We make sure they get the extra-special food. It helps them get nice and strong."

Along the outside of the cages sat one-gallon plastic jugs filled with a dark purple liquid. Hand-lettered in magic marker were the words *B-Complex, Liver & Iron*. Next to the jugs, I saw a brown glass bottle labeled *Energy Steroids (for horses only)*. I turned away.

"Tell 'im about keeping 'em in the dark," Aubrey said with that dead look in his eyes.

"*Si, si.* We keep them covered in the darkness, eh. The only time they see the light is when we bring them out, and when we bring them out we hold them down while another bird attacks them— pecks at him, stabs at him with a knife. This way, when we ready to fight the bird, he sees the bright light and is ready to kill, eh. Look, they do it right now."

Curtis and Jesse cradled their birds in one arm and held onto the back on the neck feathers with their free hand. Tyler strolled over with a rooster held outstretched in both hands. This bird attacked one of the upcoming contestants, and with its beak, pulled out a couple of neck feathers and landed some pointed pecks to the head.

The handler then put his fighter on the ground, placing its rear end high in the air, facing center. Tyler's bird swooped down and attacked again, this time with its sharp claws.

The rooster on the ground screamed and desperately tried to flap its wings free. When this ordeal was over, Tyler gave the opposing cock the same treatment.

"See, señor, this is what we call flirting the cocks. It gets them pumped up and ready to cause some trouble."

I heard Sven, but I was too busy watching Yo-Yo Harrington's sweaty face to answer right away. Beth still had her arms around his large waist, but he had stopped playing with her. His eyes beaded on Tyler antagonizing the second game cock. He rubbed his hands, ready for the action.

Then it hit me.

"Sven, what did you say this was called?"

"Sí, now you interested! We call it flirting."

"Oh, Christ . . ." I couldn't believe I'd almost been played for a sap.

Aubrey Barnes cried out: "All right! Fight! Fight!"

Curtis and Jesse released the cocks at each other. Up they went, a good three feet high. They met violently in the air and came down together in a flurry of attacks.

The beginning of this battle looked like the end of a pillow fight. Small white feathers filled the air like snow. People's fists flew in the air. Cheers, shouts, yells, and whistles echoed through the sweltering air of the basement. I looked at my watch: four minutes past midnight.

Maybe I should have realized this before, but all of a sudden, I didn't like the place where I found myself standing. Pinned with an excitable mob in front of me and the cages to my back, I knew I had to find more open ground.

I decided to move closer to Mathers, but when I looked over his way, he was gone.

I scanned left and right. There was no sign of him.

Even Beth had begun to retreat. Step by step she backed away from Yo-Yo. His whole body shook. His face turned an even brighter color of red. Sweat rained from his stringy hair. Beth didn't notice any of this. She had her stare pinned somewhere else.

I followed her line of sight. Her eyes landed on Lawton over at the drug tables. He looked more alert than ever.

Then I noticed the yelling. Yo-Yo Harrington's distinctively fat, whiny voice bounced off the walls at full volume. He shouted some choice words at Tyler, words that usually come out of sailors, truck drivers, and young rock stars.

I asked Aubrey what the hell was going on. He fidgeted with more life in him than I had seen all evening as he attempted to describe the situation.

"Man! The green leg had the yellow leg dead to rights, but now—as you can see—the yellow leg is down for the count. But now there's trouble: the green leg won't drag; he keeps running away. Now, the rules have it that he automatically loses, like when you sink the eight-ball out of turn in pool." Aubrey pulled out a red handkerchief and swiped it across his brow. "But for some reason Tyler isn't calling the fight. He's *making* the green leg fight. It looks like Yo-Yo, loser that he is, actually bet money on the yellow leg. By all accounts, he should win this fight. But if Tyler keeps this up, I don't know . . ."

A strange notion nestled its way into my brain, and I had to ask: "The cock that's running away, do you know the name of its owner—the guy who entered him in this fight?"

Aubrey turned to Sven and Sven turned back to me.

"*Sí*, some guy named Blackie something."

"Yeah, that's what I figured. Somehow that just seems to fit."

"Oh no, señor! No! No!" Sven cried out.

I turned around to the worst-case scenario: Yo-Yo Harrington had pulled out his gun.

Anytime this many gangsters gather together in the same place, you have a powder keg primed to blow. And Yo-Yo just lit the match.

A garden of guns instantly sprouted and steel blossomed in nearly every bare fist. A chilling silence echoed through the basement. Everyone seemed frozen in place.

Yo-Yo broke the spell. "Tyler!" he screamed as he pointed his snubnose .38 straight into Tyler's masked face. "What's got into you? Forget the rules or something? You call this fight right now!"

Most of the other guns were pointed in Yo-Yo's direction, but a few folks, probably the other fools who had also bet on the almost dead yellow leg, seemed to be on his side. When all the rage in this place erupted, there would be a bloodbath at the Friday-night cockfight.

The time had come for me to exit, and fast. I fought through the crowd, making my way toward the rear door. I looked over my shoulder to see if the stand-off had progressed. Tyler didn't speak; he just stood there calmly, his hands at his sides, staring at Yo-Yo through masked eyes as if daring him to shoot. Who was this guy?

"Goddamnit!" Yo-Yo erupted and switched his aim from Tyler to the green leg hatch, which now strutted proudly about the ring. The gangster's whole body shook with rage.

He squeezed the trigger, and a roar boomed through the room.

The powder keg exploded.

At the last second, Stash Mulligan slapped Yo-Yo's pistol hand, and instead of hitting the bird, the bullet ripped a hole in Jesse's chest. The handler's eyes opened up real wide. He looked down to see a rapidly spreading spot of blood flow across his T-shirt as his body began a slow tumble backward.

As the unlucky pit hand's body flopped into the dirt, the deafening roar of gunfire filled the room. I ducked down low, pulled out my Smith & Wesson Model 637, and made a mad dash for the safety of the rear exit. The last place I wanted to die was in a grungy basement in the middle of nowhere with a stray bullet buried in my back.

I'd almost reached my goal when the weird albino-like fellow appeared out of nowhere right in front of me and just stopped. He stood with his back to me, just staring up at the ceiling. A small part of me wondered what he saw up there, but the rest of me just wanted to get out of the firefight. I shoved him aside, but he didn't budge. I shoved again, more forcefully. Instead of getting out of my way, he turned toward me with clenched fists. I didn't have time for this joker.

This hadn't been my idea of how to spend a relaxing Friday night. I'd been teased, used, and tormented, and now I found myself the target of what seemed like a thousand guns. Violence came easy, and before I knew what I was doing I gave this poor fellow two quick lefts across the jaw. That made him take a step backward, stunned and weaving. I gave him a third set of knuckles to the temple. He crumpled to the ground like someone had cut his feet out from underneath him.

I ran past him and gained the safety of the shallow alcove of the back door. I didn't know what my next move would be. Burning cordite filled my nostrils, and the brief cacophony of exploding guns had been replaced by the moans, screams, and whimpers of wounded men.

I peeked out from my hiding spot and took a look around the chaos of the basement. It had turned into a massacre. A majority of the gangsters were sprawled on the dirt floor, which was now a muddy, blood-slicked morass. A few of these prone hoodlums still moved, and fewer still fired their guns at the handful of guys who still stood.

Yo-Yo Harrington was among the apparent dead, his flabby body a blood-spattered mishmash of tortured flesh.

The green-legged rooster that had started this mess jumped and squawked, occasionally attacking a wounded thug with vicious pecks and stabs from the knife on its leg.

My eyes fell across my albino adversary. The right side of his face swelled nicely. I felt bad that my anger had gotten the best of me, but at least he was on the ground and out of the way of a bullet. I tried telling myself that even though I busted his face, I probably saved his life. It didn't do much to make me feel any better.

I didn't see hide nor hair of Trout Mathers or Beth Hrubi among the dead or living.

My sweep around the room continued to the drug tables, now overturned and riddled with bullet holes. Blackie Lawton popped up from behind one of the bullet-scarred shields and cracked a wide, devilish grin. Three other fellows stood up close beside him. All four peered around the room, then started to laugh and slap each other on the back. Suddenly Lawton whipped out his twin automatics and filled the bodies of his fellow survivors with bullets until his guns clicked empty. The poor guys didn't stand a chance.

After holstering his guns, Lawton opened two beat-up suitcases, then snapped them back shut and took a last look around. Again he flashed an evil grin, snatched up the luggage, and headed straight toward the rear exit.

Straight toward me.

I'm not normally a man hell-bent on revenge, but being pushed around all night had my dander up. I had most of this caper figured out, but I needed a few answers to get the whole story.

These three crooks had conspired to steal a couple of suitcases full of dope. I had no problem understanding that. But why? Trout Mathers and Beth Hrubi weren't around to answer. That left Blackie Lawton.

I slipped out the back door into the cool early-morning air, flattened myself into the shadows of the wall, and waited.

Lawton stumbled out the door seconds later, still carrying a suitcase in each hand. He glanced around frantically and cursed violently. He must not have seen what he was waiting for, so I thought I'd give him something else to worry about.

"Hey, buddy," I called, stepping from the shadows, my small .38 aimed at his chest.

He whirled around and fixed his crazy eyes on me, huge pupils filling almost his entire eyeball. It didn't take a doctor to know that he was wired to the gizzard.

"Hey . . . the vacuum guy," he clucked. "There's a big mess inside, y'know. You might wanna go on in there and get cleanin'."

"The way I see it, all the cleaning that needs doing can be done right here."

"Yeah? Well, the way I see it, I gotta wonder what business a salesman's got carrying a piece—and a woman's piece at that."

"You never know when you might run into trouble," I said. "Now why don't we have a little chat."

"A chat? Whatta we got to chat about?"

"The scam you're trying to run."

"Scam?"

"Come on, Blackie. I'm no idiot."

"Says you. You ain't got the first clue about our plan."

"I got enough to know that you're not the brains of the operation."

"Shows what you know. Who do ya think told Trout about this Flores shipment?"

"Come on! Trout doesn't deal in drugs."

"There's no deal here. He just wanted to throw a monkey wrench into the Flores cashflow after Manny's boys messed up his last score."

"Nothing like a little revenge. So how does Beth fit in?"

"That gal sure got under your skin, huh? I don't know nothin' about her. She came with Trout."

"Where's Trout now?"

"Hell, I got no idea. All he cared about was messin' up Flores's Mexican Brown shipment, and I got the goods right here." Lawton hefted the two cases slightly, emphasizing his point.

"Well, why don't you drop those and lay down on the ground there," I suggested, pointing with the short barrel of my gun.

"Sure thing. After all, you got the gun, clean-up man. That makes you the boss."

I just nodded as Lawton slowly set the cases on the ground and began sinking down to his knees. Quick as lightning, though, he was back up and reaching for his guns.

"Hold it, pal," I snarled, cocking my weapon for emphasis.

Lawton's hands stopped, still on his holstered pistols.

"I think you're out of ammo there, Blackie."

Lawton laughed, rolled to the left, and came up with his guns pointed right at me. When he squeezed the triggers, all we heard were twin hollow clicks.

Lawton swore and threw his guns at me. I dodged them, then squeezed off a round in his direction, but my step to the side had thrown off my aim. I didn't have time for another shot before Lawton's bulk tackled me. He hit me low in the gut, and the wind blew right out of my chest. As I struggled to breathe, we slammed against the wall of the building, and my teeth rattled to their roots. Although it didn't do wonders for my spine, at least it got some breath in my lungs.

I didn't have any desire to duke it out with a drugged-up hoodlum, and just as I got ready to smash Lawton on the back of his head with the butt of my pistol, I realized my hand was empty. I must have dropped my gun when we hit the wall. Time for a new plan.

I clapped my hands over Lawton's ears as hard as I could. He howled with pain and backed off, giving me time to breathe.

"I'm gonna kill you," he crowed.

I didn't waste my breath with needless banter.

He rushed forward, throwing a heavy right fist at my head. He moved slowly and sloppily, so I had no trouble blocking it with my left forearm. The blow stung; had it connected with my head it would've hurt pretty good. I followed through with a solid right fist to the bridge of his nose. The crunch of fragmenting bone echoed through the night.

He staggered backward, trying desperately to keep his footing. Blood poured freely from his fractured beak, staining his clothes red. He held his hands over his face and squawked with pain.

Lawton may have been good at a lot of things, but an accomplished pugilist certainly didn't make the list. His howling left him wide open.

Unable to resist, I rushed forward and slammed a rapid left-right-left combo deep into his solar plexus. With a strangled cry he fell back further, still on his feet but weaving heavily. He could barely stand, so I stepped in and finished him off with a solid left across the jaw. I felt the punch all the way down my arm. I'd bet that Lawton felt it to his toes.

He stood a moment, wobbling and squinting at me. Then his eyes rolled up into his head, and he toppled over backward. He went down hard.

I rubbed my raw knuckles and wondered how I'd be getting home. I ran my hand through my hair, turned around, and walked over to where my hat had fallen.

As I bent down to retrieve it, a solid punch pounded the base of my skull. My legs went out from under me and I fell, sprawling facedown in the dirt. A viselike grip held my hair and repeatedly slammed my face into the ground. Flashing lights danced woozily in front of my eyes.

I pushed up with my arms in a desperate bid to roll over. I'd used up most of my energy, so every move I made now took twice the effort. I finally succeeded in getting myself off the ground, managing to throw off my assailant in the process.

I scrabbled backward, crawling crab-like to get away from whoever had bushwhacked me.

A battered and torn Blackie Lawton pounced on top of me and began pecking me in the face with his fist. Cold sweat dripped off his clammy skin and into my eyes. His fists moved fast and my hands were full trying to ward off his merciless blows. The night swam around me.

He focused his attack on my head and didn't really notice the rest of my body. I slipped my leg under him and gained enough leverage to flip him off me. I scrambled back to my feet as quickly as I could. It wasn't quick enough.

Before I could recover he was on me again, raining blows all over my body in a cocaine-fueled fury. He growled like a wild animal, pounding me in the face and chest. His blows soon overwhelmed me.

A solid blow caught me square on the chin and sent me sprawling into a pile of old rags. I fumbled to get up, but my body had turned to rubber; my limbs wouldn't do what I told them. Then I saw Lawton standing over me, pointing my own gun at my face.

"Say goodnight," he screeched.

I stared down the barrel, cursing myself for having turned my back on the man. I knew better than that. What a stupid way to die.

A loud, pulpy thud filled my ears.

Lawton stood, looking at me, unmoving. Then he went cross-eyed and fell forward, my gun slipping from his fist.

Right behind Lawton stood Aubrey Barnes, a three-foot two-by-four in his hands.

"I was rootin' for ya there, Ben, but ya weren't doing too good near the end. Figured you could use a little help."

"Thanks. I appreciate it."

"No problem. I could tell you were a good sort of fella."

I chuckled and struggled to pull myself free of the rag pile.

"You need some help gettin' up?" Aubrey asked.

"No, I'm almost there," I answered, before my arms gave out on me and I collapsed back into the pile. "On second thought, maybe I could use a hand here."

Aubrey reached down and pulled me up. Once I got to my feet I'd be fine. I'd taken worse beatings and lived.

"Thanks again," I said, collecting my gun from the ground and slipping it into my holster.

"Say, you know where I can get my hands on a little rope to tie this up?" I kicked Lawton in the ribs. He didn't make a sound.

"I'd like to say I got a length of baling twine on me, but I just don't." Aubrey tossed his makeshift club on a stack of boards piled against the side of a building.

I frowned. After what I'd been through I didn't want Lawton waking up and walking away.

"But, say, some of them rags might be just what ya need there." Aubrey pointed at the pile of grease-stained rags I'd been laying in.

A wide smile broke across my face. "You're a good man, Barnes."

"Thanks," he said, patting his hands on his pants pockets. "You just remember that when you to tell the cops what went on here. Be best if I didn't make it into that conversation."

"No problem at all. As far as I'm concerned, we've never met." I dug through the rag pile, selecting the thinnest strips I could find.

"That's right." Aubrey pulled a pack of cigarettes out of his hip pocket and lit one. "'Sides, you're gonna have enough trouble with that girlfriend of yours."

I dropped my rag selection on the ground by Lawton's head. "What are you talking about?"

"That girl you were with tonight."

"What about her?"

"She's Manny the Rose's girl."

"What?"

"Or at least she used to be. Word has it they're on the outs."

"Oh man, what a night."

I got down to business and started binding Lawton's limbs together with my best knot know-how.

"You should be more careful, Ben. Women'll get you into trouble."

He blew a long stream of smoke straight up into the night sky. "They're bad for the health."

"This from a guy who knows, eh?" I replied.

He turned and vanished into the night.

I finished tying up Lawton; he wouldn't be going anywhere when he came to.

Aubrey's lingering smoke smelled good, so I took a moment and lit a cigar while I tried to figure out what I would be doing next. That's when I realized something was missing . . .

"Hey, big boy."

I glanced up and saw Beth Hrubi leaning against a black MG, slim cigarette in one hand, car keys twirling around a finger of the other. She still looked like dynamite, only now I knew she was just as dangerous.

"Looks like you handled yourself okay after all."

"Yeah, you know me. See a mess, clean it up."

We both laughed.

"Say, I suppose a ride would be out of the question. All I have is me and my baggage." I gave Lawton another good kick in the ribs. I smiled when he moaned this time.

"I'm sorry, darling, but I only have one seat, and it looks like I already have some passengers tonight."

She opened the door of her car and climbed in. I saw the two beat-up suitcases sitting in the seat next to her. Just what I'd forgotten about.

She tossed her cigarette into the night. I watched it tumble until its bright glow winked out.

"Don't worry, I'll let the cops come pick up you and your playmate. Anyway, you've made quite a killing here. You're probably going to be a hero."

The car's engine purred to life.

I didn't know who she thought she was fooling. I was sure I'd be spending a lot of time in the interrogation room tonight.

She smiled, shifted gears, and left my life in a cloud of dirt.

Case Three
A Cold-Blooded Kidnapping

"They took my girl! They took my Georgia!"

The high-pitched whining set my teeth on edge. I yanked the telephone receiver away from my head in an attempt to save my eardrums a load of pain. I was too slow.

"Just calm down, sir." I tried my best to sound reassuring. "We'll find her."

I took a deep breath. The man on the other end did the same. Having just walked into the office, I was hardly ready for this call. I hadn't even poured myself a cup of coffee, though I knew the pot in the kitchen would be almost empty now except for a thin layer of boiled-down sludge.

"Let's start with a few details." I spoke slowly, hoping to keep him calm. My eyes were busy assessing the new stack of papers on my desk, on top of which was a new manila folder.

"Bobby Regardie!" He shouted this as if it was some strange command.

"Excuse me?"

"My name is Bobby Regardie, and you have to help find my Georgia!"

Oh boy. I opened the folder, quickly scanning its contents. I tripped across the name Bobby Regardie. Apparently, he was some kind of animal expert at the Gesner Wild Animal Park, a sort of unofficial zoo Testacy City shared with Las Vegas.

I got back to the details: "When was the last time you saw her?"

"Just yesterday evening. She was all curled up in her favorite spot, right by the pool."

"Uh-huh. And how do you know Georgia was kidnapped?"

"It's obvious!" he ranted, his ire rising once again. "The lock on her door was broken, her place was all messed up, and *she is not inside!*"

Those last four words vibrated out of the receiver like air rushing from a leaking balloon.

According to my folder, he had first called the Always Reddy Detective Agency earlier that morning with this abduction story. Hal Reddy, the big man in charge, had assigned it to me—no doubt because it had taken me a little extra time to get into the office. That never made Hal real happy. But I had my excuses. I had been feeling a little down the past few days, so I stopped off at the haberdashery and picked myself up a new fedora—a nice tan Borsalino that looked like a million bucks.

Buying a new hat always raised my spirits a little. Talking to hysterical men knocked them right back down.

"Okay, just relax. Have there been any ransom demands?"

"No, no . . ." He was so worked up his voice trembled. "I'm so worried about her."

"I'm sure you are, Mr. Regardie. Does she have any enemies that you know of? Anyone who'd want to see harm come to her?"

Little huffs of breath came at me from the other end of the line while my man struggled for an answer.

"I don't think so," he finally said. "I mean, sometimes she gets a little cranky, especially when she hasn't eaten in a while."

My eyes rolled up to the ceiling as I scratched behind my ear with the eraser end of a pencil. I'm no expert on females, but I'd say that line safely describes just about every one I've ever run across.

He continued: "But she hasn't eaten for nearly two months. She's bound to be very hungry . . . and very cranky. Probably really, really cranky!"

I paused, listening to the hiss of static on the telephone line, and let his last statement sink in. I once again flipped through the thin case file Hal had left for me, searching for what was now all too obvious.

"Ah, Mr. Regardie—"

"Please, call me Bobby. I'm more comfortable with that."

I closed the file, shoved it across my desk, and creaked back in my chair. I got the feeling this case was a big joke that everyone was in on but me.

"So what you're saying, Bobby, is that one of the animals at the park is missing."

A snort of derision came at me. "She's not just 'one of the animals at the park.'" His voice took on a harsh tinge of irritation. "Georgia is our reticulated python—one of the park's star attractions!"

"Right. A python." Somehow this particular detail was left out of the file. Hal's idea, no doubt. His sense of humor was known for being more than a little offbeat. Every agent in his employ fell victim to one of his jokes at one time or another.

Not that a missing snake wasn't something to laugh about. With difficulty, I managed to hold in my guffaws. Somehow, I didn't think Bobby Regardie would be able to see the humor.

Now that I had a better idea of what the case was really about, I asked Regardie some more pointed questions that might actually give me useful answers. Then I arranged to meet him at the zoo later that afternoon.

After I hung up, I grabbed myself the last quarter-inch of tar from the coffee pot and checked in with Hal.

"A python?" he asked, feigning ignorance only for a second before letting out a hearty laugh. He pointed his cigar at me and told me that's what I got for not getting in early enough. I sighed. Always the same old story with Hal.

I grabbed my coat and hat from the desk and drained my coffee cup before letting Rhoda Chang, the agency's receptionist, know that I'd probably be gone the rest of the day. Then I was out the door.

As I walked toward my car I ran into Harper "Pappy" Meriwether, one of the best ops (and certainly the oldest) working in Hal's outfit. He whistled as he strolled down the sidewalk, the youthful spring in his step belying his age. Even though he was pushing seventy, I'd seen him take out two-hundred-pound thugs—using only his trusty cane—without breaking a sweat.

"Good morning, Ben, my boy," he greeted, as I opened the door of my dependable Galaxie 500. "What do they have you working on this fine day?"

"A snakenapping, if you can believe that," I answered, managing to keep a straight face.

A long playful laugh tumbled from between his thin lips. "You wouldn't fool an old man now, wouldya?"

"No way," I assured. "I know better than to rib you, Pappy. Somebody swiped a big snake from the Gesner Wild Animal Park."

His blue eyes sparkled brightly in his sand-colored face. "That's gotta be the weirdest thing I ever heard of."

I pulled out a J. Cortès, one of the small, dry-cured cigars I liked to smoke, and gave it some flame. "I don't pick 'em, I just solve 'em." I exhaled a mouthful of smoke. "How about you? Anything juicy on your end?"

Pappy had been working on a high-profile murder for the past couple of weeks. A bus driver had found a dead bum on a bench at one of his stops, big needle sticking out of his arm. Someone had tried to make it look like an overdose, but to everyone at the agency, it sure looked like murder. Especially with the multiple knife wounds in his chest.

Turned out the bum was really Travis Kohen, a delivery boy for Mexican mob man Manny Flores. Travis was also the son of Testacy City's senate-bound, crime-busting politico Kris Kohen. Daddy wanted to see justice done, so he turned to Hal's agency. Lord knows, if you want justice done in Testacy City, you don't go to the cops.

"All my leads are coming up dry the past couple of days. I got one more place to turn. After that . . ." His words trickled off into a shrug.

"Well, let me know if you need any help."

"Thanks, I just might with this new cop in town. He's a real hard case."

The big news in the Testacy City underworld was the recent arrival of some homicide hotshot from Atlanta. He'd only been on the job a short while, and already the rumors were flying. Despite all the talk, I had yet to hear any solid information.

"So you've met him?"

"I've only run into him once so far," Pappy said. "He's one flashy dresser, that's for sure. Goes by the name of Duke Wellington. And he let it be known he's not fond of playing ball with us dicks."

"Well, that figures," I muttered. "I'd better hit the road. Good luck to ya."

He nodded his head and started walking. Then he stopped and looked over his shoulder. "Hey, Benjamin . . ."

"Yeah?"

"Take it easy on those smokes. Those things'll kill ya."

I took one last puff, then dropped the stub on the pavement and ground it under my heel. "Sure thing, Pappy."

Pappy nodded again, then resumed his whistling and began mounting the steps to the Always Reddy office.

I climbed into my car and headed for the highway.

A little past noon, I blew by the *Thanks for Visiting Testacy City: Come Again Soon* billboard. The sun streamed down as if it had something to prove, making the road ahead of me shimmer like a lazy river. Waves of heat washed over my car, baking me inside. It was going to be a hot ride.

The Gesner Wild Animal Park rested smack dab in the middle of the desert between Las Vegas and Testacy City, about an hour's drive southwest. It was the pet project of a group of desert-loving zoologists who felt the American Southwest needed some sort of wildlife preserve to protect its vanishing resources. But, typical of how things work in Testacy City, local politics corrupted what had started as a noble cause. By the time the whole thing was built, it had turned into a large, fully stocked zoo, complete with lions, tigers, kangaroos, exotic birds, otters, and even a single polar bear, the poor bastard.

Maintaining each animal's natural habitat proved to be an expensive endeavor, and since the park was funded jointly by taxpaying citizens of Vegas and Testacy City, the result had a lot of people not fond of its existence.

There was even one renegade group that existed solely to protest the park, something to do with animal rights. Stealing a giant snake would certainly fit their agenda, so they immediately made the suspect list.

After making my way through the serpentine pathways of the park's private roads, I pulled into the K section of the parking lot, right beneath a blue sign painted with a white koala.

I caught the Tiger Tram, a little safari-style wagon train all done up in orange and black that promised to take me to the front gate. The scenic drive could have been a lot faster for my purposes.

After arriving at the entrance and waiting in line behind a group of screaming kids, I finally stepped up to the ticket booth. A young woman with bored eyes but an otherwise pretty face stood on the other side.

She was about to charge me admission when I explained, "I'm here to see Bobby Regardie."

She just stared at me.

"I'm Ben Drake." I slid a business card to her through the little opening in the cage they kept her in. "He's expecting me."

She looked down at the card and her eyes grew large.

"So you're a detective, for real?"

"That's what they tell me."

"You must be here about Georgia!" she bubbled with bubble-gum enthusiasm.

"Hey," I grinned, "maybe you should try some detective work yourself."

Her smile melted into a scowl as she picked up the phone that hung on the wall next to her. She slouched into the receiver and muttered a few monotone syllables before turning those bored eyes back my way.

"He'll be out in a minute. Just wait over there." She pointed toward a little bungalow-type building that held the gift shop, stroller rental, and restrooms.

She handed me a little sticker that read *Park Pal* and featured a panda in a typical panda pose. She told me to wear it while I was in the park, so I slapped it on my lapel.

I thanked her and strolled over to a carved stone bench with a nice view of the flamingo pen, started in on a cigar, and waited for Bobby Regardie.

I'd never been to the park before. My wife and I had often talked about visiting when the time came for us to have kids. But the drunk driver that killed her assured I'd never live out that fantasy. I sort of forgot about the park after that. Oddly, I found it had a calming effect on me, despite all the people milling about on this warm spring day. It seemed like a good place to get some thinking done.

A voice interrupted my reverie: "You must be Ben Drake."

I looked up, shading my eyes against the intensity of the afternoon sun. Standing above me was a tall, thin man wearing what I took to be the park's uniform: a bluish-green jumpsuit affair with a lot of pockets. I stood up, dusting off my trousers.

"That's right. I take it you're Bobby?"

He tapped the patch above his left breast pocket with a long, slender finger, emphasizing the *Bobby* stitched there in gold-colored thread. "That's what the sign says," he chortled.

What a cornball.

"Then I'm pleased to meet you."

Shaking hands revealed a cornball with a firm grip.

"I could tell you were Ben Drake by your hat," he explained. "Not many folks come here wearing such a nice-looking hat."

"Good observation there, Bobby."

"I pay attention to what's going on in my park, don'tcha know."

"Well then, let's go see where you kept this boa constrictor of yours."

"Well, y'see, Mr. Drake . . ." He reached up and took off his park-issued cap and rubbed his free hand through his tousled curly brown hair. He snapped the cap back on.

"Now, we gotta get something straight. She's not a boa. No sir. She's a python."

"Right, right. Of course."

I asked myself what the hell the difference was, and, almost like he heard me, Bobby launched into what would be the first lesson of the day—the differences between pythons and boa constrictors. He spoke fast, his long fingers dancing wildly in the air as he told me about the animal kingdom.

"Boa constrictors are members of the family *boidae*, which includes anacondas, but pythons are members of a different family altogether: *pythonidae*. Boas are ovoviviparous, but pythons are oviparous. There are also anatomical differences, mainly in the skeletal system; although, males of both species have what you call an anal spur which—"

"Okay, Bobby," I interrupted, my hands in the air, surrendering. "My apologies. I won't make that mistake again."

"I'm just, you know, making sure you know what's what, Mr. Drake."

"I think I got it. Let's get a look at where you keep Georgia."

"Sure thing, Mr. Drake. Just follow me."

I snuffed out my cigar in the metal ashtray half hidden behind some gladiolas. Something told me that Bobby wouldn't let me smoke around his animals.

"A lot of the guys here drive around in the golf carts, but I like to walk around. Gives me a chance to be close to the animals," Bobby explained. "You don't mind walking, do you, Mr. Drake?"

"Not at all," I lied. "Lead the way."

We began our jaunt to the reptile house. He shot off across the park, his long legs keeping him moving at a good clip. I almost had to run to keep up with him. Thankfully, Regardie would stop every so often to relate some arcane animal fact. One thing was for sure, Bobby knew animals.

After trekking through the park, we came upon a strange-looking structure consisting of a group of interlocking hexagonal buildings that Bobby identified as the reptile house. As we entered, I found its odd shape gave it a mazelike feel. The snakes and other reptiles lounged in cages replicating what I guessed would be their native habitats. A sheet of Plexiglas kept them separated from the pointing fingers of curious park patrons. A series of wooden slats had been built around the entire place, effectively diffusing the direct sunlight and allowing the park to more easily control the climate of each reptile's home.

"Here's where Georgia stays." Bobby stopped in front of an empty cage, easily the largest in the reptile house. It even outsized some of the shotgun apartments on Testacy City's south side.

A continuous stream of water trickled down the rock wall at the back of the cage, flowing steadily into a nice shallow pool. A few thick logs, along with a number of heat lamps in the ceiling, rounded out the habitat.

I whistled, "That's a big cage."

"Georgia is a big snake."

"How big?"

"Well, she's still growing. But last time we measured her she checked in at about sixteen feet long and 250 pounds."

"So then it's safe to say this was the work of more than one person."

"More than one person? Re-he-hur-hur-hur!" His whole upper body arched back as he let loose the strangest bit of laughter to ever come my way. I took a step back. He continued.

"Of course it's 'safe to say' this was the work of more than one person. When we bring her out for exercise—snakes need exercise too, don'tcha know," he chided in that annoying tone of his, "when we bring her out, it usually takes six or seven of us to carry her."

"Hmmm," I nodded. "Can I get a look at the other side of this cage?"

"Righty-right. Just follow me."

Regardie walked over to a door painted the same mud-brown as the rest of the reptile house and pulled a big ring of keys out of his pocket. He unlocked the door and held it open for me.

I checked the lock on the door as I went in. No sign of foul play.

The room had many walls that zigged and zagged every which way, giving the space an odd shape. Habitat doors of various sizes, each sporting its own padlock, covered each wall. A stack of metal cages filled with rabbits, rats, and mice sat in the middle of the room.

I pointed at the stack of cages. "This what you feed the snakes?"

"Woo hoo! That's right, Mr. Drake. You're a good detective, I can see that. The smaller snakes, like Anastasia, the jungle carpet python, get the mice; your middle-sized snakes, like Roscoe, our ball python, get the rats; and the big snakes, like Georgia, get the rabbits."

"Seems to be plenty of rabbits here, Bobby."

"Absolutely there are, Mr. Drake. We keep pretty well-stocked on all our rodents."

"Okay, but on the phone you mentioned that Georgia hasn't eaten for something like two months . . ."

"Well, you're right again there, Mr. Drake."

He adjusted his hat in the special way that let me know I was about to get another lesson.

"Y'see, snakes don't eat like mammals. No sir. Let's take Georgia for instance. She doesn't really need food that often." As he talked he pointed from rodent cage to snake cage and back again like a broken circus puppet. "When we feed her, it's usually two rabbits at a time, and that keeps her pretty satisfied until she's ready to eat again."

"And that's two months later?"

"It depends on the time of year, really. In the spring and summer she eats more often, but in the fall and winter, two months is pretty normal."

"So that's why you think she's pretty hungry by now."

"Oh yeah. I've never known Georgia to go much longer than a few months between meals, except for once when she was sick. And when she's ready to eat, boy oh boy is she hungry."

"I bet that's something to see," I mumbled.

"It sure is, Mr. Drake. Say, it's about time for Roscoe to eat. Do you want to see him in action?"

"That's all right, Bobby. I'd rather take a look at the door to Georgia's cage, if you don't mind."

"Not at all. You're all business, I can see that."

Regardie strolled over to the biggest cage door.

"I've left everything just as I found it this morning."

I took a closer look. A pair of bolt cutters had sliced the padlock cleanly open. And with the lock out of the way, access to the inside of the cage was no problem.

"You can't think of anyone who might have done this?" I thought I'd let fly with the routine.

"No, no. No one at all. Do you have any ideas?"

"Yeah, this was done by someone who works at the park."

His eyes widened and he gasped, putting a hand over his mouth. "An inside job?"

I nodded in friendly agreement. "Who else has access to this room?"

It took a moment for him to answer. "Anyone with a key, I guess."

I rolled my eyes. "Of course. And who would that be?"

"All the animal handlers . . . the maintenance staff . . . I guess that would be about it."

"Can you get me a list of those people?"

"Sure as sunshine I can, Mr. Drake, but it might take a little time."

"I can wait. And while you're doing that, is there someplace I can grab a bite to eat?"

I realized I hadn't had anything but coffee past my lips all morning. And that realization got my stomach to complaining. I always work better with a little food in my gut.

"Hungry, eh? Well, no need to worry about that, Mr. Drake. We got some of the best cooks right here at the park's cafeteria. Yes sir. You're in for a real treat."

Regardie locked up the reptile house before we hiked halfway across the park to the staff cafeteria, a squat, unimposing building next to the noisy aviary.

All this walking wasn't helping to ease my hunger any.

"Here you are, Mr. Drake. Why don't you go on in and get yourself a nice meal, while I head to admin and get you that list."

"Sounds like a good plan, Bobby."

I started through the door, mouth watering at the prospect of food.

"Say, Mr. Drake," Bobby called to me.

"What is it, Bobby?" I replied, slightly annoyed.

"Ummm . . . well . . . I was just wondering if . . . if it's okay if I call you Ben," he stammered. "I mean, 'cause we're buddies now . . . right?"

"Sure, we're buddies. Of course you can call me Ben," I sighed.

"Wowie, Ben . . . thanks!"

Bobby bounced off to get the list, finally leaving me to fend for myself in the cafeteria.

Unfortunately, as it was well into the afternoon, the cafeteria had finished serving lunch; all they had left was a selection of appetizers. It was better than nothing, so I helped myself to a plate of deep-fried mushrooms, mozzarella sticks with marinara sauce, and some delicious-looking crab cakes. And of course, I rounded out the meal with a big cup of coffee.

A few other folks hung out in the cafeteria, most of them reading the paper and drinking coffee; all except for one fellow, a big blond gorilla whose green eyes kept drifting my way. After a little while he came over and pulled up a section of bench next to me.

"Hey, I haven't seen you around before . . . friend."

It wasn't a greeting. It was a threat.

"Yeah, I'm just visiting." I showed him the sticker on my lapel. "See? I'm a Park Pal."

"Yeah? You got business out here . . . pal?"

He was trying to scare me, but I don't scare easy. I stopped eating and looked at him. His pale lips twitched behind his unkempt beard. He wore a grease-stained, dark gray work shirt with the sleeves cut off. A tattoo of a coiled cobra writhed on his huge bicep. He gripped the edge of the table with a white-knuckled hand. The air between us crackled with raging testosterone. He wanted to start something, and not something pretty.

I calmed myself, keeping my eyes on his.

"As a matter of fact, I do—looking into the disappearance of Georgia."

"That snake?"

"That's right. Know anything about it?"

His eyes flicked downward before he responded. "No."

Just then Bobby Regardie breezed through the cafeteria's swinging doors.

"Hey, Ben! I got that list for you."

He moved my way with a sheet of paper clutched in his fist, then took note of my companion.

"Oh, I see you've met Kirby Doyle. He takes care of all the official park vehicles around here."

I looked at Doyle. "That so?"

"Yeah, that's so." Doyle stood up and rolled his shoulders. "See you around."

"Yeah. See you around."

I took the list from Bobby and scanned it. About thirty names filled the page. Kirby Doyle's was one of them.

"What do you know about this Doyle fellow?" I asked Bobby.

"Not hardly a thing; he keeps pretty much to himself. I hear he's a real good mechanic, though."

Initially politics seemed like a reasonable reason for the crime. However, after my run-in with Doyle, the motive started to smell like money.

"Bobby, how much is Georgia worth?"

"How much is she worth? She's priceless!"

"To you, sure. But let's say someone wanted to sell her."

He gasped. "Do you think . . . ? Oh, God, I'll never see her again!" His rag-doll body dropped down on the bench next to me. His fingers dug into my shoulder and he flopped his face against the back of his hands like he was going to cry.

"Relax, Bobby." I palmed his head like a basketball and lifted it from my shoulder. "Try to work with me here. What could someone get for her?"

"Well, it's hard to say. Not many pythons of her size are in captivity, so if a collector really wanted one that big—I mean really, really wanted one—they'd probably pay more than ten thousand dollars."

"That's a lot of cash to own a snake."

"Yeah," he agreed. "But let me tell you, Ben, Georgia's a lot of snake and worth every penny. I'd pay that much to get her back."

"Good to know. Thanks, Bobby."

He stood up and collected himself. "No sense falling to pieces; I've got to be strong for Georgia." He paused a moment, taking a deep breath and furrowing his brow. "What's our next move, Ben?"

"I've got a few people to talk to. After that, well, let's just say I have a few hunches."

"Wowie, Ben! Already? You sure do work fast, I can see that."

"I'm just doing my job. Say, Bobby, if I want to come back out here to follow up on some clues, is there an easier way to get into the park than going through the main gate?"

"Sure thing, Ben, just follow the signs to the employee lot. You can park there. I'll let the security guy know that you're okay."

"I appreciate that, Bobby." Despite being a little odd, the guy was jake in my book. "You're okay too."

Bobby grinned and his face turned a bright crimson. For once he seemed speechless. I stood up and clapped him on the back.

"I'd best get going. It's getting late, and I still have work to do tonight."

It was early evening when I got back to my car, still waiting for me under the blue-and-white koala sign like a faithful pet.

My whole body ached after following Bobby all over the park. I opened the door and slipped into the driver's seat. Not counting the leather easy chair in my apartment, this was the most comfortable seat I owned. I closed my eyes for a moment and thought about snatching a little rest. I didn't have time to waste, though; I had a case to solve.

I cranked the ignition, and the car roared to life. I shook my head in a futile attempt to energize myself, then began the job of navigating back to the highway.

Keeping my eyes open on the drive back to town wasn't easy. The sun was sitting low in the sky, washing the desert with a red glow the color of a fire's smoldering remains.

I was rarely in the open desert at sunset, but when I was, it always made me want to smoke. I indulged myself; it kept me awake as I drove the rest of the way into town.

Darkness had settled upon the city by the time I arrived. I had some thinking to do, so I headed to the agency. Everyone had gone home. The place was pretty quiet—just how I liked it.

I sat down at my desk and noticed I still wore my *Park Pal* sticker. For some reason it amused me. Maybe it was the image of Kirby Doyle calling me pal. Or maybe it reminded me of my wife. Either way, I peeled it off and stuck it to the side of my old typewriter.

I slid open the bottom drawer of my desk and pulled out a fifth of Old Grand-Dad. I checked my cup; a tiny brown ring of dried coffee rested in the bottom. I poured myself a little nip anyway. The bourbon's sweet sting soothed my aching muscles and helped me think about my next move.

I picked up the phone and dialed "Steady" Freddie Edison, a fence I knew in Las Vegas. I heard a soft click as someone picked up the line on the other end. Then there was nothing but the low hum of long-distance static. It was Freddie all right.

One of Freddie's rules is that the caller talks first. If Freddie doesn't know you, he hangs up. Another rule of Freddie's is that he doesn't do business with strangers. Luckily, we weren't strangers.

"Hey, Freddie, it's Ben Drake."

"Ben, baby! How's life up in ol' TC?"

"Pretty good, Freddie, pretty good. How's business?"

We exchanged a few more trifles before I got around to the reason for my call.

"I'm wondering if you've heard anything about someone trying to sell a stolen snake."

"A stolen snake? I've moved some weird goods in my day, but that's tops."

"So you've heard nothing."

"Zip. Zilch. Nada. Why? What's up?"

"Someone swiped a big snake from the Gesner Wild Animal Park. I'm thinking they're going to try to sell her."

"What sort of dollar figure we talking about?"

"Around ten thousand, give or take a little."

"For a snake? That's too crazy!" he spluttered. "Besides, ten large is way too south for most of my customers."

"That's what I figured, but I know you got ears. Let me know if you hear something, will ya?"

"Shall do, my man. You keep cool, now." I heard him snap his fingers at me before he hung up.

I eased back in my chair, sipped my bourbon, and closed my eyes. I couldn't get Kirby Doyle off my mind.

I pulled out my copy of the Testacy City phone book—a thin volume that combined the yellow and white pages. I set the book on my desk and opened it to the D section of the residential listings. I found thirteen Doyles, but not one of them had a Kirby next to it. I didn't want to do a door-to-door tonight, so I thought I'd try a different approach. I flipped until I got to the *Pets* heading in the yellow pages. Testacy City boasted three pet stores: Desert Fish and Pets; Fins, Feathers, and Fur; and Jan's Pets.

A fierce rumbling started up in my stomach. I glanced at the watch I kept tacked to the wall next to my desk. Eight o'clock was about to break. No wonder: the only meal I'd eaten all day was the grub at the animal park, and those small servings didn't satisfy my appetite.

I ran my eyes over the store listings again. Looked like Jan had set up her pet store right downtown, not too far from the office. It wouldn't be a bad idea to swing by the place, just in case it was still open. After that I'd grab a burger or something from the malt shop down the street.

I poured the rest of the bourbon down my throat and left the office to the roaches.

* * *

I found Jan's Pets right where the yellow pages said I would: at 9337 Oak Street in downtown Testacy City, just around the corner from the police station. It inhabited a nondescript, two-story building stuck between a dry cleaners and a liquor store. I must have passed it a million times before but never paid much attention to it. Then again, I don't have any pets.

A *Closed* sign hung at a rakish angle on the wood-and-glass door, but the lights still blazed brightly inside the small shop. I peered in, looking for any sign of life. A lot of movement caught my eye, but nothing human.

I tapped on the glass a couple of times with a quarter, hoping to attract some attention. I did.

A woman appeared from somewhere near the back of the room and walked toward the door. Her dark brown—almost black—hair tumbled down to her shoulders in gentle, natural waves, making her bright blue eyes seem that much brighter. Her red-checked dress, which sort of resembled a Purina dog food bag, didn't do much to hide her pleasantly plump figure. I got the impression she liked it that way. She had a country-gal wholesomeness; I wouldn't have been surprised if she'd been raised on a farm. In short, she was an attractive woman.

A tiny brass bell jangled as she opened the door. It was a wonder I heard the bell with all the racket going on in the joint. The dogs barked and the birds screeched—even the fish seemed to be making noise.

The place had the same earthy sort of smell as every other pet store I'd ever been in: a combination of fur, dried food, and the sharp tang of animal waste.

"Evening, ma'am," I said, tipping my hat like a gentleman. She seemed to inspire that sort of behavior. I offered her a business card. She took it.

"Good evening." A genuine smile beamed out from her broad, attractive face.

"I closed awhile ago, but I guess I have time for one last customer. Please come in." She held the door open for me.

As I walked into the store, her smiling eyes left mine while she read the contents of my card.

"A real detective here in my store!" she exclaimed. "Well, what can I do for you, Mister . . ." her eyes flicked back to the card for a second to grab my name, "Drake?"

"Please, call me Ben, Miss . . ." I went fishing for her name.

I caught it: "Just call me Jan, Ben."

"Jan it is, then."

"Now, I bet you're here for a dog. You look like a dog sort of fellow to me." She started down an aisle to the left. "Follow me," she coaxed.

I never had a dog, and although I had wanted one when I was a boy (what boy doesn't?), I couldn't see having one right now. I'd watched Rhoda Chang's dog once when she went out of town, and the thing nearly destroyed my apartment. No, there was no way I could have a dog. The demands of being a detective kept me away from home too much.

Nevertheless, something about the way Jan walked prompted me to follow her down the aisle. She stopped in front of a cage and lifted out a little dog. I had to admit it was cute.

Jan introduced us. "Ben, this is Rufus."

Rufus squirmed and wiggled in her arms as I reached out to pat him on the head. His long tongue flicked out across my hand. As I said, cute.

"What sort of dog is he?"

"She, actually. Someone mistook the poor dear for a boy, and now it's too late to change her name without confusing her. Isn't that right, Rufus?" Jan put Rufus back into her cage. Rufus whined at the prospect of further imprisonment. I certainly couldn't blame her for that.

Jan locked the cage and turned around, straightening a few boxes on a nearby shelf. "She's a Jack Russell terrier. Good breed."

"I'm sure it is, but I'm afraid I couldn't get a dog right now."

"Well, that's too bad, Ben." She smiled that winning smile again. "Then what brings you down here to my little shop?"

"I was hoping you could help me with some information."

"I'll try. If it's easy, I won't even charge you," she winked.

"I'm sort of wondering what you'd feed a python . . . or is it a boa constrictor?" Bobby's explanation of the differences between the species had the two types all twisted around in my head. "Either way, what you'd feed a big snake."

"Well, depending on the size, either rats or rabbits."

"Ah, this is a pretty big one."

"Then I'd say rabbits."

"Do you sell rabbits?"

"Normally, but little Billy Wilkins bought my last two earlier this week. That kid loves his bunnies. Keeps a hutch out in his backyard. Says he's going to be a world-class rabbit breeder."

"Good for him. How about rats, then?"

"I only have a few rats left. I sold a whole bunch to a couple of guys earlier this afternoon . . ." She wrinkled up her pretty brow. "Come to think of it, those boys were asking about snake food too. You wouldn't be looking for them, would you? Being a detective and all?"

I was hoping if I threw out some lines, I might reel in a lead. Looked like I got a bite. This was one savvy pet store owner. I told her so.

"Thank you very much, Ben. I pay attention to what goes on in my little part of the city."

"You'd be surprised how many people don't," I commented. "Any chance on one of those boys was a big blond fellow with tattoos?"

"No, no big blond fella. It was a bald guy and a dark-haired guy—he was a real dirty one. They both had plenty of tattoos, though."

"Hmmmm. So they drop any hints about where they might be found?"

"As a matter of fact, they did. They kept asking me if I wanted to go out for a few beers with them. They were going to something like . . . the Crowbar?"

I was willing to bet this would be Jake and Al's Crow Bar, a rough-and-tumble biker dive down on Solitaire Road.

"I see you didn't go with them."

"They didn't seem to be my type. Besides, I have to go home and take care of my animals. I don't get out much these days." She gave me a little shrug. "You know, I'm a pet lover."

"I guess that would keep you in on Saturdays, huh?"

"Not all Saturdays." Again with the wink. "Anyway, what did these guys do that you're after them?"

"They stole a snake named Georgia from the Gesner Wild Animal Park late last night."

"You mean the reticulated python?"

"That's the one."

"What a beautiful snake. I hope you catch them, Ben. If I can do anything else . . ."

"Thanks, Jan. I'll let you know. And thanks for all your help. If I ever need a dog, now I know where to go."

I tipped my hat and left the comfort of Jan's Pets, retreating to the comfort of my Galaxie 500. I spun the wheel and pointed the car toward the Crow Bar.

A flashing neon sign blazed in the night, a beacon leading me down the unpaved Solitaire Road. Its words lit up in sequence, first *Crow* then *Bar* then *Crow Bar.* The only trouble was that the *w* was burned out, so it looked like *Cro Bar* when completely lit up.

In the glow of a floodlight mounted high on a pole, I could just make out a fading painted sign towering above the neon. It sported two cartoon crows in biker gear, winglike arms around each other in buddy fashion, stubby cigars hanging out of their beaks. Their free hands held beer bottles of the brand XXX. In an arc over their heads the sign read, *Jake and Al's Crow Bar.*

The chrome from a dozen or so motorcycles, parked in a neat row in front of the bar, gleamed in the light.

I drove slowly around the building and slid into a spot behind the bar between more bikes and a handful of souped-up hot rods. My car was pretty out of place at this joint, so I didn't want to park in front in case anyone came in after me and started asking who the blue Ford belonged to. And I didn't want to be parked too far from a door in case I had to hotfoot it out of the place.

I took off my new hat and set it on the passenger seat before I climbed out of the car. I didn't need too much unwanted attention coming my way. As it was, I worried my suit and tie would attract enough trouble for the evening.

I stowed my worry at the back of my brain and walked toward

the bar. I didn't lock my car, another step to aid a quick getaway. Besides, these boys were interested in bikes and muscle cars, not my beat-up sedan.

Easing my way through the back door, I found the inside of the Crow Bar to be nearly pitch dark. I could barely focus on the outline of a bar to my left and a few booths off to the right. Rock music came at me thick and heavy like honey. It wasn't anything I recognized. Mingling with the notes were the twin sounds of laughter and conversation.

Normally in a situation like this I'd just belly up to the bar and get myself a drink, but considering I was a fish out of water here, I opted for the seclusion of a booth instead.

The seat of my pants picked up something sticky from the vinyl seat. Another suit for the cleaners.

As my eyes continued to adjust to the gloom, I noticed the two pool tables further toward the front. Both had plenty of action. A serious game of darts off in the corner kept a few other folks busy.

During my surveying, a peroxide blonde wearing a tiny leather skirt, along with matching halter top and boots, walked over to me. She carried a round tray holding a few empty bottles. Seeing her surprised me; I wouldn't have figured the Crow Bar as the kind of place that had a waitress.

"If you're sitting here, you gotta buy something. House rules."

"Wouldn't want to break the rules, now, would I? Old Grand-Dad, if you got it. Three fingers."

She shook her head. "We don't stock that stuff, mister. You drink anything else?"

There were many reasons why I usually drank at the H.M.S. Pandora: the soothing wood decor, the real leather seats, the way your arm fits right into the groove of the bar. But the best reason for me was the fact that they always had Old Grand-Dad on hand. It contained a little more rye than your more common bourbons, and it had a strong, spicy taste that really hit the spot.

"Jim Beam then?" I asked hopefully.

She thought a moment. "Yeah, we got that. Be right back."

I continued to look around while I waited for my first drink. Photos of women in swimsuits advertising numerous brands of beer and motorbikes lined the walls.

My waitress came back, carrying a watered-down Jim Beam on the rocks. A far cry from three fingers of Old Grand-Dad, but it would have to do.

"Three bucks," she demanded.

I went for my wallet. She started in with the questions.

"Say, you waitin' for someone tonight?"

"Nope. Just hanging out."

"Well, if you don't mind me sayin' so, you don't really fit in here."

"I don't mind you saying it." I set a five on the table in front of her.

She crinkled up her button nose. "Then why come here? This don't seem to be your sort of hangout."

"I've had a rough day. I wanted to be somewhere where no one knows my name."

A high-pitched giggle leaped from her throat. "That's funny," she chirped as she took the five and returned two ones in its place.

I lifted my glass and tilted it at her, then took a sip. I came here to do a job, so I got down to it. And to be effective, I needed to keep a low profile. I moved as much into the darkness of the booth as I could and slouched down over my drink. I hoped that if anyone did notice me, they'd think I was just another drunk.

The entire bar buzzed with conversation, rising like filthy waves over the rock 'n' roll only occasionally. I had my ears full trying to listen everywhere at once with little success. I caught snippets about bikes, broads, beer, and billiards, but nothing about boas.

My waitress, who I found out went by the name of Peggy, kept the watered-down bourbon flowing from the bar to my glass, and as long as I had a full glass I kept on sipping.

On one trip over, Peggy let me know that some of the folks in the bar were wondering if I was a cop. Looked like my low profile wasn't so low after all. I told her I was no cop, just a guy looking to get lost. She let me know that if I needed help getting lost she was available. I let her know I appreciated the offer.

I really hadn't planned on drinking all that much, but it kept going down smooth, real smooth. Too smooth. Add to that my minimal food intake, and it became more and more difficult to concentrate on the task at hand as the babble continued to swim around me.

I decided to cash in my chips for the night. I staggered a straight line to the men's restroom, which had a bulgy-eyed cartoon crow holding its crotch painted on the door. Beneath the bird, someone had scrawled *rooks* in permanent marker.

Some biker threw me a shove before I could even try the door. "There's a line, pretty boy, and you're at the end of it," grunted the voice behind the shove.

I glanced at the guy. A thick upper lip of hair weighed down his face, and his sideburns, which extended into ridiculous mutton-chops, didn't help any.

I slid out of his way, and perched on the edge of a stool along the back wall. I was just about to skip the john when two leather types brushed past me. One of them said something that caught my attention.

" . . . all those rats?"

My pulse quickened, and a shiver shot down my spine. My hand went to my forehead, and I leaned in to listen.

"I tried to drop them off, but no one was around."

The guy on the left, a squat, hairy hoodlum, checked his wrist then scratched his chin through his thick, black beard. "Where the hell could he be?"

"Damned if I know," said his pal, taller and as hairless as his buddy was hirsute.

My friend from the front of the line, the one fond of shoving, turned to add his two cents. Apparently, he was part of the party.

"How about that dress today?" He sent nudging elbows at his buddies.

"Yeah. Man, she was good enough to eat." A wolfish smile flickered through facial hair. "I wouldn't mind seeing more of that. Might have to buy me a dog."

"A dog? Man, that's too much work. Get yourself a turtle or something."

"A turtle? What kind of pet is that?"

"A lot better than a giant snake."

All three let loose with big belly laughs. The bathroom door opened, and a slight man in leather spilled out, stumbling off toward the bar.

The hairy one leaned against the wall, crossed his arms, and scoped out the room. In the process, his shifty eyes fixed right on me. I averted my gaze, trying my best to make it seem like a natural gesture. I failed miserably. My heart pounded fast and heavy in my chest.

Looked like I got the lead I was searching for, and it came with a load of trouble. I needed to get out of the spotlight and find a place to watch without being watched. I retreated toward the back door.

Out of the corner of my eye, I saw the hairy guy follow me. I knew if I ran he'd be right behind me, so I decided to play it cool. If my cool failed me, I had a loaded gun.

I moved toward the gaudy liquid lights of the jukebox. I looked up as I plunked a few coins into the slot. My adversary stood a few feet away, fists clenched tight, ready for action.

I glanced down at the selections the jukebox offered. I couldn't read a single word. I'm sure I wouldn't have recognized anything anyway. I punched a few buttons as my mind raced to find a way out of this jam.

His eyes burned into me, and I was compelled to meet his gaze. We stood there, eyes locked. He was all I could see through a rage-filled stare.

I could feel the leather holster under my arm rubbing against the skin over my ribs. It itched, begging me to move, but I couldn't.

Just as I was about to whip out my revolver, my target snapped his head to the side. I got a grip on my fury and my vision widened.

His bald buddy had just smacked him in the arm and pointed toward the front of the room.

"He's here! It's about time, eh?"

A commotion erupted from the front of the bar. Kirby Doyle had just walked in.

He seemed to be pretty popular in the Crow Bar. A lot of people went out of their way to wave or say hello. Many offered him a beer.

No way could I confront him here and now. I'd had a moment to cool down, and I could see that the odds weren't in my favor. So I spun my shoulders against the back door and headed out.

I pulled out of the lot and parked behind a row of shrubs that hid me from sight but still offered a clear view of the Crow Bar. The big floodlight illuminated the front door nicely, allowing me to see who came and went.

Stakeouts were my least favorite aspect of detective work, but at least the cover provided by the bushes allowed me to smoke, so I lit up and took a hard look at my situation.

My best plan had me waiting here until these thugs finished their carousing for the evening, then following them to where they held Georgia. Case closed. Problem was, there were four of them and only one of me. If I took a risk and got to a pay phone to call in some backup, I stood a good chance of losing my quarry. I'd just have to figure out who to follow when the time came.

Doyle seemed like the ringleader of this gang, but my knuckles were itching to pop a couple of teeth out of Hairy's head.

I sat there for hours, watching the slow stream of people come and go. I still hadn't caught a glimpse of Doyle, my buddy with the beard, or the other two guys. My eyes started to droop, and I shook my head to keep them open.

Even though the sharp sting of tobacco was still thick on my tongue, I lit another cigar, needing the routine more than the nicotine. All I had to do was stay awake . . .

The first light of morning woke me up. A half-smoked cigar rested neatly in the ashtray on top of three small stubs of rolled tobacco. I cursed violently and pulled myself out of the car. Looking down I noticed ashes covered my gray suit, rumpled from a night in the front seat. My muscles, still stiff with sleep, complained as I brushed myself off. A quick glance at my wristwatch gave me the time of almost six a.m.

Angry that I'd lost the chance to make my move at night, I pounded a fistful of frustration into an open palm. I wanted to catch these punks with the goods sooner than later. If they found out I was on their tail, they'd skip town with Georgia in tow.

I may not have known where they went last night, but I knew where to find Kirby Doyle this morning.

After a quick rinse off and change of clothes, I made a stop at Lepke's Diner for a hot cup of coffee, a plate of steak and eggs, and a fresh bear claw. One of Testacy City's best-kept secrets, in my opinion, was the pastry-making skill of Costas Papademos, Lepke's owner and top cook.

Soon after breakfast, the still-early morning found me back on the highway speeding toward the Gesner Wild Animal Park.

I pulled in through the back gate, dropped Bobby's name to Gus, the pear-shaped security guard who surveyed the zoo employees' lot from his threadbare lawn chair, and drove in. Surprisingly, only a few cars populated the small lot, and I found an open spot right in front of the motor pool.

I found Kirby Doyle bent over the open hood of a Tiger Tram car, his head out of sight in the engine block. I could see the muscles bulge and ripple across his back as his arms did their unseen work.

I knocked on the edge of the open steel door and entered the garage. Doyle raised his head just enough to peer under his arm. When he saw it was me, he turned around, setting his socket wrench on a metal tray off to the side.

"Hey, if it ain't my pal." He shot me a grin of pure malice. "What brings you to my part of the zoo?"

He walked over to a long bench littered with tools, pulling a Zippo lighter out of his pants and a cigarette from the breast pocket of his grubby shirt. The cigarette found a perch on his lower lip as he leaned back against the bench, looking too much like a wild animal about to strike.

"Well, Kirby, I've been doing a little follow-up on that snake that's gone missing."

With a quick flick of his wrist the cigarette burned brightly and the Zippo disappeared. He spat an angry cloud of smoke my way.

"Yeah? Find anything . . . juicy?"

"Oh, it's juicy all right," I purred. "You see, I think *you've* got it."

A low, cruel laugh rumbled out of Doyle. "What makes you think that?" he snarled.

"How about the rats your boys bought for snake food."

"My boys?"

"The knuckleheads you went drinking with last night."

His face sprouted splotches of red. "You been followin' me?"

I smiled in response. His eyes squinted to slits.

Doyle took one last, long drag from his cigarette before flicking it toward me. "I don't like bein' followed," he growled.

The spent cigarette looped through the air before landing gracefully at my feet. A small shower of cinders erupted near my scuffed Stacy Adams.

I looked up just in time to see a giant crescent wrench swinging straight for my face.

I ducked.

The wrench grazed my scalp, but only enough to make me a little woozy. As I stumbled backward in a bid to regain my balance, I heard a heavy thud; the wrench in Doyle's double-fisted grip buried itself deep into the wall, my brand-new hat wedged in there with it.

I pounced. My knuckles found the soft spot of his kidneys—once, twice—before he backhanded me with a thick paw that sent me to the cement floor spitting blood.

I scrambled to get to my feet.

Doyle moved faster. He planted a heavy boot in my gut.

A crunch echoed in my ears. Breath left my chest with a rush. I curled up, gasping for air, holding my arms over my face.

Doyle picked me up by the lapels, held me steady, aimed, and clocked me a good one across the jaw.

The force of the blow sent me spilling into the grillwork of the dilapidated Tiger Tram. A heavy clang rattled my teeth as my head collided with the bumper. Blackness rushed in from the edges of my vision.

I remember thinking that Pappy was going to have some choice words for me. I'd fallen for one of the oldest tricks in the book.

I gave in to the blackness.

My consciousness returned slowly. As I lay there, lacking the strength to pull myself to my feet, I inspected the damage. Dried blood from the wound in my scalp felt like cement in my hair. A huge bump grew on the back of my head. My jaw, though not broken, felt like it was. It hurt to even breathe. I was a mess.

I looked down and saw my wallet, still open, resting on my chest. After a quick check, I discovered the small amount of cash I carried hadn't been touched, but the registration card for my car was missing.

I checked the holster under my arm. My .38-caliber Smith & Wesson Model 637 still rested there. I didn't even think to draw it; after all, I'd been spoiling for a good fight since last night's washout.

After a while, I managed to stand. I hobbled over to inspect my hat, still stuck firmly between the big wrench and the wall. Despite the fact that it was brand new, I felt like I'd lost an old friend. I sighed and walked out into the sun. I wondered what time it was. I checked my watch only to find it broken.

I got to my car and flopped down on the seat. It felt good to be in a familiar place. I opened the glove box, broke out a fresh tin of cigars, and slid one into my mouth.

No matter how bad I felt, smoking always made me feel better.

I had no idea how long I'd been lying in the motor pool, and now Doyle had a good head start on me. I needed to get to his place fast. I was thinking about calling Rhoda Chang and having her find me an address, when I realized my answer was right here in the park.

I limped over to where Gus kept his vigil next to a little wooden booth. To his credit, he didn't say a word about my appearance, which was a small victory of sorts. I knew I wasn't pretty; I didn't need to be told. I asked him if he could get ahold of Bobby Regardie for me.

He jumped on a two-way radio. Moments later, Bobby's chipper voice crackled across the line. Gus slapped the radio into my open hand.

I gave Bobby my twenty, asking him to come and meet me. I told him to hurry, then handed the radio back to Gus and sat down on the curb.

A little while later Bobby pulled up in an animal park golf cart. When he saw my condition, he went pale.

"Holy cow, Ben! Someone sure beat you to a pulp!"

"Yeah, your pal Kirby."

"You mean the Kirby who works here?"

"That's right."

"Hold on there, Ben." He lifted both of his hands, palms outward, and waved them frantically. "Now, I want you to know that he's no pal of mine. No sir. No pal of mine would do something like this to another pal of mine." Suddenly, a puzzled expression clouded his eyes. "Why'd he do this, anyway?"

"Because I figured out that he's the one who stole your Georgia."

Bobby sat paralyzed for a moment, then stammered, "What? . . . but . . . I mean . . . we have to get him!"

"I know, and we will. But to do that I need to know where he lives."

"Where he lives? Well, heck, Ben! That's easy!" His voice was rich with triumphant glee. "We can get that from admin!"

I managed to stand up. "You go get it. I'll wait in my car."

"Righty-right, Ben! You can count on me!"

He sped off to get Doyle's address; I waited in the Galaxie's soothing comfort. Me, my smoke, and my pain.

This ordeal had left me numb, but that was wearing off. Now my anger was taking over. And that meant me thinking about taking down Kirby Doyle. This time I wouldn't forget about my gun.

Bobby returned and climbed into my passenger seat. It took him three tries before he could spit out Doyle's address slow enough for me to understand it: 1546 Ruskin in Testacy City. I knew the street. It was in a south side neighborhood not known for its upstanding citizens.

I turned the key in the ignition. Instead of the expected gentle roar, I heard a hideous grinding sound.

I tried again. More grinding.

I didn't know anything about fixing cars. Neither did Bobby. I popped the hood anyway, peering inside the engine compartment. Bobby pointed out a few loose wires, cut clean.

I slammed the hood shut. Kirby sure didn't leave anything to chance. I had to catch up with him before he blew town.

"Don't worry, Ben. We can take my van."

A beeline across the parking lot brought us to Bobby's white Econoline van. It had seen better days. In fact, I'd hazard a guess that it was a couple miles shy of being scrapped. But we were running out of options, so I climbed in and strapped my seat belt around me, hoping we'd get all the way to Testacy City in one piece.

As Bobby nursed his van onto the highway, I eased back in the bucket seat and nursed my anger. The way this hulking mass moved, it was going to be a long time before we got to the city, and I didn't want to lose my edge before I found Doyle.

It seemed an eternity before we arrived. The entire way Bobby chattered at me, but I couldn't tell you a word he said. Being sore and badly in need of a good stiff drink, I didn't really pay attention.

I navigated Bobby through the city to the ramshackle duplex on

Ruskin. 1546, the left half of the building, looked to be boarded up tight. A Mustang, its trunk wide open, was stationed in front of the closed garage door.

The Mustang's trunk was empty; the garage door, locked. I made a quick circuit of the house, peering in through the dirty windows for some sign of life. I didn't see a thing, so I headed for the front door and eyed up the lock. Bobby came running up to me.

"Ben, what are you doing?"

"What's it look like? I'm going inside."

"Well . . . don't you need a warrant or something?"

"I'm a detective, Bobby. Not a cop."

"But . . . ummmm . . . then it's breaking in, isn't it? You just can't break into places, Ben!"

I pulled a slim leather case from the breast pocket of my coat. "I'm not breaking in, Bobby." I flipped open the leather case and selected a pick. "I'm sneaking in."

"But . . ."

"Look. This guy took your snake. Do you want her back or not?"

"Of course I do, but—"

"Then let me do the job you hired me to do. If it makes you uncomfortable, go wait in your van."

"Okay, Ben, I'm sorry." Finally, he caved. "How about if I just wait out here, like a lookout?"

I nodded and got back to work. A few minutes later I stood inside the home of Kirby Doyle.

It didn't take me long to investigate the small one-bedroom. As I would have guessed, cleanliness wasn't one of Doyle's virtues. A locker-room smell hung in the air. Filthy clothes piled up everywhere, and a mound of dirty dishes sat in the sink. I don't think he'd ever cleaned his bathroom.

There was no sign of man or snake, but plenty of insects crawled through the house.

Based on the layout, I figured out the door just off the tiny kitchen led to the garage, the only part of the house I hadn't yet searched. I tried the door. Locked.

I took a step back and kicked, right where the latch held the door shut. The crack of splintering wood rewarded me. I kicked again, and this time the door flew open. I dropped to one knee and pointed my gun inside. What I saw made me shout out, "Jesus!"

Heavy footfalls sounded behind me.

"What is it, Ben?"

I pointed inside with my pistol. Bobby peered in. Now it was his turn to shout, "Oh my God!"

He pushed past me into the garage. I didn't want to go in there, but I sure as hell didn't want Regardie's hurricane hysterics causing any more damage.

I went after him.

The narrow garage looked a lot like the motor pool at the animal park. Short benches jammed with tools lined three sides. More tools hung from the walls.

Unlike the motor pool, though, Doyle kept a half-dozen snake cages—complete with captive reptiles—along the far wall.

Numerous white rats scurried all over the garage. Most of them had splotches of blood on their fur.

The wire cage I assumed the rats had been kept in had toppled off a workbench and landed on the ground. Next to that, an enormous canvas bag covered part of the floor. It looked red and wet, having soaked up a good bit of the pool of blood it was swimming in.

Also in that pool lay Kirby Doyle's body. A snake, one that could only be Georgia, stretched out on the floor right next to him.

Mentally, I knew that Georgia was a big snake, but I still wasn't prepared for seeing her in the flesh. Easily twice the size of Kirby, she took up almost as much floor space as a small car. Yeah, she was one big snake.

And she had swallowed Kirby Doyle's left arm up to the elbow.

Bobby stood over the body, his eyes darting all over the garage.

Doyle was flat on his back with his legs, bent at the knees, curled under him at an awkward angle. A clean, deep slice in the flesh of his neck, right through the jugular, still gurgled a little blood. I almost pitied him.

"What the hell happened?" I wondered aloud.

"I told you Georgia gets cranky when she's hungry," Bobby answered. "She might be big, but she's fast. I'll bet he was trying to move her, and she wasn't happy about it. So she snapped at him. Pythons have some pretty sharp fangs, don'tcha know."

"Good aim too, from the look of things. Then she decided to eat him?"

"She didn't mean to hurt him, Ben. She didn't want to be moved, and she was hungry." His voice took on a whining that made me wince.

"If she was hungry, why didn't she go for the rats?"

"They're fast; hard to catch. Kirby's arm, though, it's bigger and just laying there—"

"It was probably twitching at least a little," I guessed.

"Even better. It was a bigger, easier target. There isn't an animal in the world that would pass up an opportunity like that, Ben."

"All right. I guess it makes sense. I'd better call the cops. Stay here, and don't touch anything."

I went back into the house and found the phone. The police told me someone would be along shortly. Standard routine.

I returned to the garage to give Bobby the update. I found him about to cut off Doyle's left arm with a hacksaw.

"Bobby!" I shouted. "What the hell are you doing?"

"I don't want her to eat too much, Ben. She's not used to this much food!" His eyes pleaded at me.

"Put down the saw, Regardie. Christ, the last thing we need is for you to get taken in on suspicion of murder."

"But I didn't kill him, Ben."

"I know that, but the cops don't."

"But—"

"Just put the damn saw down." I slipped my arm around him and walked him over to the nearest bench. He reluctantly dropped the saw.

"Thanks, Bobby. Let's go wait outside."

As we left the garage, he looked back over his shoulder and whispered, "It'll be all right, Georgia. Just hold on, girl."

We sat in front of the house in silence.

I smoked.

Bobby chewed his fingernails.

We got to our feet when a squad car pulled up, followed closely by a plain brown Dodge.

Two officers got out of the black-and-white and went inside the house. Two detectives climbed out of the other car and headed over to me and Bobby.

One of the detectives, dressed in a cheap brown suit, I recognized as Mark Weisnecki. I'd dealt with him a few times before, and I didn't trust him.

Weisnecki's partner sported a deep-blue suit combined with a pink shirt and a floral-print tie. He even had a deep-blue porkpie hat and floral pocket square to complete the ensemble.

Although I'd never seen him before, I knew who he was: Duke Wellington, the new cop in town. He stormed right over to me.

"Who the hell called this in?" He pointed at me like he was pointing a gun. "Did you call this in?"

"Yeah, I'm Ben Drake." I held out my hand. He ignored it.

Weisnecki pointed at Bobby. "Why don't you come with me," he drawled.

"Where are we going?" Bobby asked with a quivering voice.

"Got a few questions for ya," Weisnecki said.

Bobby looked at me, uncertain what to do. I don't think he'd ever been on the receiving end of this sort of thing before. Me, I was an old pro.

"It's okay, Bobby, just tell him what happened. Don't leave anything out."

Bobby nodded. Weisnecki led him to a spot just out of earshot and started in with the third degree. Poor Bobby.

That meant I got to go a few rounds with Duke Wellington. For a long moment he just glowered at me. I had to hand it to him, he had a steely gaze. He rumbled a question at me.

"So you're a dick, huh? A private dick?"

"Yeah, I'm a detective. I work for the Always Reddy Detective Agency."

He snorted through his wide nostrils. "I'd watch your step if I was you. This is my city now, and I won't put up with your mischief." He nodded his massive head, more for his benefit than mine. "That's right, it's Duke Wellington's city, and you'd better watch your step."

"So you're this new detective I've been hearing so much about."

"Look, I ain't here to make idle chatter, Drake. That's not my game. I'm here to solve a murder. I come to this here town, and what do I find but people stabbin', shootin', stranglin' everybody else. I say to myself, *Duke Wellington, this city's got trouble comin' out of the wazoo—* that's w-a-z-double-o. Wazoo." He cracked his knuckles. "So why don't you tell me what happened here."

I could see what kind of guy I was dealing with, so I gave him the facts, just as they happened. I didn't think Bobby had it in him to lie, so I even threw in the bit about the hacksaw. Then we switched dance partners and Weisnecki asked me all the same questions, all over again.

Our stories must have matched to their satisfaction. In the end, they obviously didn't find enough evidence to call Doyle's death a murder. The final nail in the coffin arrived along with Testacy City Medical Examiner Rebecca Hortzbach.

Rebecca and I were good friends. She'd helped me with more cases than anybody, even my fellow ops. I wasn't used to seeing her in the field; I mostly ran into her at the county morgue. But every so often she would pull a roving coroner shift just to get out of the basement.

She looked at the scene and pretty much confirmed Bobby's account of Doyle's death verbatim.

Naturally, this didn't make Duke Wellington too happy. He surprised me by consenting to let Rebecca cut off Doyle's arm so we could load Georgia into Bobby's van.

Duke Wellington had the last word before we drove off; he told us to keep ourselves available, just in case he had any more questions.

Bobby dropped me at my apartment, then turned his jalopy for home, giant snake and all.

My apartment was cool and comforting. I poured myself a glass of Old Grand-Dad and collapsed into my easy chair.

I'd send a mechanic down to get my car tomorrow. I certainly didn't feel like making the drive again tonight. Besides, it had been a busy few days. Tomorrow I'd rather work out of the office and catch up on my paperwork than drive all over the desert trying to get my car fixed.

Although it looked like I'd be late again. After all, I had to buy a new hat.

Case Four
Midnight Train to Nowhere

"Hey, Drake, my man . . . seen the paper yet?"

Mike Manetti had a way of taking the most common question and making it sound like the lead-in to a bad joke, a habit that never failed to annoy me. Besides, he always picked the worst time to be buddy-buddy.

"No, Mike," I sighed as I slapped shut a manila folder and tossed it into my out tray. This particular Wednesday morning, Manetti found me trying to catch up on a few old cases before my boss called me into his office to assign me another. Usually I looked for any reason I could find to avoid paperwork, but one of the few things I liked less than filling out old case files was listening to Manetti's attempts at small talk.

I leaned back in my chair and looked up at him. "I just got in."

"Yeah, me too."

I breathed out my exasperation. "I'm trying to do some work here."

He screwed up his face at me, trying to get his mind around the concept. I drained the last few drops from my coffee cup and didn't wait for him to finish. "I suppose you're going to tell me—"

"Wait'll I tell you this, Drake. It's Trout Mathers. That's big news, huh?"

That name. Trout Mathers had done a fine job of keeping quiet since our last run-in. I spent a fair share of time wondering when we'd cross paths again.

"Mike, I don't have all day. If you're going to tell me something, you've got to let it spill."

"Aw, man, I'm getting to it." He leaned back with boyish indignation and stuffed his hands into his faded jeans.

Before I could get in another jibe at him, I heard: "You better make it quick, son, 'cause Ben Drake's a detective with not a lot of time for dilly-dallying."

This voice belonged to the agency's patriarchal detective, Harper "Pappy" Meriwether.

"Pappy! I didn't hear you come in."

Pappy smiled at Manetti's comment. He knew that at seventy he could still sneak silently into a room, even with his trusty cane. The fact that a fire engine could sneak up on Manetti didn't seem to lessen this victory in Pappy's eyes.

"Yes, I came in all right. Heard you talking the talk about Trout Mathers."

Every detective in the group knew Mathers, a notorious gangster, the sly type with a penchant for banks and broads, the type who always managed to keep from getting nabbed. They also knew that not long ago he'd slipped away from me.

I'd had enough of the small talk.

"So did they finally catch him with the goods?"

"Catch him with the goods?" Pappy's top lip curled up as he glanced back at me. "You could say that," he chuckled softly. "Yeah, I guess you could say that all right."

"That's what I've been trying to tell you, Drake!" Mike Manetti's eyes grew large as he tilted his head back and finally spat out, "He's dead!"

Pappy picked up the story and ran it home. "Not just any ol' kind of dead, Ben. The kind of dead we call murder. They found him, face beaten raw and strangled with his tie, in the Purple Knights Motel."

Well known for the management's wayward eye toward the rampant prostitution and drug use behind its closed doors, the Purple

Knights was an infamous south side hot sheet. Sex and drugs added up to fun for some people, but for others they added up to a whole lot of death.

"The papers name his killer?"

I knew the odds were next to nil of that happening, but asking just seemed like the natural thing to do.

"They had a bit from Duke Wellington about it most likely being the work of a jealous husband," Pappy reported.

"Okay, whatever," I said. Everyone underground knew that Manny "the Rose" Flores had been after Mathers ever since he fouled up one of Flores's drug deals.

"Any word on the street from the Flores camp on this killing?" I asked Pappy.

Without warning, a low voice came rumbling through the room: "If you boys were going to have a chew-the-fat party, how come you didn't ask the boss to join in?"

Hal Reddy, owner of the Always Reddy Detective Agency, stood just outside his office and stared at us through smoldering eyes, his hands firmly planted on his hips.

"I didn't think you'd have time to stand around and talk, Hal," Manetti quipped.

Hal strode across the room toward Manetti, moving his bulk faster than it looked like he could. He cracked the kid along the backside of his head.

"Manetti, you dolt! I *don't* got time to stand around, and neither do my detectives! Now get to work on the Gompers case!"

Manetti nodded and slinked off, rubbing the back of his head.

Hal looked around. "Where the hell's Goiler?" When he didn't get an answer, he turned toward Pappy. "Harper, how's the Travis Kohen body dump coming?"

Pappy spoke with reverence to Hal, even though he was more than a few years Hal's senior. "Not much has turned up, other than the kid's body. We know he was one of Flores's runners, but that whole drug angle doesn't seem right to me. I'm digging around his father's history to see if he's got any enemies that might—"

"For Christ's sake, Harper, this is a hot one!" Hal exploded. "Don't turn this thing any more political than it already is. Forget the kid—and his father. The real meat is Flores! If you don't got hard evidence to back that up, then get some!"

Hal had a hot temper, but he didn't normally lose it with Pappy; it clearly took the old detective by surprise.

"Sure thing, Hal. I'm on it," Pappy mumbled as he ambled off to his desk. Pappy had been a detective for well over forty years, and I could tell he wasn't too happy to be told how to run an investigation.

The Kohen case, one of the biggest and most sensitive ever to come to the Always Reddy Detective Agency, had Hal under a lot of pressure. Travis Kohen had turned up dead one morning, an empty heroin needle deep in his arm. But the overdose setup was betrayed by the multiple knife wounds in his chest.

The kid's father, Kris Kohen, a hometown crime-busting politician bucking for the senate, was determined to turn his personal loss into poll results. He openly blamed local Mexican mob boss Manny Flores for the killing and had hired the Always Reddy Detective Agency to back him up.

One thing was certain, Pappy wasn't a puppet detective. He'd find the real killer, and that would be that.

"Rhoda!" Hal called out to the agency's gal Friday. She hurried to his side, and he whispered something in her ear. Then he turned his attention toward me. "Okay, Drake, your turn. Follow me to my office. There's some folks I want you to meet."

I sure didn't want the wrath of the boss man coming down on me. I did what he said and, a moment later, shut his office door behind me.

Two clients sat in the twin chairs in front of Hal's steel desk.

The woman looked like she had just come from a funeral. She wore black from head to toe: a long dress, high-heeled pumps, and a classy hat complete with a lace veil. I couldn't make out her features through the dark shroud, but I could see she'd been crying, thanks to the tear-stained monogrammed handkerchief she grasped in a black-gloved hand.

The man, however, looked like he'd just come in from herding cattle. Decked out in grubby jeans, a flannel shirt, a well-worn leather jacket, and dust-covered cowboy boots, he gave the impression of being a little rough around the edges, a little older than the woman, and more than a little uneasy about being in a detective's office.

Hal dropped down into the chair behind his desk. He grabbed a half-smoked cigar that rested in his ashtray and slipped it between his teeth. Then he did the introductions.

"This is Sissy Hathaway, widow of recently deceased Eli Hathaway. And this is Eli's brother Jasper." He gestured my way. "This is one of my best men, Ben Drake."

I nodded a greeting and pulled up the last chair in the room, a scrawny wooden affair that creaked loudly as I put my weight on it.

"Jasper and Sissy here are hiring us to investigate Eli's murder," Hal calmly spelled out.

"That's right," nodded Jasper.

"Tell us about it." Hal struck a match and held it up to relight his cigar. Then he glanced at Sissy and changed his mind, blowing out the flame and dropping the dead match into the ashtray. The cigar remained clamped tightly in his mouth.

"Well," Jasper choked, "Sissy found the body late Monday night. Some thug plugged Eli in the chest four times."

A low moan escaped Sissy's lips, and she began to sob. Jasper patted her hand. She pulled it away.

I remembered reading something about this mess in yesterday's papers. The murdered Hathaway had been some rich real estate mogul. I leaned forward and tried to put some polish on the brief statement Jasper had just handed in.

"So if the papers got it right, you found evidence of forced entry but nothing stolen?"

"That's right," Sissy muttered.

"Do you two have any ideas on who'd want to see Eli dead?" I asked.

"Well, if we knew that, we wouldn't be here!" Jasper snapped. "If we knew who it was, I could take care of things myself. That's how it's done where I come from."

"And where is that?"

Jasper's brow furrowed in confusion. "Where is what?"

"Where do you come from?"

"Back at the Hathaway Ranch," he explained. "In Wyoming."

Sissy got her sobbing under control enough to explain better: "Horse racing was my husband's true passion." She sniffed and dabbed her eyes with the already moist handkerchief. "It's in the Hathaway blood, you see. The family has a long tradition of breeding race horses."

"That's right," Jasper blurted out. "Eli took care of the buying and selling here in the city. And since I'm no good with math, I took care of the training and breeding back at ranch. I'm real good with animals."

"So you're just visiting Testacy City? Vacation or business?" I asked.

He frowned. "These questions ain't helping you find out who killed my brother!"

I never enjoyed dealing with people who thought they knew how to do my job. I got up and walked behind these two. Hal stared at me with confidence. I put a hand on the back of each chair and leaned into Jasper.

"Okay then," I spoke evenly, "what else can you tell me about your brother's murder?"

"Well," Jasper said as he turned and scooted his seat away from me, "I don't know much. I wasn't around that night."

"Where were you?"

"I couldn't sleep."

"Insomnia, huh?"

"Yeah."

"So where'd you go?"

Jasper stood up and threw his face at me. "There, you're doin' it to me again with all these questions! I went out to get some grub. Is that a crime?"

"No, Mr. Hathaway, there's no crime in eating," Hal responded. "Is there, Ben?" The timbre of the big man's voice cooled the situation. Jasper returned to his chair; I returned to mine.

"No, Hal, there isn't." I didn't feel like pressing the brother any harder on his whereabouts just yet, so I directed my next question to the widow. "Sissy, were you at home that night?"

"No, she was—"

"I can speak for myself, Jasper." Sissy turned toward me. I could just make out her green eyes piercing through the dark veil. "I was at the opera. Alone. Eli hated the opera."

"Okay. Was there anyone at home besides Eli? Do you know if he had any visitors?"

"I know . . . I know that when I left to go to the opera, he was home and working in his study. That's where I found his . . . body." She paused a moment. "As for visitors . . . I honestly don't know." She sniffled. "You'd have to ask Kenneth—he's our butler. If anyone would know, he would."

"Yeah, and you better check him out real good," Jasper snarled. "We all know that butlers and murder go together like horses and horseshoes."

"You might rather take a closer look at Norman Gneiss," Sissy offered.

"And who would that be?" I asked.

"He is . . . or was . . . Eli's business partner at Hathaway & Gneiss. He and Eli had been fighting a lot lately . . . not to mention that Norman has, shall we say, affiliations outside the law."

Jasper coughed, and I expected him to add his two cents. But after he cleared his throat, he kept silent.

"Right," I said. "I'll check this Norman Gneiss out. Anything else?"

Another moment of silence filled the room before Sissy responded, "I wish I could think of more, but right now . . ."

"Yeah, me too," Jasper added.

"Any more questions, Ben?" Hal asked.

"None that spring to mind. I'll get to work on this right away."

Our new clients looked at each other, then got up to leave. Jasper held out his hand to help Sissy up. She didn't take it.

I gave each of them a card as they left the office. "Let me know if you think of anything. My home number's on there—call me anytime, day or night."

Sissy took my hand and looked up at me. Again I tried to see through her veil, and again I could only make out her eyes.

"Thank you, Mr. Drake."

"My pleasure, ma'am."

Jasper glowered at me as he shuffled Sissy out the door.

"What do you think?" Hal asked me after the office door swung shut. He had rapidly relit his cigar, and smoke began to fill the room.

"Well, Jasper sure is carrying a torch for Sissy," I said. "And I don't think the feeling is mutual. Plus, he's not being totally straight with us."

"Neither is she, Drake. Don't fall for the helpless-dame routine. There ain't nothing fair about the fairer sex."

The old man picked up the phone and barked into it: "Rhoda, you got that stuff . . . ? Well, bring it in, girl."

Rhoda was quick through the door. She handed him a thin folder, nodded, waited to see if he wanted anything more, then scurried back to her desk. But before she closed the door, she threw me a wink.

"After Mrs. Hathaway came in and I saw how young she was, I had Rhoda check up on her. Smells like money to an old hard case like me." He turned the file around and tossed it to the far end of his desk. "Have a look. The number's not as big as I would have expected, but the broad will do all right by herself."

I picked up the folder and checked out its contents. Hal certainly had a point. I don't know what amazed me more: Hal's snap judgment or Rhoda's ability to dig up information at the snap of a finger. Still, I didn't buy that the girl was the bad guy.

"Come on, Hal, take it easy. I definitely got more to find out about them. I just want to talk to both of them someplace they feel a little more comfortable."

"What about the butler and the business partner?" Hal reminded from behind a bluish cloud.

"Yeah." I didn't need reminding. "I don't buy the butler story. I'll check him out later when I visit the house. I'll play the partner angle first. See what I can't get out of him."

Hal grunted a dismissal and knocked thick ash from his stogie into the ashtray.

The offices of Hathaway & Gneiss took up space in an expensive high-rise in downtown Testacy City. I rode the elevator to the fifteenth floor and found myself facing a classy office done up in glass, dark wood, and brass. In a way, it reminded me of the H.M.S. Pandora. Perhaps it was still too early for me to be thinking about my standing Wednesday night get-together with Pappy at the Pandora, but I couldn't wait to talk to him about Trout Mathers and Manny Flores.

Shaking my head, I regained focus on the present. An old man in a white uniform wielded a thin brush, meticulously painting *Gneiss Property* on the pane of glass in the door. Norman Gneiss certainly hadn't wasted any time erasing the Hathaway name from the business.

I excused myself and stepped around the old painter into a spacious reception area. The place gave off the deep smell of relaxation.

An unctuous young man sat behind a low partition on the left side of the room, mumbling into a phone. Behind him stood a built-in bookshelf filled with thick leather-bound tomes, all identically colored in red and black.

Just to the right of where he sat, a shadowy hallway extended back into the depths of the building. A deep leather couch squatted against the right wall, right behind a low table that held a small collection of neatly arranged architecture magazines. A few healthy-looking potted plants dotted the landscape for flavor.

I wasn't looking for flavor, so I strolled over to the oily fellow on the phone and stood in front of him. He did a fair job of pretending to ignore me. I didn't mind; I'd been ignored by the best.

"Oh please, Marion, I couldn't possibly . . ." He tapped the table frantically with the first two fingers of his right hand as he talked. "Oh, for God's sake. Hold on." The tapping stopped as he sneered up at my presence. "Yes?"

I flipped a business card in his direction and said, "Ben Drake to see Norman Gneiss."

He gave the card a quick read and nodded his head. A smile blossomed on his face, and his eyes brightened. "Oh, of course." He pushed two buttons on his phone in quick succession. "He has been waiting for this."

"Waiting for what?"

He looked down at the phone, as if he were addressing it directly, and switched his tone from arrogant to reverent. "Mr. Gneiss, a Ben Drake is here to see you." He paused. "A detective." Another pause. "Right away." After a few more rapid button pushes, he returned his attention to me. His arrogant tone came with it. "Ever since we heard the news we've been waiting for someone to see us about . . . the accident," he explained, lowering his voice to a whisper when he uttered the last two words of his sentence.

"It was no accident," I corrected.

"Of course it wasn't. But if you're on the case, you'd know that, wouldn't you? Just go on back." He waved nonchalantly to the darkened corridor. "Last door on the right."

"Thanks. And, ah, say hello to Marion for me." I sent a snide smile his way before I disappeared down the hall.

At the end of the walkway, I found a thick oak door that stood slightly ajar. I pushed it open and stepped into a huge corner office that overlooked downtown Testacy City. Norman Gneiss, a rotund man—well-dressed in a tailored three-piece charcoal-gray suit, complete with a blue shirt and multicolored power tie—waited for me behind a massive mahogany desk. A dozen diplomas and certificates hung framed on the wall behind him.

He took a moment to size me up. I returned his scrutiny with some scrutiny of my own. Determining his age proved difficult. His brown eyes, deep with experience, looked like they belonged in the head of an old man. Conversely, his shiny black hair belonged on the head of a man in his twenties. His face, free of wrinkles, glowed with an infant's healthy pink.

He gestured a chubby hand toward an open chair. "Please," he uttered with a deep, rich voice.

I slid into the cushioned comfort of the leather chair. "Thanks for seeing me on such short notice, Mr. Gneiss."

"I'm a busy man, Mr. Drake," he returned.

"I understand that, so I promise I won't take much of your time. I just want to ask you a few questions about Eli Hathaway's murder."

"Yes . . ." He drew the end of the word out into a hiss. "An unfortunate incident indeed."

"Can you tell me anything about it?"

"I wish I could help you, Mr. Drake, but . . ." He threw me a smug shrug.

"No jealous business rivals?"

"None whatsoever. You see, this is a very dignified profession."

"I don't doubt that, Mr. Gneiss, but this morning his brother and widow came to see me—"

His laugh cut right through my words. "His brother couldn't think his way out of a paper bag, and Sissy," he paused and waved a perfectly manicured hand in the air, "let's just say she didn't know how good she had it . . . though she certainly has it even better now, yes?"

He rubbed his right thumb and forefinger together. His smarmy accusation made it hard to keep calm.

"Okay, let's say that," I snapped. "Let's also say that she told me you'd been fighting with Eli lately."

He smiled cruelly and leaned into his desk. "I see where you're driving this conversation, Mr. Drake, and frankly I refuse to take that ride. Yes, I was at odds with Eli. We didn't see eye-to-eye over the convention center I've proposed building for downtown Testacy City."

"Yeah? What was the problem?"

"A simple one, really. Eli didn't want it built. He said it would make Testacy City into another Vegas. Now I have to ask you, Ben, would that be so bad?"

"To be honest, I'd have to say it would be, Norman."

Gneiss blew out a deep sigh of disgust. "Another man with no vision. So many of you in this town."

I decided to go for the direct approach. Beating around the bush was getting me nowhere. "Now I have to ask you—got an alibi for Monday night?"

He stared at me. I stared back. We sat like that for a few moments, two cats ready to fight. He gave in first.

"Very well, then. Monday I was gambling. All night. I had a beautiful blonde on one arm and a redhead on the other. There's no way I was going to leave them alone to shoot poor Eli. Besides, I was winning big."

A smile oozed its way onto his broad face, daring me to speak. I didn't give him the satisfaction.

"Naturally, if I have to repeat that in court, you'll find me with an entirely different alibi. Airtight, of course." He leaned back in his thick leather chair and folded his hands across his ample belly. "You see, I'm a respectable man in this town, Mr. Drake. I can't be seen gambling, cavorting with prostitutes, or conspiring to murder. That just wouldn't do."

I nodded. "I do appreciate your honesty, Mr. Gneiss."

"Mr. Drake, honesty is my policy." With this he rose to his feet, squeezed out a patronizing smile, and extended a hand toward the door. "Now, please. I really must get back to work."

"Right. I've got a few things to do myself. Thanks for your time." I pulled myself out of the chair.

"If you need anything else, my assistant Rex will gladly be of service." If Rex was the fellow I ran into out front, I somehow doubted his assistance would come gladly.

I quickly found my way back to the reception area. I wanted to ask my friend with the phone a few questions before I got out of there. This time, instead of the phone, he was playing with an issue of *Business Week*. I cleared my throat and pointed down the hall with a jerk of my chin.

"Quite some guy, your boss."

His head snapped up out of the magazine as he quipped: "Yes, he is, isn't he?" His voice swelled with pride. "He's the Bugsy Siegel of Testacy City, you know."

I failed to stop a short burst of laughter from jumping out of my mouth. "Those his words or yours?"

His lips formed a slippery smile. "All mine."

I nodded. "So, Rex, is it?"

"Yes, Rex Mayer."

I've always found that a man with integrity offers his hand for a shake when he introduces himself. Rex made no such offer.

"So, Rex, did you interact much with Eli Hathaway?"

"Of course. Until Tuesday, I took care of his needs as well as those of Mr. Gneiss."

"And you got along with him?"

"Yes, yes." He dismissed my question with a wave of his hand, much in the same fashion as his boss.

"What about Mr. Gneiss?"

"I get along with him very well."

"No, I mean did Gneiss get along with Hathaway?"

"Of course they got along. They were partners."

"Your boss told me he and Hathaway weren't seeing eye-to-eye lately."

"Well . . . that's sort of true, I guess. Though they didn't argue nearly as much as Mr. Hathaway and Mrs. Hathaway did."

He just sat there, grinning up at me, trilling his fingers on the desk.

I'd had enough of his cute self-righteousness. "Where were you Monday night?"

"Not at the Hathaway house," he chuckled. "Mr. Gneiss will vouch for my whereabouts."

The phone jangled loudly, interrupting this dead-end conversation. Rex, still grinning, snatched it up. "Gneiss Property."

Nice indeed. Nice as a pit of vipers. I wasted no time getting out of there.

I steered my powder-blue 1965 Galaxie 500 through the dusty streets of Testacy City. I was born here, had spent most of my life here, and still loved this place. Sure, it had more than its fair share of crime, but it had loads of character as well. A Vegas-style convention center would strip that character clean away, leaving Testacy City nothing but the soulless husk of a tourist trap.

If Eli Hathaway stood against that, then I was truly sad to see him go. It was too late for me to prevent his death, but there was still time for me to bring his killer to justice. So I skipped lunch, deciding I'd rather head to the office and try to throw some more pieces of this puzzle into place.

I climbed the familiar steps of the William Kemmler Building, thinking about which piece to play with first. I wanted to follow up with both Sissy and Jasper, preferably separately. I didn't think I could trick Norman Gneiss into letting something slip, but I could certainly outthink Rex Mayer. A return visit, however distasteful that seemed, was definitely in order. And I still had to talk with Kenneth the butler, probably when I looked over what remained of the crime scene. Not to mention that I needed to learn more about Eli's death from someone who could give me some straight facts.

As I pulled open the door to the cluttered office of the agency, Rhoda Chang handed me a slip of paper with a message from Sissy Hathaway. Rhoda had checked the little "please call" box with one of her perfectly shaped check marks.

Once I settled into my desk chair, I flipped to a clean page in my legal pad and dialed the number on the slip. A man picked up the phone on the first ring.

"Hathaway residence." He spoke in a rich, honeyed voice with a slight British accent. I guessed this would be Kenneth.

"Sissy Hathaway, please. This is Ben Drake, returning her call."

"Yes sir. Just a moment, sir."

The receiver thunked down, and I heard a man's heavy footfalls fade behind the low hiss of static that crackled over the phone. A moment later, the smooth old voice returned.

"Unfortunately, sir, I'm afraid that Mrs. Hathaway is not presently at home. She did, however, leave a message for you, Mr. Drake."

I waited for him to continue. When he didn't, I spoke up. "Well, are you going to give it to me?"

"What is that, sir?"

"The message Sissy left for me."

"Absolutely, sir . . . ah, hold on, please . . . I had it here just a moment ago . . . yes, here we are, sir. The message reads: *Please inform Detective Drake that I request his company for dinner at the Long Mile Supper Club, tonight at seven. Tell him I hope to discuss Eli's death someplace less intimidating than a detective agency.*"

"That'll be no problem," I replied. "Say, is Jasper Hathaway there?"

"No sir."

"Do you know where he went?"

"Ah, let me think . . . if I remember correctly he was accompanying Mrs. Hathaway when she departed."

"So you're not sure if they left together?"

"No sir, they did leave together. I'm sorry, it's just that I've been quite distracted lately. This whole business has been extremely dreadful."

"Murder is never anything *but* dreadful," I responded.

"Yes sir. Again, please forgive me. I'm under a bit of a strain."

"No need to apologize, I've been there myself. Tell Sissy I'll see her at dinner." I hung up and laced my hands behind my head and got to thinking.

I had signed up quite a cast of characters for this caper. I needed to get a few more hard facts, and they needed to come straight from Eli Hathaway himself. I snatched up the phone again. This time I dialed the county morgue.

The line rang about fifteen times, and I was just about to hang up when it stopped. A voice came over the receiver: "Morgue."

The voice, full of authority yet soft and inviting, belonged to Rebecca Hortzbach, Testacy City's ace medical examiner and a good friend of mine. I first met her years ago when a drunk driver killed my wife. Rebecca helped me deal with her death and get on with my life. For that I will always be grateful to her.

"Hey, Rebecca, it's Ben."

"Ben! Sorry it took me so long to get the phone, I was just finishing up looking at last night's casualties."

I heard the familiar tink of a Zippo lighter, followed by the sizzling of a freshly lit cigarette. Rebecca chain-smoked like no one else I'd ever met. I don't think I've ever seen her without a cigarette stuck in her mouth or dangling from her fingers. I always reasoned that working all day in a building reeking of rotting flesh gave her the right.

The sound of the burning tobacco made my mind hungry for a cigar. I propped the phone between my chin and shoulder and dug out my tin of J. Cortès Grand Luxes from my suit coat pocket.

I popped it open, took out a slim cigar, and stuck it between my teeth. "Then you saw Trout Mathers?"

"Sure did. Asphyxiated. Never a pleasant way to go—and with a necktie no less." Rebecca took a long drag on her cigarette. "So, how are you? They keeping you busy these days?"

"Busy as ever," I answered, sliding the words around my cigar as I struck a match and got my own smoke burning. It tasted good.

"Did you just call to talk about dead bodies, Ben? Or are you calling to chat this time?"

"Actually, I need your take on another murder."

"Figures," she grunted.

Rebecca was always after me to take her out to dinner or out for a few drinks. I'm not quite sure why, but I always dodged her. I did find her attractive; she had tiny features, sort of like a cat, and the glasses she wore, pointed at the corners, made her seem all the more feline. This appearance, coupled with her innate curiosity, earned her the nickname of Cat Lady from the police. Though it sounded cute, it wasn't intended to be complimentary.

"So, you got any particular murder in mind, or can I just pick one?" Her sly titter tickled my ear through the phone.

"Very funny," I drawled, unable to keep myself from chuckling. "What can you tell me about Eli Hathaway?"

"Eli Hathaway, let's see . . ." She paused to take a few puffs of smoke. "Yeah, I remember that one. Came in early yesterday morning full of holes."

"That'd be him. Any good details? Time of death and all that stuff?"

"Hold on. I still got the file here on my desk." Papers rustled and flapped about. "Okay. Your man was shot at close range—four times—between ten p.m. and two a.m. while sitting in a chair. Three of the bullets went clean through his body, and the fourth lodged in his spine. His left lung took two of the slugs, and his heart took the other two. Even if someone had found him right away he wouldn't have made it to the hospital alive. The bullets were .44 caliber— fired from a Smith & Wesson revolver, probably a Model 29 with a six-inch barrel. That's a pretty big gun to take out a frail man. Bet it made a hell of a noise too."

Rebecca liked her guns. I think it was probably her favorite part of the job.

"That the best you can do on the time?" I asked.

"Hey! What do you want from me? A miracle? I can only tell you what the body tells me."

"Okay, okay. Anything on the shooter?"

"Judging from the angle of penetration and considering the size of the gun, definitely a man. I'd say anywhere from five-ten to six feet tall, 180 to 220 pounds."

"Hmmm. That's not very specific. I think you're starting to get sloppy, Rebecca."

"Wait a minute, now. I didn't exactly have ideal conditions to work with. Besides, you know how many of these I do each day?" I could hear the irritation start to crack her voice.

"Hey, take it easy. I was just kidding you," I apologized. "But now that you mention it, I'm curious: how many?"

"Too many." Again she let a giggle slip out. "But really, I've got to get out of here for a little while. What you say we take in a show, Ben?"

"Say, speaking of shows, I keep meaning to tell you about this case I handled awhile back. I think you'll find it pretty interesting."

Rebecca was a serious collector of conspiracies, no matter what the shape or size. And I just remembered one that I could add to her collection.

"Yeah? I'm all ears."

"This guy—a ventriloquist of all things—went missing, so his wife hired me to find him."

"You found him, of course."

"Of course. And he was one odd bird too. Anyway, he lets me in on a little secret about the history of ventriloquism."

"Hold it, let me guess. This is that whole Orpheus/Alexander Graham Bell thing."

"Uh . . . yeah." I rocked back in my chair. "How is it that you . . . ?"

"Ben, that thing is old as the hills."

"Man, you never stop surprising me, Rebecca. I swear your mind operates on a whole different level than most people. Maybe you should consider detective work."

"That's your job, and I couldn't do it nearly as well. But I will give you my gut reaction on this Hathaway killing."

"Great. Let's hear it."

"All evidence aside, I'm telling you this was a pro hit."

"Really?"

"Yes." She paused for a long drag on her cigarette. "You don't go breaking into a random mansion with a loaded .44 for backup. You know what I'm saying?"

"You got a point. I'll keep it in mind."

"And Ben," she paused again, "I always like hearing your stories, even if I know how they turn out." She laughed like a little kid.

One thing about Rebecca, she never failed to make me smile.

After I hung up the phone, I pulled out the paperwork I hadn't finished that morning; then on second thought, I put it right back. I was itching for action, so I looked in the file for the Hathaway address—124 Sycamore Circle. A quick glance at the time told me I still had plenty of time before dinner.

That reminded me: my new evening plans would cut out my regular drinking get-together with Pappy. I jotted down a note for my old friend and left it with Rhoda. As I headed out of the office, I felt a little guilty checking out on him this evening. He would understand that work had to come first; after all, he and I came from the same mold—we were both detectives through and through.

Sycamore Circle sat smack in the middle of the richest section of Victory Gardens—the wealthiest part of Testacy City. I didn't have many occasions to go visiting up there; still, I knew my way around pretty well.

I left my car parked at the top of the empty circular driveway in front of the impressive Hathaway mansion. It stood a modest two stories high and extended far back on a lush piece of property. I'd seen huge houses before, but I still had to think, *Who needs a house this big?*

Moments after the pleasant doorbell chimes rang out, an old man in a dark-gray suit greeted me.

"Yes sir? How may I help you, sir?"

"Hello, I'm Ben Drake, the detective Sissy hired."

"Oh yes, of course. I'm afraid that Mrs. Hathaway is still not at home," he said in his slow, mannered way. "She did, however, leave a message for you."

"Another one?"

"No sir, the very same one I read to you over the telephone. I thought perhaps you had forgotten about it."

I had to stay relaxed to deal with this butler. "I remember dinner all right. I just thought I'd drop by early to have a look around, maybe ask a few questions. I'm investigating the murder of Mr. Hathaway, you know."

"Investigating the murder. Right you are, sir. Please do come in then."

The door opened into a short but immaculate hallway with a high, arched ceiling. Old, unglazed vases—probably from another century—stood waist-high on either side of the hall.

This entrance opened up into an even more impressive foyer. The white polished marble floor seemed like a smoky sea beneath my feet. At the other end of the room, a bulky staircase curved up to the next floor.

I put the butler's age at a little over sixty. His bald pate shone brightly in the light of the foyer chandelier. What little gray hair he had circled the back and sides of his head just above his ears.

"You must be Kenneth," I said.

"Yes, that's correct—Kenneth Galbraith."

"Pleased to meet you. Is there a place we can sit and talk? I won't take much of your time."

"Very well. If it's all right with you, sir, I should like to go to the kitchen. I feel most comfortable there."

"Lead the way."

In the kitchen he offered me a drink. When I asked for bourbon, he left to go get some out of the liquor cabinet. This gave me a good chance to do some snooping. Sadly, it seemed to be a kitchen with no secrets—nothing hanging on the refrigerator with tiny fruit-shaped magnets, nothing scribbled on scraps of paper tossed on the counter, and nothing in the drawers except for utensils.

Kenneth returned with my drink. For himself, he poured a glass of cranberry juice from a refrigerated carafe. I wasted no time starting the questioning.

"Were you here the night of the murder?"

"Yes, but I retired to my room early that evening."

"Did you hear any gunshots?"

"Hear the gunshots? No sir, I did not. My quarters are located in a small cottage off of the main house. Plus, I had plenty to deal with that night, what with Mrs. Hathaway bickering with that . . ." He paused and took a quick sip of juice. "Ah, with Mr. Jasper Hathaway. That sort of emotion always wears me down."

"You've had a long history with this family?"

"I've been of service to the Hathaway family for over forty years now, sir."

"That's quite some dedication. Have you always disliked Jasper?"

"I did not say that, sir. He's nice enough when he's not angry, but . . . well . . . he's nice enough when he's not angry."

He took another sip from his glass; this time he drank too fast, and he began choking. His soft eyes looked up at me. In that moment I got a small sense of what the murder in this house must have done to him.

"I'd like to check out the study; that's where they found the body, right?"

"Correct, sir. The police have combed through it, but you're welcome to take another look."

Kenneth escorted me upstairs to the scene of the crime, then disappeared to attend to his duties.

I spent the better part of half an hour digging through the details of the study. Not only did I find nothing suspicious, I found nothing even remotely interesting. Most other studies I'd poked around in held all sorts of goodies: bankbooks, business correspondence, even love letters, but the police had picked this scene pretty clean.

In my experience, cops have a lot to do when they find a body, and sometimes they get sloppy. Usually that means they miss something. Not this time.

As I left the room, a feeling nagged me: I knew this house hid something that I would find interesting. I resorted to an old Ben Drake trick—check out the bathroom. Over the years, I had found that you could learn a lot about a person that way.

All the doors off the main hallway were shut. I ventured down a side hall that took me farther away from the stairs. At the far end I tried the last door. It opened into a bedroom, and from the slight feminine touches and the soft scent of flowers, I guessed that Sissy slept here.

I felt like a frat boy crashing a sorority house. I saw a door at the other end of the room, almost definitely leading to a private bathroom, but I couldn't resist walking over to her dresser.

Like the rest of the house, the top of the dresser remained clean of clutter. I eyed the couple of pictures that rested there, but they showed nothing interesting.

I opened the top drawer. Inside I found a wide assortment of brassieres and panties.

I glanced over my shoulder. What I saw made me jump like a Mexican bean. Across the room, next to the large four-poster bed, an antique vanity's large oval mirror cast my image back at me. I closed the drawer as quickly and quietly as I could and made for the bathroom while I was still lucky enough to be alone.

The bathroom's red-painted walls reflected brightly off the

chrome fixtures. The red carpet screamed up at me. I felt like I was in the center of a volcano. Why would anyone decorate their bathroom like this? Nevertheless, I wished *my* john were this clean.

Lotions and creams and various atomizers of perfume filled the medicine cabinet. No brown prescription bottles. No stray razors. Nothing suspicious.

Before I left, I washed my hands with the yellow sun-shaped soap sitting on the marble counter next to the sink basin. The only other thing on this countertop was a small porcelain dish with a dainty lid.

I dried my hands off, lifted the lid, and had a look inside the dish. I picked up the item and examined it in the light—a single cat's-eye cuff link. A man's cuff link. I put it back where I found it.

The mirror above the sink caught the curl of my smile. I fixed my tie, straightened my hat, and winked at my reflection. Then I got out of there.

I walked into the Long Mile a little after six. The soft sounds of the Charles Mingus Quintet filled the air, putting a spring in my step as I strode toward the bar. I ranked this place as the best restaurant Testacy City had to offer. Not the classiest, but certainly the best: good portions, reasonable prices, and healthy servings of bourbon.

The place was cozy. A low dividing wall running just off center split the smallish room in two. The dining area, which held a half-dozen tables and eight booths, each set for dinner, occupied the space on the left side of the partition. A set of steps at the far left led to a private dining room upstairs, while a swinging door right below allowed the waitresses easy access to the kitchen.

My springing step carried me into the small bar, my second-favorite watering hole in the city, which took up the smaller area on the other side of the low wall.

I surveyed the room. A single couple, a May-December arrangement, sat dining in the back corner booth. The rest of the tables remained vacant. The place usually kept pretty quiet until the dinner rush around seven.

"Hey, Ben," Tony, the joint's regular bartender, greeted me with a broad smile. "Haven't seen you around in a while."

He reached down, pulled out a bottle of Old Grand-Dad, and

poured a comfortable amount into a glass. Two important things about Tony: he was an ex-con who had managed, with difficulty and the love of a good woman, to straighten himself out; and he never failed to pour me a good stiff drink.

"Yeah, they've been running me pretty ragged the last few weeks."

With a drink in my hand I relaxed into the padded metal bar-stool. "So how about you?" I asked. "How's the family?"

Tony and his wife were the proud parents of two good kids, Tony Junior and Becky. In my opinion, these folks had done an admirable job of raising and keeping their little ones out of trouble in a town like Testacy City.

"Good, real good, thanks for asking," Tony rumbled in response, chest swelling a little. "TJ's growing like a weed, gettin' good grades in school . . . makes his old man proud, y'know?"

"I'll bet. Linda working tonight?"

Tony's wife Linda, the best damn waitress who'd ever taken my order, also worked at the Long Mile.

"Naw, she's off with the kids. Little Becky's in this Shakespeare deal at the school tonight—*Hamlet* or something—so she and TJ went to that."

"That's great, Tony! Congratulations."

"Yeah, thanks . . ." He looked around and rubbed the dark shadow of stubble that grew along his jaw. He leaned in close and whispered: "Christ, Ben, I need to get out of the house for a while."

My brow furrowed with genuine concern. "Why's that? Trouble?"

"Naw, Ben, that ain't it," Tony sputtered waving a big paw about. "I love my wife and kids, you know that, but sometimes they just drive me crazy. I need to get out, flex my muscles. You know, get a little taste."

His eyes held big question marks as he raised his eyebrows and cocked his head at me. "So I guess what I'm asking, you got any work needs doin'?"

Every so often I'd bring Tony out with me when I needed a spare set of muscles. Tony, the sort of guy you liked to have on your side, certainly fit that bill. He stood well over six feet tall and weighed in at 215 pounds, none of it fat.

"I wish I could help, Tony, but I don't have anything big going on.

Just a lot of small stuff." I hated to disappoint the guy, so I scrambled to think of something. "Tell you what. I'm meeting some folks here tonight. We'll be having some dinner and chatting it up. The woman I'm not worried about, but the guy . . . he's one of those big angry types that could easily get unhinged. You know what I mean?"

Tony cracked his knuckles. "Oh, I know what you mean. So you want me to—"

"Just watch my back. That's all I need. Up for that?"

"Hell, Ben, you don't even have to ask. 'Course I'm up for that; I'm always up for that. But I was hoping for something a little more . . . meaty."

"As soon as I got something, Tony, you'll be the first one I call. I promise."

He gave an earnest smile, then turned to help another customer. The place started to fill up about six thirty with people who liked to stop off for a belt after a long day of tedium. Soon enough Tony had his hands full slinging drinks for the regulars.

I sat there and watched the people who liked to eat early, typically some of the older citizens of Testacy City, as they crowded into the dining room and enjoyed some of the finest steaks and chops the city had to offer.

Before I knew it, the hands of the clock pointed to seven. Shortly after, Jasper and Sissy Hathaway strolled through the door.

Jasper's outfit hadn't changed much since his visit to the Always Reddy offices: same cowboy boots, same jeans, even the same worn leather jacket. The only difference was his shirt, a crisp denim affair, topped off with a steer's-head bolo tie. His face wore a heavy scowl.

Sissy, however, looked completely different than the first time I had seen her. She had replaced her all-black attire with a long red gown and a tiny white wool half-jacket. A pair of white gloves covered her tiny hands, and without the black veil I could see the beauty in her face. The tiniest smile played across her red-painted lips as she noticed me at the bar. She headed my way, her smile growing brighter as Jasper's scowl deepened.

I had no defense against Sissy's piercing green eyes, which shot right through me. As she got closer, I couldn't help but admire her pert, upturned nose and softly colored cheeks.

She looked stunning.

"Thank you so much for coming, Mr. Drake," she cooed, taking my hand in hers like she had that morning. It sent a chill down my spine.

"Please, call me Ben."

"Of course, Ben, but only if you call me Sissy." She laughed lightly, then suddenly became serious. "Now I don't mean any offense at this, but Jasper and I found it sort of . . . difficult . . . to talk to you in your office."

"Yeah, well, a lot of people do," I assured her. "It can be pretty intimidating. We really don't talk to many clients up there."

Truth be told, we almost never interviewed anyone about a case in the office. Almost everyone gets defensive when being questioned by cops or detectives—even more so in unfamiliar territory. I always thought it was better to talk with people on their own turf, someplace they felt comfortable. Besides, it's much easier for them to slip up that way.

"That's certainly good to know," she said. "After we left, we both sort of felt, well, guilty. Didn't we, Jasper?"

"Yeah, that's right." He moved closer to her side. "Can't we continue this talking at the table? I'm hungry. Her and I had a long day."

"Relax, Jasper," Sissy scolded. She moved closer to me and placed her hand on my lapel, smoothing the fabric of my suit coat. "Jasper's been meaning to try the coulotte steak here. He tells me there's only two per cow, you know."

"Yeah, that's right," he said.

At just the right time, the hostess came over and told Sissy our table was ready. As we walked across the room, Tony looked over at me. I gave him a little nod and followed Jasper to our table.

Normally I'd be upset that all the booths had people in them; I like to relax when I eat. But tonight wasn't about relaxation; it was about work. Without being too obvious, I managed to situate myself on the far side of the table the hostess led us to. I could see the entire room from that side, and I wanted to be able to signal Tony in case of trouble.

Jasper sat facing me. Sissy took the seat to my left.

An uncomfortable quiet passed momentarily over our table.

Then at the same time both Sissy and I said to each other: "So, how was your day?"

"Jinx," she giggled. "That means you have to buy me a drink—a real drink. Coke's for kids." She moved an auburn strand of hair that had fallen across her face back behind her ear. "My day was fine but long," she said. "After I left your office, I had to deal with a bunch of . . . formalities. Now how about you?"

I blew out a big breath of air, more for effect than exasperation. "Pretty rough, actually. I didn't get too far on the case—"

"What the hell are we paying you for, then?" Jasper fired off. Sissy glared at him.

"No, it's all right," I said. "I'm getting close, though. Real close."

Jasper just snorted as our waitress came over to take our drink orders. Sissy asked for a glass of red wine. I stuck with Old Grand-Dad. Jasper followed my lead.

Sissy unfolded her napkin from the place setting and then refolded it over her lap. "So, why don't you tell us a little about yourself, Ben?"

"Me? I'm just a detective, Sissy."

"Come now," she played. "You must have a better story than that—you know: where you come from, why you do what you do."

The waitress came back with our drinks and took our orders for dinner. Sissy selected the Cobb salad. I remained true to form and selected the chicken fried steak with garlic mashed potatoes and gravy—better known as Wednesday's special. Jasper, as expected, ordered the coulotte steak, one of the restaurant's specialties. I had to give him credit for his taste.

He also ordered another glass of bourbon, after having sucked down the first one in almost record time.

I picked up the conversation: "I don't know what kind of answers you're looking—"

"I'm not looking for any one kind of answer," she interrupted by patting my elbow resting on the table. "I'm just interested in what makes you tick."

"It's like this: I don't fight the good fight for some greater glory. I don't chase criminals to impress the woman of my dreams. I certainly don't do it for the tiny paycheck and long hours. I do what I do because I'm a detective. Plain and simple."

For the first time I heard Jasper let out a small laugh. "Plain and simple," he said.

Sissy raised her glass and clinked it against mine without making a toast. I watched the wine flow past her pouting lips.

Soon our waitress carried in our dinners. As I expected, Sissy ate her meal daintily. I couldn't say I had any idea what proper dinner etiquette entailed, but it looked like Sissy had it down pretty good. Jasper, though, only understood the etiquette of alcohol.

Sissy did most of the talking while we ate. Not surprisingly, she revealed precious little about her life. Not once did she mention her late husband or his death. I had to get closer to addressing the suspicion I'd been harboring since exploring her bathroom.

"Tell me, Sissy, do you have any friends—any male friends—that you've been able to turn to in your time of mourning?"

"What are ya trying to get at, Drake?" Jasper choked on the anger he spat out.

"Come on, I'm not 'trying to get at' anything."

"Jasper, please," she said through a tight smile. "We can't expect results with that kind of attitude. Now what exactly do you want to know, Mr. Drake?"

"Hold on, you two. I didn't mean to come off aggressive or accusatory. I'm just trying to see the big picture, to see if there are any other leads I could follow to find the killer and put him behind bars."

"That's what I want too, Ben." Sissy rubbed her forehead and looked away from me. "I want the truth to come out . . . I want to find out what really happened."

She turned back to me. "Go ahead, ask me anything. I'll tell you everything I know."

"Ah, keep quiet and stop acting like a baby." Jasper pointed his dirty fork at her as he spoke. "Can't you see this guy is playin' us just like he did at the office? I told ya he'd do that again. We should get rid of this crumb. He's coverin' up for the fact that he ain't got no leads." He put his fork down. Jasper had finished his steak; now he was going to chew on me. "Ain't that right, dick?"

"Not the way I see it. I got some leads all right."

"Weren't you going to visit with Norman Gneiss this afternoon?" Sissy asked.

Jasper shook his head and loudly complained, "Sissy!" He lapped up some more bourbon.

"Yeah, I went over there and talked with him *and* his assistant."

"So," Jasper sneered, then turned his bleary gaze my way, "what did they have to say?"

"Well, they both have an alibi for Monday night, but—"

"That don't mean nothin'! If this were Wyoming, I'd for sure be takin' care of those two."

"Jasper, what are you talking about?" Sissy said, trying to calm him down. "This isn't Wyoming, and Ben knows the rules of this city. If he thinks—"

"Shut up!" Jasper howled at her. The entire restaurant fell silent as everyone in the place looked over at us. Out of the corner of my eye, I saw Tony heading our way. I motioned for him to stay.

"Jasper, it might be best for you to keep that sort of thought to yourself," I cautioned.

His head whipped around. "Why? You all outta leads so you gonna turn me in?"

"I'm not saying that at all, Jasper." I spoke in calm, soothing tones, as if trying to tame a wild dog. "All I'm saying is that if Gneiss ends up dead—"

"This is crazy talk!" Sissy's eyes started getting heavy with tears.

"Thought I told you to shut up, slut!" Jasper shouted, baleful eyes burning into Sissy. He tilted his glass and poured his latest helping of booze down his throat. He mostly missed, and the alcohol trickled across his cheek, down his neck, and under the collar of his shirt. He slammed his glass on the table so hard the silverware danced. "Goddamnit!"

I rose to my feet. Before I could say anything, Jasper's next words had already come out of his mouth.

"I gotta take a piss." He shoved himself away from the table and stumbled off toward the restroom.

I sat back down and gave Sissy a hard look, one that was meant to make her say something. When she didn't, I prompted her a bit.

"Sissy . . ."

"I'm worried, Ben," she whispered. "He's becoming more and more violent, and all day he asked me for money."

"How much money?"

"A lot of money."

"How much?"

"A hundred thousand dollars." She shivered as she uttered the figure. "What's it mean?"

Sums of that size could mean any number of things, but in Testacy City they meant trouble. Putting Jasper together with that kind of trouble was like dropping a match in a barrel of gunpowder. It made the little hairs on the back of my neck bristle.

"I don't know exactly, Sissy." I chewed the inside of my lower lip as my mind raced with possibilities. "Do you think he'd hurt you?"

"No, I don't think so, but—"

"You two talking about me?" Jasper suddenly appeared back at the table. In the space of a minute or two he'd become completely disheveled. His hair stuck out at wild angles from his head, his bolo tie no longer hung from his neck, and his eyes glowed with a crazy shine.

He thumped down in his chair, pulling out a pack of filterless cigarettes and a matchbook the color of a neon grape. He lit up and blew a cloud of smoke right at me.

"I've always been a fast pisser," he proclaimed, grinning like a madman.

Something about that pack of matches made my mind tingle. I pulled out my own smokes and slipped one between my lips. I patted my pockets pretending that I couldn't find a light.

"So what now, detective man?" Jasper asked.

"How about you give me some flame?"

He tossed me the matches. I lit up.

"So what now?" he asked again.

"I was hoping you'd tell me."

"Well, we're plum tuckered out, what with all this running around and not being able to sleep 'cause of recent events. I think we're just gonna turn in. Right, Sissy?"

"Yes, Jasper, that's a good idea," Sissy mumbled. Then she got up from the table, collected her short jacket, and lurched for the door without even saying goodbye. Like an angry puppy, Jasper followed right behind her.

And that left me with the bill.

As I sat there finishing my cigar, Tony came over to me with a fresh Old Grand-Dad and asked the question that was on my mind.

"What the hell was that all about, Ben?"

"Damned if I know, Tony. But something just isn't right."

As I drove home through the streets of Testacy City, I couldn't shake the overwhelming feeling of dread that raced down the road with me.

Jasper's pack of purple matches came from the notorious Purple Knights Motel. It bothered me that this sleazy joint had entered my life twice in the same day.

Sissy's likely infidelities and Jasper's powerful, violent, foul-mouthed temperament disturbed me. Plenty of motives moved around in my mind, but none made much sense. If either one or both of my clients had wanted to get rid of Eli Hathaway, they could have done it a lot cleaner. Their secrets formed a maze that held the answer at its center. That didn't bother me; I've always been good at separating the relevant from the irrelevant while navigating tangled investigations. But more and more I felt that the path to truth would eventually lead nowhere.

I got back to my barren apartment and poured myself a drink. I slipped off my oxfords, loosened my tie, and plopped down into my recliner—the one luxury I afforded myself.

What a mess. I reached down to rub the knots out of my thighs. I didn't know what more I could do with the case tonight. So I cracked open the copy of the collected writings of Ludwig Wittgenstein that rested on my small reading table.

I flipped to the section containing the *Tractatus Logico-Philosophicus*—the most exciting and surprising piece of philosophy ever written. Wittgenstein's attempt to reduce the entire world to logical propositions was an inspiration to me. I'd never pretend to understand it, but my detective's mind ate this convoluted mess of words right up.

Any hope that reading would ease my feeling of impending doom quickly vanished. I squeezed my eyes shut and thought about a line Wittgenstein wrote, something like: *The things we can't do anything about, we should just pass over in silence.*

I opened my eyes and realized that I *could* do something. I put the book back down and grabbed my hat. I headed out to investigate Jasper's connection to the Purple Knights Motel.

I had just locked the door behind me when I heard my phone ringing. I thought about letting it go, but something nagged at me. I quickly unlocked the door and ran to grab the phone, finally getting it to my face so I could gasp a hello.

"Ben?" Sissy's voice, frantic yet concerned, buzzed across the line.

"Yeah?" I focused on my clock across the room; it was eleven p.m.

"Ben, I need you here," she pleaded with a fright-filled voice. "Things have gone bad. Please, I need your help."

"Jasper?"

"Yes, he's gone crazy! He's tearing the house apart, throwing things . . . Oh Ben, this is all my fault."

"What? What do you mean?"

"Eli's death. It's all my fault," she sobbed. "I was . . . I was . . . having an affair. I'm so sorry, really I am. I was so afraid Eli would find out. It was the worst thing I could have done to him, the poor man. And I couldn't bear to hurt him like that, so I called it off!" I could tell her tears flowed freely now. "And I think that's what got him killed! Trout Mathers's jealous rage!"

My knuckles whitened around the black phone receiver. This happened to me all the time: people hire a detective to figure out their problems but refuse to give up the whole story.

"I wish you would have told me this sooner, sister. But we can worry about all that later. Are you safe right now?"

"Yes. I'm in my room."

"Stay there. I'm on my way."

I drove over at a breakneck pace, running red lights and squealing around corners.

I had suspected the cat's-eye cuff link I'd found in Sissy's bathroom belonged to Mathers; I'd seen him wear that sort of affair before. And I figured the purple matchbook linked Jasper to Trout, but I still couldn't play out the angles.

I made it to the Hathaway place in record time. I slammed on the brakes and parked my car in the middle of the road.

The front door stood wide open. I whipped out my Smith & Wesson.

I quickly but cautiously entered the house behind my pistol. All seemed quiet. Kenneth, dressed in striped green pajamas and leather slippers, lay in a crumpled heap at the bottom of the steps. A quick check of his pulse told me he was still alive, so I gently slapped his face a couple of times to bring him around. He sat up abruptly, spluttering and waving his hands in front of his face like my smacks were a horde of mosquitoes.

"Please, sir, please!" he shouted, as his arms flailed about. I took a step back and waited impatiently while he adjusted his pajama top. A pair of large, doe-like eyes stared at me from his heavily bruised face. "Mr. Drake! Thank heaven it's you," he exclaimed, rubbing his cheeks where I'd slapped him.

"Is Sissy okay?"

"I . . . I don't know . . . I heard gunshots from upstairs."

I turned and bolted up the steps, taking three at a time and pulling myself up with the ornately carved handrail.

I rapped my knuckles against the door to Sissy's room and waited a moment. I felt my heart stammer when no reply came back my way.

I grabbed the handle and twisted—locked.

"Damn." I paced back and forth in the wide hallway for a few moments. "Damn, damn, damn." I ran at the door and threw my full weight against it.

All that did was jar my bones. Still, I tried again. The thick wooden door didn't budge.

I emptied my gun into the lock, hoping it was a little flimsier than the door. I stepped back and kicked with all I had. A soft ping echoed gently down the hall, soon swallowed by the eruption of the door giving way.

I burst into the mess of Sissy's room. The vanity mirror sat in fragments all over the floor. Mounds of clothes were scattered about the room, a large pile on the bed. I noticed a dainty foot with meticulously painted red toenails poking out from under the heap of clothes. I gingerly pushed them aside to find Sissy.

Her face was an unhealthy dark pink. Her beautiful green eyes— once shimmering and lively, now dull and haunting—stared upward, as if trying to penetrate the lace canopy over her bed and gaze into heaven. Her tongue lolled out between her perfectly white teeth, trailed across her burgundy lips, and flopped against her cheek. A single silk stocking, knotted about her throat, pinched the tender flesh of her neck.

I held the back of my hand in front of her open mouth, then felt for a pulse, only to discover what I already knew.

Her fingernails, chipped and broken, showed she had fought the best she could to avoid a violent death. It didn't do her any good.

I turned my back on the grisly scene and headed downstairs, reloading my gun on the way. As I left the room, I noticed three fresh bullet holes, widely spaced, scarring the wall to the left of the door.

The high-pitched whistle of a teapot drew me toward the kitchen. I followed it, bringing the questions I had for Kenneth with me.

I found the butler sitting at a small table in a dark corner of the kitchen, staring into a steaming cup. When I walked into the room, he looked at me. The bruises on his face had gotten uglier since I'd woken him up; his left eye had almost completely swollen shut.

"I had to get some tea," he explained. "Would you like a cup? Perhaps some bourbon, sir?"

The poor guy was in shock; hopefully the tea would nurse him back to reality. Over the years I'd found that I could swallow a dead body a whole lot easier if I had some booze to swallow along with it. The thought of a shot or two tempted me, but not right now. I had a job to do.

"Just fill me in on what went down here."

He blew on his tea. "Well, as I recall, my duties for the evening were finished. I had just prepared myself a nice glass of warm milk in the kitchen and was enjoying a bit of Joyce before retiring for the night. I find great pleasure in Joyce's delicate turns of phrase and stream of consciousness—"

"Get on with it," I growled.

He grimaced but continued: "the sound of gunfire disturbed my reading, so I—"

"How many shots?"

"Ummm . . . Three? Maybe four? I'm afraid I didn't really keep count, sir."

"Okay, fine. Keep it coming." I rolled my hand through the air, gesturing for him to speed up the retelling.

He downed a big gulp of hot tea. This seemed to give him a little strength, which suited me just fine. I needed this butler to grow some backbone and fast.

"Well, sir, after the shots, I thought it best to call the authorities, so I hurried to the phone in the foyer. I picked up the receiver only to hear Jasper's voice on the line."

"Who was he talking to?"

"I don't know. However, I did hear him say that he'd be going to the train station at midnight. Then Jasper appeared on the stairs, saw me hanging up the phone, and . . . well . . ." His thin voice trailed off, and he slurped up some more tea. Worry and fear crept into his eyes as his shock wore off.

I took a frantic glance at my watch: eleven thirty. I had to move if I wanted to crash Jasper's party at the train station, which sat on the south edge of town right below Highway 15.

I pointed at Kenneth and said, "You call the police and ask for Duke Wellington. Tell them about Sissy and Jasper. Then get a steak from the fridge, put it on your face, and lie down. I'm off to stop Jasper."

As I bolted out of the kitchen, Kenneth called out to me: "Jasper managed to get ahold of Sissy's gun."

I stopped and over my shoulder said, "Sissy's gun?"

"Yes, Mr. Hathaway purchased it for her protection. It's what Jasper used . . . to hit me." He clenched his fists. "He was never worthy of the Hathaway name."

I'd been hit plenty in my career. I can't say I ever liked it, but I always came out okay. Even though the fragile butler looked like a tangled mess, I knew he'd be all right. I told him so.

I left Kenneth to his tea and squealed out of Victory Gardens. I sped down Pioneer Road, a twisted stretch of asphalt that cut through the length of the city, as fast as I could take the turns.

Kenneth's suggestion of alcohol still buzzed about my brain, so I grabbed the flask of bourbon I kept in my glove compartment and took a healthy swig.

I made it to Testacy City's train station, Jackson Central, in record time. At this hour the station felt like a tomb. A few bums slept on the cushioned seats that filled the center of the space. The only sign of life came from a shifty-looking fellow wearing a gray pinstripe suit who mumbled into the pay phone over by the wall of luggage lockers. Sure, he smelled like trouble, but I had bigger troubles to worry about.

I sprinted up to the tiny barred window where the small ticket master dozed in his chair.

"Where is the midnight train coming in?" I shouted.

The clerk jumped; his wire-rimmed glasses slipped off his face and clattered to the floor.

"Oh my, you startled me!" he exclaimed.

"The midnight train—what's the platform number?" I repeated more forcefully.

"It's coming in at number two. If you want to catch it, you'd better hurry! You need a ticket?"

I ignored the question and ran off through the near-deserted building, down the underground tunnel that lead to the station's platforms.

Framed posters of destinations like Las Vegas, Los Angeles, San Francisco, and Seattle lined the tunnel walls. I remembered when my wife and I once took a weekend holiday to Los Angeles—probably the best weekend of my life. Back then I didn't have a care in the world. One week later she was dead. I threw the unpleasant thought from my mind and pressed on.

My rapid footfalls sent clacking echoes up and down the long stone passageway. The tunnel ended with a sharp left, then started a steep rise up to ground level and the canopy that stood over track number two.

As I hustled up the tunnel to the tracks, angry voices raced down the ramp to meet me. I slowed my pace and hunkered down behind the low stone wall surrounding the tunnel's exit, creeping forward until I could make out two figures locked in a standoff. Each held a gun aimed at the other's midsection.

I could see Jasper's large frame clearly in the dim light that shone from beneath the ceiling of the canopy. His dance partner stood next to the tracks, face obscured by shadows.

A train's forlorn wail echoed in the distance.

I kept my head down and my eyes up, watching and listening as the drama unfolded.

"We had a deal," the mystery man snarled.

Jasper responded, half angry, half whining: "I know that, but things didn't work out the way I planned."

"I'm afraid that's not good enough. You see, no one backs out of a deal with Rex Mayer."

Rex Mayer? The more Jasper's behavior convinced me of his guilt, the more Rex Mayer slipped into the background, even though my gut had been telling me from the beginning Rex was mixed up in this mess. It pays to listen to your instincts.

"I'm finished with your deals!" Jasper barked.

"Then I'm afraid I'll be taking everything I know to the police."

"And tell them what?" I could hear Jasper's confidence start to crumble.

Another train whistle rippled through the night. As it trailed off, a cruel laugh spilled out of Rex. "I'll be telling them you killed Trout Mathers."

Now the pieces of this caper started to click into place: Jasper's Purple Knights matchbook, Trout's grisly death, and Sissy's confessed affair all tied together. But how the hell did a bumbling simpleton like Jasper manage to get the drop on one of Testacy City's most ruthless gangsters, let alone bump him off? And how did it all fit into Eli Hathaway's murder?

"You wouldn't! It's not fair!"

More laughter came from Mayer. "You're a fine one to talk about playing fair. I'd like to ask Trout just how fair you were."

"He had it coming!"

"Just because he was making time with your brother's wife? I know for a fact he wasn't the only one."

"Watch your mouth!" Jasper howled, shoving his tiny gun at Rex's face.

I felt a low tremor rattle the ground, a tremor that meant the train was close to home. I had to defuse this situation and get Jasper into custody before he could make his railbound getaway. I owed that much to Sissy. But with this revealing argument raging, I didn't want to show my hand just yet.

"Hold on there, boyo," Rex cooed, keeping calm despite the gun pointed at him. "I'm just letting you know the truth."

"Then . . . then . . . I'll give the cops the truth! I'll tell them Mathers killed my brother! And you're the one who hired him!"

Ah, the payoff. I knew Mathers—not well enough to buy him a drink, but well enough to know jealousy didn't figure as a motive for him offing Eli. But cash, that's a motive everyone understands.

I guessed both Sissy and Jasper knew Mathers had killed Eli. Somehow the dim-witted Jasper had tumbled to the Rex Mayer connection and fell victim to some devious, self-centered plan. That left poor Sissy thinking the whole mess had been her fault. So she hired the agency for proof to put her conscience to rest.

"Ha!" Rex scoffed. "Who would believe you, an uneducated country bumpkin, over me, Rex Mayer?"

"You bastard!" The gun in Jasper's hand, still pointed at Rex's head, started to shake.

A low thrum rolled off the railroad tracks and filled the air with an electric aura.

I'd heard enough to put both these jokers away, and the train was getting too close for comfort. I decided to make my move.

I drew my gun, stood up, and stepped onto the platform.

"You'd be surprised what people will believe, Rex," I sneered.

"Drake!" Rex shouted, pointing his gun my way. Jasper's automatic stayed fixed on Rex. "What are you doing here?"

"I might ask you boys the same thing, but I've heard all I need to hear. Drop the pistols, and let's go. This game's over, and the city's got a nice set of accommodations waiting for you."

"Sorry, dick," Jasper spat, "but I'm going home."

"Home?" Rex stammered, switching his aim back to Jasper, this time putting the country man's head clean in the sights. "You owe me!"

The ground started to shake as the noise of the approaching engine grew louder and the voices rose to be heard above the racket.

"Too bad! I've had enough of you—both of you—and this town!"

"I want my money!" Rex whined.

"I'm telling you, I'm going out with that train, and nothin's stopping me."

"I can't let you leave, Jasper," I warned.

"But I have to get out of here!" Jasper now waved his gun madly between Rex and me as he ranted. "This town is poison! It's turned me into a two-time killer! I can't take it here anymore!"

Jasper had built up a good head of steam, and now there was little time left to put the brakes on this situation.

"Two-time killer?" Rex asked.

"Yeah," I answered, stepping closer to Jasper. "He just killed Sissy about half an hour ago."

"You killed Sissy?" Rex giggled.

"Yes, goddamnit, yes! Trying to get your filthy blackmail money," Jasper's howl slipped to a whimper. "If only she would have understood. Oh God, please forgive me."

The small automatic tumbled from Jasper's grasp and clattered to the stone platform. He sunk to his knees and dropped his head into his hands.

"Sissy . . . I'm so sorry. Please forgive me." Desperation clogged his voice. "I love you, Sissy."

Rex's cruel laughter returned. "Love? That's why you killed Mathers?" His giggles became more mirthful and more malevolent as he pieced things together. "Out of love for that tramp? Oh my, that's rich!"

The lonely whistle of the speeding train cut through the night, and the light from the engine poked out from behind its final turn.

"You son of a bitch!" Jasper snarled, desperation turning to wrath, and lunged animallike at Rex.

The sharp report of Rex's gun broke through the night. Jasper halted in mid-attack and howled with pain as his body fell, thudding to the platform. He lay there, gulping air, holding his shoulder. Blood oozed from between his fingers, trickling out onto the porous concrete.

At the sight of Jasper's blood, Rex began screaming: "No one double-crosses Rex Mayer! No one!"

He turned his gun toward me.

"That includes, you, Drake."

A bright flash chased away the darkness as the train approached. Rex had given me a big hand by shooting Jasper. All I had to do now was get Rex under control, which I didn't think would be too hard. Sure he held a gun on me, but I'd never had a problem taking care of a pansy.

I took a step forward, aiming my Smith & Wesson at him. "All right, Mayer, drop your gun. This little party is over."

Another blast from the whistle, this time almost deafening, ripped down the rails.

Just then Rex's eyes grew large, filled with fear. I spun around in time to see Jasper pulling himself to his feet, hand still clamped over his bloody shoulder. I could see the hatred burning off him as he began a slow lumber toward Rex.

"Jasper," I cautioned, "just hold it. We'll take care of things . . ."

My words had no effect. Jasper glowed with conviction.

The train thundered down the tracks, almost on top of us. Time for drastic action.

I twisted back around and took aim at the big man, putting his hip dead in my sights. I squeezed the trigger just as he launched his body at Rex.

My single shot went wide, flying off into the darkness.

Rex stood there, paralyzed with fear. His bravado gone, a loud scream—the sort of scream you expect to hear from a woman—leaked out of his throat.

Jasper crunched into him.

A mass of tangled limbs hit the cement and rolled back and forth, teetering on the edge of the platform.

The thunder of the train consumed all other sounds.

I hastily holstered my gun and ran forward, reaching the brawlers just as their momentum carried them over the edge.

Right into the path of the oncoming train.

The train's whistle spat out a loud warning wail. I reached over and got a fistful of Jasper's coat. As I tugged, trying to pull his weight out of the shallow trench where the rails ran, he backhanded me across the face.

I didn't expect the blow and lost my balance, dropping headfirst into the trench. My feet still held onto the platform, but I could feel my heels start to kick up, ready to begin their tumble over my head—not quite how I thought I'd die.

I managed to get a hand in front of me to break my fall, slapping it down on one of the rails. My whole body vibrated with the power of the oncoming train. I foolishly looked down the track.

The train rolled close. Too close.

I heaved, pushing myself backward out of the trench. I fell back on my haunches, and as I struggled to regain my balance, I saw Jasper slamming Rex's head, over and over again, against a metal rail.

I scrambled to my feet. Jasper's hands, covered in blood, continued to pound Rex's skull into a bloody, pulpy mess.

I bolted over to Jasper.

Not much time.

Only one more chance.

Again, I grabbed Jasper's jacket.

The train whistled; roaring thickly in my ears—or maybe it was the blood hammering through my veins.

Jasper raised both bloody fists over his head and bayed like a wolf at the oncoming train.

I yanked his jacket. He didn't budge.

The train's brakes locked; metal on metal squealed. My ears sent spasms of pain down my spine.

I yanked again, as hard as I could. The muscles of my arms and back complained; something ripped, then the air of a speeding train kissed my face just before my body spilled uncontrollably across the platform.

I watched the braking train screech by, imagining the crunching of bone and the pulping of flesh that couldn't be heard over the cacophony.

The night suddenly seemed bright as high noon. I felt every bump of the ground through the rough fabric of my suit. Thunder, blindingly loud, pounded my eardrums. The taste of salt and iron trickled across my tongue. Diesel and steel filled my nostrils and choked my breath.

I lay there, feeling every muscle in my body quiver until, at long last, the train finally stopped. The screech of grinding metal still echoed in my head.

I pulled myself up to a sitting position as an engineer rushed over to me, grabbing his head.

"He didn't move!" he whined, throwing a pointed finger back at the train. "Oh my God! Are *you* okay? Please tell me you're okay!"

I spat blood out of my mouth and looked down at the scrap of

Jasper's jacket I still clutched in my fist. I stared at it, turned it over in my hand, felt its rough texture between my fingers. I let it drop to the ground.

"Please! Please, tell me you're all right!" the engineer wailed. "We couldn't stop . . . He just didn't move . . . I think we hit him . . ." He bent down to get a better look at me. "You gotta be all right! Please! Oh God!"

I brushed the grit from my suit and felt my head, hoping my hat would be there, knowing it wouldn't.

"Yeah, I'm all right," I muttered.

"I tried to stop . . . Jesus, you gotta know that! Oh, I can't believe I killed the guy . . ."

"He was already dead," I grunted.

"What? Really? You know that?"

"Yeah."

"What about the guy over here?" The engineer pointed across the platform at the still body of Jasper Hathaway. "Is he . . . ?"

I pushed my aching body over to where Jasper lay. His legs below the knees twisted in impossible directions, so much mangled hamburger. I bent down close to him. Ragged breath slipped in and out between his lips.

"Well?"

"Looks like he'll live."

The engineer pulled off his cap and mopped his brow, then collapsed against one of the canopy's pillars. He cried without making a sound.

I simply laid back against the hard, cold concrete and closed my eyes. In that moment I tried to concentrate on the one thing that made sense.

Silence.

Case Five
Raspberry Jack

I

I gained consciousness in total darkness. Stars danced in front of my eyes to the tune of the throbbing in my head. A bright strobe of pain at the base of my skull assaulted my body with waves of acidic agony. My back ached. I had no idea how long I'd been slumped in this stiff wooden chair. Slowly, my eyes adjusted to the gloom. I could barely make out the four corners and single door of a small cell.

I struggled for breath, fighting the moist heat of the claustrophobic space. Sweltering, stagnant air kissed my skin, sending sweat to dampen my clothes and plaster my hair against my skull.

The sweat slid down my face, flowing through my eyebrows and into my eyes, stinging. I blinked furiously, wanting to wipe my brow, but rough ropes bound my hands behind the chair and cut deep into my wrists.

I'd been tied up by real pros; not only had they done a job with my hands, but they'd laced my ankles to the chair's legs, then knotted the whole mess together.

What the hell was going on?

I forced panic from my mind, attempting to make some kind of sense of the situation.

What case had I been working on?

Who had I been following?

What blunder did I make to fall into this trap?

Thoughts like that wasted my energy; I pushed them aside. I needed to figure out how to get out of this mess. Then I'd worry about how I got into it.

Experimenting, I found I could sort of hop along the cement floor, moving myself and the chair with a little effort and a lot of pain.

I scraped my way toward the door, inch by inch, chair leg by chair leg.

Nearly there, victory turned to defeat: a crack in the floor caught the chair leg and sent me toppling.

I cursed. I couldn't move. The cold floor sucked the heat out of my body. I cursed again. I wiggled my hands helplessly, the only movement I could make. Embarrassing.

I struggled in vain to right my perch when I heard the click of the door's lock echo hollowly through the prison. A bone-chilling creak filled the space.

A sliver of light slipped into the room, revealing a tall, thin figure in the doorway, its features shrouded in shadow.

I'd been in tough spots before, but I'd always managed to think or bust my way out. This time, I couldn't imagine anything that would save me.

Icy fingers of fear clawed into my guts.

"Who are you?" I asked.

The dark figure cut a deep silence in the doorway. Was it grinning? Was it scowling? I couldn't tell; it remained blank, empty, faceless.

"What do you want from me?"

Again, the figure uttered no words. Instead, the black shadow slowly raised an arm, pointing a long, thick finger right at my face.

"Come on!" I bellowed with all my anger, hoping it would mask the fear in my voice. "Say something!" Then a cold sweat broke across my forehead.

That wasn't a finger pointing at me. It was the barrel of a gun.

My eyes followed the length of the barrel, finding a trigger and a bony finger wrapped around it.

I struggled, vainly. The sharp rope cut deeper into my wrists, and sticky blood flowed down my fingers.

Helpless, unable to move, I watched the finger squeeze the trigger.

The bright flash blinded me, and the gun exploded into my face with a shower of fire.

Startled awake, I bolted up in bed. Torrents of sweat covered my body, and my chest heaved as I gasped for breath. My heart pounded against my breastbone like it wanted to break free of its cage. I'd kicked the sheet off my bed, no doubt trying to stay cool in the swelter of the night and escape the horrors in my mind.

The summer heat that wrapped Testacy City usually dissipated when the sun sank below the horizon, but for the last few weeks the city had been drowned in a dismal heat wave that kept temperatures hovering around one hundred degrees day and night. Miserable weather for both detecting and sleeping.

Seldom did dreams invade my sleep—at least not that I remembered—but lately strange hallucinations had been waking me more and more frequently. My friend Rebecca Hortzbach, Testacy City's tenacious medical examiner, told me she knew a few people who could interpret my dreams for me. Rebecca collected conspiracies and peculiar instances of occult happenstance, so she knew plenty of people who dabbled in the realms of pseudo-science and magic. I told her I preferred to resist interpretation; I could get through the day easier without it.

The glow-in-the-dark hands of the Big Ben clock ticking away on my nightstand told me that six a.m. had just arrived. Way too early for me to be up, but after that nightmare, I knew I wouldn't be returning to slumber until evening.

I stumbled to the kitchen only to find that my MJB can barely yielded half a teaspoon of coffee. So instead of my typical morning caffeine jolt, I lit one of the small cigars I like to smoke. I sat at the card table where I ate my meals when I actually took the time to eat at home and enjoyed the flavor and surge of tobacco while watching the morning sun begin to stream into my spartan living room.

Normally I preferred to shower in the afternoon, a habit left over from my days as a fireman. I found it made for a nice break in the day's monotony. However, with these temperatures not letting up at night, my philosophy gave way to the comfort of a rush of cool morning water.

After I had cleaned up and dressed—choosing a gray suit, white shirt, and light blue tie, topped off with a nice gray Borsalino hat—the time had come for my day to begin. Since hunger gnawed at my belly, I got in my Galaxie 500 and steered toward Lepke's Diner, for some of Costas Papademos's pastries—the best in Testacy City.

Hopefully a full breakfast would get me ready to face the tedium of another day spying on an allegedly unfaithful husband—the most miserable task any detective could ever have. I sighed as I pulled into the parking lot.

Entering Lepke's, I saw a typical gang of transients sitting at the counter. For some reason Costas, as belligerent as he could be, put up with all sorts of bums sitting in his joint. I guess everyone's got a soft side.

It made me wish my boss would lighten up on me. Ever since my last big case ended rather unpleasantly, Hal had been dropping all the cheating-spouse cases on my desk. I hated them, but Hal said he wanted to keep me off the hard stuff for a while.

One of the weirdoes at the counter belched. He wore a thick sweatshirt with the hood pulled up over his head, drawstrings yanked tight enough to barely allow him to shovel a plate of eggs into his mouth. He cocked his head my way, and I averted my eyes; I didn't want a confrontation this early. He went back to his shoveling.

I rubbed my wrinkled forehead. I'd much rather have gotten right back into some serious cases than being awash in adultery. I didn't become a detective to sit in a car for days at a time and go peeping around in cheap hotels on the lookout for hanky-panky. These cases were driving me nuts. No wonder I was having all sorts of crazy dreams.

A nice booth in the back corner beckoned me, so I made a slow march through the place. I passed another of Lepke's regular bums sitting by himself at a small booth by the door. He stared wide-eyed into a paperback copy of Napoleon Hill's *Think and Grow Rich*. For the first time that morning, I smiled. I'd seen this beggar before; I recognized his green army-surplus outfit and the shell-shocked stare that came from near-black eyes. I think I'd even given him some change a few times.

In the booth next to him sat Duke Wellington engrossed in the early edition of the *Testacy City Herald-Tribune*. This hothead loudmouth from Atlanta had made it his mission to wipe the streets of Testacy City clean of crime. Good luck, I thought.

This morning he dressed true to form, decked out in a bright forest-green suit and yellow shirt with a purple-and-blue patterned tie. A matching green Panama-style hat hung on the hook next to the booth.

Duke Wellington didn't take kindly to private detectives; he saw them as obstacles in his bid to clean up the city. Naturally, because he pit himself needlessly against me, I enjoyed doing my best to aggravate him. His fuse burned short and hot—and, man, was it ever easy to light.

As I walked by his table, his big head snapped around to look my way. When he recognized me, he grumbled, burying his head deeper into the morning news.

I thought about throwing him a jibe about his sense of fashion but decided to pass; my mood was all off.

My tired body fell into the booth, and I couldn't wait to have a cup of hot coffee. Finally, a waitress named Donna Dust plodded over to me.

"Morning, Donna," I said.

"Yeah, mornin'," she grunted in return. "What'll you have?"

"Three eggs, scrambled, with a slab of steak, well-done, and a bear claw to finish it off."

"Uh-huh. Anything else?"

"Yeah." I pointed at the pauper with the paperback. "Get that guy a bear claw too. It's on me."

"You wanna buy Spuds a bear claw?"

Something about hearing his name made me more content in my decision. I nodded a silent confirmation.

Donna pulled a set of silverware, wrapped neatly in a flimsy napkin, out of her apron and tossed it on the table. Everyone had their bad days, but Donna had never been this grumpy before.

"Say, you all right?" I asked.

"Yeah, I guess. It's just this weather. Brings out the nut cases, and they all come here. And they all take it out on me," she muttered, before wandering back behind the counter to retrieve a fresh pot of coffee.

Another small smile danced across my face when Donna took the pastry over to Spuds and filled his coffee cup. He looked up at her with questioning eyes, and she pointed at me. He raised his cup in a toast; I returned his salute, and we sipped together. I savored the hot sting as it slid down my throat and nestled in my belly.

Sometimes the smallest things make you feel good.

I watched Donna as she ambled over to Duke Wellington, refilling his cup as well, and reached down for his plate.

"You still workin' on this?"

"No, it's all yours. Go ahead and take it away." The police detective didn't bother looking up; he just waved her off.

"But . . . you didn't finish your danish," Donna said.

Spuds swung around and, with his mouth stuffed full of the last bits of his bear claw, spat out: "If he don't want that danish, Miss Dust, I'll be glad to take it."

"You already got your free meal today," Donna scolded.

Duke Wellington pulled his bearlike head out of his paper and trained his glowering eyes on Spuds's slight frame. "You don't really want that danish," he rumbled.

"Sure I do!"

"No, you don't," Duke Wellington countered. "It's filled with berries that're way too tart. You don't want nothin' to do with that danish."

"I don't?"

Donna scurried out of the way of Duke Wellington's tirade and disappeared behind the double swinging doors that led to the kitchen. Smart girl.

"Let me just ask you why in good God's holy heaven you'd want another one of these here danishes."

"Well . . . 'cause . . . well," my friend stammered, wiping his balding head with a thin napkin, "these pastries are the best!"

"The best? The best? You gotta be kiddin' me! Who told you these pastries are the best?"

"No one told me, I thought everyone knew it." Spuds reeled in confusion.

"Everyone, huh? And just who's this 'everyone' think he is, goin' round and spinnin' this garbage?"

Just then Costas Papademos burst out from the kitchen, wiping his hands angrily on his apron. He stormed across the floor toward the argument. I could almost see the smoke rising out of his hairy ears. He got up close, right into Duke Wellington's face, and shouted: "Garbage? I baked that pastry fresh this morning, like all my pastries!"

I may not have known this new cop that well, but I knew he wouldn't let himself be outshouted by a cook. He rose to his feet and, towering over the tiny Papademos, bellowed down at him: "Fresh is not that pastry's problem! What we got here is a seriously under-sweet baked good. What I'm saying is, this pastry's too damn tart!"

"If you want sweet—go to the candy store!" Costas screamed.

The two opponents stood there, eyes locked.

"Yeah," the forlorn Spuds mumbled, licking his fingers quizzically, "maybe they aren't that good after all."

Costas erupted into Olympian rage. "What? You come here every morning begging and annoying my customers—and now you listen to this fool and insult my pastries!"

"No, it's not like that at all, Mr. Papademos." Spuds smiled confidently. "I'd love another danish."

Costas pointed a finger at the diner's door. "Get out before I tear you limb from limb! You and your begging! I could kill you!"

Spuds slunk out of the restaurant, casting a helpless gaze my way before he disappeared out the door.

"You'd better tone it down, chef," the policeman warned. "I don't like hearing threats thrown around like that, even if it saved that old man from eating another of your pastries."

"That's it! I have had it! Out of my diner, you! Right now!"

"But I haven't paid my bill . . ."

"Fine! Your money is no good here! Get out! Out! Out!"

Duke Wellington hurriedly retreated from the crazy chef, beating a path toward the door. He left so fast I didn't have time to say goodbye.

Costas stood in the doorway and shook a knobby fist at the detective. "I never want to see you in here again! If you ever come back to my diner, you'd better have a damn good reason!"

An uncomfortable silence filled the small diner for a few moments after the door slammed shut. Costas slumped down into a booth and dropped his head in his hands. Then the fuming Greek looked around, seeking another target. He stared right at me.

"What do you want?" he snarled.

"Hey," I slurred around a mouthful of coffee, "I just want my steak and eggs, that's all."

He gave a low grunt. "Okay. They'll be right out."

I'd been working this one case for almost a week; my fourth or fifth infidelity investigation in a row. I'd been staking out the business-day activities of a gent by the name of Richard Keevil. For the better part of a week, my prey hustled from office building to office building, conference room to conference room. He showed all the signs I'd come to expect from this type, but he did nothing I could use to prove his unfaithfulness.

Today, though, he got sloppy and reverted to cliché. He took an extra-long lunch at the Purple Knights Motel with a long-legged blonde. You don't have to be a detective to realize she wasn't there to take dictation.

I collected the evidence I needed. There's never any satisfaction in a job like this. Now came the worst part for me—presenting the facts to the jerk's wife, letting her know her suspicions weren't unfounded. I called and told her to meet me at the Always Reddy office.

Mrs. Keevil took her time; denial, I suppose. She arrived hours later, sometime near dusk. Well, some women cry, some throw things, others act like it doesn't even bother them. This one fell to pieces the moment she saw me, and I had to resist the urge to play hero and put the pieces back together.

That's not how this game is played. It hurt me to admit, but I'd finished my part of the job. The rest was up to her.

I couldn't wait to get home, sink into my favorite chair, and soothe my depression with a glass of bourbon. Maybe Hal would give me some real meat tomorrow.

The short drive back to my place seemed to take forever. I pulled into a parking spot and sighed. I was glad to be out of the car. Comfortable as it was, I'd spent entirely too much time inside it lately.

As I climbed the few outside steps to my apartment, a streak of black hurled out from the darkness and collided with my leg. I looked down to see one of the neighborhood stray cats at my feet. He meowed at me with a sense of urgency.

"Hey, buddy, you have something to tell me?" I asked, reaching down to pat his sleek fur.

I hadn't expected the little guy to be wet. I pulled my hand away; no telling what sort of trash this kitty had gotten into. I looked at my hand in the dim light. Squinting, I could see that my palm was covered in red.

I glanced down the side of the building from where the cat had sprung. A dumpster for the apartment complex rested along the wall. Beyond it, the narrow alley stretched into blackness.

After wiping my hand off on my handkerchief, I dashed back to my car, popped the trunk, and got out my pocket flashlight. When I crept around the dumpster and down the side of the building, I found a man lying on a dirty mattress, covered with a few sheets of newsprint.

I shined my light on the prone figure and called out: "Hey there! You okay?"

He didn't respond.

I took a few steps closer and tapped the bottom of one of his heavily worn shoes with my foot.

He didn't move.

Fearing the worst, I rolled him over slightly to feel his pulse, and when I did I saw that his neck had been sliced wide open. Blood, still fresh and red, covered the front of his green army-surplus outfit and soaked into the mattress.

Vacant eyes—eyes that belonged to Spuds, my pal from the diner—stared lifelessly back at me.

No need for me to check for a pulse—Spuds was dead.

Then I noticed the purplish mark etched on his forehead: a capital letter R. Strange . . . I wondered what it meant.

I never liked finding dead bodies, especially when they turned up in my own backyard. Dead bodies meant police, and police meant Ben Drake in the hot seat. And lately Duke Wellington had been the one to do the roasting.

Nevertheless, I stumbled to my apartment and called the cops. They said they'd send someone right over.

I poured myself a shot of bourbon, downed it, and pulled out a small cigar. Even though I've seen a lot of dead bodies, they always make me a little queasy. Smoking always makes me feel a bit better.

I went back outside to sit on the front steps. There I stayed: waiting, smoking, sweating.

A good while later, a patrol car pulled up, lights blazing bright, and two cops got out. The driver walked with a swagger that told me he had years on the force. The other guy, a kid really, looked around like he didn't know what to do.

I stamped my almost spent cigar beneath my heel and went to greet them.

"You the guy who found the body?" the veteran asked me.

"Yeah. Ben Drake. I'm a private detective."

The veteran rolled his eyes. "Show us where he is."

I nodded and led them to the body of poor Spuds. The older cop had a little trouble squeezing by the dumpster, but when he shoved his way past, he pointed at the corpse.

"Your work?" he asked.

"No. I found him just like this."

"You touch anything?"

"I sort of rolled him over to see if he was sleeping or what," I answered. "That's when I saw he was dead."

"Christ. Billy, get this place sealed up. We don't want anyone else mucking things up before homicide gets here."

"Sure thing, Chuck." The young cop scurried off.

"Say, why don't you get out of our way," Officer Chuck told me. "Stick around though; the detectives will want to talk to you."

"Sure thing, Chuck."

I extricated myself from the cramped alley and found that a crowd had started to gather, no doubt drawn into the open by the twirling red-and-blue lights of the patrol car.

A lot of people gabbed back and forth, speculating on what sort of crime had taken place in their neighborhood. Most people guessed murder, but I wouldn't be doing anyone any favors by confirming their suspicions.

Just as soon as the boys in blue threw up a makeshift barricade, a brown Dodge pulled up behind the patrol cruiser.

Mark Weisnecki, a big, tall, shapeless detective, climbed out from the passenger seat and flicked his cigarette butt onto the ground. His new partner, Duke Wellington, came out from behind the steering wheel. The hot-tempered cop jammed his green Panama hat on his head, then began yelling, "What the hell is going on here? Why in God's name are these lights flashin' like this? All you're doin' now is drawing a crowd, an' the last thing we need here is a crowd! Would someone tell me what's going on?"

The older cop stepped forward and shouted at his partner: "God-damnit, Billy! Shut those lights off!"

The rookie did as he was told, and Chuck laid out the scene to Duke Wellington. He finished the conversation by jabbing a chubby thumb my way.

I could feel the anger pressurize inside Duke Wellington from twenty feet away. He and Weisnecki walked past me on their way to check out the body. Wellington trained his finger on me as they strolled by.

I lit another cigar and waited. Soon enough, they were back. Wellington got right into my face.

"I got a mystery for ya, Drake. How come every time I come callin' on a dead body in this town, I gotta deal with the likes of you?"

"I guess you're just lucky," I suggested.

"No jokes, Ben," Weisnecki cautioned. "Why don't you tell us how you came to find this one."

"Sure. I got home and this cat—"

"A cat? A cat? That the best you can come up with?" Duke Wellington waved his arms up and down and spun in a circle of disbelief.

"Come on, detective, if you'd let me finish . . ."

"All right, Drake. We'll let you finish. And it better make some good sense or we're taking you in, and you can tell it to us at the station. You can finish there till you get it right."

Weisnecki gave me a look that was both calm and threatening. I ignored their stage antics and laid out the tale of how I had found the body. I don't know what Wellington and Weisnecki wanted me to give them, but the story I spat out must have been good enough. Still, they weren't happy. Now they had to do something they weren't all that good at: detective work.

II

The heat made it almost impossible to sleep, and again I woke too early. Despite the weather, I felt a chill of fear. I wanted to retreat to the safety of my blankets, but pulling them over my body would have been unbearable.

I sat back in bed and grabbed a quick smoke. I couldn't get poor Spuds off my mind. Who would kill a guy like that, a harmless guy with no money? It really rankled me that with Duke Wellington and Weisnecki on the case, his murder would likely go unsolved.

I didn't feel a lot of motivation to go to the office and get handed another rookie job, so I took my time getting ready. Even though my stomach told me I needed to get a little breakfast, I didn't want to visit Lepke's this morning. I grabbed a couple cups of coffee to go from some other joint and headed to the one place where I wouldn't be bothered by food: the county morgue.

When I got there the place was busier than I'd ever seen it. Then I realized I had never been there so early before.

When I finally saw Rebecca, she scurried over to me with a scowl on her face, a cigarette between her lips, and a bloody apron wrapped around her waist.

"I brought you a cup of coffee," I said. I could tell my attempt to be social wasn't going to fly, though.

"Not a good time right now, Ben," she sighed. She shot a glance to her watch. "What the hell? What are you doing up so early anyway?"

"It's the heat . . . Well, it's a lot of things. Look, I don't want to go into it if you're busy, I just need some info on a bum that came in butchered last night."

"Which bum?"

"Older guy, throat slashed . . ."

Her scowl started melting. I threw out one more plea.

"I just need a starting point; you know, the standard Rebecca rundown. I could call you later . . ."

Her smile turned pointy like the cat's-eye glasses she wore. "All right. Five minutes, and then I've got to get back to it. Let's go outside." She called out to her assistant: "I'm going to take a smoke break!"

He gazed up at her with a puzzled look.

Once outside, she took a sip from the Styrofoam cup I'd brought her. "As much as I like you, Ben, I would've made you call back if I hadn't already sewn up this corpse of yours."

She pinned me with her conspiratorial eyes and gave me the quick stats on Spuds: multiple stab wounds in the neck region—laceration of both the jugular vein and carotid artery, perforation of the larynx and trachea. No prints found either on the body or at the scene. She finished her analysis with: "This guy knows how to cover his tracks."

"What about that mark on his forehead?"

"That's the good part." She took one last drag, then stubbed her cigarette butt into the cement and exhaled.

I raised an eyebrow at her.

"It's just a simple letter *R* scrawled on his head with permanent ink, light purple in color," she stated.

"Like from a marker?"

"Yeah, just like that."

It was my turn to exhale. "Any idea what it means?"

"Nope, but there's the starting point you wanted. I'll call you later if I find anything else out, but right now your five minutes are up."

If I didn't know what to make of the mysterious letter *R*, chances are neither did the cops. God knows I couldn't trust the police to handle a parking ticket, let alone find a potentially psychopathic killer.

That meant it was up to me to find this lunatic.

Solving Spuds's murder topped my list, so I sure didn't want another trivial assignment from my boss. Still, I needed a little help on this one, the kind of help I could find behind the doors of the Always Reddy Detective Agency, so I decided to brave going in.

Rhoda Chang greeted me with the same sympathetic look she'd been giving me the last several days. I pulled her aside and told her I needed her research assistance to find whatever she could on any recent killings involving writing on the victim's body.

She nodded eagerly, her wide eyes flashing. She loved to dig up arcane facts and unearth bizarre clues, and no one could do that job better than Rhoda.

The other thing I wanted to do at the office was talk to my friend and confidant, Harper "Pappy" Meriwether. I found him writing perfectly formed cursive script in his worn green leather casebook. He noticed me right away and held up a single finger, telling me to wait.

He slipped his casebook into a drawer, then stood up and motioned for me to follow him. He led me through the narrow corridor into the agency's often-deserted file room—a good place to get some privacy.

"What's going on, Pappy?" I asked, curious at his furtive behavior.

"Well, Ben, my boy, I finally figured out this Travis Kohen case, and let me tell you, it's not very pretty." He shook his head. "It's downright nasty, in fact."

"How so?" I asked, taking a sip from the cup of bitter coffee I'd grabbed from the office machine.

"You remember when that bus driver found the Kohen boy all hacked up, heroin needle sticking out of his arm . . . ?"

"Sure. We all guessed the needle was a plant."

"And of course we were right." He tapped the top of the short cabinet he leaned on to punctuate his point.

"What we didn't know was the who and why. The papers, the police—even Hal—had their fingers pointed at Manny "the Rose" Flores; after all, he's the big drug runner, right? Well, someone had to sift through the muck and come up with the truth."

Pappy had been playing with this particular case for quite some time, and it had frustrated him to no end. I was glad he'd finally cracked it.

"Good job!" I exclaimed, feeling a rush of excitement—a rush I always felt when closing a tough case. A rush I hadn't felt for a while.

"So what's the real story?" I asked.

He scratched at the thinning patch of gray above his ear, savoring the moment. Then he pushed a pointed finger my way. "The boy's own father did it, both the murder and the cover-up."

I almost spit out my coffee. "What? That's insane!"

Travis's father, Kris Kohen, was Testacy City's first serious politician, a hot candidate for senate. His whole platform revolved around cleaning up crime, starting with Testacy City. I guess that didn't include him. He'd been the one to hire the Always Reddy Detective Agency to solve his son's murder, spearheading the accusations against Mexican mob man Manny Flores. Maybe a lesser detective would have bought the red herring, but Pappy was all aces.

"So how does Flores fit into this?" I asked.

"Not one bit, except that Travis used to work for him, which figures as Kris Kohen's motive. He must not have liked having a son openly associated with crime—that didn't fit too well into his political aspirations. So he hired some drifter named Finch to take care of his son and throw the blame on Flores."

"That's more than nasty; that's downright sick," I said, tasting the last of my coffee.

"You can't underestimate the power of the sympathy vote," he responded with a slow shaking of his head.

"So our client turns out to be the dirty bird . . ." I murmured.

"Yes. This whole mess is bigger than the agency, so I've decided to turn it over to David O'Dare of the TCPD. I'm meeting with him tomorrow night to fill him in."

"What did Hal say when you told him that?" I didn't think Hal would be real happy about losing a big case to the cops, let alone being wrong about who committed the crime.

"I haven't told him yet. He's out today, some business in Vegas."

I nodded, hunching against a low table, throwing my fist into my palm. My mind wandered; I thought of Spuds.

Pappy noticed that I had slipped away from the conversation, and he knew me well enough not to keep quiet about it.

"You're hungry for another one, aren't you, Ben? Hungry for another big case . . ." Then, as he looked at me with his wizened face, his smile widened. "Why, you little rascal. You're onto something, something big, aren't you?"

I told him about finding Spuds. "It's not fair, Pappy, that a guy like that gets put down and nobody stands up to fight for him."

"Precious little in life *is* fair." He laughed his usual dry, raspy laugh. "But you don't need to hear my clichés. Go do your job and give this Spuds a proper funeral by finding his killer. It's the right thing to do."

I wanted to do Pappy proud, but the whole day passed, and I had gained little ground. The time I'd spent on skid row talking to transients who knew Spuds yielded me only that he had been in the war. All the local VFW offered me was his real name of William Turgall; the "Spuds" nickname apparently stemmed from repeated turns on potato-peeling KP duty during the war.

Turgall had been married, but his wife left him before he returned from overseas; no one even knew her name. Her desertion hit him pretty hard. He had no remaining family, no one he could call a friend, and—most important to the case—no real enemies.

Still more news to bring down my spirits: Rhoda's search for similar murders turned up a big goose egg. She said she would continue to look, but somehow I knew that road wouldn't go anywhere.

So I wore a heavy brow when I walked into the H.M.S. Pandora.

Barton Bourke's irritating presence weighed down the bar. He had an old paperback mystery gripped in one hand; his other hand rested on his head, fingers scratching his scalp. He let out a wide-mouthed yawn, his tongue wiggling around like a worm on a rainy day.

Normally, the only way I could put up with Bourke's inanity was with Pappy at my side; if I came in alone I'd always sit at one of the Pandora's comfortable leather booths. But tonight I just wanted a single drink before hitting the sheets—getting up early had started taking its toll on me—so I saddled up to the bar and got his attention.

"Hey, Barton, is this a library or can I get a drink here?"

"Drake! I was hoping you'd come in tonight! Wait'll you see what I got to show you." He dog-eared his page and tossed the book onto the back bar.

"How about showing me my drink first."

"All right, all right. Hold your horsehairs."

After he poured my Old Grand-Dad, he reached beneath the bar and pulled out a newspaper that had been folded up into a neat rectangle kept together with rubber bands. He threw it down on the counter and slapped it with his thick hand for emphasis.

"Get a load of that."

I took a slug of bourbon and looked at the paper, the morning edition of the *Testacy City Herald-Tribune*. Tiny classified ads filled the page. Barton, presumably, had circled one in blue ballpoint. It read:

> Dear Mr. Detective:
> The game is afoot.
> —Jack

"This could be you, Drake!"

"Come on, Barton. It could be any number of detectives."

He threw his hands up defensively and moved them back and forth like he was doing push-ups. "Okay, okay. I know this is all circumstantial and all. But it's a clue, nevertheless, so mark my words. Follow up on it, Drake."

"How am I supposed to follow up on it? Place a reply ad in tomorrow's paper?" I gulped down the rest of my drink.

"Of course. That's what any good pulp detective would do."

Christ. "I've gotta get out of here." I put some cash on the bar. "Keep the change . . . and your advice. Have a nice night, Barton."

On my way out I couldn't help but shake out a little laugh. Barton had probably been showing that damn paper to every dick who walked into the place that day.

I yawned and struggled to keep my eyelids from crashing down. When I poured myself into my car, I was tempted to put the seat back and snooze right there on the street. But I didn't live that far away.

The loud roar of the engine woke me up a bit. As I focused through the windshield, I saw a slip of paper tucked under the wiper blade. I didn't feel like reaching out and trying to grab the handbill while I drove, so I watched it flap in the wind all the way home.

Once I got my car parked, I noticed the flier wasn't a flier at all but a note written on a folded page from a steno pad. Despite my curiosity, my eyes hurt and the parking lot's dim light wouldn't do them any favors. So I crumpled the paper into my coat pocket and headed upstairs.

Inside, I flipped the light switch and read the note.

I see you appreciate my work.
Don't worry, there'll be more soon.
—Jack

I suddenly felt off-kilter. A ruthless ring from the phone shook through the quiet room, rattling my nerves even further.

I snatched it up but didn't even get the chance to say hello before Rebecca's urgent voice raced through my ear.

"Jesus, Ben! Thank God you're finally home! I've been trying to reach you all night."

"What's up? Find something else?"

"More like something else found me. Another body turned up. You've gotta come check this out."

Despite the warm air, I shivered again. "Hold on, what do you mean 'another body'?"

"I mean another body with a letter written on the forehead."

I didn't need to hear any more. I dropped the phone and sped to the morgue.

Rebecca waited for me on the front steps, smoldering cigarette in one hand, steaming cup of coffee in the other. Heavy lines of exhaustion circled her eyes.

"Hey, that was fast." Her voice had the rough quality that comes from not enough sleep, too many cigarettes, and too much coffee.

I shrugged, mounting the steps. "After such an enticing invitation, how could I not rush? What do you have?"

She finished her smoke and flipped it out into the street, then held the door open for me. The stench of death and decay assaulted my nostrils and settled in the back of my throat, making me gag.

"Pretty typical slasher-type murder," she answered, "except for the capital *E* scribbled on her forehead."

"This time it's a woman?"

"Yeah, a young girl, about college age."

"Man, that's rough. How'd they find her?"

"Some guy walking his dog through Jackson Park found her draped over the branch of one of the big willows down there. Numerous stab wounds in her chest and neck, *E* on her forehead, pretty much the same MO as last night's bum."

We rounded the corner, walked past the twin metal doors leading to the autopsy room where Rebecca did most of her work, and entered the large refrigerated vault filled with dead bodies resting on wheeled gurneys.

"Here she is," Rebecca said as she pulled back the sheet that covered one of the bodies.

A spasm of sentiment ripped through me, and I quickly spun

around, gesturing to Rebecca with broad swipes of my hand. "Cover her up . . . please."

"You know her?"

I spat out a cough, half from revulsion, half from emotional overload.

"Yeah, she was a waitress at Lepke's named Donna Dust. Good kid."

"Looking at the severity of her wounds, I'd say our boy had something to prove."

"What do you mean?"

"Her injuries came at the hands of an angry man." She paused, sparking up a cigarette. "And I'll tell you something else, Ben. This mess is just beginning."

III

My head hurt, and I felt the pressure right behind my eyes as I took a slow drive home.

Spuds, Donna—there must be a connection . . . but what? Other than being in the same restaurant at the same time, what do a helpless veteran trying to keep food in his belly and an innocent waitress trying to make an honest buck have in common? Maybe they saw something . . .

I was grasping at any scenario I could imagine; the heat and my fatigue led me down plenty of likely dead ends. One road I kept coming back to made me wince—these strange notes flying at me played into this somehow, and that put me uncomfortably in the middle of things.

At home, I peeled off my clothes and tried to grab some sleep. I could close my eyes, but the sleep wouldn't come.

Damn the heat. Damn this killer.

Every time my body gave in and I drifted off, some nightmare would haunt my mind.

Damn my dreams . . .

At six a.m., Lepke's Diner had just started to come alive. Nearly every seat at the counter held a different kind of customer, from lawyers and construction workers starting their days to drifters and ruffians just ending theirs.

Then there was me, somewhere in between. I took the first open spot at the counter and tried to wave down the frantic Costas Papademos.

"Hey, Costas, I've gotta talk to you," I called out as he rushed by, delivering orders to hungry breakfasters.

"What is it with you people? You gotta talk to me, and so does everyone else in my place. I'm busy, so wait your turn!"

"This can't keep, my friend . . . the game is afoot."

I played a hunch, a test to see if this crazy cook could be my mysterious messenger. Costas just stared at me like I was an idiot as he collected a stack of empty plates.

"What are you talking about? Why this foolishness? Can't you see I'm short staffed today? This girl who works for me doesn't come in, doesn't phone—"

"She's dead."

"Who's dead?"

"Donna Dust."

He stopped in his tracks, dirty dishes stacked on one arm. I had his attention now. "You're not funny," he snorted.

"I'm not trying to be. I saw her body last night at the morgue."

He looked at me through squinted eyes, cocking his head to one side. I paused, knowing what I had to ask would be difficult.

"When's the last time you saw Donna?"

"Yesterday, here at work!"

"Two days ago when I was in here, she acted awful depressed. You know why that would be?"

He set his stack of dirty dishes on a wheeled cart and wiped his hands on his apron, then turned back to me.

"I do not pry into the personal lives of my employees."

"Any weird people bother her the last few days?"

He held his arms out wide and shook them in the air for emphasis. "Look around you, there are always weird people in my place, begging for meals, dirtying my restroom."

"How well did she know Spuds?"

"Spuds?" He crossed his arms over his chest. "I do not know any Spuds."

"Sure you do, he's the old bum you threatened to kill—"

"Are you accusing me?" he accused.

"Hold on, that's not why I'm here; I'm here to get some answers," I promised in my best reassuring voice. "You were probably with some friends last night, or maybe your wife?"

He clenched his teeth, trying to hold back his emotion. He couldn't, and exploded: "I certainly wasn't out killing my waitress so I could cook, clean, and take orders by myself!"

By now the entire restaurant had stopped eating and stared at our little exchange.

"I'm finished with you," he spat hotly. "I have work to do."

He turned on his heel, pushing the cart with the dirty dishes through the swinging doors into the kitchen.

I'd had enough of Costas, and after a few more sips of coffee, I'd had enough of Lepke's.

Getting into the office early was turning into a bad habit for me. I hadn't had much sleep the past few days, and my limbs complained as I walked down Fielding Avenue toward the William Kemmler Building, home of the Always Reddy offices.

A plain brown Dodge sedan was parked in front of the building; Duke Wellington sat inside. He pulled himself free when he saw me coming, and by the time I got to the steps leading up to the offices, he stood on the sidewalk, glowering at me.

I stopped when I got near him. Neither of us said a word. With a flourish, he whipped out that morning's paper and brandished it in my face. The headline read: *Sick Raspberry Killer Strikes Twice! Testacy City Gripped in Fear!*

Only then did he start in with the typical Duke Wellington routine: "You been talkin' to the papers, Drake? If you been talkin' to the papers, you better pray to God Almighty I don't get wind of it. You ain't ready for the kind of trouble I'll be bringin' down around your ears."

Two photos, side-by-side shots of Spuds and Donna, jumped out at me from beneath the headlines.

"Hell, DW, I seldom find the time to read the things, let alone talk to them," I cracked back.

"Don't be wise with me, Drake. The cat lady—"

"Her name's Rebecca."

"I don't like it when people interrupt me, Drake. But let me tell you right now, I'll call her what I want to call her, an' I call her the cat lady. She tells me you been askin' around about the vagrant and this dead waitress, so don't be thinkin' you're wise at all."

"I'm not wise, DW, just trying to solve a couple of murders."

"You just keep in your mind that this is police business. Now last time I checked, you ain't got no client, so you ain't got no business here. This case is all mine. You keep lookin' into this, we'll be haulin' you in."

"Threats won't keep me from cracking this case."

"An' your wise mouth won't keep me from crackin' your head. Just back off, Drake. This is my case."

He returned to his car, keeping his finger pointed at me until he climbed behind the wheel and sped off.

Despite Duke Wellington's visit, I didn't plan on abandoning the case, but it was clear I had to keep myself off his radar. I had enough real trouble to worry about.

My stomach sank when I found two manila folders, new cases handed down from above, sitting right in the middle of my desk. I knew what they held, and I didn't want another tedious case or two distracting me.

"Mornin', Ben," Mike Manetti yawned. "You've sure been in early lately."

I didn't really like Manetti, the agency's greenest detective. He dressed badly, didn't use his head, and couldn't hold his liquor. But when push came to shove, he'd be there to watch your back. If only I didn't have to listen to him talk.

"Yeah, trouble sleeping the last few days."

"Insomnia, huh?" Manetti thrust his hands into the pockets of his grubby jeans and leaned against my desk. "Hey, you seen the papers today?"

"I had the headlines waved in my face," I grunted, picking up my new case files. I started to crack one open to take a look, when I noticed a white envelope sitting on my desk, peeking out from its hiding spot underneath the folders.

"How 'bout that killer? Brutal stuff, eh? Hey, that whole business with the letters in raspberry-colored ink—that's how the guy who found the girl described it in the *Trib* anyway—it's pretty strange, wouldn't you say?"

I took a closer look at the envelope; someone had carefully addressed it using cutout letters to: *Ben Drake*

"Yeah," I mumbled, setting the files down and picking up the envelope instead. It didn't hold much . . . perhaps a single sheet of paper.

Manetti still buzzed away: "That sort of thing'll keep a fella up nights . . . Hey, maybe that's why you're not sleeping so good!"

I needed to get into that envelope, but I didn't want to do it with Manetti standing around.

"Look, Mike, I've got a lot to jump on today, so I'm going to get to it, all right?"

"Right, I gotcha, Ben." He pulled himself off my desk. "Hey, I'm a little light today, so if you need anything just give your man Mike a holler."

"Then hold on a second," I blurted out, reaching for the two files on my desk. "I'm getting jammed up here, can you take these two cases? They're pretty routine."

"Yeah, sure thing. I'll check these out and get 'em back to you when I got 'em all sewn up."

I nodded as he strolled away, then grabbed my letter opener and slit the envelope open. A sheet of steno paper was tucked inside.

Glad to see you're playing.
You won't guess my next play,
so let me help you out.
Get over to Cedar and Fifth.
You just might be able to catch me.
—Jack

I found Rhoda and asked her if she knew who had delivered the note. She told me she found it when she opened up that morning; someone must have slid it under the office door.

I didn't have times for guessing games. I had to get across town.

I drove through the intersection of Cedar and Fifth, just four blocks west of where they'd found Donna's body in Jackson Park. When nothing suspicious jumped out at me, I parked and got out to investigate.

Silent duplexes stared at me on the west side of Fifth Street. The east side held vacant lots; the houses that used to be on this block burned down a few years ago. Looked like no one had bothered to rebuild, and now the grass grew tall—waist-high in some places.

The late-morning sun pounded down on me. Other than the occasional chirp from birds, the street remained silent. Just what was I supposed to find here? Maybe I beat my friend Jack to the punch.

A thought jumped into my head: maybe I was *supposed* to get here first. Nervous energy buzzed through my body, and I instinctively checked my gun. I should have figured this for a setup, but this case had the inside of my head all twisted up.

I spun in a slow circle, carefully scanning each house and scrutinizing each empty lot. Again, nothing suspicious jumped out at me.

Something on the street caught my eye, though; I looked down to see a lipstick case. Its cap was missing and the bright red lipstick stuck outward, melting in the rising heat. Not too far away, just on the edge of my vision, I spotted a single black shoe—a high-heeled number with a strap designed to wrap around the ankle. It rested against the curb, right in front of the empty land on the southeast side of Fifth.

I looked out across the lot. The tall grass swayed in the light breeze. I played a hunch.

It didn't take me long to find her. She lay where the grass grew the tallest, gazing up at the sky with glassy eyes.

Bright red lips—slightly parted to show off dainty white teeth—still begging to be kissed.

Her throat had been slit, and the drying blood had spilled across her porcelain skin. On her forehead, just below her neatly cropped, jet-black bangs, a reddish-purple letter V advertised her killer.

As always, Beth Hrubi dressed in black.

She held a single piece of steno paper in her left hand. On one side, Jack had scrawled a crude drawing of a heart being punctured by a knife. On the other, he'd written me a note: *Meet me at Lepke's.*

This cat-and-mouse Jack and I were playing had been personal, but I hadn't fully realized that until the moment I'd found Beth's body.

I considered her a friend, although we'd only met that one night at the H.M.S. Pandora when she dragged me into a cockfight that doubled as a den of crime. Of course, I knew she had ulterior motives: what was supposed to be a simple takedown turned into a bloody mess.

It had required all my skills to get out of that joint alive. I'd had to ruffle some feathers on my way out the door, and more than a few guys had tasted my knuckles that night.

Beth got out without a scratch, stranding me high and dry in the desert to sweep up her mess. When I found out she used to be Manny Flores's girl, I figured she probably always got out all right—but now I found her butchered and left to bake in the hot sun, a pawn in some game I didn't understand.

I imagined Beth's bright red lips whispering in my ear words from the note her dead hand held . . . *Meet me at Lepke's.*

I hated being led around from body to body, task to task, like an errand boy. I decided I'd keep playing along, but I'd have my own set of rules.

I wouldn't be doing myself any favors by letting Duke Wellington know I was a step ahead of him, so I dropped an anonymous tip to the cops from a nearby pay phone—after all, that's what pay phones are for.

I wasn't done. I dialed another number. Tony, the bartender at the Long Mile, picked up on the first ring.

"Ben! What's up? You need a hand?"

"That's why I'm calling, I need some backup."

"What's the job?"

"I'm meeting someone. Things might get messy, and I want a guy I can trust in my corner."

"Where do I gotta be?"

"Lepke's Diner. You know it?"

"Yeah, I been there. When?"

"Right now."

He hung up without saying goodbye.

The lunchtime crowd packed Lepke's to capacity. A quick scan of the room didn't register any familiar faces except Tony, who sat in one of the small booths at the rear of the restaurant, drinking a cup of coffee and slurping a bowl of soup. He didn't even look my way, but I knew he'd be ready for action the second it came.

I stood at the front until a booth opened up. Then I ordered myself a cup of coffee, cracked open the paper, and pretended to read, keeping an eye on the room as I waited for my mysterious messenger to show his mug.

Two waitresses hustled from table to table doing what waitresses do, and two cooks scurried behind the grill doing what cooks do. I didn't see any sign of Costas Papademos.

Though I tried, I couldn't keep Beth Hrubi's frozen face from floating around in my mind.

Finding her dead body tore up my insides real bad. In a city full of cheap dames, Beth Hrubi had been a classy lady, and even though I'm not the type to chase skirts, something about Beth got me running. I've always fallen for the bold, dangerous type, and she knew it. She played me for a fool the night of the cockfight, and I played along—half knowing she wanted me around for more than my company and the other half knowing she was up to no good. We both knew what we were doing though. She may have been a crook, and I may have been a crook chaser, but we played by the same rules.

I'd already sucked down four cups of coffee when Costas Papademos, wearing an ugly, ill-fitting plaid jacket, burst through the front door and disappeared right into the back room.

Moments later he emerged, now dressed in sparkling white T-shirt, pants, and apron. He moved behind the counter and started wiping down the Formica.

Just as I pondered how strange it was that he wasn't saying anything, let alone shouting at his staff, the piercing sound of squealing tires drowned out the murmur of conversation running through the restaurant.

All eyes watched the brown Dodge screech to a halt in front of the eatery.

Two patrol cars pulled up as the pair of homicide cops exploded through the door. Costas, so angry he almost ignited, rushed forward to meet Duke Wellington and Weisnecki.

"How dare you come in here like this!" Papademos shouted. "You are bothering my good customers!"

Tony sat rigidly in his booth, ready to strike. He had no fondness for cops, especially Mark Weisnecki. I hoped he wouldn't do anything rash; I'd feel pretty bad if he landed in the cooler while on my payroll.

Duke Wellington stood tall, hands on his hips, and scanned the room, meeting every eye in the place. "This city, as well as God Himself, has put us on the righteous path of justice," he lectured, "and we have come here to dispense that justice."

I'd never seen the big cop so calm. It was downright eerie.

Costas, now right in front of Duke Wellington, stuck a finger straight at his broad nose. Before more words could escape the angry cook's mouth, Weisnecki snatched up the offending digit in his doughlike grip.

"Don't you ever point at my partner," Weisnecki slurred, giving Costas's arm a little twist.

The cook couldn't help but spin around as pain lanced up his arm.

He gasped—surprise and agony paired on his face—and shouted: "What do you think you are doing? I pay my taxes!"

Weisnecki slapped a pair of cuffs around the pastry chef's wrists and began to hustle him toward the door.

"We're taking you in, sucker, that's what we're doing," Duke Wellington snarled as he followed Weisnecki.

I jumped to my feet, hurrying after them. I could feel Tony hot on my heels. I bolted through the door and shouted for Duke Wellington just as he stuffed Costas into the backseat of one of the patrol cars.

He pulled himself to his full height and turned around, hand reaching for his gun. When he saw who had yelled his name, he cracked a wide grin and walked my way.

"What the hell is going on here?" I demanded.

The twin prowl cars pulled away, and Weisnecki leaned against the unmarked Dodge, watching our confrontation, cooly content.

"I don't have to explain myself to anyone, Drake, let alone a private dick—but I'll tell ya, 'cause I'm in a good mood. I'm always in a good mood when we solve a big case."

"What case?" I cried.

"What case? *The* case, Drake. We're closing the book on these sick murders." He nodded his big head. "That's right, we're closing the book tonight."

"You've got the wrong man there, DW. This guy isn't your killer."

Duke Wellington pulled a neatly folded peach-colored handkerchief out of the pocket of his shimmering lavender suit and mopped his massive brow.

"You see, that's where you're wrong, Drake. What you don't know is we've been watching this guy. We've got a whole dossier on him."

"Dossier? You work for the feds or something?"

"I'm talking about evidence here, Drake, tons of evidence."

"Come on! Like what?"

"Like I said, Duke Wellington ain't in the habit of explaining himself. But, 'cause I'm happy, I'll give you the basics—let you in on the secret of how real detective work gets done."

Please. I opened my mouth to cut him down, when his list of "secrets" cut me off.

"First off, this guy threatens to kill a harmless bum one morning, right in front of a cop—hell, Drake, you were there for that."

"Get serious," I said, not able to fully fathom this guy's ignorance. "You know he didn't mean it like that! You can't use that as evidence!"

"I can and I will; it sounded damn genuine to me. Number two: the next day, who turns up dead but his waitress—and this guy shows not one ounce of remorse when we tell him about it. He wasn't even surprised. And three: just now some coward phones in another body, and this one's holding a note that ties this restaurant right in with the whole wang-dang-doodle. Like I said, case closed."

"That's thin, DW. It'll never wash."

"Oh, it'll clean up real nice. Just give me one night." He turned his back on me and strolled to his car. Weisnecki climbed in behind the wheel, and Duke Wellington slipped in to ride shotgun.

"Sorry, Drake, you lose this one. This round goes to Duke Wellington."

I kept him from rolling up the window with a shout: "What about the raspberry letters?"

"Oh, we'll find that out, Drake, don't you worry. We'll find that out."

The car spun a U-turn and peeled off. Tony, who'd been waiting just on the inside of Lepke's, came outside and watched as the car vanished down the street.

"What was that all about, Ben?"

"Results, Tony, at the expense of justice."

"That Weisnecki is no good."

"Yeah, I know. But until now, I honestly thought his partner was better."

Costas Papademos was in for a long night of abuse—verbal and physical—and all for nothing. I didn't mind giving out a few lumps to a chump who deserved it, but I knew Costas was innocent. And deep down, so did Duke Wellington. While I certainly didn't get along with him, I always thought he would be a decent cop. This incident left a bad taste in my mouth.

I needed to crack this case for real.

Tony and I headed back inside. The place felt like the morgue. No one made a sound, except for the occasional clink of forks and knives.

I walked up to the shell-shocked waitress behind the counter and settled the bill for Tony and me. As I turned to leave she called out: "Wait! I almost forgot! Some guy left this for you."

She handed me a blank envelope. All the hot coffee I'd drunk that afternoon didn't keep my stomach from freezing over. I knew what it was—and what it meant.

"When did he leave it?"

"Just before Mr. Papademos came back from the bank. I meant to give it to you right away, but I got busy and sort of forgot about it. Then the cops stormed in here and—"

"What'd this guy look like?"

"Just a regular guy."

"Seen him before?"

"Sure, he comes in a couple times a week. Quiet type."

"Know anything about him?"

She thought a moment. "No, it's like I told you, he's just an average guy."

I sighed, and uttered a terse thanks.

Tony and I left the little diner, avoiding the chaos that was sure to come.

Outside, Tony pointed at the message I grasped in my fist. "What's in the envelope?"

"Bad news."

"You gonna open it or what?"

I ripped open the flap, took out a slip of green steno paper. It read: *Don't forget to throw out the trash.*

"What the hell does that mean?" Tony asked.

"It means death!" I cursed angrily. "Trash . . . trash . . . trash . . ." I ran the possibilities through my head.

Tony interrupted my thoughts: "How 'bout we check behind the diner? I'm sure they've got a dumpster of some sort."

We looked at each other for a brief moment before we bolted to the back. A narrow alley ran behind the small diner. Next to the alley, butting up against the eatery, rested a green dumpster.

Tony pointed at it. "That's where I'd put the trash."

A collusion of flies and rancid smells filled the air. Tony waved his way through the dense insects and lifted the bent metal lid.

We peered inside.

"Oh, hell!" I shouted, stumbling back.

I expected to find a dead body.

And I did.

I stood in the middle of the alley, no balance, world spinning around me. I could vaguely hear Tony calling my name.

I expected to find the corpse mutilated, stab wounds lacing its chest and neck.

And I did.

I staggered backward, arms flailing, until I crashed into the chain-link fence bordering the alley.

I expected to find a slit throat and blood-soaked clothing plastered to the front of the lifeless body.

And I did.

I slid down the fence, ripping my coat, landing in a ragged heap on the alley's rough pavement.

I expected to see a letter drawn in raspberry-colored ink on a cold forehead.

And I did, the letter *E*.

Tony shook me, slapped my face, forcing me back to some sense of awareness.

But I didn't expect to see who I saw.

I coughed a couple times and shook the cobwebs from my head.
Harper Meriwether.

Damn this murderer.

Oh, dear Christ. Pappy.

I choked back the tears threatening to pop my eyeballs.

Pappy had been like a father to me. My own father died when I
was young, a relationship I didn't know I missed until I'd met Pappy. He taught me nearly everything I know about detective work,
and quite a bit of what I know about life. He helped me exorcise the
ghosts of my past, just by being who he was.

I couldn't fight it anymore.

The tears flowed.

IV

After I'd found Pappy, I sort of wandered aimlessly through the city,
eventually ending up at the H.M.S. Pandora.

The dark interior and cool wood, once comforting to me, now
seemed harsh and uninviting. Inexplicably, Barton Bourke didn't
stand at his usual station, and without him and Pappy the place took
on a foreign air of depression.

I ordered three fingers of Old Grand-Dad from the rube bartender and sat there, slowly sipping my bourbon, trying to regain the
feeling of home.

It never came. That was the last drink I ever had in the Pandora.

I spent the rest of the night driving, drinking, thinking—trying
to make some sense of it all. But everywhere I went in Testacy City, the
dead faces of Spuds, Donna, Beth, and especially Pappy haunted me,
so I drove into the desert and guzzled bourbon until my bottle ran dry.

By the time I staggered up the steps to my apartment, the first
shimmers of dawn started to reclaim the sky, and things made less
sense than when the night began.

I unlocked my apartment and pushed the door open, then froze.
Something felt wrong. I couldn't tell what bothered me, but all my
instinctual alarms shook my senses.

Pappy taught me the importance of listening to your instincts,
and if I'd learned only one thing in all my years as a detective, it was
that Pappy was right about most everything.

I took in the silence, letting all my senses work overtime. Something was wrong all right, but I could also tell I wasn't in any danger—at least not in the immediate sense. Still, I slipped my pistol into the palm of my hand, just to be safe. It fit there like an old friend and gave me the strength to slink into the foreboding darkness of my home.

As I peered through my tiny apartment, I could just barely see him sitting in my favorite chair, shining like a ghost in the faint light.

"Good morning, Mr. Drake," he greeted in a rich, spicy voice. His ethereal shape shifted, and I heard the clink of what could only be ice in a now-empty glass. "I took the liberty of fixing myself a drink," he explained. "I hope you don't object—though I must say I question your taste in alcohol."

I sniffed. The thick scent of rosewater wafted through the air. "How long have you been sitting here in the dark?"

"Long enough to settle for whiskey."

I grunted and flipped on the light.

Manny Flores smirked in my leather recliner, playing his role as a swarthy Southern gentleman for full effect. He dressed in a spotless, perfectly pressed ice-cream suit over a white shirt and midnight-black tie. White-gloved hands rested in his lap. His dark hair was slicked straight back across his head, and a flawlessly trimmed thin, oiled mustache sprang from beneath his slim nose, emphasizing the fullness of his lips. He bent his head and sniffed the bright red rose pinned to his lapel, then uncrossed and recrossed his legs. He wore a pair of polished black-and-white wingtips on his feet. He didn't wear any socks; for some reason, this struck me as odd.

He gestured toward a kitchen chair, not so mysteriously relocated to my living room. "Please, have a seat, Mr. Drake. We have some business to discuss."

"Business?"

"Yes, business. I have some information—and a proposition—for you." A wicked playfulness danced in his dark, wide-set eyes. "But you'll want to take this sitting down."

I didn't trust Manny Flores, yet here he sat, alone in my home—atypical behavior for a notorious mob boss. I decided to play the hand out. I reholstered my pistol.

"Let me get a drink first." I tilted my head at the empty glass in Manny's hand. "Refill?"

"Please. I don't suppose it's possible to switch to tequila?"

A "no" masquerading as a chuckle escaped my lips.

"Another whiskey then. With ice." He handed me the glass. I filled it, then mine, taking a long pull before I settled into the kitchen chair. I took out a tin of cigars, offering a smoke to Flores. He declined with a wrinkled nose. I offered a smoke to myself. I accepted.

"You're a man of complexity, Mr. Drake."

I extinguished my match with a flick of the wrist and drew in a big mouthful of smoke. "Yeah?"

He merely nodded and sipped his bourbon. The slightest grimace crossed his face. And this guy drank tequila?

"So, to what do I owe this visit?"

"Let me be blunt," he responded. "Beth Hrubi told me that Ben Drake is a stand-up guy."

Beth. Of course.

"She was a stand-up gal."

He smoothed his mustache with a gloved hand. "She told me if I ever found myself in a jam, Ben Drake would be a good man to call on."

"Huh. Well, I'm sort of booked up at the moment."

"You remember that cockfight of mine you busted up?"

"That isn't exactly chapter and verse, but yeah. Is that what this is about?"

"Yes, but not how you think. Let me tell you a story."

He sipped his drink again, never taking his eyes off me. I followed suit.

"Once there was a woman with the heart of a girl . . ." He set down his glass and leaned forward, his hands waving in pace with his story. "She didn't want the limelight. She didn't want the glory. She only wanted the fun. Despite all that, she had responsibilities. Oh, she hated responsibility, simply hated it. You see, that's where I came in. People think I'm the heavy, but I'm no heavy. Yes, I participate in some illegal activity. Everybody breaks some kind of law now and again; I just make sure I profit out of these occasional transgressions. I'm an opportunist."

He shrugged his shoulders as he reclined back into the chair. He picked up his glass and grimaced another gulp of booze.

"That's why I worked for Beth Hrubi," he said. "The city belonged to her."

I didn't say a word for a long time, and neither did Flores. I felt like a patsy, played for a fool. But if I'd been duped, so had the entire city.

"You telling me Beth ran Testacy City?"

He grinned. "The best-kept secret in the Southwest. Now let me tell you another. A much darker secret about the ultimate betrayal . . . I'm sure you know of the esteemed Kris Kohen . . ."

A cold spider crawled under my skin and up my spine. "Sure." I fidgeted in my chair, wishing he'd get on with it.

"Oh yes, everyone does. But most people don't know that Mr. Kohen is more than a politician on the rise. He's a crook—a real crook: drugs, prostitution, even slavery. His people are the ones who bring drugs up from Mexico into Testacy City."

I sent a quizzical gaze his way, and he held my stare. He knew what raced across my mind: Manny Flores was known as the biggest drug runner this side of Vegas.

"Sure, I deal in drugs, but all I do is move them through this city, routing the shipments to the coasts. I don't distribute a thing in my backyard; Beth and I agreed to that. You don't defecate where you eat, Mr. Drake. I'm more of a gambling man myself.

"However, the elder Kohen had no such scruples and decided to cut me out of the loop for a bigger slice of the pie. So Beth hatched a plan to send a little message his way. We orchestrated her split from my camp; she played off a few grudges, and set up that business that went down at the cockfight. That heroin belonged to Kohen."

"A lot of people died that night," I said.

"True, and as much as I regret it, you can't fight a war without losing some soldiers. Most of them were out-of-towners on Kohen's payroll, anyway. All we really did was gum up the Kohen works for a while."

The cold feeling spread from my spine, washing across my whole body, numbing me; if Flores spun me the straight dope . . .

"Kohen killed his own son . . . in retaliation?" I took a shot at filling in the blanks.

"You're a man of surprises, Mr. Drake, given what you know and what you don't know. Kohen hired a freelancer named Finch, one nasty customer for the deed, then framed me."

I rubbed the back of my hand across my stubbled chin, thinking about all the insanity of the past few weeks, and how it suddenly seemed to make some sort of sick sense.

"What did Travis Kohen do for you?"

"The ultimate irony, almost nothing. I liked him. Smart, a good kid, a true showman with real talent. All he wanted to do was perform, so I put him in charge of the cockfights."

My jaw dropped open. Again he flashed a grin. He liked dropping the hammer on me.

"That's right, you knew him as Tyler."

"Look. What do you want from me?"

He gave me a deadpan gaze, all the playfulness from his eyes now gone, replaced with cold, frightening malice. He uttered: "I want you to get this Finch character and get him to tell the truth about me, about Kohen. I want my name cleared, my reputation restored." His voice grew louder, sterner. "If I didn't need his confession, I'd have taken care of him myself."

"I'd help you except for two important things: one, as I already told you, I'm kinda busy at the moment; and two, I don't work for criminals."

"You don't have to work for criminals!" He stood up. "And to sweeten the deal, I'll leave town—there's nothing left for me here. All you have to do is finish the case that Mr. Meriwether put together and bring in Jack Finch!"

Numbness washed over me. Jack Finch? Jack? Oh hell . . .

Spuds. Donna. Beth.

And Pappy.

My numbness gave way to white-hot rage. My half-empty glass of bourbon slipped from my hand, shattering on the wood floor of my living room.

I turned and paced away from Flores, letting my body sink against the support of the far wall. I crashed my fist into the plaster. I spun back around, screaming: "You knew! You knew he was the killer, and you didn't do anything! You could've whacked him. You could've stopped him before . . . before . . ."

He stood there frozen.

"What if I kill him?" I said.

"You won't. You're a man with integrity."

I sped toward my destination, heedless of stop signs, pedestrians, and other traffic. Every nerve in my body fired off a feeling that I had to get to Squirrel's Mini Storage before it was too late.

If this nightmare was going to end, it would end there.

Manny Flores had given me his offer, and I'd finally accepted, perhaps more for personal reasons than I cared to admit.

After he left, the scent of rosewater lingered in the air. I cleaned the broken glass and whiskey off the floor, then cleaned myself up.

I desperately wanted to feel better. Putting on a clean suit helped—enough to make me ready to get to work. Trouble was, my body craved sleep, and I didn't know where to find Finch.

Next thing I knew I snapped awake from my slumped-over position at the kitchen table. The sun had gone down. I had scribbled some notes that I couldn't read. If only I could ask Pappy . . .

A bit later, I was at the office, sitting at Pappy's desk. I poured over various scraps of paper, clues from previous cases and notes for the memoirs he'd always meant to write when he retired. Strangely, I couldn't find his casebook, but I did notice a hastily scrawled name in the upper corner of his desk blotter.

I picked up the phone and called David O'Dare, the cop Pappy talked to the day before he died.

I thought of all this as I raced toward my destination, squealing around a hard corner and pressing the accelerator to the floor. Out of nowhere, a glaring red light forced me to skid my Galaxie 500 to a halt just in time to avoid hitting a downtown-bound semi.

The light flicked green; I stomped on the gas and resumed my breakneck scream through the night.

I had received a little of the typical runaround from the police operator when I called, but thanks to a little Benjamin Drake charm, she finally patched me through to O'Dare.

His partner, Peterson, answered the phone and told me O'Dare wasn't around. After I dropped the name of Finch, followed by

Harper Meriwether, he reluctantly gave me the goods: O'Dare had gone out to meet an informant at Squirrel's.

My instincts buzzed because I knew the storage scene smelled like trouble. Thankfully, Manetti still hung around the office. I told him to wait by the phone. If I didn't call him in a half-hour, he was to ring the cops and get them over to the storage building.

Nearly at my destination, I ripped through the ramshackle south side neighborhoods. The speedometer told me I was roaring along just under ninety; the dashboard clock told me I was blowing into eight p.m.

I screeched to a stop in the near-empty parking lot; another lonely car waited by the front of the three-story facility, its engine still crackling with heat.

I drew my Model 637, cocked the hammer, and rushed into the building. A small, darkened room sat to the right, with a *For Service Ring Bell* sign on its metal door. Straight ahead of me, roughly in the center of the building, lay David O'Dare's crumpled body.

Looming above him stood a pasty, youngish figure with long white hair. He wore a grubby hooded sweatshirt over blue blood-stained overalls. He brandished a thick, blood-slicked, Bowie-style hunting knife in his left fist.

Jack Finch.

"Hold it!" I screamed, thrusting my gun straight at this bastard's face. "Drop the knife!"

Wait a minute . . .

Finch slowly lowered his knife to the ground.

His hooded sweatshirt triggered my memory . . .

He slowly wiped the bloody blade clean on O'Dare's flannel shirt. Something familiar . . .

He reached for the bright silver badge clipped to O'Dare's belt.

Lepke's! He was sitting in Lepke's, shoveling up his breakfast, the morning Spuds had been killed!

He plucked the badge off the butchered cop's body.

"I'm not joking around here, Finch!" I warned with a low growl.

Déjà vu nagged my brain; that wasn't the first time I'd seen him . . . Lost in thought, I cocked my head and peered at him closely. That white hair and pale skin, almost albino-like . . .

He moved fast, throwing the badge at my head.

I ducked out of reflex.

A big noise from my small gun ripped through the night.

Finch bolted, vanishing into the darkness of the storage lockers as I remembered where I'd first laid eyes on him.

The cockfight.

That night, chaos and confusion ran through the basement gathering, erupting in slaughter. He'd been in my way as I scrambled to get out alive, so I'd clobbered him hard and broke his face. The night of the cockfight.

Jesus . . .

I stepped over O'Dare's lifeless body and slipped into the dark, mazelike corridor of lockers. I had just enough light to see a few feet in front of me. Beyond that, nothing.

On the wall at the beginning of this hallway, my scouting fingers felt a small dial. Above it, in painted stencil, the word *Lights* caught my eye.

I gave a twist and light flared on, but only down the single row of lockers immediately behind the dial. This provided enough light to see that each row featured a similar knob. A loud ticking filled the air, keeping time with my racing pulse, as the dial's timer wound down. I knew the lights would wink out again when it reached the end.

If I used the lights, Finch could easily keep track of my movement, and in these labyrinthine passages, it would be too easy for him to sneak up behind me.

I swallowed hard and rushed down another dark passage. After a few rows and a few turns, I realized my mistake. There was nothing to keep Finch from escaping back out the front. Cursing my stupidity, I retraced my steps as best I could. I'd gotten all turned around in the dark. I found the main corridor just in time to see Finch step into the building's industrial-sized elevator.

I ran toward him.

He grinned at me as the metal grate slammed shut. I fired another shot, but it bounced off the grate and ricocheted about the room.

Two wasted shots. Goddamnit!

I reached the elevator and slammed my fist against the steel cage. Why didn't he run?

The elevator didn't stop at the second floor; that meant he'd be riding to the top. I did a quick check; behind me I found a steel door leading to a set of steps and rushed upward—trying to climb faster than the elevator.

I hit the top floor, kicked open the door, and pointed my pistol right at the elevator. Empty. No sign of Finch.

Darkness, even thicker than two floors below, filled the slim corridors.

I knew I had to play this smart. I couldn't afford to lose my way. If I did, I'd be Jack Finch's next victim.

I paced forward, pistol extended in a double-fisted grip, until I reached the end of the corridor. The wall in front of me held windows. The dim light from the moon illuminated this narrow walkway ever so slightly.

I paused. I listened. No sound. I turned left.

I moved down along the outside wall slowly; taking a step, pausing, then taking another, trying to hear something besides my beating heart and ragged breath.

Step . . . Pause . . . Listen . . .

Step . . .

The scream of a wild animal shattered the darkness; Jack Finch burst from the shadows. I squeezed off a shot, realizing it went wide as I yelped from a burning pain searing my arm.

I fired again, a reflex, but stood alone. Hot, sticky blood ran down my arm from the deep cut across my left bicep. Shooting pain engulfed my entire body. I couldn't look, knowing if I dropped my eyes to check my wound I'd feel a knife across my throat.

I'd been careless.

My gun held five shots; I only had one left. I'd often remarked that if I didn't hit my target with five shots, the sixth wouldn't do me any good. Until now I'd always meant that as a joke.

Step . . . Pause . . . Listen . . .

I started to feel a little dizzy as I rounded the next corner. My concentration slipped, flowing away with the blood trickling down my arm.

Step . . . Pause . . . Listen . . .

I heard noises all around me now; my pulse quickened with every rat skittering along the floor, every roach scurrying through the walls, every cricket singing its mournful song in some dark crevice.

Step . . . Pause . . . Listen . . .

A click-clack echoed behind me and I spun, raising my gun, vowing not to waste my final shot.

I pointed it at empty air.

My eyes roved through the darkness, anxiously searching.

I didn't see him until he grabbed my arm and slammed my hand, gun and all, through the window. Shattering glass sprayed all around me as he beat my gun-clenched fist against the thin wire framework covering the window on the outside.

A thousand tiny knives lanced into my hand. I winced; my gun, still with its single bullet, slipped from my grasp and thunked to the floor. A quick kick from Jack sent it spinning into the black depths. It clanked against metal somewhere deep in the maze. I guardedly took a few steps back, tensing for Jack's next attack.

"Why me? What are you after?" I cried.

The low whine of sirens reached my ears; way to go, Manetti!

His answer came at me, a knife glittering in the low light. "Revenge!"

A tight swipe flew at my face; I jumped back and ducked, then came up and pounded a glass-pierced fist into Jack Finch's temple.

I'm no boxer, but I know how to use my fists. A punch—full of fury and packed with malice—rattled Jack Finch's teeth to their roots.

He crumpled, landing on his hands and knees—wheezing, spitting blood.

Sirens screamed louder.

I smiled.

My solid oxford slammed down on Finch's left fist. A grunt rewarded me. He tried to dig his hand out from beneath my foot; I ground a little sole against his knuckles, then smashed a heel against his fragile phalanges.

Bones cracked. I stomped again. Another grunt. The knife slipped from his fingers.

Flashes of blue and red burst through the windows, joining the piercing, oncoming sirens.

I bent to pick up the big knife. I knew Rebecca could confirm it was the instrument that had taken my friends from me. Just before I touched it, Finch's head hammered into my skull, toppling me backward.

Voices shouted outside—voices belonging to cops.

The air blew out of my lungs as Finch pounced on top of me. His knife stabbed down at my face. The half-severed muscles of my right arm screamed as I blocked his strike.

I twisted his wrist backward and, prying the knife from his grip, hurled it off to join my pistol. Jack responded with soft blows to my head; he was better with knives than with his hands. I ended that nonsense with a deep uppercut to his gut.

I threw him off me and scrambled to my feet.

Jack got his balance and hustled off, trying to escape. I ran after him, gaining ground; neither of us moved too fast. Sure I felt pain, but I ignored it.

I tackled Finch, and we tumbled into the low light that spilled out from the elevator. I noticed the metal grate was still open as Jack got both hands around my throat. In turn, my fingers managed to wrap themselves around his windpipe.

That's when I saw Duke Wellington standing in front of the door to the steps, his big .45 aimed right at us.

"All right, boys, fight's over," he rumbled. "Now, I want the both of you to stand up real slow. An' when I say real slow, I mean real slow. Got it?"

Through some unspoken communication, Jack and I haltingly let go of each other at the same time, each sliding away from the other as we followed Duke Wellington's orders: taking it slow, standing up.

I held my hands in the air, palms outward. Thick blood covered my left hand and quills of broken glass stuck out at odd angles from my right.

I nodded at Duke Wellington, and he gestured with his gun for me to get to the stairs. I limped a step forward, then paused. My ears caught the soft hiss of metal on metal, and the corner of my eye caught an evil glint.

I recoiled, pulling my legs up to my chest.

A bright flash blinded me as Duke Wellington's gun exploded with a shower of fire.

I tried to turn into a ball. The killer was almost on top of me.

Torrents of pain ripped through my head.

Jack's shoulder erupted in a wet firework of blood.

His albino rag-doll body flew through the air, into the elevator car. But the shot came too late.

The hilt of Jack's butterfly knife stuck out of my thigh.

I hit the floor, hard; the pain kept coming.

Jack Finch crunched against the back wall of the elevator and slid to the floor, painting a bloody smear above him.

I pulled myself to my feet, wincing as the knife in my leg scraped against my femur. I decided I'd be better off leaning against something solid.

Duke Wellington held his smoking gun on Jack Finch.

I pointed at the pale-skinned murderer.

"There's your raspberry killer, DW," I coughed, spitting out a gob of bloody phlegm. "He killed Travis Kohen too."

"What's that?" Duke Wellington asked, walking over to Finch, keeping his gun trained on the killer's head. "Get on your face," the big cop commanded.

Finch flopped over onto his belly. Duke Wellington cuffed him. Hard.

"Yeah, I know it's tough to believe, but Kris Kohen paid this guy to kill his own kid," I explained.

"You got proof of that, Drake?"

"No, not me, but I'll bet your man downstairs had enough to bury Kohen *and* Finch. That's why he's dead."

"And what about the raspberry letters, Drake?"

"You'll have to find that out, DW. You'll just have to find that out. Looks like the score's even, huh?" I grinned.

I didn't see it coming.

Duke Wellington's boulder-sized fist rocketed off my skull, sending me sprawling to the floor.

"Now we're even, Drake, now we're even. Let's get you to the hospital."

It's the last thing I heard before I passed out.

V

A wind had come into town, cooling things off considerably. It did nothing to lessen my troubled dreams. I was so hopped up on pain-killers the last couple of days, my mind could barely focus on the nightmares.

I pulled myself together for the funeral. I put on a clean black suit over all my bandages and limped to the taxi waiting to take me to the cemetery.

Hal and the other detectives stood in a solemn row, their heads down, their hands clasped in front. I gave a nod to Manetti, who showed up in a suit; I hadn't thought the kid owned one.

Rhoda dabbed a handkerchief to her tears as she shook her head back and forth.

A handful of cops, including John McCluskey, stood on the other side of the freshly dug hole. McCluskey, one of the few officers on the TCPD whom I considered a friend, showed up in his best uniform. His polished shoes shined as bright as sunlight off a placid lake.

Sometimes the smallest things make you feel good.

His wife Kathy walked alongside him, holding his arm. I went to high school with Kathy all those years ago. I actually introduced her to John after he and I sparked up a friendship back in my days as a firefighter. They were a good couple.

"Hey, Drake. How you holding up?" John asked. He stuck out his hand, and I shook it, although the cuts from the broken glass made me wince.

"It's been rough, these last couple days," I said, trying to get my voice out of my throat.

"We're really sorry, Ben," Kathy said as she gave me a soft hug.

"Thanks, Kath." I did my best to put on a game face and give these guys whatever smile I could. "So, how are you two doing?"

"Keeping busy with work, like always," Kathy said. "You know, we've been meaning to have you over for dinner. If you feel up to it, we'd love to see you later this week."

"Thanks, I appreciate that. How's things at the station, McCluskey?"

"You know me, I'm a tiger," he countered. He pointed toward the grave with his solid chin. "He was the best. The whole city will miss him. I'll miss him." He gave me a supportive clap on the shoulder.

"Yeah . . ." I breathed in deep and long. "I'll miss him too."

"I just want you to know, Ben, Finch is behind bars. Once we got him inside, he sang like a bird—based on the case Pappy and O'Dare had put together. And another thing . . ." His head swiveled on his beefy neck, first left, then right, as he glanced over his shoulders, confirming that no one was close enough to hear him whisper. "We brought Kris Kohen in this morning, and it doesn't look good for the bastard. Not too many juries are going to give him any sympathy."

I kept going with my forced smile. Finch and Kohen and all the goddamn criminals in the world could go to hell.

I took my place next to my fellow detectives as the ceremony began. We all muttered a prayer in unison. The coffin was lowered into the ground. We each took our turn tossing a spadeful of dirt over the grave. All that should be said was said. The crowd dispersed, everyone heading off their separate ways. Some returned to their jobs, some returned to their families.

Not me. I stood there until the sun sank low in the sky, wondering why life is so unfair. I continued to wonder as I walked over to the familiar plot of my wife's grave. I missed her more than ever.

At last, with the coolness of the evening settling in, I limped toward the small chapel, soaking up the cemetery's solitude and isolation.

I called a taxi from a pay phone. I had a few more moments to myself before it arrived and took me back to the world of the living.

Once home, I found a single red rose resting on my doorstep. I picked it up and sniffed. Its gentle aroma lingered in the air as I entered my apartment and poured myself a drink.

A PUNCH IN THE GUT AND A BAG FULL OF ORANGES

(2000)

Buck Bixel's wrecking-ball fist rock-eted into my gut, choking me on the air I'd just sucked into my lungs and sending my innards painfully sloshing against each other.

I had to admit that while the guy didn't look too bright, he sure knew how to throw a punch.

My feet flew out from under me, and I teetered over backward, heading for a hard slam onto the rough gravel. As I fell, Bixel crossed his arms and glared, daring me to not collapse at his feet. He would have been scary if he didn't look so damn goofy; his skin drooped off his massive frame like a pinkish prune, and he wore an oversized suit that hung loosely on his doughy body. Hard to believe this guy was one of Testacy City's toughest tough guys.

I crumpled to the ground and thousands of tiny rocks dug into my back. Wincing, I rolled onto my side and managed to wheeze some air into my lungs, but trouble came on all over again when I tried to blow it back out. A vise cranked tight around my chest as waves of nausea and pain fought for the right to take over.

I wanted to laugh. I wanted to throw up. I couldn't do either.

"You've gotta be gettin' a little tired of this, Drake," the diminutive Zef Ehrenreich wheezed as he stepped forward to loom over me.

The tiny thug, the civilized half of Small-Tooth Kelley's main muscle duo, whipped out a cigarillo and set fire to it, then cocked his head and bored his narrow, sparkly eyes into mine. He looked like a chimp in a cheap suit, but I knew he could be every bit as deadly as his giant partner.

How'd this happen to me? I'd been feeling good when I left the Long Mile earlier that night—too good, it turns out. And that's why these thugs got the drop on me and dragged me out here to the dump. A tight spot to be in; people didn't get hauled here to play cards. I've been in plenty of tight spots before, but I'd always known the score. This time, the worst of it was that I honestly had no idea what these guys wanted from me.

Ehrenreich jabbed me in the belly with his foot. "Eh? I asked if you were gettin' tired, Drake," he said, this time with a rising edge of violence in his voice. His scuffed shoe anxiously pawed the loose gravel as he spoke. "Hell, we are, ain't that right, Bixie?"

Bixel's floppy jowls waggled back and forth when he grunted an affirmative.

I tried to grunt my affirmative, but it felt like a big hand had wrapped around my heart and squeezed, so I just moaned.

Ehrenreich slid his tiny bowler far back on his head, then squatted down and stuck his mousy face right into mine. He stank of cheap gin and even cheaper tobacco.

"Now, I'm gonna ask ya this one last time, Drake, and I ain't gonna fool around no more. You get me?"

I nodded, but I knew things didn't look good, no matter what I said.

"Awright then . . . Mr. Kelley wants to know where them oranges are at. You care to help us out, Drake?"

If you can't breathe, it's not that easy to answer questions, especially when you really don't know the answer.

I managed to croak out a short, fractured sentence telling Ehrenreich I had no idea what he was talking about. I knew it wouldn't make him happy, but he'd be a lot less happy if I made something up. At least I'd be a lot less happy if I made something up.

The little guy let out a big breath full of smoke as he stroked his pencil-thin mustache, then drew himself up to his full height, which really wasn't all that much.

"Well, Bixie, looks like our boy ain't too good at learnin'."

He tossed his half-smoked cigarillo to the ground right in front of my nose, snapped his fingers, and spun on his heel, heading across the lot and back to his black sedan.

Bixel unfolded his arms and took a clumsy lumber closer to me. I squinted as his size-15 wingtip came sailing at my face.

I knew it was going to hurt.

The crickets woke me up; at least it seemed like they did. My head throbbed, and after a while I dared to open my eyes.

I struggled to my feet and took inventory. My ribs hurt, my back hurt, but most of all, my head hurt. I probed the tender and moist spot above my left eye that had met with Bixel's foot. Fresh blood on my fingers told me he got in a good kick.

The dump was about ten miles outside the city. Stranded without a car, I started the long trudge back to town. Every so often someone whizzed by me, going too fast down the road, but no one stopped. I didn't expect them to; Testacy City wasn't the type of town where you pulled over to pick up strangers.

By the time I limped my way downtown to the William Kemmler Building, my left eye throbbed and had swelled so much it felt like it would pop right out of my head.

I took the steps to the second floor, then slipped through the familiar door that read, *Always Reddy Detective Agency*. Rhoda Chang, the wily receptionist, had long since gone home; the small waiting room where she did her work was dark, but it still felt comforting.

I walked past her desk and crept through the door that led to my office, wishing Bixel hadn't swiped my Smith & Wesson Model 637 before he beat me up. I half-expected to find someone waiting for me in my chair, so I flicked on the light, clenched my fists, and got ready for action.

But my chair was empty. Instead, a medium-sized, beat-up cardboard box waited for me on my desk. A note, written in Rhoda's carefully penned handwriting, read: *Manetti brought this in. Said you'd know what it was for.*

I decided to wait a few minutes before I took in whatever bad news the box had for me, so I filled the sink in the corner full of cool water, stripped down to my T-shirt, and washed my face. My left eye stung something fierce as the water splashed over it. I took a look in the mirror; I sported a deep gash, right below the eyebrow. Bixel had done some damage all right.

After I dried myself off, I poured three fingers of Old Grand-Dad into my office coffee mug and took a healthy swig. Then I sliced open the top of the mysterious box.

Nestled inside was a mesh bag full of oranges.

Great.

Now what the hell was I supposed to do?

Mike Manetti answered the door only after my fist pounded on it a good six or seven times. I didn't care about waking him; if he had answers, I was ready with the questions.

"Drake? Ah . . . are you crazy, man? It's like not even morning yet."

"Yeah, I'm crazy—crazy enough to wear these bumps, bruises, and bandages like cheap earrings on a hooker. And crazy enough to think your shenanigans got me this way."

The bandages were courtesy of my friend Rebecca Hortzbach, the city's ace medical examiner. I had cabbed over to her place straight from my office. She liked to take care of my wounds, and always told me that fixing me up was a lot more fun than stitching up her regular customers. I didn't mind; she kept my hospital bills low.

"Whoa, hold on, Drake! Your man Mike wouldn't . . . I mean, what are you saying?" His knuckle rubbed at the sleep in his eye, while his other hand scratched his ribs.

"I'm saying I want you to tell me about the bag of oranges that's sitting on my desk."

"Well, yeah. It's . . . It's got to do with that thing I'm working on."

"What thing?"

"You know, that thing."

"Manetti!" I invited myself in and offered him a seat.

"Okay, I'm still waking up, man. Come on, you remember that job I was working, the one with the worried mother hen thinking her son was up to no good?"

"Yeah?"

The young detective leaned back in his grubby love seat. A smile leaked onto his tired face. "Well, he was up to no good."

A busybody type by the name of Emma Twitchell had placed a call to my office about a week ago, expressing some concern that her teenage son, Timmy, was running with boys from the other side of the tracks. I didn't expect much to come of it, so I'd shoved the tail job off on Manetti. Looks like he found something juicy; now all I had to do was get him to spit out the facts.

"Mike, all this talk is getting me no closer to explaining a bag of oranges that seems to inspire thugs to use my body as a punching bag."

"I was just getting to that, Drake," Manetti said. "I followed that Twitchell cat all over Testacy City until we ended up south of 15 in the warehouse district. Know what he was doing? He was picking up a delivery. Now, I know what you're thinking, probably the same as I was thinking—what's the big deal with picking up a delivery of a bag of oranges? That's what I was thinking."

His hand reached into a greasy white paper bag and fished out a cold french fry. "My mind couldn't take all the guessing and speculating—and I know that us private dicks want results. So when the kid stopped at the gas station for a pack of smokes or something, I swiped the oranges right out of his car."

I knew I wouldn't get anything else from Manetti that morning, so I spent a little time chewing him out for such bone-headed eagerness, leaving a job incomplete, and poor follow-up. But that's the past, and I'm not the kind of detective to dwell on mistakes. Assess the situation, collect the evidence, and make your move.

So I made my move with a few phone calls. A couple hours later, I was in my office staring at Small-Tooth Kelley's evil, small-toothed grin shining at me from across my desk. The gangster clicked out his question between dry, chapped lips: "So, Drake, what's it gonna be?"

I took my time answering. After all, it was my move, and I had this whole thing planned real nice. After leaving Manetti's apartment, I'd ducked into my place, cleaned up, grabbed some coffee, then strolled back to the office to give this bag the once-over in the light of day.

All night I had wondered what criminal activity could come from a bunch of oranges. Poisoning? I'd laughed, thinking of some comic book supercriminal planning to poison the city with toxic fruit. Not likely. Smuggling? A safer bet, but no, the plastic mesh of the bag had held nothing but oranges. Sure, a bag of oranges were often used by professional muscle to deliver a beating without leaving a mark. Though I didn't think such workman citruses would be valued so greatly.

Then I'd taken a closer look at the bag itself. Pretty standard: a bright orange net of plastic with a white label around the middle that wrapped the whole affair like one big piece of sealing tape. Lost in thought, I'd absentmindedly flicked at the label's top edge. And wouldn't you know, that label wasn't slapped on there too well at all.

With the thin blade of my Leatherman, I had peeled back the label, and a smile had broken heavy across my face, much like the one I was using on Small-Tooth Kelley right now. I could tell it unnerved him.

"One more time, Drake," he repeated, "what's it gonna be? You got my oranges or don't you?"

He was smug and tense, but I wasn't worried—even with my two dancing partners from last night flanking him. I had muscle of my own. Tony, the bartender at the Long Mile, was standing behind me, arms crossed. They were the thick arms of an ex-con gone straight. Like I said, I wasn't worried.

"Oh, I got your oranges. I guess a pasty guy like you needs his Vitamin C, huh? You know, Small-Tooth, they got pills for that now."

Kelley clicked his angry tongue through clenched teeth.

"No need to get mad," I said. "You'll get your oranges. But first, I want three things in exchange."

"You're in no position to make deals."

I had to keep from laughing when Tony cracked his knuckles in response. He was good at that.

"There's no threats here, just a simple set of requests among gentlemen. First, I want my gun back."

Small-Tooth's reply was interrupted by the tiny, spiteful Ehrenreich: "Give us the information first!"

The backhand from the boss hit Ehrenreich's puffy face swift and hard. "You keep your hole shut; I'm doing the negotiations here. Bixel, give the man his gun."

Bixel pulled my .38 out from one of the sagging pockets of his department-store suit and handed it over.

"Thanks, Bixie," I said. "Now, number two. The Twitchell kid, he's out of the business and left alone. For good."

Kelley sat up straighter in his chair and showed all his tiny teeth. "Of course, Drake. Not a problem, not at all. And now—"

"Hold on. I said I had three requests." I pulled the bag full of oranges from my bottom drawer and laid it on top of my desk. "You got a whole bag of oranges here, and they seem pretty valuable to you. So I'll be taking one. Think of it as payment."

His smile—the broadest smile I'd ever seen on his narrow face— told me he was buying my game. "You drive a tough bargain, Drake, but . . . I think we can deal with these terms."

I nodded and handed the oranges over to Bixel, and, like a trio of roaches, the scoundrels scurried from my office.

I leaned back in my chair and kicked my feet up on my desk. Tony's eyes flicked down as he poured some whiskey into an empty coffee cup, and when they flicked back up he saw me peeling my pilfered orange. He knew me well enough to know that I usually had a good reason for doing what I did.

I bit into the pulpy flesh of the orange; its juice ran down my chin. Tony smiled and sipped his liquor.

"Something tells me that orange ain't quite as valuable as you were making it out to be."

"I'll say. Tasty though. Want a slice?"

"I'm not much into fruit."

"Suit yourself." I tossed a small note, about the size of a business card, his way. "Read this out loud."

"*Beast Benton falls in the fourth.* Hey, ain't that the guy fighting Samson Sanders tonight?"

"That's right. And when our buddies peel the label back on that bag of oranges, they're going to find what they were expecting: a card just like this one inside a small envelope. Too bad the one they have says Sanders is the one hittin' the mat."

"Going to put some money down on Sanders?" he asked.

"I'm thinking about it."

He passed me the cup. I knocked a shot back.

"Hell, Ben, when those guys find out that you've screwed 'em—"

"Yeah, that could be a problem. That's why I told old Mrs. Twitchell to take her kid and get out of town. No matter how the cards fall, they'll be better off somewhere other than Testacy City."

"I'm more concerned with you. Small-Tooth Kelley won't be too happy that he's lost a fight on your account."

I popped the rest of the orange into my mouth, then lit up a cigar. Not a bad day's work, and it wasn't even noon.

"Don't worry about me, Tony. I'll take care of myself."

FAZE OUT

(2002)

Henry Goiler worked the fabric of his cheap brown tie until it collapsed into a sloppy knot. Frustrated, the detective jerked the tie's thin end from the tangled bunch and unraveled the whole mess. He opened and closed a fist of fat fingers in his right hand. The joints radiated a small throbbing, enough for him to shake his head in disgust.

Christ, Henry Goiler thought, *I'm not even forty, and I've got arthritis.* Normally he could ignore the pain, faze it out like it were some trivial thing, But lately, no matter what he did, he could still feel the pain pulse, tight and hard, in the back of his brain.

"What's the matter, baby?"

His eyes flicked up in the mirror and looked across the room at the slim black hooker lounging naked on the small room's bed. She smoked a cigarette with fury, as if it would be the last one she ever smoked. That was how Lucinda did everything—with fury. Not too long ago, just looking at Lu would get Goiler's engine running hot. But lately, he had trouble making it through even a brief afternoon diversion.

"You shouldn't be so tense," she said.

"Yeah? Well, I am."

The phone rang. Eyes narrowed, he looked at Lucinda. She gave him a shrug. It rang again. Who the hell would call him here? Maybe his buddy Bo Stickler had decided to give him a jingle with a little change in plans. When Goiler went boozing, he went with Stickler, and tonight he intended to booze it up hard. He reached for the phone as it rang a third time, then stopped. He flexed his chubby digits, hand hovering just above the phone.

"Ain't you gonna answer it?" Lu asked.

He shot her a malevolent glance that told her to shut up. He remembered that he hadn't told anyone where he planned to spend his lunch break, so no one, not even Bo Stickler, knew he was shaking time at the Purple Knights Motel. At least no one who didn't follow him there. Warning bells went off in his head as he grabbed the receiver and put it to his ear.

He heard giggling, then a woman's voice on the other line: "Hello."

"What do you want?" he asked.

She giggled again, then asked if she could get some champagne.

"Champagne?"

"Yeah, you know, like in those little bottles? Isn't that the complimentary champagne that comes with the fantasy suites? Can you bring some down to 254?"

"This ain't no front desk, lady." He slammed the phone down and mopped his round forehead with a dirty handkerchief.

Goiler sat down on the bed. He hunched forward, placing his forearms on his knees. "Gimme one a them cigarettes," he said.

Lu snubbed out her butt and grabbed the pack from the side table built into the padded bed frame. She crawled to him feet first and wrapped her legs around his waist from behind. She put her arms over his shoulders and shook a smoke from the wrinkled pack. She slipped the cigarette between his lips then lit it.

"You in some kind of trouble, Henry?"

"What's it to you?"

When she ran her hands front to back through his thinning hair, he lifted his head to look into the mirror he faced. She rubbed her nose along the edge of his ear without breaking eye contact with her reflection.

"It's just that you're so tense all the time these days. Always in a hurry. You used to take your time with me. . ."

She fixed his tie for him, pulling it tight—but not too tight—

against his unbuttoned top button, the way he liked it. He blew smoke at the ceiling.

The phone rang again.

He got up, knocking the hooker back across the bed like a losing lottery ticket. He shook his fingers and made a quick fist. The bones in his hand let out a popping sound. His fist opened and grabbed the phone from its cradle.

"I tol' you this ain't the front desk!"

"If you're done fooling around, Goiler, I need you to do some work," the man on the line said.

The cigarette dangling from Goiler's lips stood erect as he took a quick pull from it. He held the receiver up as he blew smoke out the corner of his mouth. "Hal, I . . . I'm ready. Gimme the lowdown."

"The only kid of some rich family has been kidnapped. The family is being blackmailed for her return. They don't want to take any chances, Henry. They're going to pay, but they want to make sure they get the kid back. They need a courier that can guarantee the job's done right. You're it."

"Yeah."

Hal Reddy, Goiler's boss at the Always Reddy Detective Agency, gave the rest of the details point by point and no more. The pickup: an address in the west hills. The briefcase: full of money. The drop: a phone booth in an isolated part of town, south of Highway 15.

"Yeah, got it. There anythin' else you want me to do?" Goiler sucked in the last drag of his smoke so close it burned the filter.

"Just the standard stuff," the boss said. "You have a problem with that, Henry?"

"No." He peered up at the mirror and saw Lucinda behind him. She hadn't even started to get dressed. She was on her back and her legs were spread open like high holy heaven.

"Say, Hal, you gonna tell me how you found me here?"

Hal Reddy had already hung up.

Goiler screamed out the window of his four-door sedan: "Come on already!"

"Yo, chill down, a'ight? I couldn't get away from the bitches."

Bo Stickler pounced onto the vinyl passenger seat and slammed the door shut as the car pulled away. Already he had both his head and his long, scrawny arms waving out the window like a tattered flag. He blew raspberries back toward his home, but no one was at the door to receive them.

"Did you do like I tol' you?"

Bo brought his body back in the car. His bloodshot eyes brimmed over with tears from the wind. He wiped them away as he said, "What's dat?"

Goiler snapped his fingers in Stickler's face. "Faze out, Stick. Faze out. When the dames realize you ain't listenin', they just give up. Then you're free."

"Got it." Stickler rubbed his hands together. "Just like that *Bugs Bunny* shit. Big cartoon grizzly come after Elmer Fudd, and his ass is down, spread out, flat on the ground. Playing possum. All nervous and shit. Goddamn that's funny, Henry."

Goiler didn't laugh.

"Yeah, that shit's funny," Stickler said to himself. "That some funny shit."

The car's engine kept a steady noise running. They passed the bar. Stickler watched as it went by like a fading memory.

"Hey, Henry, I thought we was drinking?"

"There's work to do first. See that briefcase back there?"

"Filled with cash, init?"

The detective smiled at his drinking buddy.

Goiler opened the car's ashtray and picked out a butt with still a little tobacco. A great flame jumped out of his Zippo and lit what was left of the end.

"I got smokes," Stickler said.

Goiler eyed him again. "I coulda left you the one waitin'. Picked you up all pussy-whipped and ready for drinkin'. But I figure with you with me, we do this drop, then we go huntin'."

The car's engine seemed farther away now. Its noise was no less steady. Stickler leaned against the passenger door and shot his drinking buddy a cockeyed look.

"You want to go huntin', Stick?"

Bo pulled out his Camels, took one for himself, then offered one to Henry.

* * *

Goiler carried the briefcase in his left hand in case he had to pull his gun. He walked alone down an almost empty street. Mosquitoes swam heavy in the thick air, and Goiler fanned the air around him with a frantic arm to keep them away. He hated bugs.

Before he reached the corner he got to a dusty vacant lot. Construction trailers huddled along one side. He looked up at the sun; telephone wires drooped like an old hag's tits against the yellow sky. His eyes followed them down the pole to the dented gray phone booth.

Goiler worked against the tight springs and forced the door to the side. He plopped the case to the metal floor and shook the feeling back into his left hand. The door snapped closed in his face. Searching the ground, he found a piece of broken wood and jammed it in to keep the door open. Then he walked away.

He could almost feel the eyes boring into his back. They were out there.

When Goiler turned the corner he picked up his pace, circled back, and met up with Stickler to grab a vantage point from where they could watch the phone booth.

Bo Stickler had picked up a stone and was marking time by scraping at the mortar of a building's brick exterior. Stickler thought that erosion was every man's duty.

They didn't wait long before some twenty-something with dirty strawberry hair strolled along, stepped inside the phone booth, and checked the briefcase. The cash was there, all there, so he snapped it up and started walking away.

The kid's neck kept twisting left and right as he looked for his tail. He was doing more looking than seeing. Goiler and Stickler had no problem following him down a couple streets, zigging and zagging until he got to an abandoned-looking two-story house.

This structure stood as a lost attempt at revitalizing this sad area; the house couldn't have been more than twenty years old, but already the neighborhood had repossessed it. To the left of the entrance the garage door, all crumpled and off-center, looked like it had fallen down a flight of stairs. On the other side of the front door, the picture window displayed shards of glass and bits of curtain.

Standing on the small cement porch, the kid with the suitcase looked all around one last time. He disappeared inside.

"What's the plan, Henry?"

"This ain't breakin' outta Alcatraz and it ain't no presidential election. We go in there and get what's ours."

"Don't I git a gun or nothing?" Stickler said.

Goiler paused and gave Stickler a hard once-over with his eyes before he pulled out a .22 with the handle wrapped in black electrical tape and passed it over.

"Now that's better," Stickler said. "We gonna go in there and git what's ours. And that's the shit." He stuck the gun down the front of his pants. "You know what I'm saying?"

No question. Goiler slowly twisted the doorknob. The door was unlocked. They walked straight inside.

The first thing they saw was the set of stairs in front of them; next to the stairs, a small hallway with a closed door at the far end. On the door someone had painted 9:00 in yellow.

Muffled voices whimpered and moaned from behind this door. Stickler moved toward the sound. Goiler snapped his fingers; Stickler stopped and glanced back at the detective who made a motion that they should circle around.

The small foyer they were in spilled over into a large vacant room to the left. Broken pieces of the window were embedded in the pile carpet; dirt and sand had blown in to mix with the stains on the floor.

They followed a short, tight hall from this room to a dirty empty kitchen. Beer and whiskey bottles stood on the counter like a miniature glass cityscape. Several ashtrays sat stacked in the sink.

Goiler had just walked past the cracked Formica counter that jutted out into the center of the room when he heard a scraping sound behind him. He turned and pointed his Beretta at Bo Stickler, who was opening and closing some kitchen drawers. He leaped at his friend and shoved his shoulder hard.

"What the—"

"I'm just looking fer clues, man."

"What are you, Sherlock Holmes? We don't need no damn clues!"

Stickler stared at him without humor. He wanted a drink. The sweat on his skin felt clammy, and he started to shiver. He broke off the stare and motioned his head to the next room, past the counter.

Twenty or so metal folding chairs were lined up against the far wall next to a battered door with a window that looked out at the next house over. On the floor by the counter lay several metal film reels; next to them were several shoe boxes filled with red, white, and blue poker chips.

The right wall of this room held wooden double-wide sliding doors. Goiler and Stickler didn't need to be all that close to hear the muffled voices coming from the other side.

Goiler motioned to Stickler, who took the hint and stood with his back to the wall next to the doors.

With his left hand Goiler rolled open one of the doors. It moved quickly and cleanly. He waited for the gunshots and waited to shoot back.

The only thing that shot out was the flickering light from the tiny 16mm projector in the center of the room. It was busy projecting against the wall opposite the double doors.

Stickler entered after Goiler and stood slack-jawed.

From what they could see against the thick red velvet curtain that covered the wall, the movie was an amateur stag film.

Goiler went over to the curtain and ripped it aside. It led to a recessed room with a large projector screen on the wall. A little girl was gagged and tied to a chair. She blinked through tears as pornographic actions were projected all over her. Transparent images of wet pubic hair tattooed her face like bruises; the oversized glossy red lips cut across her chest like an open wound.

The clicks and clacks of the projector now seemed louder than the whimpers and moans of the film's ugly participants.

Bo Stickler stuck his gun back in his pants and said, "Damn."

A noise from behind the door to the right side of the room made both men jump. Goiler snapped his gun arm in the direction of the door. It remained closed.

Stickler spoke up: "Yo, let's split, a'ight?"

"Stay with the girl, Stick. I'm going upstairs."

"But Henry, don't you want to go drinking?"

"Stay with the girl."

A deep breath, a crack of his knuckles, then Goiler charged through the door. He ran down the hallway until he was back in the foyer with the stairs to his right. Seeing no one here, he went up.

At the top the path split left and right. The left curled around to the back of the house; the right stood short and sweet and ended in a closed door.

Goiler smiled for the first time since he'd been in this house. Whoever took that girl downstairs was going to pay, and not because Henry Goiler felt any moral obligation to right the wrongs of the world. But because kidnappers, killers, pimps, and pushers who put themselves on the wrong side of the Always Reddy Detective Agency became his prey. And that made his engine run hot.

Then he heard the gunshot from below.

He turned to run back downstairs, but stopped. A small clicking sound caught his attention, something from the room at the end of the hall. He stomped toward it with no effort to conceal his heavy footfalls. He reached the end of the hallway, kicked the door open, and started shooting.

The red-haired kid with the briefcase didn't even have time to look up. His body jerked against the impact of the bullets; his head snapped up and down like he was agreeing that this was the end.

Henry Goiler picked up the briefcase and headed back down the stairs.

The stag film was over, and the sex sounds were replaced by the clack-clack-clack of the single spinning reel. The light from the projector flooded the scene. The girl sat twitching against the ropes, her head quivering, snot running down her nose and onto the gag still in her mouth.

At her feet, facedown, lay Bo Stickler.

"Jesus H.," Goiler muttered.

He peered across the room. A ghost-faced punk stepped gun-first out of an open closet. "Drop it! Drop the money, drop the gun, bro!"

Goiler's eyes went down to his left fist. He twisted his wrist so the bones made a popping sound.

"You're makin' me tense," Goiler said.

"I said drop—"

Bam! Bam! Bam! The sound of Goiler's gun alone would have

dropped this delinquent, but several bullets in the stomach did the job proper.

"I ain't your goddamn bro," Goiler said.

He went over to the girl and undid her gag and started untying her arms and legs. She didn't move and had no more tears left to cry.

At that moment, Bo Stickler got up and said, "Now *that* was close."

Goiler almost fell back. "What the hell?"

"Wait till you hear this one. Kid with a nine jumps outta the closet, a'ight?" Stickler said, while dusting himself off for effect. "How come we didn't check the closet? Don't ask me. So he jumps out and shoots at the Stick Man. Shot musta gone wide, I tell ya. I hit the floor. Then I went all Elmer Fudd–like and just played possum."

"I don't wanna hear another word outta you or I'll shoot you myself." Goiler picked up the gag and threw it at him. "Grab that briefcase and get back ta the car."

Stickler grabbed the case and lowered his head to look at the girl. "You watch any of that *Bugs Bunny* shit, kid?"

She pulled her legs to her chest and sank her face into her knees.

"Don't listen ta him, girl. Faze him out. Faze it all out. You'll be home soon."

He took her hand in his. It fit like a key into a lock that wouldn't turn.

"by the bells" 3-17-98: RoR

BY THE BALLS

(1998)

Chapter One
Another Miserable Day
in Testacy City

Rain clouds hung low over the flat expanse of the desert town, spewing forth torrents of water that turned the dirt-caked streets into rivers of mud. I've spent most of my life in either Testacy City, Las Vegas, or somewhere in between. Living in the desert has taught me to hate the rain. I prefer the dry air and near-constant sunshine that you normally find in the American Southwest. When it rains, trouble comes down.

The trouble started last night. I'd worked late, tracking down leads on a big jewel heist, and had come away with nothing but a name and a severe hangover. I thought I could handle my detective work better than that; hell, I thought I could handle my drinks better than that. A name, a hangover, and now I was late. And it was raining.

I climbed the steps to the offices of the Always Reddy Detective Agency, on the second floor of the William Kemmler Building at 1341 Fielding Avenue, right smack in the middle of Testacy City's business district. The newspaper I'd bought that morning, which had tried its best to shield me from the rain, was a sopping wet mess. I didn't own an umbrella; I didn't think anyone in the city did. I tossed the news in the trash as I entered the office, nodding to Rhoda Chang, the agency's gal Friday, and made my way down the hall to my corner. It was my little plot of workspace real estate, less than an office yet more than a cubicle. The place where I took calls and would hang up pictures of my wife and kids, if I had a wife and kids. I did have a wife once, but seeing her picture this morning wouldn't have helped my spirits any.

"Drake!" Hal Reddy's wrecking-ball-on-concrete voice smashed through the cluttered agency offices, finding me just as I arrived at my desk.

"Yeah?" I shouted back.

"Get in here! Now!"

Normally, I didn't like to keep the boss waiting, but I needed to take a little detour through the agency's small kitchen for a somewhat fresh cup of coffee. And with that small solace, I entered the smoky confines of Hal's office.

The boss sat behind his desk, chomping on a smoldering Antonio y Cleopatra, one of those dime-store cigars that come five to a box. He was a short, broad man with a wide nose and huge ears that stuck out at right angles from his craggy, bald head. The top half of his left ear was missing (a remnant of his days working homicide in Los Angeles back in the '60s), which made his right ear seem that much larger.

"Sit down, Drake."

He inhaled deeply from his cigar, and it sprang to life. Hal looked like a bear, and his squinty little eyes gave the impression of ignorance. But if you could hold his gaze—and few could—you'd see the cold fire of intelligence burning there.

"Know anything about bowling?" Hal asked, as he added to the volume of smoke that drifted about the office.

"Not much beyond the basics."

"The name Gentleman Joe Biggs mean anything to you?"

"No. I take it he's into bowling?"

"Not just *into* bowling; as far as Testacy City goes, he *was* bowling: PBA tour, endorsements, the whole bit."

"You said *was* . . ."

"That's right. Was. They found him dead at Penny's Lanes this morning. What's the matter with you? Don't you read the papers?" Hal punctuated this point with a deep draw on his cigar.

"Christ, give me a break! I just got in."

"Then you should get in earlier." He pointed at me with the glowing tip of his stogie.

"Come on, Hal. You didn't call me in here to bawl me out for being late. What gives?"

He took one of the many manila envelopes that littered his desk and pushed it toward me.

"I'm giving you the Biggs case."

"What? But I'm working on the Haufschmidt jewel heist."

"Yeah, I know that. Tell me how far along you are."

I winced at the thought of letting Hal down; I didn't have nearly enough to justify him keeping me on the case. I was half-tempted to lie but knew that wouldn't play with the boss. Hal was the best detective I knew. He had plenty of experience with lies—both telling them and seeing through them.

"Just got started. I did a little digging yesterday and came up with Marcel the Mangler."

"Isn't he that French jewel thief who got sent up after he strangled a street mime?"

"That's the one. The word on the street says he's in town, recently out of Leavenworth."

"You got any leads on this French fry?"

"Nope. It took me all night just to shake his name loose."

"That's what happens when you read the morning paper in the afternoon: you lose the jump shot," Hal chided. He leaned back in his chair. "I gave that case to Henry Goiler this morning."

"Goiler?"

I had nothing against Goiler, even though he was a slob and a braggart. He'd worked a couple of jobs with me, and I found him to be handy on a caper. It just rankled me that I was being replaced on a case.

"Yeah, he's already got something on Marcel," Hal explained. "Apparently, they did the cat-and-mouse a couple of years ago."

I couldn't really argue with that, plus the truth of the matter was I didn't really like the case. I didn't have a whole lot, and I'd had a rotten time getting what little I did have.

"Fair enough," I relented. "So now I've got the bowling alley butcher. What do we know?"

I flipped open the file. Except for the facts that Joe Biggs was five feet ten, 207 pounds, fifty-four years old, and dead, it was nearly empty.

"That's about it," Hal said, indicating the folder. "Biggs was found about nine this morning by the guy who cleans the place. His head was in the ball return on lane 13, smashed between two bowling balls."

"So who's our client?"

"The mother, Elizabeth Biggs. She lives at the Desert Flower Retirement Complex. The cops gave her the impression that they were more interested in running Joe's name through the mud than finding his killer."

"Any other family?"

"I hear he's got a wife. Don't know much about her. No kids. He's got a house in Victory Gardens."

Victory Gardens was a high-class suburb of Testacy City. If you lived there you were money—old or new, it didn't matter.

"So he was doing all right, huh?"

"Guess so," Hal shrugged. "Get out and interview the mother. See what she's got. Then talk to the widow."

"I'm on it."

I grabbed the sparse Biggs file and left Hal to his smoke. There's something about a new case that really gets the blood pumping. I grabbed my hat and hit the road, blowing Rhoda a kiss on the way out.

Chapter Two
The Crime Scene

A few minutes later I was navigating Testacy City's barren streets in my powder-blue '65 Galaxie 500, heading toward Penny's Lanes. I didn't necessarily agree with Hal's plan of visiting the mother first. I thought my time would be better spent at the crime scene, especially since the body was discovered only a few hours ago. I was pretty sure the mother wasn't going anywhere fast, but I couldn't say the same thing about any evidence still at the scene of the crime.

I took a left off Broadway onto Dickerson and drove past the bowling alley, slow enough to take in the details but fast enough not to raise suspicion. Just another rubbernecker. The place was crazy with cops; there were six black-and-whites parked out front and four uniforms managing the barricade.

I parked my car in the next block. The rain had slowed to a misty drizzle. It still didn't make me happy, but at least I could walk a block without getting soaked. I pulled my hat low on my forehead and started off.

It's no secret that cops and private eyes don't always get along. But this morning I didn't see any unmarked cars in front of the alley or in the parking lot of the diner next door. Without any detectives around, the direct approach might work best.

My gut feeling paid off. John McCluskey, a friend of mine in the Testacy City Police Department, was on duty outside the barricade. We go way back to my days as a fireman; his wife was a high school friend of mine.

He saw me coming. "Hey, Drake! How are ya?" He stuck out his hand. I shook it.

"Good, thanks," I lied. "How about you?"

"You know me, I'm a tiger," he countered. He pointed toward the bowling alley. "Hell of a thing for a Monday morning, huh?"

"Yeah. You got the skinny?"

"Well, first I gotta warn ya. Duke Wellington told us that no one but officers and witnesses go in."

Homicide detective Duke Wellington wasn't fond of private dicks in general and me in particular. Awhile back I took a case he'd solved and solved it right. He hadn't forgotten about it.

"He mention me by name?" I asked.

"No, but it's no secret you're included."

"That was expected, I guess. Can you at least fill me in on what went down here?"

His head swiveled on his beefy neck as he confirmed that no one was close enough to hear us talk. "You didn't hear it from me," he cautioned.

"Not a problem." I meant it.

"Okay then. The janitor, a guy named Dino, found the body at about nine. It's been here since early this morning, probably about two or three. They just removed it about fifteen minutes ago."

"What was this guy doing here at three in the morning?"

"According to Dino, the guy liked to bowl from one a.m.—when the place closes—until about three. I guess it was easier for him to concentrate on his game."

"Right," I chuckled. "I don't suppose you can look the other way for a second or two . . ."

He slowly shook his head no. "This place has a set of rear doors," he continued. "We think the killers used them to get in and out quick and quiet."

I took the hint. "Thanks, John. See ya around."

"Sure thing, Drake."

I ambled away and headed across the diner's parking lot, making my way toward the back of the alley. A couple of cops were milling around, but there were also enough parked cars to make it look like I had business being there.

I got to the back of the building and tried the double doors. Locked. Damn. As I moved away to contemplate my next move, I heard the distinctive cla-clack of a steel door opening. Out walked a mousy little guy in his late forties. He was rail thin, dressed in a denim shirt and pants, lugging a huge bag of trash. He looked like a convict. I shook the dice and took a guess that this was my man.

"Yo, Dino!" I rolled.

He turned around, jumping a couple of feet in the air. It's always good to be right. He shifted himself into a stance that suggested he might know how to deal a little damage. I was too pressed for time to try him out.

"Morning. I'm Ben Drake." I extended my hand.

He took my hand and pumped it, relief etched on his face. He seemed a little skittish.

"So whatcha want?"

"I'm a private detective." I handed him a card.

He turned it over in his hands before shoving it into his back pocket. "A PI, huh?"

"Yeah, the genuine article."

"Mebbe I can help ya."

"That's what I'm hoping," I encouraged. There's a part of every-one that wants to be a detective.

"Let's go inside where it's dry," he suggested after thinking things over. Just the invitation I was waiting for.

He led me into the eerie, industrial atmosphere of the back room. Ahead of us, down a short set of steps, row upon row of identical robots with gaping maws of steel lay silent and motionless. A narrow catwalk built atop the machines and an equally narrow walkway—little more than a crawl space—between the back wall and the machines were the only paths available to get from one side to the other. I could only imagine the noise and madness that filled the air back here when the alley was in full swing.

"Take a right here," Dino instructed, just as I was about to enter the guts of the alley.

Instead we walked past a long workbench littered with a wide variety of tools and went through another door into the part of the bowling alley that most people see. We weren't alone; a handful of forensics types and a few blues were hanging about. I tried to act inconspicuous, but a guy in a fedora and a rumpled suit is bound to attract attention sooner or later. Especially in a bowling alley.

"Mebbe I can shadow someone for ya, like in the movies?"

"Maybe." I was feeling rushed. "Tell you what I need right now, though—"

"Yeah? So I can help?" Dino interrupted.

"Yeah." I talked fast, suspecting I wouldn't have much longer. "Here's what I need you to do. In my experience, cops got a lot to do and sometimes they get sloppy. It's almost a guarantee they miss something at the crime scene. So if you see something suspicious, give me a call."

Dino looked a little disappointed. "So—"

"Aw, sweet Jesus, Mary, and Joseph, don't tell me that's Ben Drake!" a booming voice bounced off the walls, cutting Dino off. "Someone gimme a stick so as I can beat the man who let this rapscallion onto my crime scene!"

Duke Wellington was heading right at me, eyes filled with hatred. He wore a wine-colored suit with a bright green neon tie; he looked more like a pimp than a homicide detective.

He closed the thirty-foot gap between us with a few strides of his long legs. "You got no business being in this building!" He shoved a huge finger in my face. It was attached to a huge fist; a fist I'd felt once before and was not anxious to feel again.

"Easy, man. I'm just working a case, like you."

"You're working this case? You're working this case?" He was the type who liked to hear himself talk. "Now who in high holy heaven hired you?"

"You know I can't tell you that, DW. Client confidentiality and all."

Duke Wellington's dark skin began to blossom red. The muscles of his jaw jumped out from his face as he clenched his teeth. I could tell he wanted to hit me. He turned toward Dino instead. "You don't be talkin' to this guy." He gestured in my direction with a wild waving of his arms. "You find anything, you talk to me, Duke Wellington! Got it?"

"Yeah, but . . ." Dino started.

"But nothin'! I'm the guy you talk to, understand? I am the guy."

"Yeah, yeah. No problem," Dino caved.

"Good," Duke Wellington purred before his attention swung back my way. "You get outta here."

"Come on. I've gotta earn my paycheck," I pleaded. I didn't think it would get me too far.

"O'Neal!" Duke Wellington shouted toward one of the uniformed cops. "This guy seems to be lost. Help him find the way out."

A brawny cop with a cruel mouth headed toward me, drawing his baton and gesturing my way. "Let's go, buddy," he ordered.

I shrugged at Dino and began the trek toward the front door. O'Neal marched behind me, prodding me with his stick.

On the way out I heard Duke Wellington giving Dino the third degree. Wellington was a good detective; he had a keen sense of deductive reasoning. But that's only one thing a detective needs. What he lacked was people skills. You can do all the deductive reasoning you want, but it'll get you nothing if people won't talk to you. I didn't mind that Wellington had kicked me off the scene; I got what I came for. I had a man on the inside.

"Now beat it, tough guy," O'Neal commanded when we reached the front door.

I walked the block back to my car, stopping at the diner for a cup of coffee to go. It was just about noon, and I was feeling good about my progress, especially after the dead end I'd hit last night.

I hadn't had a cigar all morning, so I pulled out a tin of J. Cortès Grand Luxes. These aren't big stogies; they're quite small, close to the size of cigarettes. I never seem to have enough time to finish off a nice Churchill, so these do the trick.

I fired up a smoke, then I fired up my car and headed out to see my client, Elizabeth Biggs.

Chapter Three
The Grieving Mother

The Desert Flower Retirement Complex was a pensioner's community a stone's throw north of the city. I wasn't really looking forward to this interview. I didn't expect Elizabeth Biggs to be able to tell me much about her son's death, and it's never any fun dealing with relatives of the recently dead.

The sparse traffic on the road made my drive go quickly, and before long I pulled into the barren gravel lot and parked my car. It didn't look like this place got too many visitors. I opened my car door, then paused and sat for a moment, pulling out my cigars. I contemplated smoking one but decided against it, realizing I was stalling. I began a slow walk to the gated entrance, the gravel of the lot crunching under my shoes.

I went through a door underneath a small tin sign that told me it was the office. I was alone. On the right, a couple of lonely padded benches rested below a paint-by-numbers flower picture. Straight ahead, a short hallway opened into a large room filled with ill-arranged furniture and a small television against the far wall. To my left, the office proper reminded me of a dentist's waiting room. Above the narrow counter was a pair of sliding glass windows, beyond which was a small room with desk and chair. But no receptionist.

I waited a moment, the silence antiseptic around me. Losing patience, I slapped the metal bell that sat on the ledge. Its tinny sound seemed too loud in the emptiness.

Sooner than I thought, but not as soon as I would have liked, the door on the opposite side of the small office opened and a plump woman wearing a gray nurse's outfit and too much hairspray stumbled in. She looked annoyed.

"Yes?" She glared at me as she smoothed the wrinkles in her skirt.

"I'm Ben Drake, a private detective." I pressed my card to the glass. "I'm looking for Elizabeth Biggs."

"Oh, this must be about her son?" It was a statement, but she turned it into a question.

"Yes, that's right. Where can I find her?"

She bent over the desk and consulted a long list of names that lived under the clear blotter. "Uhhh, she's in D-109." More smoothing.

I waited to see if she'd give me directions. It seemed that was too much to ask. I started to doubt this woman's ability to help the elderly. "And where can I find that?"

"Go out the door there," she said, indicating the door I came in. "Take a right, and it's the third building on your left."

"Thanks."

I turned to leave. She stopped me.

"By the way, there's no smoking in the Desert Flower Retirement Complex, sir."

"I'm not smoking."

She flashed me a smile that wasn't a smile. "Just for your information."

I flashed back. "Right. Thanks." I turned again. This time I got out.

I followed my friend's directions and took a right down the path. I knew I was going to have a little trouble. The crooked trail ran around and between the eight buildings that randomly littered the courtyard. I couldn't tell which building was the third on my left, and I sure wasn't going back to ask for directions again, so I forged ahead.

The courtyard was a regular Garden of Eden. A variety of well-tended plants and trees grew along the curving path, filling the air with a not unpleasant fragrance. Some would have called it serene. Others would have described it as pastoral. To me, it was just a confounding maze. Occasionally, I bumped into an elderly Adam or Eve, wandering about as if they were on a mission to wander.

I'd been wandering for a while myself, when I noticed a big *F* on the building in front of me. I turned around, retraced my steps, and it wasn't long before I was pushing the button labeled *109* at the front door of the D building. An old woman's voice crackled through the small speaker.

"Who is it?"

"It's Ben Drake, ma'am. I'm from the Always Reddy Detective Agency."

"Oh, I'm glad you found me. Hold on a second." I waited until the buzzer sounded to let me in.

Her room was easier to find. I knocked on the door.

"Who is it?"

"It's still Ben Drake, ma'am."

"Oh, come in."

I grasped the doorknob. It resisted my attempt to turn it. "Ah, could you unlock the door, please?"

A moment passed before the door opened. "I'm sorry, this horrible business has me in a state."

Elizabeth Biggs was a small, white-haired woman, but she was far from frail. She wore a navy cardigan over a conservative white blouse and tan slacks. On her feet were a pair of orthopedic shoes, the type nurses wear. Although her smile beamed brightly under her sapphire-blue eyes, it didn't hide the pain.

"No problem, ma'am. Can I come in?"

"Oh, yes. I'm sorry. I've forgotten my manners. I just put on a new pot of coffee." She gestured toward the kitchen. "Could I offer you a cup?"

Apparently she hadn't forgotten them for long. I accepted.

She switched off the television and told me to take a seat on the sofa, which filled most of the small living room. The opposite wall was nothing short of a shrine to Gentleman Joe, with numerous portraits of him at various ages, pictures of him in action, and pictures of him brandishing trophies large and small.

There was something missing, though, and I couldn't quite put my finger on it.

My thoughts were interrupted when Elizabeth brought in a tray holding two steaming cups of coffee along with a pitcher of cream and a bowl of sugar. She placed her burden, appropriately, on the coffee table and sat down next to me.

"Now what did you want to ask me, Mr. Drake?"

I selected my cup and began with the basics: "I know the police came by earlier—"

"Those hooligans!"

Judging from that, I guessed it was Duke Wellington who had paid her the visit. "Yeah, the police don't know how to treat a lady. What'd they say to you?"

"Only the most terse and uncouth comments about Joey."

"Such as?"

"They wanted me to believe he was into bad things like gambling . . ." She paused and made a face as if she had just eaten something disagreeable. "And drugs."

"We know that isn't true." I did my best to sound matter-of-fact.

"Absolutely not. He was a perfect gentleman. I raised him myself, you know. Ever since my husband Barry passed away. He's the one who taught my Joey to bowl."

"Did Joe have a lot of friends?" Somehow I couldn't bring myself to call him Joey.

"Friends? Sure. Everybody was Joey's friend . . ."

I sensed she wasn't quite finished talking, so I took a sip from my cup. It was a pause I regretted; she started to cry. It made me feel like leaving, but I knew I had to stay.

I got up and grabbed a couple of tissues from the box on the end table. As she took them, she struggled to compose herself.

"Thank you. He really was a good man. He was all I had."

"Did you see him often?"

"All the time. He came by and spent some time with me every day."

"So you were close, then?"

"Oh yes. I raised him, you know. Barry, Joey's father, died when Joey was only ten. That's how he got into bowling."

"You said that Barry taught Joe how to bowl."

"That's right. But Barry, God rest his soul, was not that good. Not that he was bad, he just wasn't good enough to bowl professionally. After he died, Joey practiced real hard every day. He was a natural, they said. He got on the pro circuit when he was nineteen—the youngest bowler ever on the tour. And he won. I was so proud of him. And I know Barry was too."

As interesting as this was, I had to get to the heart of the matter. I needed to know if Joe had any enemies. I started to transition with the old standard: "I know this is a hard time for you and his widow . . ."

Without warning, the soft warmth of Elizabeth's face grew hard and cold—looked like that was the wrong thing to say. Then it hit me. I realized what was bothering me about the Joe Biggs photo gallery: no pictures of him with his wife—nor any other woman for that matter. Maybe it was the right thing to say after all.

"Ooooh! I don't like her." Elizabeth's voice was filled with hatred now. "She's such a spiteful woman. I've known plenty of women like her before, always looking for something for nothing. And she's the type who always gets what she wants.

"I used to live with Joey—until he married that fast-moving hussy," she continued. "They got married two years ago, and she moved in with us. She didn't like having me around, so she told Joey it was either me or her, and Joey stuck me here. Not that I blame him. He was in love. We do such stupid things for love."

I told her I couldn't argue with her.

"You talk to that girl, Mr. Drake." It wasn't a request. "If I were a gambling woman, I'd bet good money she had something to do with Joey's death."

"I plan to do that later today, Mrs. Biggs," I assured her. "Look, I'd best be going. I have a few things to do before I talk to her."

"Oh, won't you stay just a little longer? There's more coffee . . ."

I glanced at my watch. I did have a little time to kill. And the coffee was good. Damn good. "All right. I'll have another cup."

She smiled, delighted, and took the cup from me as she hurried into the kitchen. Any trace of her anger over Suzi Biggs had disappeared with my decision to stay. And I found myself feeling good about that.

"Let me show you some pictures, Benny," she invited when she returned with my coffee. Only two people called me Benny, my grandmother and my wife. Both were dead. It was hard to take, but if I was going to let anyone call me Benny, it would be Elizabeth Biggs.

After showing me all the framed photos of Joe, she started in on the photo albums. We were halfway through the second album before I'd finished the pot of coffee, and it was time for me to go. It was still a fight to get out the door, and I felt a small pang of guilt about leaving.

I wound my way back through the courtyard, lighting a cigar as I got to my car. Then I headed back into town. Like I'd told Elizabeth, I had a few errands to run before I took on the widow Biggs.

Chapter Four
In the Cutting Room

Eventually my errands took me to the county morgue, a facility that smelled like stale cigarettes and dead bodies. Laid out in front of me on an aluminum autopsy table was the lifeless body of Gentleman Joe Biggs. His broad chest was neatly stitched with the traditional post-autopsy "Y." His head was deformed, with a strange, oblong appearance and eyes that popped out, giving him a permanent expression of cartoon-like, eternal surprise.

My tour guide was Testacy City's medical examiner, Rebecca Hortzbach, a woman of academic beauty, the type of girl you find attractive but are afraid to approach. A bob of red hair framed her pale, lightly freckled face. Over her bright green eyes she wore pointed glasses that accentuated her already feline appearance. A lit cigarette was almost always dangling from her mouth—even when she talked. Today was no exception.

"The proximate and immediate cause of death was extreme trauma to the head," she explained, indicating Biggs's misshapen skull. "And I mean *extreme* trauma to the head."

Rebecca wiped her hands on her white lab coat and sucked in a lungful of smoke. "In layman's terms, his head was crushed between two bowling balls. I'd say sixteen pounders."

She had an uncanny eye for detail. She had solved more cases for the TCPD by simply looking at the crime scene than they'd care to admit. The police often referred to her as the crazy cat lady, as much for her curiosity as for her appearance. It was not meant as a compliment. Although I didn't care for the nickname, I had to admit she was a little freaky. There was something about a cute gal who likes cutting up dead bodies that gave me the willies.

She was also a collector of conspiracies and arcane facts. Every time I visited, she launched into some crazy theory. My last time here, she told me the story of how, in 1933, the US government made a secret deal with the Illuminati to bring the country out of the Depression. In exchange for their aid, the Illuminati demanded their thirteen-story pyramid appear on the reverse of the new dollar bills. She went on to say that this pyramid represents the impending destruction of the Church and the establishment of a one-world government in its place.

"Any questions?" she asked.

By the look of his corpse, Biggs kept himself in pretty good shape. It would have been quite a task to wrestle him down and stave in his head with a pair of bowling balls. It made me wonder: "Was he drugged?"

"Toxicology shows no drugs or alcohol in his system. The guy was in excellent health. Hell, when I cut him open, his lungs were bright pink." The cigarette between her lips bobbed and danced as she spoke. "You normally only see that in kids."

"So, he just lay there while they cracked his head open?" I asked, hoping for her take on the murder. I got it.

"Probably not. Here's how it went down. This contusion," she lifted what remained of Biggs's head and pointed at a black-and-blue spot at the base of his skull, "is the result of him getting whacked from behind by a blackjack. My guess is that someone kept his attention while a second guy came up from behind and brained him.

"Then while he was down, they bound his hands behind his back and propped him in the ball return. Look here." She indicated Biggs's wrists. "You can see ligature marks from where he was tied. I found fibers of common household twine embedded there."

"Seems like a lot of trouble to go through to rub a guy out," I offered.

"Maybe not," she postulated. "My guess is that he knew something our perps needed to know, otherwise why tie him up? When he came to, they grilled him again. He still wouldn't cave, so smash!" She slammed her hands together. "They caved him."

I nodded. It was a good hypothesis. I had the how, now I just had to find the who and the why.

"Do you want to see the crime scene photos?" she invited.

"Sure."

Although I didn't expect them to show me anything I didn't already know, I followed her into her office. She handed me a folder that contained numerous black-and-white snapshots of Gentleman Joe at the crime scene taken from a variety of angles. It was a grisly sight. Biggs's head lay in the ball return, a single black bowling ball on either side. His body was stretched out, arms tied behind him, with something—I guessed a small stool—supporting his back. Blood was spattered everywhere. The ball return track and the top third of Biggs's bowling shirt were dark with blood. His pants were undone, revealing a pair of boxers, complete with cartoon bowling pins emblazoned upon them. For some reason, this disturbed me more than the manner of his death.

"Why are his pants undone?"

"That happens with a lot of dead bodies." She finished her cigarette and ground its remains into an overflowing ashtray. "Mainly men."

"No kidding. Why would that be?" I asked, a mix of dread and anticipation in my voice.

"I don't know for sure, but here's my theory." She lit another cigarette. "It's a red herring. There's this long-standing tradition among more accomplished criminals to throw off medical examiners by introducing a bit of absurdity to the crime."

"Come on," I doubted as I joined her in a smoke. I had to get the smell of death out of my nostrils. "You can't expect me to believe that."

"Believe what you want," she dismissed with a wave of her hand, "but it's true. This goes back to the 1800s when forensic science was not so exact, and it was easier to throw a pathologist off the right track."

She looked at her watch. "Say, Drake, you wanna grab some dinner? I haven't eaten all day."

I liked Rebecca. A lot. She was funny, intelligent, attractive—everything a guy like me looks for in a girl . . . if I were looking.

"I'll take a rain check," I responded truthfully, holding out for a meal that didn't happen right after I'd seen a dead body. "I've got to see the mourning widow before it gets too late."

"Next time, then." A smile of disappointment.

"Next time," I promised. I sent her a smile of encouragement, tipped my hat, and left, footsteps echoing hollowly off the walls.

I exited into the chill evening air, feeling a little depressed. I'd never be caught dead in cartoon boxer shorts.

Chapter Five
The Mourning Widow

Victory Gardens is all money. Looking around at the houses, you'll see either modern opulence punctuated with an occasional Victorian quaintness or monuments to old money updated here and there with the best of contemporary detail. It all boils down to how you were raised and what you're expecting. Me, I was expecting a bowler's house and a bowler's widow. When I navigated the car past the carved stone entranceway of Victory Gardens, I knew I was in for some surprises.

I pulled up to 300 Pine Lane and exhaled the last breath of smoke from my tiny cured cigar. The smoke formed lingering swirls in my car as I turned off the ignition and rolled up the window. Something made me want to stay there one moment longer. I sat looking at the façade of the Biggses' residence until I instinctively grabbed for another smoke, then I knew my moment was over. So I brushed off my lapels, got out of the car, and headed up the walkway to meet Mrs. Biggs.

Next to its neighbors, the Biggs house looked small and old—someone involved in real estate might say cozy, though I was sticking to small and old. If I were forced to be poetic, I'd have said it was like a gingerbread house. But thankfully, no one was forcing me.

I cringed a bit when I saw the *Beware of dogs* sign, dogs being the scourge of mailman and detective alike. And even though the rain had stopped, it was still plenty wet. Just thinking of wet dogs made me cringe again.

At the front door, I pushed a small pearl-colored button. A low two-tone gong sounded, as if even the doorbell were grieving. I heard the yipping of dogs: small dogs, the kind you can kick if they get in your way. When I had begun debating whether to endure the doorbell again or simply pound on the door, the locks clicked and the door opened. And there stood Mrs. Suzi Biggs.

"Hello," she said, wearing a skimpy red negligee meant to barely cover her, and doing a good job of it. "Can I help you?"

"Yes, probably you can."

I could detect the lust in the air, but that had nothing to do with the fact that I'm a good detective and everything to do with the fact that I'm a man. When it comes to emotional distress, there's nothing like a mourning widow. And let me tell you, Suzi Biggs was *nothing* like a mourning widow. She was more like a morning window. I could see right through her.

"I'm Benjamin Drake of the Always Reddy Detective Agency. I'd like to speak with you about your husband's death."

"You mean murder!"

"Yeah, that's what I mean."

"Well, come on in. Don't mind the dogs. They're friendly." Then, more for my benefit than for the dogs, she commanded, "Laza! Apsos! Settle down, you two! This man's here to help us." Back to me. "You *are* here to help, right?"

"Sure."

I set my hat on a tiny table near the door, then she led me into the main living room, the damn dogs nipping at my heels. We sat down in a pair of matching red leather armchairs. I tried to stay focused despite the number of trinkets, trophies, and other bowling knickknacks scattered about the room—and despite her skimpy red negligee.

Before I could start my questions, she came at me with: "So, how can I help you, Ben—that's your name, right?"

"What do you know about murder, Mrs. Biggs?"

"Only what I read in the novels," she giggled, and turned coyly away with a hand to her smile.

I didn't know if she was trying to be cute or if she was tipsy. I knew she'd been drinking; I could smell the faint tang of alcohol in the room.

"By the way, you can call me Suzi." She stopped talking and looked around the big colonial-style living room, her smile fading into melancholy. I noticed her gaze stop on a portrait of Joe over the fireplace. Her mood changed quickly and melodramatically. "And of course, I know my husband was murdered."

"Of course. Know anybody who'd want him that way?"

"If you're asking me if I know who killed him, the answer, Ben, is no. This wouldn't be a detective story if I knew who the killer was."

I hadn't wanted the questions to start out antagonistic, but since we were already warming up with the verbal fisticuffs, I tried this combo: "Funny, when I talked with his mother, she said you—"

"Don't even tell me she said I did it!" Suzi was on her feet, her pink-nailed fingers rubbing her temples. "That bitch!"

"Hold on, young lady. Don't get all excited and start jumping to conclusions. Now, it's no secret how you gals feel about each other. Why don't you give me the Suzi Biggs side of the story."

"I'm sorry for acting like that. Ben, she makes me crazy. And it's her who doesn't like me; I don't have a problem with her other than that." She was already heading for the liquor cabinet when she turned this trick: "If you want us to have a real discussion, you're gonna have to drink with me."

"Not going to argue with that."

"What do you want?"

"Old Grand-Dad, if you've got it."

She threw me a look that said try again. Before I could, she asked, "Is that some kind of brandy?" How did I forget she was twenty-four?

"Ah, it's bourbon. Do you have any bourbon?"

Her laughter kept me company while she worked the drinks. She brought over a goddamn water glass full of hooch. Looked like she was going to shoot tequila. Brave. And it could play to my advantage.

"So, why doesn't the old lady like you?" I started in again.

"You must not be a very good detective if you can't figure that one out. I'm . . . what some people would say . . . 'significantly younger' than Joe. Mama Biggs couldn't understand our love. She thought it was all about his money."

"But it was really true love?"

She downed her second shot, still managing to pause long enough to make me suspect.

"Well, yeah. When I met Joe, I never thought I'd fall for a bowler. But he really was a gentleman. He really paid attention to me, treated me like I was some kind of important person." Her eyes were drifting off. She was getting full of drama again.

"I believe you, Suzi," I lied. "Just one more question."

I took a long pull off the bourbon, giving her time to have more of the Mexican poison. She seemed to enjoy my attempt at conversational tension.

"Can you think of anyone else, besides Joe's mother, who may have been unhappy about your marriage? An old flame, maybe?"

"Nobody." She hung on that word as she licked the lime juice off the tips of her fingers, seemingly lost in thought.

Liquor makes people either talkative or unreasonably quiet. It was clear what camp we were in. I wasn't going to get any answers, and until I had more of an angle, I didn't really have any more questions. I took my last swallow of bourbon, set the glass down, and said, "Well, Suzi, I just have one favor to ask: may I use your bathroom?"

She escorted me to the first-floor bathroom. True enough, I had to use it; but over the years, I'd found that you could learn a lot about a person by using their john.

Here was the layout: deep-basin sink, round mirror above, standard head, no shower, hardwood floor, mauve throw rugs, matching mauve hand towel, lots of plants. The thing that most caught my attention was a framed photo of Gentleman Joe wearing nothing but a Speedo. He was striking a weight lifter's pose in the midst of an array of fallen bowling pins. Cute.

Before I flushed, I figured I'd try something. With one hand on the door to steady it, I slowly, silently turned the knob with the other. When I got the door open, I could hear Suzi's voice. Stretching my neck to catch a glimpse of the scene, I saw her motioning to someone I couldn't see. Her hushed voice seemed to be telling this mysterious third party to stay put.

Now that I had a clue, I slipped the door back into place, flushed, then audibly opened the door. When I reentered the room, Suzi looked as if nothing were going on; in fact, too much so.

"Are you done with me, Ben?"

Her smile was playful, almost enticing; paradoxically, her body language exhibited the most modesty I'd seen since my arrival. She stood legs crossed, elbows pinned inward, trying in vain to cover herself, or at least giving the illusion of caring to. This girl knew her game.

"I'm done asking you questions, for now." I turned to the door and retrieved my hat. Then, giving her the game right back, I said, "You know, it's not a good idea being alone at a time like this. Maybe you should call somebody, like a mother or a sister."

"Why, Ben, that's awful sweet of you to think about my needs like that. Oh, but my mama's dead, and I'm an only child. I'll be all right. I . . . I can call you if I have any problems?"

"Of course you can. I hope you do . . . if you have any problems, I mean." I handed her my card, and then I was out.

The bourbon made me want to smoke, but for whatever reason I didn't feel like burning the tobacco in the Biggs house. I've got a deep-down respect for the fairer sex. Sure, she wasn't playing straight with me. But in this business it doesn't take long to realize that nobody tells the truth, at least not all the time.

I would have plenty of opportunity to smoke in the car, because my next move was crystal clear. It was Suzi who made a passing joke about this being a detective story, and as it goes in all good detective stories, it was now time to stake out the widow's house to see what might develop. Especially considering she most definitely had a mysterious visitor.

My small cigar had not even reached its end when out from Suzi's door came yet another clue: a young chap, tall, clean-cut, and good-looking. He was wearing a checkered button-down shirt opened in front with a white T-shirt underneath. What most caught my attention were the nice pair of black-and-white saddle shoes. You can't tell whether to trust somebody based only on his shoes—though this was one fella I wasn't trusting; still, you gotta like a guy with a fancy set of soles.

He kept twisting his head left and right, looking like he was trying to spot someone—probably me. I'd have to be extra careful shadowing him. If I could let him get out of Victory Gardens without him picking up on my tail, I'd have him.

When we were both on the open road, I knew I was out of his mind. One of the Ben Drake rules of shadowing is not to be overly focused on your target; it's too easy to show your hand. I eased back just enough and peered up over the road. The Testacy City sun was setting low in the sky. It made the sand swirling off the plains glow red like neon dust.

The moment we hit the city, I had that strange feeling of knowing where we were going. I'd be damned if we weren't headed right back to the bowling alley. Good ol' Penny's Lanes.

Chapter Six
Jerry Goes Bowling

When I entered the bowling alley, the low rumble of rolling balls and the crash of falling pins immediately overwhelmed me. Some twangy country-western music played in the background. Lane 13, with its lights off, was noticeably vacant. Maudlin bowlers had piled dozens of colorful bouquets at the foul line. I guess everyone did love Gentleman Joe.

Our man went over to a locker and pulled out his own ball and shoes. I was still new to this bowling stuff, but my keen detective skills were telling me that this guy was a serious bowler.

The last thing I wanted to do was stand around in a bowling alley. I already stuck out like a hitchhiker's thumb. I figured this would be a good time to ask around, get the lowdown on the scene.

I walked past an effeminate shoeshine boy. He called out to me, "Shine, mister?"

I looked for the guy I'd tailed here from the Biggs house. He was just hitting the lanes; he wasn't going anywhere soon. I climbed up into the chair.

"Wow. Nice shoes, mister," he said with a mischievous smile across his young, light-brown face.

"Thanks. You can call me Ben."

"Okay, Mr. Ben."

"What's your name?"

"Enrico."

"Pleased to meet you, Enrico." I lowered my voice just enough to match his mischievousness, though not low enough to sound suspicious. "Say, who knows the score around this place?"

He looked up at me as he snapped his rag over my shoes. "There's lotsa scores here, Mr. Ben. Everyone's got a score."

I pulled out a twenty and set it on the chair next to me. "I'm thinking of a guy who might know the big score. You know who holds that scorecard?"

The twenty disappeared in a flash.

"You might wanna go talk to Mr. Spence." Enrico was glancing over behind the shoe rental booth at a solemn-faced man in a sharp, black leather cap, the kind with the snap on the front brim that's left unsnapped. "Mr. Spence Nelson. He's the guy that gives out the ugly shoes."

I looked again and saw this particular fellow heading for the bar. Enrico saw me giving the guy the eyeball. He nodded that I'd spotted the right Mr. Spence, then added a little twitch of his eyebrows to make sure we were on the same page.

It's always good to attack in one's natural element. So I climbed out of the chair and set my course to the bar.

"Thanks, my man. Nice job on the shoes. How much?" He gave me a price of three bucks. I gave him a five.

On my way to rendezvous with Mr. Spence, I made a visual check on our friend from Suzi's. He was knocking back his second Budweiser. I don't know jack about bowling technique, but I know plenty about anger. Here was a guy trying to blow off some steam.

Just then a cute little brunette number in a tight sweater and short skirt came over to him and started with the conversation. It was pretty clear they didn't know each other. When it was clear that they were going to get to know each other, I moved along.

The bowling alley bars I remember from my childhood in Las Vegas were not like this beauty: At the Penny's Lanes bar, dim lights reflected cooly off the burgundy leather covering the high-backed curved booths. Smoke hung around in the upper corners. The bar counter had a cushion along its edge wrapped in the same well-worn leather. That edge snaked around the room at random angles, making the bar top look like a dancer's stage at a strip club.

Behind the old lady working the bar were rows and rows of bottles with the prices written on them in black felt-tip. Possibly the best part of the whole scene was the scarcity of drinkers. The joint was almost empty except for some lush in the back corner, Spence Nelson, another guy with him, and me.

Luckily, this Spence character hadn't ordered a drink yet. Buying a fellow a drink is a great ice breaker as long as you have something to follow it up with. He had just finished talking with the other guy. Neither of them looked like he belonged in a bowling alley. When Spence turned to pony up to the bar, I was in the stool next to him.

"If you're Spence Nelson, I was told I should buy you a drink."

"If I were this Spence Nelson, I would think that I would like to know who this stranger is that so freely offers me a drink."

"I'll give it to you straight. My name's Benjamin Drake, and I'm a PI. I'm working the Biggs murder. I've been through the standard Q&A regarding this scene. Now I'm looking for more stimulating conversation that might bring up some points that wouldn't normally show up on a crime report. You want that drink?"

That little old lady bartender was waiting for our order. I told her to bring me three fingers of Old Grand-Dad. Then I glanced over at the man I was hoping could give me some answers.

"I will have a Zima."

A grin broke loose on my face, and knowing that I wasn't hiding it, I decided to ride him a bit: "You actually like that stuff?"

"Yes, I do like that stuff. But more than liking it, I admire it. Zima has character, admittedly a much maligned character, but that is part of the charm it holds for me."

I offered him one of my cigars. He declined, pulling out a beat-up pack of Lucky Strikes from his blue jeans pocket. He was quick with a book of matches. After he lit his cigarette, he held out the flame for me.

"I will tell you some things, Drake." He paused to take a leisurely drag. "But first you must tell me something."

"What kind of something?"

"Oh, anything. I can judge a fellow by the quality of story he tells. I am not necessarily looking for information that would be perceived as useful. I am through with useful information. I have a PhD in genetics from Tulane, if you can believe that. Now I am interested in the mundane."

I gazed at him incredulously. "You have a PhD in genetics and you work in a bowling alley?"

"Your first lesson from me: the currently accepted lingo is 'bowling center.' Many people now believe 'bowling alley' to have a negative connotation, as in back alley or dirty alley. As for genetics . . ." This time he paused to drink. "Genetics is a dead end. I procure much more enjoyment from the renting of shoes to eager bowlers; though I, myself, am not a bowler."

This was one Zima drinker I could drink with. Though he hadn't provided me with anything but entertainment yet. I discreetly tipped my glass toward the guy I was tailing.

"Let me ask you, Spence, do you know that bowler—"

"You have not given me my requisite piece of trivia. Tell me something, and I will answer your questions."

"All right, here's your bit." I took a moment to gather my thoughts, then I laid this on him: "Four years ago I was on a case involving a man named M.N. Fallaby. His wife hired me because she suspected him of having another woman on the side. Story she gave me had him spending several nights away from their nest with no reason or explanation given. So I tailed him. He was a small, bookish man. Funniest thing, he acted like he knew he was being followed, though it was not as if he was going to shake me. I followed him to his nighttime destination. And do you know who the mysterious other woman turned out to be?"

Spence Nelson's small eyes, like black marbles floating in heavy cream, stared right through me. "There was no other woman," he guessed.

"Right. He was alone at the public library of all places. After I watched him pore through books for close to two hours, I went over to talk to him. Flat out I asked, 'What are you doing?' I fingered him as the type that, given a reason and enough time, would be able to come up with a yarn to try and throw me off. But if I hit him dead-on, he'd let the soup spill, beans and all.

"Turns out he was an amateur ornithologist and was trying to formulate a theory for the flocking patterns of birds. He was eager to talk. Any of the paranoia I noticed earlier was gone, or at least well hidden, possibly under his slight stutter.

"So after we had been chatting it up, after he brought up how much he loved his wife, I gave him the line on her hiring me to sniff out an affair. I put the question to him: 'Why not just tell her the truth?' I'll never forget his response: 'I am a . . . weak man. And for there . . . to be danger, there . . . can be no weakness. And for . . . there to be beauty, there must be . . . danger. It's better if my . . . wife suspects me, just enough to thrill her, not . . . enough for her to leave. It's the best . . . the best way for the . . . relationship I'm trying to develop to . . . bloom.' Of course, I assumed he meant his marriage. Thinking back after the case had been filed away, I can't help wondering if maybe he meant his relationship to birds."

I turned away to keep my eye on the dope I was following in the here and now. He was still playing with the brunette. She had her hands all over him.

"Bravo, Mr. Drake!"

Nelson had relaxed his posture now that my story was done. It was his turn to talk. I helped him along.

"Did you know Gentleman Joe?"

"Indeed, I did. A better question would be who in this place did not know Gentleman Joe." Realizing that I was looking for more than a yes or no, Nelson understood my silence and continued. "He was one rich bowler."

"Really?"

"The man was loaded. Of course, I place that in the respective context of other bowlers."

"How about his wife?"

A slow, dismissive laughter came out of Nelson's mouth, following a lungful of smoke from his Lucky Strike. "His wife is nothing but a bowling groupie who married."

"There are bowling groupies?"

Before he answered, Nelson turned his head toward the couple I was watching. The guy's game looked like it was improving; he had just thrown a strike. His lady friend bounced up and down, clapping her tiny white hands in quick bursts.

"Why not? I could present you with an extended social theory, but suffice to say, if you take a group with a shared, specialized interest—add to that money and fame, however relative—you'll find individuals trying to sleep their way up the perceived ladder, like salmon swimming upstream."

"I was asking you about that guy over there, the one bowling with the brunette."

"That would be one Jerry Iverson. He was Gentleman Joe's protégé. A fine bowler with a skill level that comes from more than nightly practice; skill like that, my friend, is genetic. And as you can witness, he is popular with the ladies too."

"Joe have any other friends? Any non-bowling friends? You know what I'm getting at—anybody you think'd want him dead?"

"There is nothing, except for the certainty that he is, in fact, dead, that would suggest somebody would want to do him wrong. Gentleman Joe had an enormous number of friends. People loved him—especially women." Spence smiled a testosterone smile. "He treated them nicely; that is how he got his nickname. Non-bowlers, though, I don't know. He was known to patronize Van Winkle's when he was not at Penny's Lanes."

"The bar over on Cosgrove?" I'd never been there.

"Yes, a lot of bowlers drink there."

A swarthy-looking man came conspicuously into the bar and gave Spence Nelson the eye. Spence nodded, almost imperceptibly.

"Now, Mr. Drake, I must take my leave. Business calls."

It was pretty clear he wasn't talking about the business of renting shoes to bowlers. Whatever bad business he was in, it wasn't my concern. At least not yet.

"No problem. Thanks for your time."

There was no need for me to get up. I had a good view of Jerry from this stool, and he was still throwing balls with the babe.

Spence made a final comment while scratching the little patch of hair growing below his bottom lip: "That was a good story you told. Were you to ever need some more questions answered, I would be happy to let you buy me another Zima."

I took my time finishing my drink. Things seemed to be progressing for Jerry. After what I figured were about three games, he and his young bowling groupie—I was still amused by the concept—headed for the exit together. I wasn't far behind.

Their trail led to an apartment complex on the west side of Testacy City. Jerry parked the car in a convenient space right in front. The couple hastened up the cement steps to the building's main entrance. They groped at each other, their smiles acknowledging the awkward glee of the moment. I sat in my car and watched. I was old enough to roll my eyes at their youthful display of lust, but young enough to feel a pang of envy.

An hour passed. My watch said it was only eleven p.m. In contrast to the last case I'd tackled—it was hard to believe that was just the night before—this one held promise. Though I didn't have a lot of details, it was more than I started with, and the getting was easy.

I wanted to celebrate. The drumming of my fingers on the steering wheel got me thinking about my next move. I had just enough liquor in me to want some more. And I knew the place to go.

A call to the Always Reddy Detective Agency from the pay phone on the corner got me a stand-in op. They were sending me Mike Manetti. Truth being the truth, Manetti's not very smart, he's not a helluva good detective, and I don't like the way he dresses. He's okay to have around when you have to rough up a few birds, but when it comes to sitting and waiting, he can't always cut it. Unfortunately, I didn't have time to be picky. Besides, my gut told me that Iverson was in for the evening, and I needed a set of eyes to prove me right. Looked like Mikey would be the big winner.

Soon, but not soon enough, Manetti's El Camino rolled up to the curb. Under the light of the streetlamp I could make out that he was wearing a grubby T-shirt and dirty jeans. Not really an issue when all you're doing is watching a door all night. Nevertheless, it lacked style.

I filled him in on the situation, told him to watch apartment 3G—I'd picked up the number from the registry at the front of the building—and let him know I'd be back in the morning, before six a.m. He assured me he had it under control, so I left him to his task and got into my car.

Like a moth, I followed the light of the moon. I knew it would lead me to Van Winkle's.

Chapter Seven
What Van Winkle Knows

Van Winkle's was a small, dark bar on a small, dark street. Over the heavy wood door hung a burned-out neon sign of a bearded man asleep with his back against the stem of a martini glass. A neon *Open* sign blazed in the plate glass window. I squinted to get a glimpse inside, but I could only make out a vague sense of movement.

I pulled the door open and entered a crowded, noisy room filled with the bluish haze of smoke and the strains of Sammy Davis Jr.'s voice in the background. Thirsty patrons clogged the long bar on the left side of the room. On the wall behind the bar, a collection of bowling fliers and pictures covered every non-mirrored surface. A little shelf overflowed with trophies, and a pair of beat-up, red-and-blue bowling shoes hung over the antique cash register.

The right side of the narrow room featured a number of small booths occupied by what I'd come to recognize as the bowling type and their groupies.

Intermixed with the typical alcohol advertisements were a number of old-style paintings of Rip van Winkle. In many he slept under a tree while a group of dwarves cavorted in the background, playing a game of ninepins. In others he played a little ninepins himself.

I felt the heat of a hundred eyes as the door slammed behind me.

I licked my lips and approached the bar. The bartender did his best to ignore me. He finally got the hint I wasn't going anywhere and moved my way. Maybe it was the twenty in my fist.

"Help ya?" He looked at me as if to ask what I was doing there.

"Bourbon. Old Grand-Dad."

A chuckle. "Don't have it."

Damn. "Jim Beam?"

"Don't got that either."

What kind of place was this? "What do you have in the way of bourbon?"

"Only one bourbon here. Van Winkle's."

"Okay," I grinned, the absurdity cracking my composure. "Give me three fingers, straight."

He went away and came back with the smallest three fingers of bourbon I'd ever seen. And I'd seen plenty. When he told me what I owed him I thought I should have asked for fewer fingers.

"Kind of pricey."

"I don't set the prices." He took my cash and headed off again. He poured a few more drinks before I got my change.

I thought I'd throw a few questions at him. "Did you know Gentleman Joe?"

"Sure. Everyone here did."

"How often did he come in?"

"Couple times a week. Sometimes more, sometimes less."

"He drink with anyone in particular?"

A sigh. "Look, man, I'm just paid to pour drinks. You want answers, you gotta talk to the boss."

"Yeah? Where can I find him?"

"In the back booth." He jerked his thumb over his shoulder as he popped the cap off a Bud. "That's where you can always find him."

I glanced toward the back of the tavern. "Pretty crowded back there. Who am I looking for?"

"Walter Wilson. He's a little guy."

"Thanks."

I left the guy a tip and made my way through the packed club. It was a nice crowd; no one went out of their way to let me by. At the back of the bar, ten people crowded around a large table, listening to a raw-throated voice scratch out a story. All of the listeners were typical of the bowling type I'd been spending time around today. All of them, that is, but one. She was a blond bombshell, the kind you see in the movies. Her skin was too perfect. Underneath her flowing blond hair she had large, ruby-red lips over unbelievably white teeth and blue eyes that held a vacant stare. She wore a black sleeveless top that showed off her ample bosom and a short, black skirt that showed off her alabaster legs.

The storyteller sat in her lap, a hood ornament to the blonde's mannequin. He was a hatchet-faced midget, his dyed-black hair, slick with pomade, combed straight back over his skull. His ears were large and grew so close to his head they seemed pinned together from behind. His right hand was missing its thumb and forefinger. I figured this guy for Walter. He talked fast and gesticulated wildly, keeping his audience enraptured as he spun his yarn. I lit a cigar, determining that I came in somewhere about the middle of the story.

". . . So Dvorkin steps up to the line, ball in hand. He pauses and looks down the lane. A full set of pins waits for his smoke gray–pearl OutRage. He'd just bowled eleven strikes in a row. If he got this strike, he'd have a 300 game. But remember, so far Reado had bowled a perfect game too, and was riding high with nine strikes."

He paused while he surveyed his audience.

"And Reado was the better bowler. Dvorkin began his approach. It was perfect, right down to his follow-through. The ball made a beautiful curve and hugged the right side of the lane, kissing the lip of the gutter. At just the right moment it swung to the left and hit the head pin in that sweet spot. Pins went flying . . . and when the table dropped, there was nothing left for it to pick up."

Walter stopped for a dramatic sip of beer. The entire table followed suit. This Walter had juice.

"It was a 300 game, but Dvorkin only got a smattering of applause." Another sip, the blonde kissed the top of his head, then he resumed. "Now it was Reado's tenth frame. The crowd cheered wildly. He stepped up to the return, rolled his shoulders, and crossed himself—he was quite religious, y'know."

Everyone around the table nodded. They knew.

"He hefted his ball and focused somewhere beyond the pins. Reado had been bowling for a long time, and it was mostly reflex for him. His first ball of the tenth was a solid strike. He turned and bowed to the crowd as they cheered. He wiped his hands, then his ball, and did a quick pray before he quickly rolled another strike—his eleventh. One more strike and it was a tie game.

"Now the way the bet was set up," Walter explained, "the odds were stacked against Dvorkin. If the game was a tie Reado still won. Dvorkin had complained about that, but that's what happens when you challenge a champ.

"Even though Reado was good, he was still worried. He waited for his ball to come up the return, drying the sweat off his hand with the blower. He wiped his face and hands, then his ball. Once more he crossed himself and stepped up to the line, his fire-red Primal Rage in his hand. He stood a long time, just staring down the lane. When he moved, it was sudden. The ball was out of his hand, headed toward the pins with his trademark arc. It hit dead on; he threw the ball with a lot of spin so he always got great pin action. This time was no exception; those pins were flying every which way—"

"He missed it, didn't he?" one chubby-faced guy blurted out.

Walter pinned him with a steely eye. "You telling this story, Larry?"

"No, no, Walter," Larry apologized, hands in front of him defensively. "I just got excited, that's all."

"Yeah, well, you keep your mouth shut." Walter scanned the crowd for any other excitable types. "Now, where was I?"

"Great pin action, baby," the blonde got him back on track.

"That's right, that's right. Thanks, sugarplum." He paused, taking a moment to recreate the tension that had built up before the interruption. "Those pins were flying every which way, a strike for sure. We all thought it. Everyone was up, cheering, screaming Reado's name. But someone—I don't remember who—shouted, 'Look!' and pointed down the lane.

"And suddenly everyone stopped cheering. There was dead silence. There wasn't a pin standing; not a whole pin anyway. The seven pin had split in two—right down the middle—and only half of it was up. I swear to God. Everyone in the place just stared. Well, they had to get the judges in on this one, and they ruled that Reado had bowled not a 300 as everyone expected—but a 299 and a half." Walter finished his beer in one gulp, slamming the empty mug on the table. The slightest smirk colored his face. The story was over.

"I don't believe it!" Larry cried out, looking around for supporters. He found none.

"Too bad, tough guy"—Walter's face was getting a little red—"because that's just how Diamond Dan Reado lost the bet and fell from grace. No one's heard from him since."

Before this Larry could get himself in more trouble, I walked up and tossed a few business cards on the table and introduced myself. "You Walter?"

"Yeah, an' this is my joint. What can I do for ya?"

"I'm looking into the Biggs murder." I had the attention of everyone in the place now. It was just me and Sammy singin'. "Wondering if I might ask you a few questions."

"Shoot," he answered, leaning back against his flesh pillows, throwing his feet up on the table. He was wearing the tiniest bowling shoes I'd ever seen.

"How about we talk alone?"

"These here are all my friends. Anything you got to say to me can be said in front of them."

I knew I had to stir up a little trouble. "Why would anyone want to kill a bowler?" I got blank stares as an answer. I tried again, turning up the heat. "Gentleman Joe was into drugs, wasn't he?"

"You better watch your step, *dick*."

"I'm just saying that he was chock-full of drugs when he died." I heard a few chairs scrape back as angry bowlers got up behind me.

"Now don't be lyin' here, we know Gentleman Joe was clean," Walter cautioned.

"I was at the morgue. I read the autopsy report." Now it was my turn to pause for effect. "He was loaded."

Action exploded around me. I was hit from all sides by bowlers defending the honor of one of their own. Fists clubbed my kidneys and plowed into my gut. A set of knuckles slammed into my jaw, bringing with it the tang of blood. It was a good punch. It sent me reeling backward into the bar, where I knocked over a couple of stools and scrambled to gain my footing. Everything went into slow motion. Through hazy vision I saw an angry mob approaching.

My hand had just found comfort in the butt of my Smith & Wesson when I heard a voice shout out, "All right, you bunch of jamooks! This is no place for a row!"

The crowd turned to look at Walter Wilson standing crimson-faced on top of the table.

"Get back to drinking, or get the hell out!" Walter commanded, his little hands balled into fists.

The crowd reluctantly obeyed. When he saw that the violence was over, Walter jumped to the ground and walked over to me.

"Are you soft in the head or somethin'? I want you outta here!"

"Okay." I rubbed my jaw where I'd been socked. "But I still have to clear up a few points."

A stream of obscenities spouted from Walter. "All right! I'll talk with ya outside, but none of this nonsense about Joe bein' dirty."

"Fair enough."

We went out the back door—the path to the front being too hostile. Once outside, I didn't waste any time showing this little guy I meant business.

"Okay, Walter, Joe was clean. That's the problem. He was too clean. In fact, that whole bowling alley is."

"So you've been there?"

"Yeah."

"You meet Spence Nelson?"

"Well, now that you mention it, I got the feeling he dealt in a few illicit things on the side."

"A few? That boy's got a regular drugstore set up in the men's room! Anything you want, he'll get it. A lot of the boys carry for him. He wanted Joe to help out, but Joe wouldn't bite. And he's only the beginning of the trouble at Penny's Lanes."

"You mean the bowling alley is a center for crime?"

"No, I mean the bowling *center* is a center for crime." He held up his three-fingered right hand. "Believe me, I know."

I nodded.

"Now you get outta here!" Walter shouted. "And steer clear of Van Winkle's."

That sounded like good advice to me. I hit the road.

* * *

I cruised to the nearest pay phone and called the office, leaving a message for Rhoda Chang to check on the records of Gentleman Joe Biggs, Jerry Iverson, Spence Nelson, and Walter Wilson. Hopefully I'd have a little reading to do in the morning.

Rhoda was Always Reddy's best source for hard-to-get information. Although the agency kept pretty extensive records that were shared with other detective agencies across the country, we didn't have everything. Sometimes we needed police records; when that happened Rhoda magically delivered. We didn't know what her private life was like, and we didn't ask questions.

I hung up and eased on home. My adrenaline surge was wearing off into a somber melancholy, making the pain of my short but thorough beating harder to ignore.

Soon enough, I climbed the steps to my apartment, a small one-bedroom number in a low-profile part of town. No one bothered me here. I flipped open the lock and out of habit took a quick survey; everything seemed to be in place.

I headed straight for the bathroom, where I dressed my wounds and swallowed a couple of vitamins. Then I made a stop in the kitchen to swallow a little Old Grand-Dad before I plopped down in my favorite chair. The table to my right held a banker's lamp and the book I'd been reading: Immanuel Kant's *Groundwork of the Metaphysics of Morals*. The older I got, the more I came to appreciate simple reason, pure deduction, optimistic enlightenment. That's some of what I got out of reading Kant.

I grew up reading science fiction, mostly, although I took to anything I could get my hands on. Included in that lot were plenty of so-called modern writers. I used to be keen on ambiguity and uncertainty, used to think that life's problems were giant structures that required dismantling. Of course, when you tear apart a structure, the discarded pieces pile up and form other structures. That's a fancy way of saying that when you focus your attention on one problem, others creep up around you.

I realized this after my wife died. I was a firefighter back then. One night I was going up against a particularly nasty burning building. We thought we had everybody out, but a hysterical woman was crying for her baby. Well, I'm a sucker for a woman in tears. Out of some sense of duty, I reentered the inferno. Eventually I found the little girl. She lived.

That night, that building—it was the longest I ever worked a single fire. The boys were calling me a hero. I just wanted to go home. I'd play big-shot hero fireman tomorrow after I got some rest.

The police intercepted me at my front door. My wife's mangled body was at the morgue. She'd been smashed to pieces in a car crash. The police phrased it more tactfully, but not by much.

I was supposed to have met her for dinner at some restaurant, but she knew I was on duty, and when I didn't show up, she had headed home. Often I wonder: if I hadn't gone searching for the little girl, if I had let her die, would I have been able to be at the restaurant in time to save my wife?

The answer was probably not to be found in Kant. But his cold, convoluted language soothed my mind, like the post-national anthem static following a long day of television programming. And my mind, my body, my whole person needed rest.

After all, I planned to be back at Jerry's early. I cracked open the book and read until I drifted off into unconsciousness.

Chapter Eight
Sleeping in the Nude

My eyes snapped open just after six thirty on Tuesday morning. I cursed under my breath; I'd wanted to be back at Jerry's by now. I splashed some cold water on my face, ran a comb across my head, threw on a fresh shirt and tie, grabbed my hat, and hurried out the door.

About thirty minutes later, after stopping for two cups of coffee to go, I pulled my car into a spot a few spaces behind Manetti's El Camino.

I knew I'd find him sleeping. It took two hard raps on his window to pull him out of his slumber. He sat up fast and, though he'd never admit it, scared. He fumbled with the big automatic sitting in his lap before he noticed me.

Relief flooded his face. "Drake!"

"Sleeping on the job, Mike?"

"No way, man. I was just resting my eyes."

"Uh-huh." Idiot. "Fill me in."

He got out of his car, yawned, and stretched like he was in his bedroom.

"The chippie left by six. I figured you wanted me to keep an eye on . . ." He stopped talking, noticing the pair of steaming coffee cups resting on the hood of his car. "Aw, Drake, thanks!"

He reached for a cup, but I stepped in his way. His brow furrowed. My actions were too much for his intellect.

"It's not for you, Mike."

"What? You gonna drink both of 'em?"

"I could, but I'm not going to. One's for me, the other's for Iverson."

"You got the pigeon some joe but nothin' for your man Mike?"

"It's like this," I sighed. "I'm going up there to play a little game of good cop–bad cop with Iverson. I might have to get rough, and that'll make me the bad guy. The coffee," I pointed at the twin cups, "will be the good guy."

He didn't understand, but I didn't really expect him to. I told him to go home and get some sleep. He hopped into his car and sped off, tires screeching as he turned the corner.

I trudged up two flights of stairs and stopped in front of the door marked 3G. I set the coffee on the railing behind me and pulled a black leather wallet out of the inside pocket of my coat. I sized up the lock, selected the right lockpicks, and got to work. I wasn't an expert at this, but I was no slouch either. In about five minutes I had the satisfaction of feeling the tumblers roll into place. I grabbed the coffee and slid into the apartment.

A typical bachelor pad, a little fancier than most. The living room was sizable, with a huge entertainment center against the far wall. Above it was a wide shelf holding five trophies. Framed bowling posters hung on the other walls. The clothes Jerry was wearing the night before, including those slick saddle shoes, were strewn about the floor.

I set the coffee on the counter that divided the living room from the kitchen and made my way down the hall, past a set of sliding doors that opened onto a balcony, until I reached Jerry's bedroom.

The door was wide open. Jerry was sleeping on his king-size bed, wrapped around a bowling-themed comforter. He was totally nude.

I bent down, lifted the mattress, and flipped it over. I drew my gun. I carry a Smith & Wesson Model 637. It only holds five rounds, but it's easy to hide and, at this range, has plenty of stopping power.

Getting tipped on his can woke Jerry right up. He sprang to his feet, fighting mad. He extricated himself from the unwieldy mattress and brought his fists up into boxing position. He made a move to attack, but seeing my gun made him back off. Then he realized his goods were hanging out in front of God and everybody, and his attack completely fell apart. The red of embarrassment spread across his face.

"Morning, Jer," I greeted cheerfully. "I brought you a cup of coffee."

"What gives?" he asked, covering his privates with his hands. "Who are you?"

"Let's go to the living room and have a chat." I made an "after you" gesture with my free hand. "After all, that's where the coffee is."

"At least let me put on a pair of pants first," he whined.

"There's a pair in the other room."

The friendly gesture didn't work, so I waved him out with my gun. This time he obeyed.

"Y'know, I used to sleep naked until I started doing detective work," I explained. "Now I wear boxers, at the very least, when I sleep. Sure, it's not as natural, but that way when someone busts into my house in the middle of the night, I'm not too embarrassed to deal with it. Trust me, you feel much more manly if you're wearing pants."

When we got to the living room, Jerry climbed into his jeans and sat down on his ugly gray-green couch. I brought him his coffee and took mine over to a comfortable leather recliner. I kept my Smith & Wesson in plain sight; you never can tell when a guy might decide to fight.

He took a sip of coffee. "I'm pretty sure you're not here to rip me off—"

"Many crooks bring you coffee?"

"No, but I don't get many friends busting in at seven thirty either," he snapped back. "And you still haven't told me who you are."

"Ben Drake, PI." I sent a card flying in his direction. "I'm investigating the death of Gentleman Joe Biggs."

"Oh," he answered before he took another sip of coffee. "It's a damn shame."

"What can you tell me about it?"

"I don't know nothing but what's in the news."

"I understand you knew him well," I prodded.

"Yeah, he was like a big brother to me. He taught me everything I know about the game. But that don't mean I killed him!"

He was getting defensive and that didn't do me any good. I needed Jerry to be free with his speech.

"Relax, Jerry. No one's pointing the finger at you." I strategically sipped my coffee. "Know who might want to see him rubbed out?"

Jerry shook his head. "Everyone loved Joe. I can't imagine who might want him dead."

So far all these conversations had been pretty much the same. Everyone loved Joe, no one wanted him killed. Well, I had news for these people: someone did. I thought I'd try the male-bonding approach.

"Cute girl you were playing with last night. See her often?"

"No, that was the first time . . . probably the last."

"So you don't have a steady girl?"

"What's it matter? They're all the same." He dismissed women with a wave of his hand and a gulp of coffee.

"Same as Suzi Biggs?"

"Joe's wife?" His eyes popped wide, incredulous.

"You know another Suzi Biggs?"

"Guess I only know one Suzi Biggs," he confessed. "I'm just wondering why you'd bring her up."

"I don't think you're that dumb, Jerry, and don't make the mistake of thinking that I am," I cautioned.

"Whatever." What I assumed to be his everyday bravado was slowly creeping into the conversation. I was hoping this know-it-all attitude would make him careless.

"She and Joe get along?" I sipped from the Styrofoam cup.

"Sure. Joe really loved her, y'know. She was his first wife, and he just adored her. I don't know if she felt exactly the same way, though."

"Why do you think that?"

"I got my reasons."

"Share 'em with me," I coaxed.

He paused, thinking it over before he started. "Joe was always kind of self-absorbed. The guy slept, ate, and breathed bowling. And he was always nice to the ladies, but when it came to relationships, they always took second place to bowling . . . and his mom."

He paused and took in another dose of caffeine. "Sometimes people have other needs, y'know?"

"Are you telling me Suzi was fooling around on Joe?"

"All I know is she's been trying to get into my pants for . . . seems like years."

"But you didn't go for it?"

"Don't get me wrong, I like the ladies." He puffed up his chest like a rooster. "It's just that I couldn't sleep with Joe's woman. I always figured she was half-joking. Besides, it wouldn't have been doing right by him. Anybody else's wife, sure. But not Joe's."

"When's the last time you saw—"

"Joe? Sunday night at the center," he answered fast.

"Actually, I was going to ask about Suzi. When's the last time you saw her?"

"Man, I don't know. I don't keep a datebook. Couple of days ago?"

"You're lying to me, Jerry. I know you were at her house last night." He looked to the floor and muttered, "Man . . ."

"What were you doing there?"

"I just wanted to see if she needed anything. Y'know, after Joe's death."

"Uh-huh. Fight about anything?"

"Fight? Why would we fight?" The faintest line of sweat beaded his brow.

"I was hoping you could tell me."

Jerry glanced away, out across his balcony. He answered without looking at me. "Nope. We didn't fight about a thing. I just wanted to see if she needed anything."

"Did she?"

"No . . ." His voice trailed off.

I sensed he had something else to say, so I let the quiet sound of the waking neighborhood fill the apartment.

After a few moments, Jerry looked over at me. "So, you wanna find out who killed Joe?"

"That's why I'm here."

"You might wanna check out Jack Walker," he whispered.

The name sounded familiar, but I couldn't quite place it. "Who's that? Some bowler?"

"C'mon, everyone in Testacy City knows who Jack Walker is."

"You mean the ball bearing guy?"

A bit of a local celebrity, Jack Walker was the head of Walker

Industrial, Testacy City's sole big industry which manufactured ball bearings.

"Yeah, the ball bearing guy."

I laughed. The idea was ludicrous. "That's the best you can do, Jerry?"

"No, really, man, I'm giving it to ya straight," Jerry insisted.

"What do you know that would connect him to this?" I was still skeptical.

"Couple of years back, he and Suzi used to be an item. He bought her all sorts of fancy things, told her he'd leave his wife for her, but never got around to it. Suzi got bored with him and hooked up with Joe. Walker never really could let her go, though, and he's been trying to get her back ever since. Joe didn't know about it. Hell, no one knew about it."

"Then how'd you find out?"

"Suzi told me, man."

"Why?"

"She trusts me. We're pretty close in age, we like the same music. We get along."

I got out of the recliner and slid the Smith & Wesson back into its hiding place.

"All right, Jerry, go back to bed," I said, backing out of the apartment. "And for chrissakes, put on a pair of boxers."

As I walked down the steps I had to wonder about Jerry. I didn't believe everything he told me. And I think Suzi Biggs left some things out of her story as well. Something between these two was missing.

Jerry's bit about Jack Walker intrigued me, though. No one really knew Walker, except for what the magazines and papers reported about him. Everything printed told of a guy who was a pillar of the community: good family man, contributor to local charities, member of the Knights of Columbus. Not the kind of image that immediately brings to mind adultery. But now that the idea had been forged, it seemed fairly believable. Definitely worth checking out.

First things first. My stomach, which had only had booze and coffee since yesterday morning, was telling me it needed something a little more substantial. I headed down the block toward the diner on the corner for a spot of breakfast.

Chapter Nine
Lunch in the Commissary

I dropped some silver into the metal box outside of Hopper's Diner, and took out a copy of the *Testacy City Herald-Tribune*. My eye caught the Biggs headline on page one. I'd have time to digest it once I'd put some food past my teeth.

Inside Hopper's I grabbed a counter seat. I was barely situated when a young, gum-chewing doll with pink lipstick placed a coffee mug in front of me. I nodded toward it. She poured.

I opened the newspaper, searched for the page with the crossword puzzle, and refolded the paper into a manageable shape, like I was doing some oversized origami. Completing a crossword puzzle always brought me a healthy dose of joy. Easy puzzles helped warm up the mental muscle, and the *Herald-Tribune*'s were never very difficult. This morning's topic: entertainment.

The waitress was back. I noticed her name badge said *Dierdre*.

"Dierdre. That's a pretty name," I told her.

"Thanks. It's the only one I got. You ready?" She had her ballpoint aimed at her pad.

"Steak and eggs, please."

"How you want them?"

"Well-done for both. Eggs fried over hard. Tell the cook I don't mind if they're crispy."

"I'll tell him."

I let the facts that I had about the Biggs case wrestle themselves in my noggin while I occupied my lesser faculties on this joke of a puzzle.

It was hard for me to be distracted by the crossword today. Jack Walker's name kept ringing between my ears, and the more I thought about it, the more I believed Jerry's story. It's hard to get that big and powerful without getting dirty—especially in this city. Testacy City was corrupt all right. It took the place left vacant by the old Vegas once the strip became some sick family entertainment complex.

Going up against Jack Walker wouldn't be easy. Getting information out of him would be like springing a guy from Sing-Sing—while not completely impossible, I didn't want to do it.

Dierdre brought me my plate of breakfast and topped off my coffee. I asked her if she knew an eight-letter word for hairless.

"How about 'balding'?"

"That's only seven letters."

"Then I guess I don't know." She cocked her head in the direction of the kitchen. "Hey, Emil! Word for hairless. Eight letters." She peered back at me. "What's it begin with?"

Caught off-guard and slightly perplexed, I glanced back at the puzzle. "Ah, the letter *g*."

"Begins with *g*!" she shouted to the cook.

A funny, guttural sound came from the kitchen: "Glabrous!"

I stared at the waitress. She made a loud snapping sound with her gum. "He knows everything. Go ahead, ask him something else. His name is Emil."

I figured it was worth a try. "Hey, Emil, you know who killed that bowler, Gentleman Joe Biggs?"

A funny, guttural sound came from the kitchen: "No!"

Several comments came to my mind, but I let them stay there. Dierdre had already gone off to wait on somebody else. I dug into my breakfast, not wanting it to get cold.

After breakfast I went to the office. One of the worst things about being a private eye is having to get up early. That doesn't fit well with my habit of staying up late. Some mornings I wish I had a nine-to-five. But then I'd need to shower in the morning. This way I can wait until the afternoon. It's a good way to break up the day.

On my desk I found reports on Joe, Jerry, Spence, and Walter.

Joe was clean as a whistle. That matched everything I had heard, guessed, or already found out about him.

Jerry was slightly dirty: shoplifting, minor drug possession, driving without a license, disorderly conduct—that sort of thing. This Iverson character was a walking, talking misdemeanor. These petty crimes either belied some larger offense that he was just waiting to get caught at or served testament to a sloppy life. Either way, I wasn't done keeping my eye on Jerry.

Spence's record had a playlist of possession charges. Looked like the dirt I got from Walter was dead on. Though I was certain drugs didn't play in this murder, that didn't mean Spence and I were through with each other yet.

Walter, surprisingly, only had a drunk-and-disorderly beef on file from his younger days. That was flat-out no help.

I put the last file down on my desk, then looked up at the clock. It was nine thirty. Time to call Mr. Walker.

I dialed the main number to Walker Industrial. I got an operator who, when I asked for Mr. Walker, transferred me immediately. That meant I was going to be dealing with his assistant.

Sure enough, a perky non-Jack Walker voice picked up the line.

"Jack Walker, please."

"I'm sorry, Mr. Walker is busy. May I take a message?"

"I think he'll want to talk to me."

"Who's calling?"

"Benjamin Drake. I'm a private investigator. I'd like a few moments of Mr. Walker's time to—"

"Hold on." Her sigh, barely discernible, started to drift my way before the line cut off, and I found myself listening to the soothing sounds of Testacy City's Light FM. I would have expected—and preferred—a classical station. Adult contemporary never made me happy. I'd use that unhappiness to my advantage.

The assistant returned. "No, I'm sorry, he's all booked up."

"Well, never mind. I just wanted to congratulate him on keeping his name out of the papers—you know, with Suzi Biggs's husband dead and all. Wish him good luck in the future for me." I paused just long enough to see if she'd take the bait. She did.

"Oh, he just finished his meeting. Ah, hold on a moment." She returned me to the "easy listening" music. There was nothing easy about it. Thankfully, she came back quickly. "We can fit you in today at noon."

"Great! Are we going to have lunch at the commissary?"

"No sir. Twelve in his office."

Too bad, I thought, I'd always heard the Walker Industrial commissary was top-notch. "Noon it is, then." I made the receptionist happy by hanging up.

I got down to a little paperwork. I heard a door slam, reminding me that Hal Reddy was always here. I was tempted to give him the lowdown on what I'd found so far, especially since the last time we spoke I'd had to admit that I came up short on my previous case. But I knew he'd knock me down a couple rungs by asking me if all my information added up to knowing who the killer was. I'd have to admit no. Letting him know all I had were a few leads wasn't worth that. It certainly wasn't worth enduring the stench of his cheap cigars.

Paperwork got dull, and I found myself at Elizabeth Biggs's place with a bag of eclairs.

"Hello, Benny! I was just frying up some Jimmy Dean. Can I get you some?"

Oh, brother. I declined the sausage, since I'd already had breakfast; I didn't mind helping myself to an eclair, though.

I was there to fill her in, but felt a little strange. A bunch of information had fallen my way since we last spoke, though none of it amounted to an answer. I settled on the simple truth—that I was making good progress.

She had been watching television and invited me to join her. We watched one of those daytime talk shows that the nighttime talk show hosts often make fun of. Now I knew why.

As casually as possible, I asked her about Jerry Iverson. She told me he was like a kid brother to Joe.

"Is he helping you out, dear?"

Iverson was helping me out all right. It was clear she didn't know anything about him and Suzi; if she had, I'd have heard it.

She kept deflecting my questions, either offering me coffee, asking if I was getting enough sleep, or remembering trivial anecdotes from her life raising Joe.

I wondered aloud if Jerry had been to see her.

"No, he hasn't. But so many nice people have sent me cards and flowers. I'm sure his is among them. Would you like to see all the lovely cards they sent me?"

I went through the cards. She was right, they were lovely.

The morning was slipping away from me. I wanted to stop home and run some water over my body before I had my encounter with Jack Walker. I knew Elizabeth wouldn't mind if I used her phone, and I'd save time if I could call the office to check my messages.

Rhoda told me that Dino from the bowling alley had called a couple of times saying he had something that might help me out. I instructed her to tell him that I'd stop by the alley as soon as I could.

I didn't have time at that particular moment. After all, I didn't want to keep Mr. Walker waiting.

Chapter Ten
Mr. Walker

I was sitting in a high-backed leather chair, and I would've been comfortable if not for the two muscles from India standing on either side of Walker's mahogany desk. I knew they were Jack's bodyguards, but to me, they were pure punishment in suits.

The room was silent.

Jack Walker knew how to keep his distance. My chair sat a good ten feet from his desk, and the desk itself was a generous three feet deep.

Behind this distance loomed the curly haired presence of a man with power. He wore no glasses. His face was clean-shaven, exposing his strong rock of a jaw. His affluent lifestyle provided him with a youthful vigor. It was impossible for me to determine his age, but I remembered reading somewhere that he was in his fifties.

The smoke from the pipe he held between his clenched teeth gave the air a rich, woodsy smell. Maintaining the silence, he leaned back in his chair. Through the smoke, his eyes were fixed on me—eyes that were deep-set below thick tufts of black eyebrows. Unable to resist the urge, I fidgeted slightly.

He knew what he was doing, and just as I was about to break this verbal standoff, he spoke.

"Is there something I can do for you . . . Drake, wasn't it?"

"That depends." I hoped that by speaking slowly I could mask my uneasiness. "Depends on what you know about bowling. And it depends on where you were early Monday morning, between one and nine a.m."

"Look around you, Drake. Do you think I'm a man who goes anywhere or does anything without a paper trail?" He made a new cloud of smoke with his pipe; a thin, distinct line rose from its bowl. "I can tell you I wasn't bowling."

"Nobody thinks you were bowling."

"And what do people think I was doing? Oh, excuse me—what do *you* think I was doing? Let's cut to the chase so I can throw you out of here."

I leaned forward in my chair. "All right, here it is: having an affair with a girl whose husband shows up dead—that doesn't look too good, Jack."

Not the kind who ruffled easily, he took the accusation in stride. I was more concerned with how his two heavyweights would take it. The expressions on their brown, sandstone faces remained frozen in permanent snarls. They were practically twins: both wore dark suits with purple sashes around their waists like cummerbunds, and both had the hair growing off their chins greased into traditional upturned Jheri curls. I half-expected them to have scimitars hidden somewhere.

"Your proof, Drake? I notice you're not here with the police."

"I'll get proof when I need it. And if you think you keep such a clean trail, then how'd I find out about Suzi, smart guy?"

I eyed the two pairs of Indian fists. Clenched, they looked like jackhammers.

Walker was still playing with me when he asked, "Please do tell me, how *did* you find out?"

"Uh-uh, that's a secret. I'll be in touch."

He waved his hand dismissively. "Get him out of here." He leaned forward to write something on a legal pad. Without looking up he added, "Butch and Schultz will show you to the front."

The Indian muscles moved like robots. I got up before they could grab me.

They came with me as I rode the elevator down to the garage, one standing on either side of me. It was a tight fit. I had no idea which one was Butch and which one was Schultz. I was tempted to ask them about their decidedly non-Indian names. I decided against it, having caused enough trouble here.

Driving away from the Walker Industrial offices, I didn't have much time to think about my encounter with Jack Walker, because I soon noticed a black Lincoln (my guess: Butch and Schultz) doing a rather sad job of following me. Apparently, I was not going to be so easily dismissed.

I had some fun trying to shake them, but even with their sloppy driving, they managed to stay with me. I could excuse the bad driving; the poor tailing technique was another matter. Obviously, these guys needed a little crash course in the Ben Drake rules of shadowing.

I started to lead them into the maze-like streets of Testacy City's west-side hills. Before I got there, the fuel gauge caught my eye: the needle was just kissing the E. The last thing I wanted was to run out of gas on some residential street. I decided to try a different approach. Lepke's was right up ahead. I figured I'd grab a bite, maybe get one of the waitresses to set up a distraction for whoever was tailing me, then bolt out of there.

More important, though, Jack hadn't bought me lunch. And that left me mighty hungry.

When I turned into the parking lot, the Lincoln quickened its approach. I scurried to get to the entrance, and the big car nearly smashed through the front door in a successful attempt to intercept me. Simultaneously, Butch and Schultz erupted from the car and started toward me. As big as the car was, it seemed too small to hold both of them. I hadn't expected them to make a play for me, especially in broad daylight.

"What's shaking, guys?" I began walking slowly backward. This was going to be ugly.

"Mr. Walker's got a lot of affairs that are very delicate, affairs that a guy like you could really mess up," one of them said, cracking his knuckles. "We're here to make sure you don't do anything stupid."

With speed I hadn't expected from their enormous size, one thug walloped me but good in the stomach. Then, out of some violent sense of balance, the other one knuckled me as well with a heavy punch upside the head, right behind my left ear. This second blow brought me to my knees, breathless. My head got all soft-fuzzy, and a high-pitched wail began sounding from somewhere deep in my brainpan.

"Consider this an advance on a beating to come," a coarse voice rumbled.

When my eyes regained their focus, I looked up to find the gorillas' car speeding away behind a thick cloud of desert dust. It was then that I realized the ringing in my ears was really the droning of a police siren.

I managed to pull myself to my feet just in time to greet the squad car that pulled up beside me. I waved the cops on, hoping they got the message I was okay. They didn't. Two boys in blue jumped out, ready for action. Too bad all the action here was finished.

"All right, buddy, you're coming with us," the taller of the two said.

I looked around, then laughed, even though it hurt.

Chapter Eleven
Police Interview

The only thing I could get out of the jokers at the police station was that Duke Wellington wanted to talk to me. Already, I'd been in the holding room for close to two hours. Various officers occasionally brought me Styrofoam cups of what passed for coffee along with a promise that they'd be right with me. It all left a bad taste in my mouth.

Finally, a cop I knew came to see me. Mark Weisnecki, a tall, mustachioed lunkhead of a detective who had the pleasure of being Duke Wellington's partner. I trusted precious few of the police in this town, and Weisnecki was no exception. But at least he was easier to talk to than Wellington.

"Sorry about this, Ben."

"Don't be. Just tell me what the hell this is all about. Better yet, tell me when I get to leave!" Raising my voice brought back the pain in my head.

"The main man wants to ask you some questions," Weisnecki said, apologetically.

"That's no good, and you know it. I want some answers."

The door flew open, banging loudly against the wall behind it. "I'll give you answers!" Duke Wellington stormed in, waving his arms, not stopping until he was inches from my face. He was in a dark gray suit, maroon shirt, and a silver tie. The smell of musk pushed its way toward me.

He continued yelling at me: "You want answers? Fast and furious, I'll give you answers, answers with big question marks at the end of them! How about this answer: what in God's good name are you doin' messing around with Jack Walker?"

"Who?"

I was tired and beat, but I always had a bit of extra energy available to yank this guy's chain.

Weisnecki intercepted, "Ben, don't give him a hard time and then expect us to cooperate with you."

I snapped back at him: "I don't want you to cooperate with me!"

Duke Wellington was pacing the room. He grabbed a chair, pulled it over to where I was sitting. He spun it around and straddled it backward.

"Okay, Drake, let me break it down for you." He rolled his head on his shoulders as if he were warming up for some exercise. Motioning to Weisnecki with his chin, he said, "Mark, break it down for him."

Mark did. "It's like this, Ben. We've been trailing you since you left Iverson's. We know you met with Walker. We know his goons were trailing you."

"Do you know who killed Gentleman Joe Biggs?" I had little patience left.

"No," Weisnecki blurted out.

"Then the truth is you want *me* to cooperate with *you*. Well, I got news for you and DW: I'm not a cop. I don't get paid to help you out, and I'll be damned if I'm going to do it for free."

Duke Wellington's loud mouth went off again: "Are you asking for a payoff, you dirty little—"

"Come on," I said. "This is entrapment!"

Weisnecki continued what he was trying to say: "We know Walker's goons were trailing you. You must have had something pretty irksome to say to him. How about telling us what you were doing at Jack Walker's office and what bit of information you gave him?"

I didn't feel like answering. Even if I did, I wouldn't have.

We stayed like that for a while: Duke Wellington sitting right in front of me, trying his best to stare me down; Mark Weisnecki leaning his hulking body against the wall; me just sitting there.

Duke Wellington was the first to start up again. "We're not threatenin' you, Drake. You'll know when we're threatenin' you."

"Oh, will I?"

"You'll know, you'll know. What we're doing here is trying to cooperate. You and us, see? Cooperate. We're trying to do our job. We're just a pair of honest cops."

I glanced at Weisnecki. He turned away.

"Give me a break."

"What were you doing at Walker Industrial, Ben?" Mark was sounding like a skipping record. He wasn't getting any happier. "What'd you tell him?"

"The fact that you want to know so badly makes me want to tell you all that much less. And," I pointed at the hothead detective sitting in front of me, "you're the last person I'll tell anything."

Wellington sprang up and tossed his chair to the side. "Maybe you'll talk to my fists!" He came at me.

I was up to meet him. "Maybe my fists'll talk to you!"

Before we could get to swinging, the calmer detective rushed over and pushed his partner out of the way. Weisnecki then took two fistfuls of my lapels and lifted my 180 pounds high enough from the ground that only my toes remained there.

He growled, "Let's get something straight: I don't want to be wasting the night with you any more than you want to be wasting it with us. You're not here to find out what we know, you're not here to ask us questions, and you're goddamn not here to throw fists at my partner." He put me down, but he kept ahold of me. "You're here to answer a few simple questions."

He walked to the back of the room and leaned against the wall, right next to the *No Smoking* sign. He pulled out his Marlboro Reds and tossed one into his big wet mouth. I licked my lips. It was going to be a long night.

"Now, how about telling us what you were doing at Jack Walker's office?"

Chapter Twelve
Girl Trouble

It was late when I left the police station. I was glad finally to be out and able to smoke. Smoking made it easier to think. The cops didn't get anything out of me. In fact, I learned a bunch of things from them, the most important being that they hadn't known about the Jack Walker–Suzi Biggs affair. They still didn't.

Another thing: they had Jerry figured as their key suspect, but for all the wrong reasons. As near as I could tell, they had him playing the jealous boyfriend role. I didn't buy it. I wasn't ready to clear Jerry, but he had too many women following him to bed for him to whack a fellow bowler, and a big brother figure at that, out of jealousy.

Spence Nelson's name didn't come up, though they made several references to the drug scene at the bowling alley. If they knew that Spence was their man, they'd probably be cooking up some cockamamie scheme to shake him down and see what he knew. I had plans to get to him before that. He liked me, maybe even trusted me. He was going to be my pigeon before he'd be one for the cops.

I had enough of thinking about murder for the day. The police detention had left me drained of everything I had, and mighty hungry to boot. My eyes glazed over, focusing on an indiscrete point on the open road as I thought about ways to relax. Maybe I'd fall back in my chair with a tall drink and an LP spinning.

I picked up a pastrami sandwich to go. As hungry as I was, I was so much more looking forward to the alcohol I had waiting for me at home.

Finally I arrived at my door. My tired hand fumbled with the key, eventually finding the keyhole. It was an effort even to turn the lock. I was beginning to feel I should pass on the pastrami and head straight for the cool comfort of my bedsheets. After I flipped on the light switch, however, I knew that possibility was gone like the darkness in my room.

Suzi Biggs, who'd been sleeping in my favorite chair in the darkness, was startled awake by my entrance.

Detectives come to expect the unexpected, but this... All I could say was: "How'd you get in?"

She yawned casually, like she belonged here. "I flirted with the landlord. Oh, Ben, I'm so glad you're home." She said it like it was her home too.

I shooed her out of my chair. She jumped up. I plopped down. The sandwich bag fell to the floor.

"What are you doing here?"

She grabbed a chair, pulled it over to where I was sitting, and in a move far too reminiscent of Duke Wellington's, spun it around and straddled it backward. "Oh, Ben, I don't want to be alone, and I didn't have anywhere else to go."

I wanted to ask her why she didn't go to Jerry's, but a lot of the fight had been taken out of me, so I didn't.

"Well all right, then. Want a drink?"

"No. You know, I'm not really a drinker. When you saw me yesterday, I wasn't really myself. I mean, I was totally denying Joe's death."

"Suit yourself. Me, I've had a rough day, and I need a bourbon." I struggled to get out of the chair. "After I get that drink, I'm going to sit down to the sandwich I brought home, and you're going to tell me what you're really doing here."

She laughed a light, playful laugh, hiding her mouth behind her dainty hand. "You're so funny, Ben. I like your style." It was such a put-on it made my brow wrinkle with annoyance.

My fatigue must have chased away the subtlety of my expression. As I turned back to her with my full glass, she drew quiet, sensing my lack of patience with her games.

My body found the chair again. I reached for the bag and pulled out the sandwich. On my lap I spread out the white butcher's paper my snack was wrapped in. Before I started eating, I offered Suzi a bite. She declined.

"How about a pickle then?" I asked, my mood lightening.

"No thanks. How are things going on the case?"

"At this rate, I won't have to do any detective work. All the clues are coming to me. I can barely keep up with them." I licked some mustard off my fingers.

"So do you know who killed my husband?"

I didn't like the know-it-all attitude she was using. I felt my good humor starting to slip away again.

"Not yet. But I do know a good detective secret—and that is to maintain a balance between action and inaction. If you're a good detective, like me, just the briefest sniffing around will bring the clues to you. So it's not a matter of me finding the killer; it's a matter of the killer finding me."

I offered a content, drowsy smile. The pastrami hit the spot, but now I was even sleepier. Still, the two long swallows of bourbon mixed with Suzi's attitude made me feel like causing a little trouble.

"You know, Suzi, I was going to ask you earlier—if you just didn't want to be alone tonight, why not go over to Jerry's place?"

I could see her face turn red. "Why would I go over there?"

"You two seem to be pretty friendly, what with him spending the afternoon at your house the other day."

Her face turned even more red as she sprang to her feet, hands on her hips. "You've been spying on me!" she accused, shoving her face into mine.

She was angry. She looked better that way; it gave her an edge.

"I'm a detective, sister. I'm spying on everyone."

She harrumphed and crossed her arms before picking a new seat on the far side of the room. She pouted there for a while as I sipped my Old Grand-Dad. The glass was getting dangerously low.

I had the feeling that she was waiting for me to apologize, but that wasn't happening. And since I didn't care if she was there or not—or even if she talked or not—the evening turned into a waiting game. I waited longer.

"So . . ." A dramatic pause. "You want to know what's between me and Jerry?"

"Sure, if you want to tell me. If not, that's no problem. See, I'm going to find out either way."

"You can be a real son of a bitch, Ben."

"I've been called worse. I thought you wanted to talk about you and Jerry?"

"Yeah, okay." She paused again, this time to take a deep breath. "It all started even before I met Joe. I went down to the bowling alley one night, now I can't even think why . . ."

I remember closing my eyes, telling myself I was still listening to her. But I wasn't, and I fell asleep.

Chapter Thirteen
Too Many Possibilities

When I was shocked awake the next morning, I was still in my favorite chair. I had been dreaming, and while I couldn't recall the details, I was left with a lingering sense of blood and violence. A result of yesterday's events fueled by a healthy dose of pre-shut eye bourbon, no doubt.

I shuddered involuntarily and looked over at the clock. It was nearly ten in the morning, and my whole body ached.

A loud ringing startled me. It was a moment before I realized the phone had roused me from my chaotic snoozing. I picked it up. "Yeah?"

"Where the hell ya been?" Hal Reddy's gravelly voice demanded.

"Yesterday was rough," I explained. "The cops needed a playmate for most of the afternoon, and I was it. We were having so much fun they kept me occupied for most of the evening too. By the time I got back to my place I was too tired for anything but bourbon and bed."

"Don't be gettin' old on me, Drake." His idea of a joke.

"No problem. What d'you want from me?" I knew something was up. Hal never called just to make small talk, thankfully. The last thing I needed this morning was the boss making a social call.

"You talked to some joker by the name of Iverson yesterday, right?" He was all business now.

"Yeah, why?"

Hal dropped the bomb: "'Cause he's dead—they found him hanging off his balcony with an extension cord around his neck."

"An extension cord?"

"Yeah, the long orange kind. You know, the industrial-strength ones."

"Sure. Who found him?"

"The dame who lives two floors below him. She came tripping home after the local bar closed and saw Iverson's body hanging in her backyard. Must've woke up the whole block with her screamin'." I could hear a tinge of glee in Hal's voice. He enjoyed the distress of "civilians," as he called them.

"What are the cops saying?" I asked.

"Looks like the initial call is suicide."

That just didn't fit for me. From what I'd seen, Jerry had too much going for him to want to end it all. "You got anything else on it?"

"Uh-huh. The cops are fingering this Iverson for the Biggs murder. You wanna check it out and see how it plays?" It sounded like he was asking me, but I knew better than that.

"Sure," I said. "I'll get right on it."

"Good. Fill me in later." He hung up in my ear.

I set the phone back in its cradle and began to strip off my rumpled clothes. My mouth tasted like something had died in it, and I was off to the bathroom for a remedy when I suddenly remembered that I wasn't alone last night when I ran out of gas.

My pistons still weren't all firing this morning, and I actually looked around my small apartment before I realized there wasn't any place she could be hiding. Suzi Biggs was long gone.

I dug through the pockets of my coat until I found the notebook with all the information about the Biggs murder. I flipped through it, found Suzi's number, and grabbed for the phone. My guts felt like they were filled with ice water as I dialed. I knew she wouldn't be there, but I had to try. My guts were right on target: no answer.

I dropped the receiver and got cleaned up. Suzi Biggs was heavy on my mind as I dragged a straight razor across my two-day growth of beard. I still wasn't positive that she didn't have anything to do

with Joe's death—or Jerry's, for that matter—but I sure had a few questions for her, like where she'd got to last night. Hell, what she was even doing here last night was a puzzle. She was playing with me, and I hadn't even figured out the game.

The way I was feeling, I was going to be no good to anyone—especially myself—without a little coffee. There wasn't any in my kitchen. I kept my cupboards pretty bare. I took a little trip down to the corner grocery and picked up a can of Maxwell House. I knew when I got back I wouldn't feel like waiting for the coffee to brew, so I also got a hot cup to go.

When I returned home I got a fresh pot going, biding my time by finishing my deli coffee and enjoying a cigar. I had a few thoughts on Jerry's death. I wasn't buying the suicide story the cops were selling. It sounded like a frame-up to me, and I needed to dig up some solid dirt to bolster my theory. The police sure wouldn't give me anything I could use, and I didn't trust the press. That left one person who could help me.

I got Rebecca Hortzbach on the phone on the first try. We exchanged the cursory pleasantries before I brought the conversation down to brass tacks.

"So, have you gotten Jerry Iverson's body yet?"

"Yeah, they brought it in early this morning." She sounded tired, not at all her normal, jovial self.

"Look at it yet?"

"Just a glance. His neck was broken and he has a deep contusion around it, but that'll happen when you take a dive from a third-story balcony with a cord around your neck. I haven't been able to take a closer look. It doesn't seem to be a priority to the cops."

"What's the general thought?"

"You mean what do the police think, or what do I think?"

"Both, actually," I said as I poured myself a cup of fresh-brewed coffee. "Police angle first."

"Word around here is they're calling it suicide."

"And what do you think about that?"

"Of course I'm skeptical, but it's feasible," she admitted. "Apparently there was no sign of struggle in the apartment, no evidence of forced entry. The techs couldn't find a single thing that would suggest anything other than death by hanging. But then again, there was no suicide note."

"Male suicides don't always leave notes, and I knew Jerry well—okay, maybe not that well, but enough to know that he wasn't ready yet to dangle off his balcony on the end of a cord. When are you going to get to his body?"

"Last night was busy, so I'm kind of backlogged down here. Since the police aren't in a rush for it, I don't know . . ." She paused. I could hear her tapping her teeth with a pen. "Maybe a couple days from now?"

"I've got a feeling about this. Could you push that up any?"

Another pause. I heard the lighting of a cigarette, followed by her inhaling, then exhaling. "I guess I can fit it in tomorrow. Wanna watch?"

"No, I've got a full day."

I'd seen a lot of dead bodies in my day, and I could handle them just fine. But there's a big difference between seeing a dead body—even a decapitation—at a crime scene and seeing the same body being taken apart in the morgue. For some reason, autopsies gave me the willies. Plus, they take at least a couple of hours.

"I'd like to stop by when you're done, though. What time do you think you'll finish up?"

"Hold on." The phone thunked to her desk and sat there for a few moments. I heard the rustle of papers before her voice returned. "Stop by about eleven tomorrow morning. I should be just about finished by then."

"Right. See ya then, and thanks."

"Anytime, Ben."

As long as I had the phone in my hand, I decided to call Elizabeth Biggs to let her know about Jerry's death. After all, if Jerry was like a little brother to Joe, he was probably like a son to Elizabeth.

She took the news pretty hard and started crying. It hurt listening to her sob.

When she got hold of herself, she wanted to know if I thought the same person killed them both. I told her I didn't know, mentioning that the police thought Jerry committed suicide. She didn't believe it any more than I did. Smart woman.

I promised her I'd visit soon and hung up.

Jerry's death kind of threw me for a loop. That made two bowlers murdered in the span of three days. Testacy City is far from crime-free, but it was definitely strange that the fix seemed to be in on bowlers this week.

I stretched out on my bed and smoked as I turned it over in my head. Compared to the last case I was on, this one was a cakewalk. I almost had to dodge the clues as they came flying at me, and now there were just too many possibilities: Jack Walker, Suzi Biggs, Jerry Iverson, and even Spence Nelson all worked into the mix. Sure, I had a lot of leads, but they all got knotted together in the middle, like one of those kids' games on the back of the menus at Denny's. I tried to unravel everything in my mind, but I felt the weariness of my sore muscles creeping into my thoughts. I quit trying to fight it and closed my eyes.

Chapter Fourteen
Crime Scene, Redux

When my eyes opened again, the sun was just going down. I dragged myself off the bed and stumbled to the phone, dialing the number of the Biggs residence. There was no answer. Not that I expected one.

Now that it was starting to get dark, I decided it was a good time to check out Jerry's apartment. Like I'd told Dino, forensic technicians sometimes get a little sloppy, especially when their days are filled with one job after another. Rebecca said last night was pretty busy. I was hoping that would play in my favor.

Speaking of Dino, it hit me that I kept forgetting to swing by and see him to pick up his "hot tip." I wasn't taking my junior ace detective too seriously, but nevertheless I made a mental note to check in with him tomorrow.

A light purple dusk had just descended on the city, and I wanted to wait until it was a little darker before I busted into Jerry's. So I steered my car onto the 15 and ended up at the Long Mile, the best restaurant Testacy City has to offer.

It's a comfortable place, dimly lit, with deep black leather booths. It's not fancy or anything, but it's dark, it's quiet, and they serve the best chicken-fried steak with mashed potatoes and gravy in the tri-state area.

John Coltrane played quietly in the background as I strolled through the tenebrous atmosphere of the restaurant, its serenity slowly stripping away my anxiety. I took a seat at my favorite table in the back. Detectives by nature are a paranoid lot. I'm no exception, and this table allowed me to keep an eye on the whole place.

I always liked to come here when, like now, I was waiting for things to happen. The place had a soothing effect on me. While this case might have been easy so far—aside from getting beat up and detained—I'd been doing this long enough to know that whoever was behind this wasn't done causing trouble.

Lynda, my usual waitress, walked up and presented me with three fingers of Old Grand-Dad straight up. Being a regular had its advantages.

"Evening, Ben. How are you tonight?" Lynda was a tall woman who looked that much taller due to the voluminous beehive of reddish-blond hair piled on her head.

"Just fine, thanks. How are you doing?"

"Y'know . . . same old, same old."

I took a sip of my drink. "How's Tony?"

Tony was Lynda's common-law husband and the bartender at the Long Mile, and although he was a better bartender than husband, he was a good man. He'd done some work for me in the past.

"He's staying out of trouble these days." She glanced over her shoulder at Tony, working behind the bar. "Barely, anyways. Wanna hear the specials?"

"Bring 'em on."

"Tonight we've got free-range fried chicken with mashed potatoes, baby back ribs with steamed vegetables, or the chef's secret coulotte steak. That comes with a baked potato."

Now I had a tough decision. Only two coulottes could be cut from a single cow, and it was a damn fine cut of meat. But I had a busy evening ahead of me, one that just might involve some running. The last thing I needed was to be slowed down by a sixteen-ounce slab of meat sitting in my gut. And like I said, the chicken-fried steak here couldn't be beat.

"I'll go with the chicken-fried steak."

"It's good to know some things never change." She laughed and ambled off, scribbling my order on her little green pad.

I lit a cigar and smoked, enjoying the silence around me. Lynda came back with another drink before she brought me my dinner. I wasn't disappointed in my choice.

After I left the Long Mile, sharing a smoke with Tony on the way out, it was dark enough for me to check out Jerry's place safely. I pulled onto Draydon Avenue and parked a little way up from the apartment where Jerry used to bed his pretty bowling groupies.

I opened the trunk. I kept a lot of the tools there that I used for jobs like this. I snapped on a pair of surgical gloves and filled my pockets with a tiny flashlight, a few little plastic bags, and some other goodies that I thought would come in handy.

For the second time in forty-eight hours I trudged up the steps to apartment 3G. This time I knew I wouldn't find Jerry sleeping in the nude, but I wasn't too sure that I would be alone.

The door was, of course, sealed with crime scene tape. I pulled out my trusty Leatherman tool and sliced through the tape with one swipe. I tried the handle; someone had forgotten to lock the door. My prospects for finding overlooked evidence seemed good.

I drew my Smith & Wesson and entered the apartment, locking the door behind me. Maybe not the smartest move, but since it was the only practical way in and the easiest way out, I'd rather not be caught by surprise. I figured I could always take a tumble off the balcony to the second floor if things got too hot inside.

I did a quick walk-through behind the security of my gun. Once I had determined that I was alone, I began a more intensive search of the place. The report Rebecca got was right—there was no sign of any struggle. The entertainment center, trophies, and posters were still all in place. The place was neat, as neat as it could be, anyway, considering Jerry's slovenly ways. The bed was unmade, but I had a feeling that wasn't unusual at all.

I moved through the apartment, shining a tiny flashlight into every nook and cranny I could find. I even creeped out onto the balcony. Apparently the cord had been secured to one of the metal bars nearest the side of the house and tossed—with Jerry attached—over the railing into the backyard area.

When I finished my inspection, I'd been in the place about forty-five minutes and had nothing. It was risky being here even this long, so I made my way back through the living room.

Right before I reached the door, I saw something on the floor glint off the beam of my flashlight. I got down on my hands and knees and discovered, embedded in the shag carpet, about seven small steel balls.

Ball bearings.

I pulled out a plastic bag and, with the help of the Leatherman, coaxed the balls into it. I sealed it and put it in my breast pocket.

Then, feeling anxious, I got out of there as fast as I could without making too much noise. I left the door as I'd found it, unlocked, and pulled a small supply of crime scene tape from my pocket to reseal the door before I headed back to my car.

Once there, I returned my tools to their hiding place and removed my gloves, rolling the left one inside the right one, like I'd seen Rebecca do. I tossed them onto the passenger seat so I would remember to get rid of them in a dumpster before I got too far.

The Galaxie 500's engine roared to life. After the strained silence of Jerry's apartment, it seemed abnormally loud. As I pulled away from the curb, I thought about how I'd got in and out of Jerry's place so easily.

It nagged at me all the way to Penny's Lanes.

I don't know why I headed there; I was just following my detective's intuition. I certainly wasn't going to do any bowling. The place was busy as ever, but it was a late-night crowd. There were no groups of kids on school outings, chaperoned by bored adults. There were no families. It seemed darker and more dangerous at night.

I went straight for the bar. I guess I needed a drink, and while I can't ever imagine wanting to bowl, I can definitely imagine drinking at this bar on a regular basis.

The bar was a little more crowded than the last time I was there, but I saw some of the same faces. The old lady bartender was still on duty, and the solitary lush was holding down what I guessed to be his regular table in the back. It looked like he was passed out; his head was on the table atop his outstretched arms, a thin line of drool leaking between his big lips.

Of course Spence was there, leather cap and all. He was seated in a booth, and it looked like he was making a deal with some shady character who had about as much business being in a bowling alley as I did.

Walter's comments about Spence and his relationship with "some of the boys" came back to me. This deal looked suspicious enough to warrant keeping an eye on.

I moved to a dark corner of the bar, opposite Spence and his playmate. I'd been watching them for only a few moments when they got up and started to leave together. I followed them, thankful there were plenty of people who chose to bowl at ten p.m., giving me ample cover.

My quarry departed through the front door and headed west. I was right behind when I got held up by a gaggle of drunk young folks coming through the front door. By the time I fought past them and made my way outside, there was no trace of Spence Nelson or his dancing partner. I took a quick stroll around the building just to be sure. I flushed out a teenage couple groping each other in the darkness behind the building but came up empty otherwise.

Next time, Mr. Nelson.

I went back in, sat down at the bar, and had a couple of Old Grand-Dads. No one except the bartender, whose name I'd learned was Mabel, said a word to me. And all she asked me was: "Want another?"

Yeah, I liked this bar all right.

Chapter Fifteen
Necking with Rebecca

The next morning I made my way downtown to the morgue. Rebecca greeted me wearing a blood-spattered apron and a smoking cigarette. She still looked good.

"Morning, Ben." She gave me a little wave. "Too bad you couldn't make it earlier; it was a lot of fun."

"I'm sure," I drawled. "What'd you find out?"

"Jerry had some interesting tales to tell. Come on back. I'm sure he'll share them with you if you ask real nice."

She led me through the bowels of the morgue to the autopsy suite. She had apparently just finished the postmortem on Jerry. His body still rested on the steel table, chest split wide open. What I took to be Jerry's internal organs were piled atop one another on a metal table at the body's feet. Looking at a mound of guts and blood, I never failed to be amazed at just how much stuff is inside the human body.

Butcher-style scales were suspended above the table—hooks slick with blood. In fact, there was blood everywhere—on the floor, on the autopsy table, even on the chalkboard where Rebecca had scribbled the weights of Jerry's various organs in neat block letters.

The room's smell was overpowering: a combination of meat just starting to rot, vomit, urine, and feces.

"Sorry about the mess," Rebecca joked.

I laughed. "That's all right. I can take it." I pointed at the body. "So what's his story?"

"Okay. He died about midnight; cause of death: strangulation. His last meal was a burger and fries about three hours earlier. *That* was kind of messy."

"Did he set himself to swinging or not?"

"Not on your life. After we spoke yesterday I made sure to pay special attention to his neck. Come here."

I followed her over to the hollow shell of Jerry's body. The vacant chest cavity reminded me of birch bark canoes I'd seen in pictures. She threw her spent cigarette into a metal washbasin, pulled on a pair of rubber gloves, and slipped on some oversized wraparound glasses.

"Here, put these on." She handed me a pair of the glasses. "Put on some gloves too."

Jerry's scalp was pulled down over his face and the top of his skull had been cut off. Inside it was just a hollow bowl with a cleanly sliced spinal cord sticking up from the bottom. Rebecca caught my expression of surprise and pointed to a glass jar filled with liquid in which a brain was suspended.

"We'll get to that in a couple of weeks, but I don't think it'll tell us anything new." She grinned. "We've got all we need right here."

She flipped Jerry's scalp back over his head. It flopped into place, sounding like a wet chamois slapping against the hood of a car.

"This," she indicated the deep line that circled his neck, "you might guess is from the ligature."

She glanced at me. I nodded. "Sure. I'd guess that."

"And you'd be right. But look here."

She took a long-bladed knife and deftly flipped the skin of the neck back. My untrained eye didn't see anything unusual, other than the deep, ugly line that ran around his neck right under his jaw.

"This contusion," she pointed at the deep line, "is where the ligature cut into the flesh. It matches the one on the outside of the neck. But these," she indicated a series of deep, bluish-purple bruise marks lower on his neck, "were made by a very powerful pair of hands."

A low whistle escaped my lips. "Would ya look at that."

"You know it. You were right again, Drake. Jerry Iverson was murdered," she confirmed. "But it was set up so that no one would think twice about it being a suicide."

As I've said before, it's always good to be right.

"So why didn't we see those finger bruises on the outside of his neck?"

"Any number of reasons, not the least of which is that our boy Jerry here doesn't bruise very easily. Plus, I believe the killer, thinking he knew what he was doing—I say 'he' because those were some damn big hands—used some sort of padding and mistakenly assumed that the ligature would effectively erase any sign of his hands."

She took off her gloves and glasses and lit another cigarette. I joined her with a cigar. I could taste the smell of the room in the back of my throat; I hoped a J. Cortès would wipe it away.

"His neck was broken a short time after he died," she said, finishing her analysis. "That happened when he was tossed over the balcony."

My mind was working overtime, sorting out the possibilities. One kept coming to the surface. "Do you think the same guy killed Biggs and Iverson?"

"All I know for sure is that both dead guys were killed by a strong individual," she said.

"There's no way you can connect them?"

"They were both bowlers," her voice took on a misty quality, like it did whenever she spoke of conspiracies, "but there's something more to this than bowling."

"Yeah, thanks. Guess I'll have to figure the rest out on my own."

"Be careful, Drake. Duke Wellington isn't going to like you upstaging him again. After you uncovered the truth in the Raspberry Jack case, you're not high on his list of favorite people."

"Hey, I couldn't have done this without you. I just had a hunch—you found the proof. You're on his hit-list too, and this discovery certainly won't do anything to get you off it."

"True, but he's used to me. And he kind of needs me around—who else would do this job in Testacy City?" Rebecca smiled, chin in her palm.

"Yeah. Well . . . I'll try to steer clear of him, but he's already got a mad-on for me, so what can I do?"

"I'm not kidding, be careful. I've got a bad feeling about this case."

I pulled into the parking lot at Penny's Lanes and eased the Galaxie 500 into an open spot. For a guy who doesn't bowl, I sure seemed to be spending a lot of time here.

Normally, Rebecca's paranoia didn't bother me, being largely a result of her fondness for finding the esoteric wrapped inside the mundane. But this time, there was something in her eyes that had me worried. I knew there'd be more death before this case was over. I just wished I knew for certain where to turn next.

I climbed out of my car, the stench of Jerry's body clinging to my clothes. The two cigars I'd had since I left the morgue hadn't done anything to get the odor out of my nostrils.

I walked up to the old guy behind the shoe rental counter—Spence wasn't in sight—and asked him if Dino was around. He sniffed and wrinkled his nose before he grabbed the microphone and paged Dino. I could barely hear his amplified voice above the sound of the alley.

"He'll be calling on that phone over there." He pointed to a small alcove about twenty feet away. There were two pay phones hanging on the wall next to three other phones: a red one, a yellow one, and a brown one. None of the colored trio had a dial.

"Which one?"

"The yellow one," he spat, as if I'd just asked him how to score a strike.

"Thanks." I headed over and waited a moment before the phone rang. I snatched it up.

"Whatta ya want?" a voice snarled at me from the receiver.

"Dino?"

"Of course it's me, who do you think . . ." A pause. "Who is this?"

"Ben Drake."

"Hey! The private dick!"

"Yeah, that's right. I hear you got something for me."

"Boy, do I ever," he whispered. "I'll meet ya in the bar in five minutes."

"Sounds good." Actually, it sounded great. I hung up and made my way to the bar.

I checked my watch. It was almost twelve thirty. I never really subscribed to that superstition of not drinking before noon. Believe me, if there was drinking that needed to be done at eight a.m., you can bet I'd be doing it. For me, the "noon rule" was more a polite suggestion. Still, I didn't like to be impolite too often.

In the bar it was me, Mabel the bartender, and the old lush in the back who was, as far as I could tell, always there. I sat at the bar and Mabel poured me a bourbon. I took a sip and felt it burning away at the bad taste in my mouth. I should have thought of this sooner.

Not long after, Dino slunk in and sat down next to me.

"Hey," he whispered.

"What's with all the whispering, Dino?" I asked.

"Shh! Not so loud." He looked around nervously. "Let's go to a booth."

This was already taking longer than I wanted it to, but I followed him to an isolated booth. When I sat down he slid a greasy paper bag across the table to me.

"What's this?" I asked.

"Evidence!" Flames of excitement danced in his eyes.

I opened the bag, and sitting in the bottom were a number of small metal balls.

"Ball bearings!?"

"Shh!" Dino hissed.

I ignored him. "Where'd you find these?"

"On lane 13, Monday morning," he said. "They were swept off to the side. Are they a clue?"

"Just maybe, Dino. Just maybe."

Chapter Sixteen
Back to Jack

I pulled away from Penny's Lanes and headed for home. I felt dirty and was tired of smelling like a corpse. I was hoping a hot shower would make me feel at least a little better.

During the drive, the ball bearings kept rolling around in my mind. After my visit to Jack Walker and the working over I got from his goons, it seemed more and more likely that the man was somehow tied up in this mess.

I ran some facts through my head. Jack Walker was probably the one person in all of Testacy City who really wanted to see Gentleman Joe pushing up daisies. Iverson was killed the same day he clued me in to the relationship between Walker and Suzi. And now Suzi had apparently gone missing. If I were painting a picture, it would look a lot like Jack Walker. Not that I think Walker would be out doing his own dirty work, but another visit to his offices might turn up something worthwhile. In my experience, guys who think they're untouchable tend to brag about how powerful they are. Walker certainly thought he was untouchable, and I was hoping that with the right persuasion he'd go off on a power trip and let something fly.

I parked and trudged up the steps to my apartment. I entered slowly, not knowing whether I'd find Suzi Biggs there. I didn't.

I got undressed and put my dirty suit in a plastic garbage bag. A little gift for the cleaners. I cranked up the water as hot as it would go and stood under the scalding stream. It felt good, burning my skin a bright pink and penetrating deep into my sore muscles, doing its best to soothe. I stood there until the water turned lukewarm. After a brisk toweling off, I felt almost normal again.

I put on a fresh suit, shirt, and tie and headed back out to face the rest of the day, stopping for a quick bite at Lepke's before I made my way to the office.

When I arrived, the place was deserted except for Rhoda. I asked her where Hal was, and she told me that he had gone to the courthouse to testify in the Lewis case. He probably wouldn't be back until late.

I hadn't called him yesterday to tell him what I suspected about Jerry because I didn't like to put guesses into my reports. But now that I was sure Jerry was the victim of foul play, I wanted to let him know. I wrote him a quick note telling him to call me at home when he got the chance and put it in his in-box. Then I left, feeling a little nervous about the prospect of coming down hard on Jack Walker.

After bluffing my way past the main receptionist, I found myself in the posh offices of Walker Industrial, dealing with Jack Walker's gestapo-like assistant, a petite woman with blond hair, a pert upturned nose, and bright blue eyes peeking out from behind her designer eyeglasses. She wore a conservative tan business suit and a superior attitude.

"I'm sorry," she sneered, "but Mr. Walker's all booked up today."

"I was just in the neighborhood and decided to stop by." I handed her a business card. "I'll only take a minute of his time."

She read my card, screwing up her face as she did so. I got the impression that she wore the glasses for effect. "He has a full schedule today, Mr. Drake. Maybe if you tried calling for an appointment?"

"That's okay, I'll wait," I said, indicating a comfortable-looking chair against the wall, right next to a framed portrait of a stern-looking man in eighteenth-century attire.

She sighed in disgust. "I told you, sir, he's all booked up."

"No problem. I'm in no hurry." I pointed at the portrait. "Who's this guy?"

The woman snorted contempt. "That's Philip Vaughan."

"And why is he hanging out here?"

"Philip Vaughan first patented the radial ball bearing in 1794," she recited, like she was giving a fifth-grade speech.

"A real pioneer, huh?"

"Yes, he was. Just like Mr. Walker."

"Right." I couldn't help but chuckle.

I sat down and began to peruse the stack of *Popular Mechanics* back issues spread out neatly on the short table in front of me. I read about electric cars, solar-powered airplanes, cryogenics, and rocket-powered jetpacks.

An hour passed. Then another. The woman behind the desk took a few calls, did some typing, and performed some other receptionist stuff. The one useful thing I learned was that Walker was obviously in his office.

I continued to flip through the magazines, encountering articles that were right out of the science fiction novels I used to read as a kid. I wondered if Rebecca ever checked out *Popular Mechanics*.

I had just started reading an interesting article about superconductors when I was interrupted by a terse voice: "It's for you, sir."

Surprised, I looked up at the secretary. She was holding the phone out to me.

"Are you talking to me?" I asked.

"Yes sir. Your card says you're Ben Drake, the private investigator. Is that not correct?"

"No, it's correct."

"Then I am talking to you. You have a phone call." She again thrust the receiver at me.

Puzzled, I got out of the chair and took the phone from her.

"Hello?"

Duke Wellington's loud voice screamed at me: "I had a feeling, since you got knuckles for brains, that I'd find you there! Don't you learn nothin'?"

"Not if I can help it," I answered. "Do you need something? Like a case solved?"

"Very funny, tough guy. The cat lady told me about you keeping the Iverson death open."

"I'm just doing your job, DW."

"You think you're so smart. You think you got all the answers. Let's try this again: what are you doin' at Jack Walker's?"

"Not that line again. Did you call to interrogate me over the phone?"

"No, I called because you figure out Iverson was murdered and head straight to Jack Walker's office. I can't help thinking there's a connection."

"Keep following my leads, DW. We'll make a detective out of you yet."

I could feel the heat of his anger burning into my ear. "We're coming down there, Drake. We're coming down. You'd better not be there when we get there, or this time I'll lock you up and forget where I put you." He slammed the phone down.

I handed the receiver back to the lady behind the desk. "Hold the rest of my calls, will ya?"

I stood there, thinking. I couldn't leave yet; I needed to talk to Walker. I had to find out what he knew. I didn't expect him to sing for me, but I could exert a little pressure and take his pulse. Like I said, he struck me as the bragging type. But I couldn't let Duke Wellington find me here either . . .

The next thing I knew I found myself standing in the affluent air of Jack Walker's office, and despite my bravado from moments ago, I had no idea what my next play was going to be.

Walker, sitting behind his desk, looked up as his assistant scurried in behind me, apologizing profusely.

"Mr. Walker, I'm sorry . . ." she whined.

His two bodyguards, bigger than ever, started to come at me, expressions of what could only be joy at the promise of violence upon their faces. The whole office seemed to shake with their approach. Or maybe that was my heart pounding in my throat. Just as they were about to grab me, I blurted out, "Ball bearings were found at both crime scenes, Jack! What do you have to say about that?" As the sentence fell out of my mouth, I realized it was probably the dumbest thing I could have said. I wasn't exactly thinking straight.

The giant closest to me was readying a fist; his twin was right behind him. I winced, expecting to feel a broad pain across my face, when Walker's voice, quiet yet forceful, said, "Hold."

Butch and Schultz stopped in their tracks, though they didn't relax. Like trained attack dogs, they were just waiting for word from their master before moving in for the kill.

"I'm . . . I'm . . . so sorry, Mr. Walker, he just burst in," the assistant stammered.

"It's all right, Ellie. No harm done." Walker smiled at me caustically. "I think we can handle Mr. Drake from here. You can go back to your desk."

"Yes, Mr. Walker." Her relief was visible. I guessed she'd fallen victim to Walker's ire in the past. "Thank you."

"Please close the door on your way out."

"Yes, Mr. Walker." She backed out of the office, closing the thick, leather-covered doors behind her with a soft thud.

I felt sweat begin to run under my arms and well up thickly under the brim of my hat.

Walker stared at me for a moment, then picked up his pipe from its stand, looked into the bowl, and frowned. He struck a match, put the pipe to his lips, and took a few puffs. When the tobacco was burning again, he blew out a few mouthfuls of smoke that rolled about the room like gentle, aromatic clouds.

"Ball bearings, you say?" Walker's voice was thick with derision.

I nodded slowly. "That's what I said."

"Hmmmm." He leaned back in his leather chair and peered thoughtfully at his ceiling. "And you think I had something to do with their presence?"

All I could do was stand there. A few responses popped into my head; they all sounded stupid. I certainly didn't need any more help in that department.

"No snappy banter, Mr. Drake?" Another puff. "Let me tell you something. I run this ball bearing manufacturing plant. I oversee the production of millions of ball bearings each and every day, many of which end up right here in Testacy City. Do you expect me, just because of my position, to keep tabs on every one that comes out of here?

"Besides, I *own* the company, I don't work in the factory. Do you for one minute think that I walk about the city committing murders with ball bearings in my pockets? The idea is," he paused, choosing his words carefully, "well, ludicrous."

"Yeah, maybe." Irritation and fury began to rise up inside me. "But let me tell you, Walker, this case stinks. I know you're mixed up in it somehow, and no one—not you, not your goons, and certainly not the cops—is going to stop me from finding out how!"

"I don't know what you expected to find when you came here, and I don't know if you found it, but I think it's time that you be going. I'm a busy man."

"You can't dismiss me this easily!" I shouted, jabbing a finger at him.

"Oh, I can't, can I?" Walker spat scorn. "I think you're forgetting that you're in *my* office, and in *my* office I can do whatever I wish. And I choose to dismiss you. Just like that." He snapped his fingers. "Now beat it. We don't need any heroes here, Drake. You'd better stick to helping Suzi Biggs play her part of the widow in distress."

I felt my face grow hot at his barb. "How dare you . . ." I started toward him, fists clenched.

I didn't get too far. My anger had blinded me to Walker's body-guards, and for my carelessness I got a face full of fist. A small light exploded behind my eyes, and I staggered backward, just in time to take a blow to the gut that sucked the breath out of me and knocked me into the leather doors. Gasping, I slid down to a sitting position, lacking the energy to look up at the fist that careened off my chin. I slumped into a pile on the floor of Walker's office.

I remember hearing the sound of his voice echo in my ears and being lifted up like a sack of potatoes before everything went black.

When I came to, I was sitting behind the wheel of my car. My head throbbed like someone was taking a mallet to my skull, and I felt a thick crust of dried blood in my nose. I fumbled with the rearview mirror until I got a good look at myself. Actually, it wasn't good at all.

The face looking back at me was all lumpy. My left eye was al-most swollen shut, and there was a deep gash on my right cheek. My teeth felt like they were hanging loosely in my jaw. A black-and-blue flower was blossoming on my chin.

On top of that I had no idea where I was.

I got out of the car and glanced around. After I took a moment to learn how to walk again, I found that I was parked just off an empty stretch of road.

The nice thing about the desert is that when you're deep in its darkness, city lights are easy to spot—if you're near any. Thankfully, I was—the lights of Testacy City shone brightly to the southeast.

The keys were in the ignition, so I started up the car and began to drive back to town. About twenty minutes later I passed the famous *Welcome to Testacy City: Diamond of the Desert* sign.

I stopped at the first liquor store I found and picked up a fifth of Old Grand-Dad. If I ever needed a drink, I needed one now.

I headed for home, thinking fondly of my bed and cursing myself for my stupidity with Jack Walker. I had let my anger get the best of me—and let me tell you, that's the surest way to failure. The crack he made about Suzi still burned hot in my brain.

I was about halfway home when suddenly a crazy notion took over. I squealed a U-turn and sped back toward the highway.

I knew no one was answering the phone at the Biggs residence, but I was hoping that if I staked out the place I'd get a lead or two on what had happened to Suzi. It was too early for me to be jumping to conclusions, but I was doing it anyway. Rebecca's paranoia must have been rubbing off on me.

I rolled past the gates into Victory Gardens and drove up to 300 Pine Lane. The small house looked positively sinister in the shadows of the night. I parked a little way down the street, in the dark space where the light from the streetlamps didn't quite reach.

Suzi first gave the impression of a spoiled gold-digger with a sense of entitlement. Conceivably, she could have had an active hand in Joe's murder, especially considering her indifference the day I met her. But with her visit to my apartment, I started to see through her act. Now, given the apparent foul play surrounding Iverson's death—and, especially, Suzi's current disappearance—it was possible that her involvement in this mess may have gotten her killed.

The thought of her turning up at the morgue made me shudder.

Too often I've befriended a person who later turns up dead. Seeing the cold body of someone you know is never easy. Even thinking about it isn't easy.

This kind of thinking always made me thirsty. I tore the seal off my new bottle of bourbon and took a slug. It tasted good. It felt good. I took another.

I don't know how long I sat there, but it was awhile. I didn't see a thing. No lights came on in the little mansion, and I didn't hear any sounds from inside.

When my bottle was more half-empty than half-full, I started up the car and drove home, smoking a cigar on the way. I don't know how I made it without wrapping the Galaxie around a telephone pole. I was relieved when I turned off the ignition, still in one piece.

I was not relieved when I opened the door to my apartment and found Duke Wellington and Mark Weisnecki watching my television.

"Drake, you gotta get yourself a bigger TV," Duke Wellington chided. "This thirteen-inch black-and-white is no good. If you're gonna make us come to your house to roust you, least you can do is have a decent TV."

I ignored him.

"And get cable, man," he continued. "This late-night stuff is just crap. You need cable for some good TV."

"You look like hell, Drake," Weisnecki said.

"Observation skills get you that detective job, Weisnecki?" I slurred, leaning against the wall by the door. I needed it to stand.

"Cool it, wise guy." Weisnecki raised his lips over his teeth like an angry dog. "You're drunk, so I'll be easy on ya. But another crack like that, I'm running you in."

"Just get out of my place," I said, trying to sound threatening.

"A night in the drunk tank might do you some good," Weisnecki threatened back—his came out with the conviction mine lacked.

"Look, believe it or not, Drake, we're here for your own good," Duke Wellington explained, nodding his head. "That's right, your own good."

I snickered. "Sure. Like I believe that."

"Really, Drake. Hear us out," Wellington insisted. "Mark, tell him about it."

"We're here to warn you to lay off Jack Walker," Weisnecki said. "For your own good."

Again I had to snicker.

"Just look at you," Weisnecki continued. "You're a mess."

I couldn't argue with that.

"A *damn* mess," Duke Wellington emphasized. "A damn mess."

"Look, I don't need your help."

"Yeah, you can get beat up all by yourself," Weisnecki said.

They got up from their chairs and headed for the door.

"Stay away from Walker." Duke Wellington stopped in front of me, accosting me with a thick finger. "Stay away, or you're going to be in a world of trouble."

"And lay off the booze," Weisnecki added as he walked by me. "Get some help, Drake."

I was glad they left so soon. I stumbled to my bedroom and collapsed on the bed. I fell asleep thinking that I was going to be damn sore the next morning.

Chapter Seventeen
Elizabeth's Offer

I woke up slowly, fitfully from a dark dream. I dreamed of a school-house on fire, a group of young girls running, their arms out-stretched, toward me. They were crying and screaming. All I could make out was the distinct plea of "Help me!" I was just standing there, helpless, feeling like a ghost.

I didn't wake suddenly; my swollen eyes merely opened them-selves to the darkness of my small bedroom. My temples beat against my poor skull. I tried to think of absolutely nothing.

What crept into my head was a story I'd read somewhere about a guy who questioned whether we should pay attention to dreams and wheth-er they could be interpreted. The response was that we should pay at-tention to everything, because everything can be interpreted. Well, the most important thing about interpretation is that you can resist it.

I had to get some coffee in me. This was the kind of morning when I actually thought about grabbing some hair of the dog. But I had that sticky taste of alcohol on my tongue, and I wanted it off.

My breaths came quick and heavy, my eyes were full of paste. When I walked into my kitchen, she scared the hell out of me.

For the second time, Suzi Biggs was waiting for me in my own apartment. My headache got worse.

"Jesus! What in hell are you doing here?" My mind attempted to catch up with what my eyes were seeing. Then I had a bad thought: "Please don't tell me you've been here the whole time."

"No, I haven't. I've been hiding out. Ben, I'm afraid for my life," she blurted out. She was hunched over my kitchen table. In her hands she clutched a paper cup of coffee from one of those gourmet joints.

"Still friendly with the landlord?" I guessed at her method of getting in here.

"No . . . I mean . . ." It took her a moment to figure out what I was really asking. "You left the door unlocked." She tried a small smile. I could see a lot of the game had gone out of her.

"I don't want to hear any more until I get some java in me. And then I want to hear it all." I moved toward the coffee maker, then turned back to her, adding, "It's a good thing I don't sleep in the nude." She didn't get it. I didn't expect her to.

After I got the Maxwell House brewing, I sat down across the table from her. Suzi wasn't looking at me; she had her head down. I figured I'd give her a moment or two to begin.

She peered up at me and said, "Do you want a sip of my coffee, Ben, while you wait for the new pot?"

I don't know what the hell I was thinking when I took her cup and put the fancy plastic lid to my lips. The moment the sickly sweet liquid hit my taste buds I knew that I should have known better.

"Aaaak, I thought you said this was coffee!"

"Oh, I'm sorry, Ben, I forgot. I have this made special for me. It's coffee that's brewed with the same Indian spices they use to make chai. And then I have them put in condensed milk on top."

She placed her hand over mine. I pulled it back.

"Is that what all the kids drink these days?"

"Is that what I am to you, a kid?" She looked hurt.

Actually, she looked pretty cute. She was wearing a black knit cap over her curly hair. She didn't have nearly as much makeup on as she had the last couple of times I'd seen her. It made her seem younger.

I shook my head. It hadn't stopped throbbing. I had to remember who I was dealing with. "Look, you've played me like one of your boy toys since I first came across you. You've lied to me, you've played dumb at me, you've tried your damn best to hide behind flickering eyelashes and those big red lips." I felt I was losing my cool, but a hangover combined with a conniving woman in distress will do that to you.

I continued: "I've spent the last couple of days getting sucker-punched by bowlers, bodyguards, and coppers. I'm about through with your girl games. You're going to start giving it to me straight, sister, and you're going to start right now!"

Suzi stood up. She beat the table with her tiny fists. Tears were welling in her eyes. "You probably think I know who killed my husband. Well, I don't!"

She ran to the other side of the kitchen and hid her face in the corner. I could hear her sobbing. Then she craned her head around to me. "I saw a big monstrous guy go into Jerry's the night he was killed . . . Yes, I said *killed*. Jerry Iverson was murdered!"

"I already know that. And if you want the killer, you better come clean and tell me everything else I should know that you haven't already told me. How about you start at the beginning."

"Joe knew how to make me feel . . . I don't know, really special. He adored me. And I loved him for it." As she paused, her eyes darted around the room. "But I got bored with his bowling. Okay, I hate to admit it, but it's bowling, for God's sake! How can you take something like that serious? I mean, please don't tell me you're a bowler, Ben. Are you?"

"Ah, no. I'm not a bowler. I'm a detective."

"Of course you are, Ben. Of course you are." She smiled, but I didn't smile back. "So I started . . ." She was tracing little circles on my table with her finger. "I started seeing what kind of attention I could get. You know, from other boys . . ."

"How much attention could you get from Jerry Iverson?"

She laughed a playful, carefree laugh, but then quickly became ice cold. It was as if she suddenly remembered something—perhaps the fact that Iverson was dead.

Her brow was heavy, and she crinkled up her lips. She was thinking about something. A moment later a cute half-smile returned to her face. "I liked Jerry. Not 'liked him' liked him. I just liked flirting with him 'cause he was kinda cute and I could always break his cool."

"The way he told it," I countered, "made it seem like you were hot to get together with him and he had to cool you down."

She laughed so hard I thought she was going to fall out of her chair. "Oh, Ben, Ben, Ben, you silly man. That's such a guy thing to say. If he told you that, he didn't want you to know that he never had a chance with me."

"Is that why he was at your place that first day I met you? Is that why you were going to his apartment the night he was given a twenty-foot orange necktie?"

"He was at my place because, because he wanted to ask me something . . . Oh, Ben, I was in no mood to play with Jerry! He wanted something from me . . . and I had nothing to give!" She was getting worked up.

"Calm down." I had little patience for hysterics, especially on a morning like this.

"And I went to see him the other night because . . . I didn't know where to turn or who to go to. I tried to come to you, but you fell asleep. I told you I don't know who killed Joe, but I think it's pretty plain that it wasn't an accident!" She wasn't listening to me; in fact, she was up from the table waving her arms about like a madwoman. "I went to see Jerry because I . . . I think . . . maybe he . . ."

"Out with it," I said, hoping for something with more meat than melodrama.

"I don't know! I don't know! Drugs? Gambling? You know how crooked this city is, Ben. It could have been anything!"

"What are you talking about? You saying that Iverson had a hand in this business?"

She slumped back down into the kitchen chair, the hysterics gone from her. "I just don't know, Ben. I don't know what Jerry had got himself into. It was something bad—bad enough to get him killed."

The phone rang. I debated not answering it, but Suzi was staring at me with an aren't-you-going-to-answer-it look. So I did.

"Yeah, Drake here."

"Let me get something straight: do I pay you to be a detective or just to run around this city causing trouble?" It was Hal. And though he usually delivered his lines with a pinch of playfulness, there was none of that now.

"Hal, you're one of the main people who taught me that being a good detective means stirring up some trouble sometimes. You got a specific bit of trouble in mind?"

"You're damn right I do. Police tell me you're busting into Jack Walker's office like some crazed vigilante. Problem here is you're not some vigilante, you're one of my men! I don't give a lazy rat's tail if you want to turn up the heat on some bowling loser, but you turn the heat up on a guy like Walker, ya know whose rump gets roasted? Mine, damn you!"

I pinched the bridge of my nose between my thumb and forefinger as I squeezed my eyes shut. I wasn't used to Hal not backing me up. Letting him down crushed my spirits.

"Hal, I know I acted, well, rash . . . but I got some information—"

"I don't care if you got a photo of the pope, the president, *and* Jack Walker all holding bowling balls over the body of Joe Biggs. Let me tell ya what I got for you: this case is closed."

"What!?"

"You heard me. The Always Reddy Detective Agency is dropping the Biggs murder. The whole thing is getting way too political for us, now that ya dragged Walker into this. The police aren't happy about that. And quite frankly, I wouldn't give a good goddamn about the police, but the old Biggs broad isn't giving us enough dough for me to want to throw the finger at the cops."

"Hal . . ." I didn't know what to say.

"Save it, Drake. Take the day off, then come in tomorrow. I'll have a new case for ya. Besides, it sounds like you need to sober your sorry self up." He slammed the phone down.

Suzi was wearing a frown of sympathy. "Are you okay, Ben? Is there a problem?"

"Yeah, there's a problem. I think the fact that you're Jack Walker's slut has something to do with this murder, and him throwing his weight around has got me—"

She slapped me harder than any girl had ever slapped me. And I'd been slapped plenty hard by plenty of girls.

"You bastard! Yes, I had an affair with Jack Walker, but that was before I met Joe. I have never been unfaithful to Joe! I might be young, I might have done some bad things in my life, but I am not a slut! How could you, Ben? I thought you could help me! All

I wanted was your help. I hate you, Ben Drake! I really hate you! You're no hero."

I stood and yelled, "I never said I was a goddamn hero!"

She ran crying into my bedroom and slammed the door shut. I could hear her loud sobs through the door. Christ, I felt like a stranger in my own home. But one thing was certain: I wasn't about to just sit there and listen to her cry.

I picked up the phone to call Elizabeth Biggs. I didn't know if Hal or anybody else at the agency had bothered to contact her, but I figured it was my duty to talk with her either way.

Being hungover, beaten up, fired from my case, and verbally belittled by Suzi Biggs must have all scrambled my brains if I thought for a moment that calling Mother Biggs would be better than just sitting there.

She knew right away something was wrong; I've said before she was a smart woman. When I told her the news, she cried and cried.

Now I had girl tears in stereo.

Just when I thought I had all the surprises I could take this crazy morning, Elizabeth threw this ringer my way: "Benny, you have to help me! Please, I know you're the only man who can put this nasty business to peace. I'll . . . I'll pay you personally to handle this."

It was the kind of offer that could only spell trouble. I'd be working outside the law, and I'd be working outside the rules of my job. It would mean me boiling down everything to the very essence of who I was.

I was a detective. A damn good detective.

I told her I'd do it.

If I was going to go underground, I would need some help. And I knew just the shoe-renting geneticist I needed to recruit.

Chapter Eighteen
Beautiful Yet Dangerous

I fixed myself some fried eggs while I let the pain in my head melt away to steel resolve. The best plan for approaching Spence Nelson had me showing up at the bowling alley near dark, which was fine with me because I wasn't about to leave Suzi crying in my bedroom.

The pressure of two murders was wearing her down, but she was still holding back. With a couple cups of coffee in me I realized the mistake I'd made with her: she was just starting to trust me enough to unburden her soul. I had to regain that trust. And I had until evening to do so.

I cracked open my bedroom door. Suzi was curled up in a fetal position, staring wide-eyed at me.

"I'm sorry I yelled at you, Suzi. I had some bad news from my boss come down on my head like one of those 500-pound Acme weights you see in the cartoons. I took it out on you. That wasn't fair. I've also spent too much time thinking about my needs and not enough thinking about what you are going through. I'll tell you something. I lost my wife in a car accident. You're handling this a helluva lot better than I did."

A smile found its way onto her sad face. I could tell she wasn't the type to stay mad at me for long.

"So, Suzi . . . It seems I've found myself with the afternoon off. Want to go grab a bite to eat, maybe get some fresh air?"

She sat up looking as though she hadn't cried a single tear. "I'm not really that hungry, but I do have a crazy idea if you're up for it."

"I'm probably up for it, and I'd be shocked if it was anything less than crazy."

"Let's go see the animals at the Gesner Wild Animal Park!"

The Gesner Wild Animal Park was what passed for a zoo in the area. Located about fifty miles south of Testacy City (and almost the same distance from Las Vegas), it was mostly composed of large expanses of natural habitat for the captive animals to run free in. Modeled after the famous San Diego Zoo, it was a much smaller version. I thought the drive there and back might be just the retreat I needed to cleanse my mind.

"Okay," I told her. "Let's go see the animals."

"We'll take my car! I just love to drive the desert highway!"

She should have said she loved to drive the highway like a demon shot out of hell. I was strapped into her white convertible Mustang, hand clamped down on my hat, wondering if I'd live long enough to solve her husband's murder. We were racing past the desert sand so fast I thought it would turn to glass.

On top of that, she insisted on playing me tape after tape of her favorite music. Every time I cringed at the onslaught of sound she sent my way, she would eject the cassette, throw it on the backseat, and try again. "Oh Ben, that song wasn't you at all. But listen to this. You'll just love this!"

Once we were in the park, she took my hand and started running, screaming, "I want to see the tigers! I want to see the tigers!"

The park's star attraction was its pair of Siberian tigers. If I was here to win points with Suzi so she'd tell me her secrets, I was in luck. I happened to know the head animal keeper, a jake I'd met while investigating a boa constrictor snakenapping a couple of years back.

We got to the ledge that overlooked the tigers' habitat and waited only a few moments for my man, Bobby Regardie. He was a tall, lanky gent wearing a pair of blue-green coveralls with *Bobby* sewn in gold stitching on his left breast. His curly brown hair sprouted wildly beneath the matching cap on his head. I made the introductions.

"Hi there, little lady!" His watery brown eyes sparkled brightly at Suzi.

"Hello, Bobby—I can call you Bobby, can't I?" she beamed.

"Sure as sunshine you can!"

She put her arm around him. "I was just telling Ben how much I love tigers, especially Siberian tigers."

"They are wonderful animals, aren't they? So beautiful," he dropped his voice to a whisper and bent close to Suzi's ear, "yet so dangerous."

Suzi gave a little start, her face a mask of mock fright solely for Regardie's benefit.

He continued in his normal voice: "They were almost made extinct, you know. D'ja know that there, Suzi-Q?"

She blushed, giggled, and pushed him away coyly. "Oh you. Of course I knew that. I know lots of facts about tigers. I know there are three reserves for Siberians in Russia. I've always wanted to go to Russia and see them."

"Righty-right you are! There's the Sikhote-Alin, Lazovsky, and Kedrovaya Pad Reserves. Wowie, you're pretty *and* smart. Hey, Ben, she's a keeper!"

I tried not to laugh. "Yeah, a real keeper."

"Bobby! I just thought of something!" She was working her eyelashes on him. This would be good. "Do you think I could . . . I mean, do you think you could let me . . . pet one of the tigers?"

"Re-he-hur-hur-hur," he laughed. He was a strange man. "You see, you see, you don't just, you don't just go up and 'pet' the animal." When he said the word "pet" he made invisible quotation marks in the air with his spindly fingers. "They're deadly killers, you know."

"Yeah, I know." She was bummed. "Deadly killers."

All in all, the trip south did what I had hoped it would: now Suzi seemed to really trust me. Several times on the ride back to the city, she would reach over and rub my shoulder or pat me on the knee. It made me uncomfortable, but I kept telling myself it was for the good of the case.

Once we were back at my place, I knew I should start in with my questions, but the sun was getting low in the sky, and I was itching to talk with Spence Nelson. I told Suzi I had to go out, that I'd only be gone an hour or two at the most, and then I'd take her to dinner.

But first I made her promise to stay put in my apartment; I didn't want to lose track of her again, not when I was this close. Only when she agreed not to stray anywhere did I leave, making sure to lock the door behind me.

After riding in the Mustang, it was good to get back into my Galaxie 500. It wasn't as comfortable as Suzi's car, but it felt like home. That and a cigar soothed my mind, readying me for another foray into the dark world of the bowling alley.

Chapter Nineteen
Spence's Party

I found Spence Nelson in the bar of Penny's Lanes, talking to an unwholesome-looking lady with dirty-blond hair. He was dressed in jeans and a leather vest, one that matched his ever-present cap. She was a rail-thin girl who looked older than she probably was. She wore a short, grimy floral-print dress and Lo-Top Chuck Taylors with no socks. She said something I couldn't hear, and Spence nodded in return, rubbing the growth of hair on his chin. She hopped off her barstool and made a beeline for the bar's exit, leaving Spence sitting all alone.

He wasn't alone for long. I joined him and pointed at his glass. "Hey, Spence Nelson, your glass is looking a little empty."

"Ah! Benjamin Drake, ace private investigator. My glass may be empty, but my soul overrunneth. What brings you down to this bowling establishment on such a fine evening?"

"Let's just say I'm looking for help."

"Intriguing. And am I to assume that I can be the provider of said assistance?"

I blew out a big breath of air. "Well, that's what I'm hoping. I'm still trying to find out who killed Gentleman Joe, and I've run into some . . . trouble with the law."

"And what is your rationale for approaching me with this dilemma?"

"Look, I know you're not exactly Mr. Clean when it comes to dealing with the authorities ..." I trailed off, hoping he'd get the point. He didn't let me off so easily.

"And you are looking for Mr. Clean? I am certainly not him, nor do I know his whereabouts. I will tell you, though: if, instead, my likeness were to be placed on bottles of cleaning supplies, many more units would be sold."

I liked Spence's humor—at least I did the first time I talked with him. This night, however, my capacity for his brand of absurdity wasn't as high. "Cut the shtick. I was making a point, and you damn well know it."

He slid his shoulders back away from me, lowered his chin to his chest, and said through downturned lips, "Just what is the point you are trying to make?"

"I know that your business—and I'm not talking about bowling shoes—puts you on the side of the law that cops don't like. There's a lot of talk at the station about drugs being involved in this case." I leaned in closer. "And that means you."

He stared blankly at me.

I continued what I had to say: "Now, I know and you know the cops are barking up the wrong tree. I also know you've got more secrets about this 'bowling center' that haven't made their way to my ears. It's high time we had a real talk. Here, let me tell you what I know—"

"I already know what you know," he interrupted.

"So you know that I'm officially off the case?"

"No." His eyes popped ever so slightly in surprise. He licked his teeth. "I did not know that."

"Well, I am. But despite that small setback, I'm still going to find out who killed Joe Biggs—and Jerry Iverson. I think you can help me."

"Of course I can help you," Spence confirmed. "In fact, I have already made up my mind as to whether or not I *will* help you. But first, tell me why you think I would lend you assistance."

I paused and collected my thoughts. I needed his help, and from what I'd seen of him so far, I figured I'd only have one chance.

"It's my gut feeling that despite your dalliances into the realm of illegality, however minor," I emphasized, pulling out all the stops, "you have what Kant would call a *duty* to do what is right."

"*To do what is right,*" he laughed. "You have not yet failed to surprise me, Drake. I had already made up my mind to assist you, but after your use of Kant as a rhetorical tool, I will do so with zeal."

"I'm glad." I breathed a sigh. "So you want to get to it?"

"In a moment. First, I have to finish a business transaction. It should not take more than five minutes of my, and likewise your, time."

"I'll be waiting right here; then we can get down to business of our own."

He walked off, heading toward the men's room, no doubt. I turned to the bar, signaling Mabel to pour me a drink.

"Say, Drake," Spence called to me from the door of the bar.

"Yeah?"

"I am willing to say that this partnership shows great promise."

"Yeah, I think so too," I laughed. "Just like Frank and Jesse James."

He laughed in return and disappeared from the doorway.

Mabel brought me a fresh bourbon. I lifted it to my lips, anticipating the sharp sting on my tongue. But just as I was about to drink, something stopped me. It was something that, while not unusual in and of itself, was strange and unexpected.

The lush who always occupied the back corner of the bar stood up.

This was the first bit of movement I'd seen out of him all week, and near as I could tell he drank more than I did. He moved across the bar with a strong, confident walk that was anything but the walk of a drunkard. Even though the bar was dark, when he got close to me I noticed that he wasn't as old as he looked from a distance. He had a strong jaw and thick muscles in his neck. He continued strolling, right out of the bar.

I wasted no time in following him. Something was wrong, and I had a bad feeling it had to do with my new partner in crime.

As I left the bar, I noticed that the few people who had been bowling this afternoon weren't bowling now. Instead, all eyes were on the cops—both uniforms and detectives—heading toward the men's room.

I heard a voice shout: "Okay, Nelson, give it up! We've got the place surrounded!"

I wouldn't have been able to hear Spence's reply even if there were one. I assumed that he didn't answer, because just then a group of cops showed up with a battering ram and proceeded to knock the door off its hinges.

I couldn't see into the restroom, so I didn't know what was happening until two cops dragged out the dirty broad in the floral-print dress Spence had been talking to when I arrived.

"He jumped out the window!" she screamed hysterically. "The window!"

"Who was on the window?" one of the detectives yelled out.

I didn't wait for an answer; knowing the Testacy City Police, I was willing to bet no one had been watching the window. I ran as fast as I could for the exit. I still needed Spence's help; I had to get to him before some too-eager rookie cornered him.

The bathroom window overlooked the parking lot, so I assumed that's where all the action would be taking place. I burst through the door into the cool evening air and paused. I could hear the sound of gunfire. I drew my weapon. It sounded like there was a party, and I didn't want to be caught without any favors.

I ducked behind the cover of a nearby car to assess the situation. About ten cops had Spence cornered behind a couple of parked cars in the far end of the lot. He was backed against a chain-link fence. His options for escape were few.

I questioned my sanity as I eased my way toward him, using the several rows of cars to dodge errant bullets, before finally reaching Spence's side.

"Drake!" Spence was surprised to see me. "What are you doing here?"

"Trying to talk some sense into you."

Spence jumped up and threw a couple of bullets out of his Glock. I heard glass shattering. "Get out of here, man. It's me they want."

"Christ, I know that, but I'm not leaving my new partner high and dry!" I shouted as Spence squeezed off a few more shots, emptying his clip. "And quit with the bullets already! You're just playing into their game! Let me talk to the cops for you. We'll let them take you in. These guys are such amateurs, we can have you out of the joint on a technicality in no time."

Spence pulled another clip from his waistband and slammed it into the Glock. He looked at his gun, then me, then the advancing cops, then back to me. Worry filled his eyes.

"Stay put, and for God's sake—don't keep shooting at them," I pleaded.

He stared at me, brooding. He held his automatic so tightly it shook in his hand. "Drake, I have something to tell you about these bowling murders, something you need to know."

"You damn well better have something to tell. And I expect you to tell me once I get you out of this mess."

I started off along the fence, hoping my words got through to him. Now all I had to do was figure out how to approach the cops without them shooting me.

I creeped past a row of cars, then turned to check on Spence. All those brains and they didn't stop him from acting stupid in a crisis. He stood up to run toward the diner. Where he thought he would go, I had no idea. I was sure he didn't know either.

"Spence! What are you—" I started to yell, but as the words left my mouth the sound of guns exploded in my ears. I watched helplessly as a bullet ripped through Spence's chest. Some son-of-a-bitch cop had shot him in the back.

He let out a sickening cry and fell forward onto the hood of a car, hitting it with a metallic crunch. His gun clattered to the asphalt next to him. He hung on the hood for a moment, then slid slowly to the ground, landing with a heavy thud.

"Damn!" I cursed fate, slamming my pistol into its holster as I ran over to him. I turned him over. The bullet had gone straight through him, exiting close to his heart. It was bad, one of the worst hits I'd ever seen. There was no doubt about it: Spence wasn't going to live much longer. I slapped my hand over his wound and pressed hard, hoping he would hold on long enough for the ambulance, at the same time knowing he wouldn't.

"Man," he moaned, pain cutting heavily into his voice, "where's that double-crossing broad?" She wasn't around. He yelled at her anyway: "Thanks for the sour persimmons, bitch!"

My mouth rattled off some obscenities of my own as my mind swam in the thought of Spence's blood. "Hold on . . . just hold on."

I was barely conscious of the booted feet that gathered around us.

Spence's eyes parted slowly and stared at me. "Drake." His voice was all raspy and weak. "I have to tell you." A spasm of coughs racked his body. Blood spurted out of his mouth and flowed freely from his damaged chest.

"What's that?" I asked, pushing down heavily on his injury with my hand, crouching nearer to him.

"Everything . . ." he croaked. "Everything is all red herring."

"What?" I shouted at him. "What do you mean by that? Spence? Spence? Answer me, goddamnit!"

There was no answer. Spence Nelson was dead.

Chapter Twenty
Backseat Driver

I was cradling Spence's lifeless body. His blood soaked into the fabric of my suit, thick and sticky on my arms, chest, and thighs. I remember thinking that my cleaner wasn't going to be very happy with me.

I felt sick. Part of me felt guilty about Spence's death. I'd only known him a short while, but if I'd ever had a kindred spirit in this business, it was Spence Nelson. I couldn't help but think he'd still be alive if I hadn't been involved. But then he'd be in custody, and prison is no place for a guy like Spence. So maybe he was better off, considering the options.

Another part of me was feeling anxious. I was worried about being caught at the scene. I was supposed to be off this case, and things would get further out of my control if Hal—or Duke Wellington—found out I'd been there.

That was when I heard footsteps crunching across the parking lot. The sea of booted feet parted to reveal a pair of beat-up wingtips and a pair of shiny new basketball shoes.

"Well, well, what do we have here?" a voice shocked me out of my thoughts.

I looked up into the face of the short, ape-like man ballooning out of the wingtips. He was all forehead and belly with a wide, flat nose and thinning black hair. He wore brown polyester pants and a cheap dress shirt—open at the neck—under a navy-blue TCPD vice windbreaker. It took a moment for me to realize who he was: Brad Makoff, half of the most notorious vice partnership in Testacy City. The other half, Leo Nolan, was standing right beside him. Nolan was a tall, broad, brown-haired guy in grubby jeans, red polo shirt, and the trademark TCPD vice jacket. His violent tendencies were legendary among the Testacy City underworld.

These two had made it their personal goal to wipe Testacy City clean of drug dealers, pimps, and pushers. At least that's what they said during press conferences. Fact of the matter is, they wanted all that action to themselves. Taking out the competition made things that much easier.

And Spence was competition.

"Hey, Drake!" Makoff demanded. "I asked you what you were doing here."

Never once did I regret upstaging Duke Wellington on the Raspberry Jack case, but every so often it was damn inconvenient to be so easily recognized by cops. It made weaving a good yarn all that much more difficult. Not impossible, though.

Ten or so cops were huddled around Makoff, Nolan, and me. None of them said or did much. If they didn't know my reputation, they certainly knew Makoff and Nolan's reputation. They were a willing audience to what they probably hoped would be some good entertainment. I tried my best to ignore them.

"Actually, Brad, you asked me what we have here," I corrected, gently lifting Spence's body off my knees and placing it on the pavement. "Well, I don't know what you've got, but I've got one dead informant."

"An' what were you doing, getting information from this scumbag?" Makoff poked at Spence's motionless body with his foot.

I stood up, brushed off my suit, and began weaving my tale. I started, like all believable fiction, with a solid groundwork of the truth: "I was working on a case." I glanced down at Spence's body again. A pool of blood began to ooze out onto the pavement under him. "He had some information that would've helped me out."

"Yeah? What sort of information?" Makoff asked.

Nolan cracked his knuckles and smiled at me. It wasn't a friendly smile.

"I wish I knew," I shot back. "But your boys killed my man before we got to talk."

"Well, that's just too—" Makoff was interrupted by a commotion from Penny's Lanes.

Three officers were dragging Spence's double-crossing customer out of the building, and they had their hands full. She was an alley-cat, kicking, fighting, biting, scratching, and spitting. It was all these three could do to keep ahold of her, let alone get her under control.

"I did my part!" she screamed. "We had a deal!"

Makoff looked up at Nolan. "Say, Leo, looks like there's a little confusion as to what we promised. Take care of that, will ya?"

"Right," Leo nodded and strolled casually across the parking lot.

When he reached the struggling woman, she calmed down a bit and started to say something to him. She didn't get the chance—he smashed her in the mouth with a ham-sized fist. I saw a few teeth fly out of her head. He followed that up with a left to her temple. She went limp and crumpled to the ground. One of the uniformed cops cuffed her and hauled her off to a squad car. Nolan turned and headed back toward us, dusting off his hands like he'd just finished chopping wood.

"Now what was I sayin'?" Makoff shoved his hands deep in his pockets and smiled. His smile was only slightly friendlier.

"You were asking me about my case."

"Right. So how's about it?"

"Look, I don't mind telling you guys anything, but do we need all these uniforms around?"

Nolan got back over to us just in time for Makoff to say to him, "Hey, Leo, we need all these blues around like this?"

Nolan took the hint and gestured at the assembled uniforms. "All right, guys, we've got it from here," his big voice boomed with authority.

The ten cops standing around us looked at each other, nodded, and murmured to themselves before rapidly dispersing.

"That make you feel better?" Makoff asked, flashing his teeth.

"Yeah, much. Thanks," I returned. "Now what do you want to know?"

"Who ya workin' for?"

"I can't tell you that." This client-confidentiality bit came in real handy sometimes. If it didn't get me killed first.

Makoff frowned. Nolan went back to cracking his knuckles.

I shifted my strategy slightly. "Okay, let me tell you this. I'm working for a concerned party that wants to stop drugs from getting into Testacy City's high schools."

"And you thought Spence was the source?"

"Well, actually, I was looking for *his* source."

This got them interested.

"And what did you find out?" Makoff drilled, almost drooling.

"Before we get into that, let's make a deal," I said with trepidation. I hoped my deal was better than the one Spence's stool pigeon got.

"What ya got in mind?" Makoff squinted his eyes to slits, as if he were trying to see through my game.

"It's like this: I give you Spence's supplier, and you keep me out of your reports."

"That's it?"

"That's it."

The two cops looked at each other, nodded, then turned their attention back to me.

"Deal," Makoff agreed. "Now tell us who you got."

"Okay, here it is: Spence gets—well he used to get—most of his goods from Jack Walker."

"Who's that?" Nolan blurted out. "Some kinda bowler?"

"No! What's wrong with you, man!" Makoff barked. "Jack Walker, the ball bearing guy!" He turned toward me. "You sure about this?"

"Not one hundred percent," I admitted. "I was meeting with Spence tonight to confirm it."

"And you think he'd tell you the truth?"

"Yeah, I do. We had a rapport going, something that took me a long time to establish, something you guys erased with a bullet."

"Well I'll be . . ." Makoff said pensively. "Okay. Give us everything you got, and we'll forget you were here."

It took me another hour to spell it all out for them, how Jack Walker, millionaire industrialist, was up to his eyeballs in drugs. It was hot and juicy gossip, the stuff that made vice cops all quivery inside. And it was all a big, convoluted lie. I figured it was the least I owed my old pal Jack.

Finally, their greed satisfied, they let me go. I wasn't all that sure they'd keep their end of the deal, but I was hoping they'd keep it long enough for me to close this case.

I headed for the Galaxie 500, dog tired. The events of the last few days had left me drained, and I felt as if I were running on fumes. After Spence's death and the subsequent grilling and creative truthing, my brain was all cloudy.

I didn't really feel like doing anything but going home and collapsing. Either that or going back to Penny's Lanes for a couple of stiff drinks at the bar. I certainly didn't feel like going home to play with Suzi. But she was waiting for me, and she had information I needed.

I closed my eyes and once again resisted the urge to return to the bar. But there could be no turning back now, there could be no rest. Very soon this business was going to come down, and I was going to follow it right to the bottom.

My hand paused a moment on the door handle of my car. I got in and concentrated: Drive home. Get Suzi. Eat. Find out what she knows. Relax and sort it all out later.

I started the engine and pulled away from the curb. The cool night air blowing in my open window kept me awake.

I twitched when I suddenly felt the chilly touch of a cold steel barrel against my occipital ridge.

"Oh, come on! I can't believe this!" I said aloud. I thought garbage like this only happened in the movies.

"Keep driving, cretin." With an accent like that, it could only be one person; actually, it could only be one of two persons—Butch or Schultz.

"Ouch, you trying to hurt my feelings? Besides, I'm surprised they taught you 'cretin' in your ESL class." This was one ride that was going to end with a lot of pain. If I didn't start acting tough now, I was dead. I might be dead anyway.

He pressed the barrel tighter against my skull.

I continued: "So, you want me to take you anywhere special? Grandma's house?"

"The quarry," he grumbled.

"A party at the quarry? But I forgot all my ball bearings at home. Have any on you?"

"It's no party. Mr. Walker wants to see you in private."

"Say . . . this wouldn't have anything to do with the Biggs murder, would it?"

I was starting to have fun, but it ended when his left hand wrapped around my throat with a grip that could have ended me right there.

Both my hands instinctively left the steering wheel and tried to break his hold. All I succeeded in doing was making the car swerve all over the place until it skidded to a stop on the shoulder. Thankfully, there was no one else on the road.

He released his grip on me. My head snapped back as I gasped for air. He spoke directly into my ear: "No more talk. Drive."

I did as I was told. We hit the highway and sped out to the old quarry, about forty miles west of the city. I kept quiet the whole way.

The night was pitch black as we neared our destination. I had no idea where I was going. Suddenly my hulking passenger told me to turn left. My headlights revealed a small dirt road immediately in front of me. I would have completely missed it had I been driving alone.

I slammed the wheel hard to make the turn, and the Galaxie fishtailed across the dust-covered road, tires complaining. The new road was pretty straight, and up ahead I saw a single white light that could only be our destination. I felt steel prod the back of my skull. I cruised ahead. A rumble from the backseat told me to stop the car underneath the light, which turned out to be a bright floodlight hanging off an old crane. Nice and convenient.

Even with the cone of light coming down, it was so dark that the moon and the stars cast a blue glow over the landscape.

The lummox in the back dragged me out of the car. Before I could adjust my eyes to the darkness, I smelled the pipe smoke. Then all I remember were fists to my head and body. It wasn't the worst beating I'd gotten in the last few days, but it still took me to my knees.

"Enough," Jack Walker's voice cut through the pain. As much as I hurt, this rich, pompous bastard made me angry enough to forget my pain.

"Bring me here to kill me, Jack? Like you killed the others?"

"No, Drake. If I wanted you dead, you'd already be dead. No, I brought you here ..." I saw his dark silhouette move out from the black toward me. "I brought you here, Drake, to give you the answers you need."

Chapter Twenty-One
The Red Herring Syndicate

"Answers? What's that supposed to mean?" I demanded, crouched on my knees beneath Walker. I didn't like being at his feet like this, but I doubted my ability to stand.

"It means that I've had my eye on you, Drake, from the moment you took this case. If you suspect me of having my hands in more things than the manufacture of ball bearings, you're right—though don't for a moment think that you can pin anything on me."

"Like the Biggs murder?"

"Damn you, Drake, listen for once instead of shooting off your mouth!" He stepped closer into the light, pointing a neatly mani-cured finger at me. "I'm telling you that I don't have anything to do with either of the dead bowlers!"

"Yeah, okay. You get your goon to drag me out to the middle of nowhere to tell me you're innocent?"

"No. You were dragged out here so I can tell you who the killer is."

I wasn't ready to buy this load of laundry. My insides felt empty, like after having dry heaves. I had nowhere to turn. I pushed: "Are you saying you have a name for me, Jack?"

"Yes, I have a name for you, but it's not exactly what you're expecting."

"What's that supposed to mean?"

"Just this: Joe Biggs's death wasn't the result of some petty act of vengeance. Rather, it was part of a complex plan designed to muddy the waters, so to speak. More specifically, perhaps, to confuse and confound a certain detective, namely you."

"You're telling me some guy was killed to throw me off the fact that he was killed? What kind of nonsense—"

"No, no, no, you buffoon. He was killed to throw you off the trail of something bigger than a dead bowler—and I don't mean that literally."

I pushed harder: "Give me the name, Jack."

He lifted one of his legs and knocked out his pipe against the sole of one of his Bruno Maglis. He placed the pipe in the outer breast pocket of his suit. When he was damn well ready, he said: "You're looking for an organization called the Red Herring Syndicate."

Spence Nelson's dying words immediately echoed in my mind. "The Red Herring Syndicate?"

"The Red Herring Syndicate, yes. It's an underground crime organization in Testacy City. Many people are aware of their activity; a small handful have heard the name. Nobody knows anything else. This concerns me only in that this Syndicate continues to . . . interfere with some good opportunities that come my way."

"Uh-huh." I felt like an old-style phone operator who'd just had all her plugs pulled from the switchboard; I could almost see the lights flashing as I scrambled to reestablish the connections. "So, how does Suzi Biggs fit into all of this?"

"Hardly at all. I'm done with her. If I can speak frankly, man-to-man, she was an . . . *enjoyable* girl to know. And I made some modest efforts to continue that enjoyment. But enjoyment comes in many colors and many flavors, if you get my meaning, old boy." He let out a deep, lecherous laugh. He tilted his head back, and the floodlight reflected off his eyes.

He looked possessed.

He moved closer to me, but not too close. "So you can have Suzi Biggs. I can be awful generous with my . . . hand-me-downs."

My throat burned with rising bile. I funneled all my anger into the energy to stand. If I had been calmer, more relaxed, I would have exploded. But I was beat down enough to be desensitized to his childish instigations. He was pushing my buttons; the only thing I could do was let him and still stand strong.

"Why tell me all this, Jack? Why all of a sudden are you so willing to play ball?"

"I've been playing ball with you from the beginning; you just didn't know the rules of the game. Don't think for a moment that I wouldn't have a troublemaker like you locked away in a jail cell, especially when the police are so eager to do it for me."

If he wanted me to be grateful for his generosity, I wasn't.

"No, I've been testing you, seeing what kind of mettle you have. After you stormed into my office, I knew that if any man could take down the Syndicate, it would be you. You have that kind of fire.

"Don't get the impression, Drake, that I like you. The truth is that I know you're in deep enough, and you're desperate enough, to go out and shake up this group of malefactors. On the one hand, any rabble-rousing that you do to help yourself helps me even more. Of course, on the other hand, whether you choose to ignore me and my gift of information or not, they'll get to you. I'm sure you haven't more than a day—two at the most—to live. Then you won't be bothering me—or anyone for that matter—anymore. Good luck," he sneered.

So I was going to be his tin soldier, wound up and let loose in the minefield.

He was good. I was wound up plenty.

One of the monkeys threw my keys at me. Then all of their figures faded into the deep black surrounding the quarry.

This whole week I'd been collecting pieces of a puzzle that didn't quite fit together. Jack Walker had taken this puzzle and mixed it up good, and suddenly all the pieces were falling right into place. As hazy as my mind was, things were finally starting to make sense to me. I was beginning to see the pattern that spread out over Testacy City.

The more I thought about it as I drove back to town, the more it scared the hell out of me.

The scariest part was that one clue was still missing. Though I had no idea what it was or where to look for it, I knew it was the piece that would bring this whole mess together.

My foot pressed harder on the gas pedal. The city lights rose in the distance. I remembered the bottle of bourbon I'd left in the car. I grabbed it from under my seat, spun the cap off with my thumb, and poured enough alcohol down my throat to make me cough.

I focused hard on the lights from town. I could imagine the whole city in flames.

That thought kept me company the entire way home.

Chapter Twenty-Two
The Missing Clue

It was a little after nine by the time I got home. I was bone-tired, but Walker's information—along with the bourbon I'd sucked down on the ride back to town—had burned away at the fatigue. I could feel that I was close to the end of this.

I opened the door to my apartment and found Suzi Biggs laying claim to my favorite chair. That, I had expected. I had also expected the two of us to hit up a restaurant and get a nice meal, then for me to figure out a way to get the last piece of this puzzle out of her.

What I hadn't expected to see was Henry Goiler standing over her, his black 9mm Beretta stuck in her face.

Last I remembered, Goiler was the detective Hal had assigned to the Haufschmidt jewel case. I'd worked with him a couple of times before, and we always had good results, even though his crude ways clashed with mine. Regardless, he was the last person I expected to be threatening Suzi in my apartment.

His crudeness was all-encompassing. Goiler was a squat little man, pig-like in both appearance and manner. Perched on his head was a brown porkpie hat that was about a size too small. In fact, all of his clothes were too small: his tan pants just brushed the tops of his heavily scuffed brown oxfords, his yellow shirt didn't quite cover the volume of his belly, and his tiny brown necktie—the short, wide kind—looked like it belonged on a teenager. Over the whole ensemble he wore a threadbare brown suitcoat that seemed as if it was about to burst its seams.

He looked like a dangerous clown.

"Goiler?!" My voice cracked with confusion. "What are you doing here?"

"Ben!" Suzi cried, panic thick in her voice. "Thank God you're here! This guy broke in here and threatened to kill me!"

I was having a hard time accepting any of this. "Goiler, what's your deal?"

"Like you don't know, Drake," he drawled out of the side of his mouth, not taking his eyes off Suzi.

"I'm not in the mood for this!" The confusion and fatigue only added to my anger.

"Funny, Drake, very funny," Goiler spit out. The way he spoke required an excess amount of saliva. It wasn't pleasant. "I don't believe that for a minute. I know the tricks you like to pull, and you can't pull nothin' over on me."

"Come on, Goiler, put the goddamn gun away, and we'll get this straightened out. Christ, man, you're with the agency."

"Oh no. The gun stays." He jabbed the Beretta in Suzi's direction. "One false step, and it's curtains for the floozy."

"Hey! I'm no floozy!" Suzi, indignant, started to pull herself up out of the chair.

Goiler backhanded her hard across the face, knocking her solidly back into the seat. "I told you not to move." He emphasized every word with a thrust of his gun.

We weren't going to get to the bottom of this as long as Goiler was waving his gun around. And when he hit Suzi, he'd crossed the line. While he was paying attention to her, I made a play. It turned out to be a lame move. My lunge across the room suffered from bad timing and poor execution. Goiler saw me coming and had plenty of time to move his bulk out of my way. I slid past him, and he clubbed me right behind the ear with the butt of his gun as I went by.

The pain from the blow jarred me all the way to my toes. I lost what little balance I had and tumbled into my television stand, sending its contents skittering across the floor as I continued into the wall on the far side of my cramped living room. I landed with a thump.

"I told you, Drake, no tricks." Goiler walked over to me, snatched my gun from its holster, and put it in his coat pocket. "For safe-keepin'." His tiny black eyes glistened like oil-covered BBs from beneath the folds of his puffy face. When he saw I wasn't moving too fast, he turned his attention back to Suzi. "Now, let's try this again. Where's the bracelet?"

"Ohhh . . ." Suzi moaned, maybe out of pain, maybe out of frustration.

I pulled myself to a sitting position. "Bracelet?" I rubbed the sore spot behind my ear. It was already starting to swell. "What are you talking about, Goiler?"

"Oh, Ben," Suzi sighed, trying not to look at the gun pointed at her. "This is what I've been trying to tell you the whole time."

"What?" I was getting more confused by the second. "You've been trying to tell me something?"

"Shut up, the both of youse!" Goiler shouted. "I'm not playin' around here!"

Suzi started to cry, putting her shaking hands over her flustered face. "Ben, I'm so sorry. It's been hard . . . so hard . . ."

"Awright, stop it with the waterworks, already," Goiler ordered. "I can't stand blubberin' dames."

Suzi sniffed and managed to get herself under control. She looked over at me. "Ben, the day before he died, Joe gave me this diamond bracelet. It was beautiful."

"Aw, for cryin' out loud!" Goiler said. "Enough with the back story. Just fork over the goods!"

I ignored the fat gunman. Now that Suzi was talking, I didn't want her to stop. "A diamond bracelet, huh?"

"It was the nicest thing anyone had ever given me. I mean, people bought me expensive stuff before, but I knew Joe had sacrificed a lot to give me this. We were so happy we went out to have a nice dinner at the Long Mile—"

Goiler broke in: "Nobody cares where you were gonna eat—"

"Come on, man, have some patience. We're not going anywhere,"

I explained, hoping to cool him off a little. "You've got the gun."

"That's right I got the gun. What I don't got is the damn bracelet!"

Suzi had been holding back with her story for so long, now that she'd started, it was all flowing out. "The next day Jerry came by. I thought Jerry and I were friends. I thought he was going to comfort me, but instead he demanded that I give him the bracelet." Suzi's tears came back with a vengeance, making it hard for her to speak. "I . . . played dumb . . . not wanting to . . . lose . . . the last gift Joe . . . gave . . . me."

"I can't believe you're telling me this now," I said.

"That's the final camel straw! I've had about enough of all this yammerin'!" Goiler pointed his gun at me. "I want the bracelet. I know she's got it on her, 'cause I already tossed her place and got nothin'."

"Don't listen to him, Ben!"

Goiler turned and belted Suzi alongside her head, knocking her cleanly out of the chair and sending her sprawling on the floor. Still sobbing, she curled up into a little ball.

"I told you to shut up!" Goiler screamed at her, sweat running in torrents down his round forehead.

Seeing Suzi get hit again made me sick to my stomach, but I was too woozy and Goiler was too hopped up for me to try anything. There was nothing I could do except convince her to give him the bracelet.

Silence, except for Suzi's quiet sobbing, filled my apartment.

"I know you got it on you!" Goiler's bloodlust was running hot. His face was a dark crimson, and the veins in his temples throbbed with impatience. "You gonna give it up, or do I gotta strip you?"

"Suzi," I said slowly and quietly. I didn't want to do anything that would set Goiler off worse than he already was.

Suzi opened her eyes and peered at me.

Goiler pulled my weapon out of his pocket and started pacing around the room, a gun in each fist, crazy eyes darting between me and Suzi, looking too much like he was deciding who he was going to shoot first.

"I don't care that you haven't told me everything," I said. "Really, I don't. That doesn't matter now. All that matters is getting you out of this safely. So please, if you have the bracelet, give it to him."

"But . . ." Her eyes pleaded with me.

"Suzi, I know this guy. He's not kidding around. Give him the bracelet."

Suzi pulled herself up into a sitting position. Goiler watched her intently, his big fish-lips twitching, as she slowly unbuttoned the top of her blouse. She reached under the fabric and dug around in her brassiere. When she pulled her hand back out, she was holding a bracelet made up of the biggest diamonds I'd ever seen. It sparkled brightly in the dim light, and tiny rainbows flashed wildly from its many facets.

It was beautiful.

Suzi held it out to Goiler, eyes cast down at the floor in shame. He dropped my gun back into his pocket and snatched the bracelet from Suzi.

"That's more like it." Smug satisfaction played across his face. "Thanks for your cooperation, Drake."

"Sure, Goiler," I sneered. "Now how about leaving us alone?"

Goiler ogled the bracelet with palpable greed. His big pink tongue flicked out and cleaned the saliva from the corners of his mouth with a heavy slurping noise. He stashed the bracelet in the breast pocket inside his coat.

"Sure, I'll be leavin' all right." He wiped his mouth on the back of his fleshy hand. "But I can't let you stick around to squawk to the cops, so we're all gonna leave together."

"Where . . . where . . . are we going?" Suzi stammered.

"We're all gonna take a friendly little ride," Goiler's words, full of malice, oozed out from between his spittle-covered lips.

"A ride? Jeez, Goiler. Can you get any more cliché?"

"Shut up, Drake," he threatened. "Let's go." He gestured us to the door with a violent waving of his gun.

With some difficulty, I managed to get my legs under me and walk over to Suzi. She sat on the floor, staring intently at my shattered television.

"Oh, Ben," she wiped tears out of her eyes, "I'm so sorry."

"That's okay, Suzi." I held out my hand, offering to help her up. "Come on. Looks like we're not quite done yet."

She looked up at me and smiled. It was a small smile, but it was genuine. "I know you'll take care of me, Ben."

She took my hand, and I helped her up. Her confidence gave me strength.

"Where we going, Goiler?"

"Well, I've got some things to finish tonight, so I thought we'd head out someplace where you two won't be able to cause too much trouble," Goiler said. "I thought we'd head on out to the quarry."

For the second time that night, I drove my car down the desert highway to the quarry at gunpoint. Goiler insisted that he sit in the back where he could easily plug anyone who, in his words, "does anything stupid." That left Suzi sitting next to me, holding tightly to my leg. She was scared. Her long nails dug deeply into my flesh.

It wasn't long before Goiler had found my three-quarters-empty bottle of Old Grand-Dad rolling around on the floor and started taking heavy pulls from it.

Goiler's reputation as a slob was second only to his reputation as a braggart. I was hoping his pride, in addition to the alcohol he was consuming, would make him open to answering a few questions. I certainly wouldn't have time later when I had to make a move.

"Say, Goiler . . ."

"Yeah?"

"I'm wondering some things." I took a moment to continue, letting curiosity build in my throat. "Now, I've figured out that you were the one who ripped off the Haufschmidt jewels—"

"Did I now?" he interrupted with a coarse laugh.

"And I'm pretty sure you offed Iverson."

Goiler tipped the bottle to his lips and sucked noisily at the bourbon. "Yeah," he belched, "well, that's what you call an educated guess there, Drake."

"But I just don't understand why. How's he tied up in all of this?"

Goiler cackled from the backseat, "And I thought you were a detective." He took another swig of bourbon. "Y'see, Iverson wanted to be connected—too many cops-and-robbers shows on TV or somethin'. Anyhow, I helped him out. He was doing a little freelance work for me. The guy had the right attitude for crime, but he lacked conviction. And he forgot the first rule I taught him: you don't steal from the big man."

Finding out that Iverson pulled off the Haufschmidt jewel heist with Goiler was one big curveball—and just when I thought I had a handle on this case. That only left one question.

"So, did you take out Joe Biggs too?"

Silence emanated from the backseat. I glanced into my rearview mirror, but all I saw was the black of the lonely highway. The barrel of Goiler's gun jammed into my head, right behind my ear. Goiler pressed it hard against the tender spot where he had clubbed me earlier.

"I think you've asked enough."

Suzi's nails dug deeper into my leg. I could feel her shaking.

"That's not something you need to know, not where you're goin'," he said. "An' you keep yappin', you're gonna get there faster."

Goiler was just crazy enough to shoot the guy who was driving the car he was riding in. So instead of talking, I started thinking how I could get me and Suzi out of this fix.

My brain needed a little lubricant.

"Okay, then," I resigned. "If you're not going to talk to me, then how about giving me a little of that bourbon?"

More silence, then finally: "Awright, fine. Just don't drink it all." He handed me the bottle.

He sure hadn't left me much to work with. I took a couple of swallows, getting a good dose of Goiler's spit in the process, and passed it back. The liquor's sweet fire started burning in my throat and rapidly spread to my brain. Now it was time for a plan.

We rode the rest of the way in silence. This drive seemed a lot longer than my last one. Finally, we pulled up under the bright glow of the quarry's floodlight.

"Well, here we are," Goiler announced as I switched off the ignition. "Let's all move real slow, eh?"

We got out of the car and started walking. Goiler was pushing us along from behind, a gun in each fist. He stopped us when we got to the edge of the quarry. We were far enough away from the floodlight so that all I could see in front of me was a yawning pit of black.

I turned around, ready to make my play.

The dust we had kicked up shimmered as it settled back to the ground, making me feel like I'd slipped into a dream. The distant light behind Goiler streamed around him, cutting a man-shaped hole into the dust. The silhouette was as dark as the void behind me.

His mood seemed positively lighter, and he chuckled with glee as he said, "Okay, Drake. You got any last requests?"

Chapter Twenty-Three
Leningrad Rules

"You kill many people out here, Goiler?" I asked, trying to sound casual.

"What sort of trick are you tryin' to pull?" He looked at me quizzically.

"None at all. I'm just wondering how often you bring people out here and shoot 'em."

"A couple of times, I guess."

"Huh. You kill many people?"

"Ben . . ." Suzi whined, confused about what was running through my head. I couldn't blame her, I wasn't so sure myself.

"What's with all the questions?" Goiler barked.

"I'm just curious, so I thought I'd take you up on that last-request offer and ask a few."

He glared at me and wiped the sweat from his ample forehead. "Yeah, I've killed a few folks, sure. Okay?"

"Doesn't it get boring after a while?" I let loose with a little chuckle. "I read that somewhere."

"What do you mean?"

"I would guess it gets boring, all that death. You've got to keep coming up with more and more interesting ways to kill people to keep it fun, right?"

"I guess so . . ." He was still trying to figure out what I was up to. I was hoping I could keep him guessing until he was too caught up in my scheme to quit.

"What's the most interesting way you've ever killed someone?"

He thought a moment before he said: "I guess once when I gave this guy a Colombian necktie—"

"That's your most interesting murder?" I interrupted. "That's pretty boring, Henry."

"What . . . what do you mean?" I was starting to rattle him.

"Goiler, your problem is you've got no style."

"Style?"

"Yeah, style. I'll bet you're always in a rush and miss the finer points."

"Heh," he said, switching to the defensive. "Well, I get the job done."

"Sure you do," I agreed, "like Jerry Iverson."

"Yeah, like him. I already told you that," he snapped, his irritation at my questions building.

"Yeah, but you messed up, didn't you?"

"Whaddya mean? He's dead, ain't he?"

"Yeah, but it was supposed to look like a suicide, wasn't it?"

"Yeah . . ."

"And it didn't. You screwed up."

Silence.

I turned it up a notch. "I bet the Red Herring Syndicate wasn't happy about that, were they?"

"What are you talking about?" Goiler exploded. "I'm part of the Red Herring Syndicate!"

"How long have you been working for them?"

"*With* them," he corrected. "I've been working *with* them for a long time. Years."

"And you're still a pawn to them, just a little man to be shoved around. Dirty work needs doing? No problem, call Henry Goiler. 'Henry, do this. Henry, do that. Henry, kill Jerry Iverson. And don't mess it up this time!' But you did."

"Why you . . ."

"And you know why? 'Cause you're a screw-up with no style."

"You want style?" Goiler screamed at me. Even in the darkness I could see his puffy face turn bright red with anger. "You want style? I'll kill *you* with style!" He leveled his gun at my head. He was so mad he couldn't hold it steady.

"How? Shoot me in the head and leave my body in the desert?" I snarled. "That's not style."

"You got a better idea?"

"As a matter of fact, I do." My throat was parched. I ran my dry tongue across my lips. "Are you a gambling man?"

"Sure." His eyes squinted with confusion. "I like to play the ponies."

"That's good, 'cause I'd like to challenge you to a game. Just me and you."

"A game?" He took a wary step backward, gun still pointed at my head.

"Yeah, a simple game." I was feeling the adrenaline pump through my veins, knowing I was putting it all on the line. "If you win, you can do whatever you have to do with no interference from me."

"Oh, and let me guess," Goiler laughed, "if you win I gotta let you go?"

"Me and Suzi. Exactly." I waited for Goiler to respond. He didn't, so I prodded him along: "So, you up for it?"

"Maybe." Goiler scratched the side of his face with the barrel of his gun. "Depends what game we're playin'."

I paused, letting the silence of the night sink in before I responded with, "Russian Roulette."

"Oh God, no, Ben!" Suzi cried. She fell down at my feet, looking up at me, pleading.

Russian Roulette was an absurd and dangerous idea, but Goiler was an absurd and dangerous man. I needed this distraction so I could catch him off guard just long enough to get the upper hand.

"Jesus!" Goiler barked. "I've known you to do some crazy things, Drake, but . . . but . . . you're out of your damn mind!"

"Scared, Henry?" I asked, whispering.

"Shut up!"

"It's okay if you are; it takes a real man to play Russian Roulette."

"I said shut up!" Goiler looked down at the guns he held in each hand, thought creasing his brow. "I ain't afraid, Drake. Not of you. And not of some silly game of yours."

He broke my gun open, carefully keeping the Beretta trained on me. With his thumb he held in one round as he tipped the gun back, allowing the remaining four rounds to fall to the dusty ground. He snapped it shut with a flick of his wrist and gave the cylinder a hefty spin.

He handed the gun to me, barrel first.

"Okay. Let's do it. You first," he rumbled, aiming the barrel of the Beretta directly at my face, just below my left eye. "And if you don't pull that trigger, I'll do it for ya."

I was gambling with my life, and that didn't bother me. What did bother me was the fact that I was gambling with Suzi's life too. But despite that, I had to forge ahead. This was the only chance she had.

I could see Goiler trembling; I couldn't tell if it was out of excitement or fear.

My thoughts flashed back to the day—was it only yesterday?— that I stormed into Jack Walker's office. That was a pretty risky move then, but I got out of it just fine. Maybe I'd get out of this jam in one piece too. I just had to stay one step ahead of Goiler.

"Wait," I said, looking into his bloodshot eyes.

Suzi's crying lessened to a soft whimper before she held her breath, waiting for Goiler to respond. The absence of her sobbing left a tension that was terrifying.

"Scared, Drake?" Goiler asked.

"No, I just need to know which rules we're playing by."

"Whaddaya mean, rules?"

"There's two different versions of the game," I explained, "St. Petersburg rules and Leningrad rules."

"What the hell's the difference?"

"In St. Petersburg rules, you spin the cylinder between every pull of the trigger, but in the original version, Leningrad rules, you spin it only after everyone playing has had a turn."

"I don't care," Goiler said. "Whatever you want, let's just get this over with. No, wait. Let's play Leningrad rules. That sounds more fun."

"Fine, then."

"Yeah, fine. Now quit stallin' and play!" Goiler ordered, prodding me with the Beretta.

As my finger tightened on the trigger, visions of my wife, alive, vibrant, and beautiful played in my head. The roar of blood between my ears was deafening. I focused on the images of my wife . . . squeezed . . . and . . .

Click.

Goiler took the gun out of my numb hand and started laughing. "Damn, Drake! I didn't think you had the stones to do it!"

"Your turn, Henry," I deadpanned. "Do you have the stones?"

Goiler suddenly stopped laughing. "Damn right I do. But first . . ." He held the gun out to Suzi.

"No . . . oh no . . ." Suzi whined, her face wet with tears. She held her hands defensively outward and frantically waved them about like she was trying to escape a cloud of insects. She backed away as Goiler approached her.

"Goiler, leave Suzi out of this. This is just you and me playing."

"I'm in charge here, Drake." Goiler's laugh took on a more maniacal quality. "An' I say she plays."

There wasn't much I could do, not while he held that Beretta on Suzi. I knew if I made a move, he'd kill her.

Suzi took the Smith & Wesson from Goiler and sank to her knees. "Please, no," she begged, looking for mercy in Goiler's cold eyes, her arms held limply at her sides. Then she looked at me. The tears on her cheeks glistened in the dim light, and her big eyes were glazed over with fear. "Ben . . . Ben . . . I don't want to die."

"Yeah, yeah." Goiler aimed the Beretta at her forehead, careful to not turn his back to me. "Just get on with it."

Suzi lifted the gun to her left temple, barely having the strength to hold it there. Her whimpering echoed out across the quarry and got deep in my ears, bringing a guilt, thick and heavy, that settled in the pit of my stomach.

"Come on, Goiler," I pleaded, "leave her out of it."

Goiler looked back over his shoulder and shouted: "Drake, she's playin'! You quit complainin' about it, or I'll finish her right here!" His voice was rich with hostility.

"Please . . ." Suzi whined.

"Pull the trigger, or I shoot you right now," Goiler growled.

I stood there, feeling powerless as Suzi's sobs brought more pain to the sickness in my stomach. After an eternity of waiting, I heard a loud click. Suzi collapsed in a heap on the ground, her body twitching in spasms. She cried for all she was worth. Poor kid. I had to end this soon.

Goiler stood over her laughing uproariously. "That was great! You should have seen her eyes, Drake. Just like a deer caught in the headlights!"

"Okay, Goiler, your turn."

"Actually," he handed the gun to me, "I think it's your turn. That was just a warm-up round."

"That's not playing by the rules, Henry."

"I decided we're playin' Goiler's rules," he answered. "And that means it's your turn."

I figured he was gambling on one of us getting killed before he even had to play. While that may have been his plan, it sure wasn't mine. I promised myself I'd do this one more time, then I'd make my move. But if he wasn't going to play by the rules, I wasn't either. And I needed better odds. I spun the cylinder.

"Hey, what gives? Who said you could spin?" Goiler squealed.

I chose not to answer. I put the gun to my head, closed my eyes, and squeezed the trigger. It was easier the second time.

A long wail erupted from Suzi Biggs that seemed to go on forever. It sounded like someone was dragging a serrated blade across her belly.

I handed the gun back to Goiler. "Are you going this time? Or are you afraid to take your turn again?"

"I'm not afraid! I'll show you!"

This was the moment I'd been hoping for—I'd jump Goiler during that second of hesitation when, holding a gun to his own head, he contemplated the consequences of pulling the trigger.

Goiler grabbed the Smith & Wesson from me, spun the cylinder, brought it to his head, and squeezed the trigger. All in one fluid motion.

Click.

There went my chance. Just like that.

"There, Drake!" Goiler tittered. "You happy?!"

"Yeah, couldn't be happier."

This bad idea had just gotten worse. A lot worse.

He turned to Suzi, still lying in a heap in the dirt, and held the gun out to her.

"Your turn again, doll."

Suzi broke down into hysterics, hyperventilating uncontrollably. "No, not again. I can't do it again. Don't make me. Don't make me. Please."

"You can thank your new boyfriend, Ben Drake, for this world of pain. This is his game. You're gonna play 'cause that's what he wants." The twisted words slithered out of Goiler's throat. "Now play!"

Suzi gingerly took the gun and held it to her head for a moment, then let her arm fall to the ground. "Wait! I can't go . . . I just remembered . . . my puppies are at home . . . and there's nobody to feed them. I can't do this! I can't die! Who's going to take care of Laza and Apsos? Who'll care for my little puppies?"

"Come on, woman, we ain't got all night!" Goiler pulled back the hammer of his Beretta. "Play the game!"

Again Suzi placed the gun against her temple.

A cold chill ran down my spine. I had a bad feeling about this. I lunged at Goiler and yelled, "Suzi, don't!"

He saw me coming and spun to meet me, firing the Beretta in the process. The shot went wide, echoing off the quarry walls. I was close enough to the gun that it set off a ringing in my ears. The night suddenly seemed wrapped in cotton.

I tackled Goiler, taking him to the ground.

We struggled, rolling dangerously close to the edge of the quarry. Goiler grunted and flailed his legs. I pinned his gun arm beneath my knee.

Inexplicably, he kept on squeezing the trigger, sending bullets off into space. He was too busy trying to keep hold of his gun to do any sort of real fighting. One by one I pried his thick, strong fingers from the pistol.

I got the Beretta out of his grasp. Now I had to put him down quick. I hauled off and belted him across the jaw with the butt of the gun. I was rewarded with a loud crack as the bone broke beneath my blow.

Goiler howled like a wounded dog and clutched his jaw with both hands. He rolled back and forth, as if that would ease his pain.

I figured that would occupy him for a while, so I bolted over to Suzi's side. She was lying on the cold ground, motionless. When I reached her I saw why.

Her blank eyes stared vacantly at me. Her mouth hung slightly open. The whites of her eyes and her pearly teeth glowed eerily in the pale, dim light. A small, charred wound marred the left side of her head. A larger, bloodier wound blew out the opposite side of her skull. A thick trickle of viscous liquid, a mingling of blood and brains, oozed from the gaping hole.

I felt like someone had turned me inside out. The sickness in my stomach rose to my mouth and sent the contents of my guts spewing out hotly onto the desert ground. I wiped my mouth on the back of my hand and watched the sand absorb my steaming bile.

I heard a scraping sound behind me, and I spun around in time to see Henry Goiler struggling to get up. He was making a strange "wuffling" noise. It took me a moment to realize that it was the sound of a man with a broken jaw trying to laugh hysterically.

My vision turned red. For a moment I hated Henry Goiler with every fiber of my being. He was a despicable wretch who deserved to die.

I shot him twice in the head with his own gun. He dropped backward and landed with a sickening thump. I fell, first to my knees, then to my back. All the strength was gone from my body. It was the first time I'd deliberately killed anyone. The first time I'd committed murder.

The events of the night played out again and again in my head. I kept changing things slightly, hoping for a better outcome, but it always ended with Suzi's death.

I don't know how long I stayed like that, lying on the ground, looking up at the stars.

When I rose, I retrieved my empty gun from where it had landed beside Suzi. I went over to Goiler and pulled the diamond bracelet out of his pocket. I kicked his lifeless body over the quarry and stood there until I could no longer hear it sliding down the steep embankment. I tossed his gun after him.

I kept glancing back over my shoulder as I trudged to my car, hoping that Suzi would get up and be all right, knowing it was a ridiculous fantasy.

Chapter Twenty-Four
Tell Me Tomorrow

Nothing could possibly shake the image of Suzi Biggs from my mind. So on the hard, lonely drive back to my apartment, I thought of nothing.

At night the desert was cold. I drove with the window down. The air that rushed into my car made the sound of a low dirge. My teeth were clenched shut, and I grasped onto the steering wheel like it was the neck of my worst enemy.

I'm not a man who takes to crying; nevertheless, I wiped my eyes, knowing that the tears were in there somewhere and that they were bound to come out sooner or later.

When I got home, the door was unlocked. I pushed it open and entered the darkness with resigned indifference. If someone was waiting to ambush me, I would put up no fight. But I knew there would be no one there.

I walked into my kitchen and instinctively opened the refrigerator. I wasn't even slightly hungry, which was good because it held nothing but condiments, sour milk, and leftovers that should have been thrown out long ago. I was barely awake enough to stand. I just wanted desperately to keep moving, away from that day, into the next.

Tomorrow this case would be over. I knew that.

I closed the refrigerator door and looked around aimlessly. I saw the paper coffee cup that Suzi had brought with her that morning. Christ, how could it have been that very morning? I thought about her slapping me and her saying I wasn't a hero. I thought about us spending the day together at the animal park, acting like kids on a date. I slammed my fist on the counter.

"This isn't fair," I said aloud, simply to hear myself say it.

I had this sudden urge to be instantly unconscious. I headed straight for bed, not even pausing to turn the lights out. I collapsed facedown on the mattress. As I dug my head into the pillow I could smell her perfume—a faint scent remaining from when she had cried there that morning.

I should have slept in my chair, I thought. Too late now; I wasn't in any condition to move a muscle. I was out cold in seconds.

Morning came, and I just let it carry on. I felt no more desire to move than I had the night before. However, now that my eyes were open, I couldn't get back to sleep.

The phone rang. I didn't answer it. Some time later, it rang some more. I still didn't answer it.

But it got me thinking. I had a plan for how this whole mess would get wrapped up. The first thing I had to do was set that plan in motion. This involved some phone calls.

I dragged myself out of the bedroom and made the three calls I needed to make. They weren't easy. I had to pretend I was more in control of the situation than I really was; certainly, I couldn't let anyone know what had happened last night. Not yet. Despite my inner uneasiness, the calls came off okay.

I jumped into a long shower. The only other thing I had to do before nighttime was stop in the office. I didn't want to have to come back here after that. So after I was cleaned up and dressed real nice, I did one final check to make sure I had everything I needed. The last thing I did was clean my gun. Spinning the cylinder to check that it was oiled right sent chills up my spine.

Rhoda Chang stood up when I came through the door. Her eyes

went big as she glanced toward Hal's office and then back at me. She exaggerated her frown so that I could see her tiny teeth.

"I take it the boss ain't too happy?" It was mostly rhetorical; if everything had been hunky-dory I wouldn't have bothered to stop in.

With downcast eyes she shook her head no.

"I don't suppose he found out that I was at the bowling alley yesterday?"

Slowly and with sympathy she nodded her head yes.

"Thanks for the warning, Rhoda."

I managed to break my stoic expression long enough to wink at her. Damn cops. When I made the deal with Makoff and Nolan to keep me out of their report, I didn't really expect them to play fair. I was just hoping to buy some time. Looks like all I bought was a fast train ticket to an earful of heat.

When I entered Hal Reddy's office, the hell I'd expected launched out of his mouth like a rocket to the morgue. All I could make out between the spittle and swear words was his distinct brand of frustrated anger.

"I'm not going to argue with any of your accusations, Hal. Right or wrong, I had my reasons; now I got to see it play out."

Hal was flicking his ear, the one with the piece missing out of it. I'd seen him do this at other times when he was frustrated and wanted to remind people—and probably himself as well—that he could take a lot and still not back down.

Hal turned down the volume of his voice, which meant he turned up the sarcasm. "I suppose you're so wrapped up in right and wrong that ya forgot ya got a boss to answer to?"

"I know this isn't going to make you happy, but I've been working straight for the mother. And I know this means I might lose my job, but I can't let the lady down. Besides, I know who the killer is."

"You know better than to play games with me. If ya got a name, then let's hear it."

"All I ask is that you believe I've got a plan that will put all the problems churned up by this murder to rest. I'm meeting with the killer at the bowling alley bar tonight. If you're going to fire me, tell me tomorrow. Tonight, I have work to do."

As I turned to go, I expected more screaming, maybe even something thrown at me. Instead, Hal Reddy just sat there fuming, his finger flicking his ear.

It was all about waiting now. A large chunk of the day was already gone, and I wanted to spend the rest of it alone. I don't remember exactly where I went. Where I went and what I did are not important.

What's important is that I walked down a dusty street into the open arms of Testacy City and became one of her ghosts.

Chapter Twenty-Five
Drinks with the Killer

I walked into Penny's Lanes Bowling Center for what I knew would be the last time. For all the hours I had recently spent here, everything felt new. I was immediately overwhelmed by the low rumble of rolling balls and the crash of falling pins. I was aware of the twangy country-western music that played in the background.

And I noticed that lane 13 was back in operation; the young family gathered there was bowling happily, oblivious to the murder that had taken place where now they stood.

I walked slowly to the bar, right past Enrico, the shoeshine kid. He called out to me, "Shine, mister?" I turned away, surprised that he didn't seem to recognize me. Though maybe he did, because he kept after me: "Come on, mister, how's about a shine? They're some nice shoes you got. I could shine 'em up real good!"

I disappeared into the comfort of the bar. It was empty.

After my first glass of bourbon, I had the feeling that the killer might be stalling, hoping that I'd drink myself out of commission before he got here. When Mabel came back to get me another glass, I switched to ginger ale. I wanted to keep a clear head, and without a steady flow of drinks to soothe my raw nerves, my small cigars had to carry that burden. Waiting was always easier with tobacco.

I kept my back to the door of the bar. I didn't want to seem too anxious. I knew the killer would show up at some point.

Shortly past midnight, after several hours of waiting, I heard a body shuffle up behind me. The foul-smelling smoke of a cheap dime-store cigar told me my hunch was right. I glanced to my right and saw Hal Reddy sit down on the barstool next to me. I said, "I wasn't one hundred percent sure it was you until now. Here." I pulled out the diamond bracelet and slid it across the bar counter toward him.

"What's this?" he asked, nonplussed.

"The missing Haufschmidt jewel, of course. I figure you were in on that too."

"You keep working on all the cases I kick ya off of?"

"Don't play dumb, Hal. Time for that is over."

"What kind of fool ideas you got cooking in that noodle of yours, Drake?"

"Goddamnit, Hal!" I said in a loud whisper, not wanting to start a commotion. "I'm trying to level with you. Now you level with me. Here's how I figure all this played out.

"You, Hal Reddy, are the head of the Red Herring Syndicate. Something must have got to you in LA back when you worked homicide. When you moved up here, the town was ripe for someone to take it over. So you got this bright idea: start a detective agency and gather as much information about the crime world as you could. Once you got set up and established a reputation and all, you brought on a select group of people you knew you could really trust—people who were in this for the long haul and not out to make a quick black buck. They do all the 'administrating,' so most people in the Syndicate, the people under them who do the dirty work, don't know who the real boss is.

"Even better is the fact that you can set up crimes and then put your own detectives on the cases to 'solve' them—the driving force behind the Red Herring Syndicate being to pull off random, almost absurd crimes that you can frame on some hapless pigeon. That way, the media's attention turns away from the big-money capers.

"This case is the perfect example. You found out that an enormous collection of jewels was coming into the city. You and your inside buddy Henry Goiler staged a heist. Though, let me tell you, Goiler wasn't the man you thought he was. But I'll get to him soon enough. Then all you had to find was a punk who was expendable in case you needed a fall guy. Enter young wannabe crook, Jerry Iverson.

"After the robbery, Mrs. Haufschmidt came to the Always Reddy Detective Agency. This was nice and convenient for you because she brought with her a list of the stolen jewelry. That's when you found out a bracelet was missing.

"Of course, Iverson is the main suspect; his first job and already he's trying to skim off the top. You get Goiler to brace him with the question, and he finds out that bonehead Jerry gave the rocks to his bowling buddy, Joe Biggs, so that Joe could keep his marriage from slipping away.

"So you had to come up with a new plan: kill Gentleman Joe with an over-the-top display of violence to take the spotlight away from the stolen jewels. The public would become obsessed with finding out who could commit such an atrocity, which means the police would feel the pressure to find the killer quickly. Then a couple days later you have Iverson killed, making it look like he hanged himself. There'd be enough circumstantial evidence to connect him to the Biggs murder, so the police would have a nice, neat package to sell to the news hounds. By that time, the jewel heist would be yesterday's news.

"Didn't count on me being smart enough to figure all this out, did you, Hal? You thought I'd be just as gullible as the police on this one. What you really didn't count on was Jerry Iverson talking to me about Suzi Biggs's affair with Jack Walker."

"What?" Hal blurted out. It was delivered with just enough surprise to make me believe that he really didn't know about it. That was good; telling him something he didn't know would give me a small advantage.

"Getting beat up by Walker's goons—that's not my idea of a good time, Hal. I'd love to knock him down a few notches. That's why we're here. I have a proposition for the leader of the Red Herring Syndicate. I was pretty sure it was you, but I had to get you to meet me here to be certain. Well, here you are, so let me give you my offer." I paused. He eyed me suspiciously. "I want in. Cut me a piece of the action."

"You're mad in the head, boy."

Hal waved the old bartender over his way and ordered a bottle of light beer.

"No way, my head's crystal clear now. I've come this far. I figured you out. Now deal me in. I've shown good faith here, returning the bracelet to you. Oh yeah, I forgot to tell you about your man Goiler. I saw Goiler tonight, and he sold you out."

"What do you mean he sold me out?"

"You heard me. He filled me in on most of the details I was missing. If you don't believe me, take a trip to the quarry, maybe his corpse'll tell you something."

"His corpse?"

"That's right. I shot him and dumped the body. He was afraid of you, afraid of what you'd do to him if he couldn't get the bracelet. That's when I saw my opportunity: I put the plug in him, drove over to Suzi Biggs's place, and got her to show me the bracelet. Then I put a plug in her. I'll tell Mother Biggs that Suzi had something to do with her husband's murder, and that she's fled the city. No one will miss her."

I wondered if Hal was going to bite. He said, "You killed Suzi Biggs?"

"That's right."

He twitched in his seat. His eyes stayed on me even as he tilted his head back to take long swallows of his light beer. He drank like a college boy. I got the impression he was trying to figure me out, and that had him on the defensive. Right where I wanted him.

I stood up. "Maybe you don't understand me, Mr. Reddy, but I've got you, got you right where I want you."

He chuckled at this.

"All right, laugh if you want to. What you have to understand is I'm not backing down. This city has Benjamin Drake's name all over it, and I'm taking hold of it. You don't want to deal me in, I'll go right through you. I bet Jack Walker would be interested in finding out the name behind the Red Herring Syndicate."

"You can't take me down." Hal pointed a finger at me. He was talking between gritted teeth.

"I can and I will, you smug bastard. That is, unless you're ready to play ball with me. Actually, forget it. I've given you chance enough; I'm going to see my new buddy, Jack."

"You little worm—I'll step on you and smear your guts on the cement."

"Why, Hal? Why did you kill Gentleman Joe Biggs?"

His eyes lit up like a maniac's. I went too far with that last line.

"Ya trying to get a confession out of me? Cops got ya all wired up? Well, you're not going to get me to confess to anything."

The fire in his eyes flickered. He pulled a huge Colt Python from his jacket. He leveled the gun at me inconspicuously enough, but it was hard to be subtle with a piece like that.

"Come on, Ben, let's go back to the office. I've got another case for you."

I leaned back against the bar. "Maybe you haven't been listening. I don't work for you anymore. Now that I figured out how you operate, I'll be calling the shots. Me and Mr. Walker, that is."

Hal's temper was getting the best of him. He lunged at me, throwing his empty left fist at my head.

I was prepared for this, and even though Hal's swing came at me fast, I managed to duck under his roundhouse, balling my hands into fists. I shot back up, bringing with me five hard knuckles to Hal's chin. Despite this solid punch, he was already sending a left jab to my forehead. It connected with a heavy thump. I stumbled back and fell to the floor.

His blow left me dizzy. Before I could shake it off, he was on top of me—the gun at my temple and his meaty, heavy hand around my throat.

My hands shot immediately to my neck and tried to loosen the grip his strong fingers had on me.

Mabel spoke up sternly: "You boys want to have a rumble, then take it outside. This is a family establishment. Don't make me call the cops!"

I could see the sweat start to bead on Hal's bald head at the mention of the word "cops." His hand still around my neck, he slammed my head to the floor. It didn't help my wooziness, but at least I was still conscious. He should've known I have a hard head.

He got up, hid his gun, and moved to the wide exit way of the bar.

As I struggled off the floor, I saw him turn to the left, then waffle nervously and go the other way. So he was rattled and in flight. Good.

When I scooted out of the bar, I did a quick eyeball of the scene; I saw what spooked him: some boys in blue were loitering to the left near the entrance. Unfortunately for Hal, there was no exit in the direction he headed.

Hal knew the layout of this place; after all, he had been here just a week before. There were two walkways on either end of the lanes that led into the back of the building. But as I knew from Dino's brief tour, the exit back there was on the left as well. Doing his best to look casual, Hal hurried down the right walkway, through the narrow door.

I didn't have time to be discreet, because I knew that once he got into the back he would bolt for the exit. So I sprinted across the lanes, jumping the gutters, sidestepping oncoming balls. Some bowlers shouted out rude names at me. Rude names I could handle. At least they weren't carrying guns.

As I went through the door Hal had used, I pulled out my piece. I let it lead the way around the bulk of the monstrous pinsetter machines. Hal was running down the narrow back corridor.

"Stop running, Hal! It's all over."

He turned to face me, his gun zeroed in on my chest, mine on his. His chin was raised in the air as he tilted his head side to side like a snake about to strike. He moved slowly toward me, his eyes drilling into mine.

"Shoulda let me walk out of here, Ben. Now I gotta put you down."

"You'll go down with me. That how you want this to end?"

He continued to pace slowly toward me. "If ya want to end it here, I'll end it here."

My gun arm felt stiff and heavy, but I kept my piece pointed at him. The closer he got, the more certain it was that we both wouldn't miss.

"Christ, Hal, you're a psychopath, you know that? You're a grade-A, certified nutcase. It *was* you that killed Gentleman Joe. You did it with your own crazy-man hands."

He got closer still. He shouted over the roar of the machinery, "And do you know why? He had integrity and conviction. He really loved that slut wife of his. He would have rather died than disappoint her." He cursed. "If I could smash those bowling balls against his happy little head one more time, I would!"

I'd had enough. "Stop right there, Hal! Drop the damn gun, or I drop you!"

He fired his weapon.

My gun flew from my hand as I staggered backward into the wall. My legs went out from under me, and I went down. I didn't dare take my eyes off Hal to look at my wound, but I knew from the pain that he'd clipped my right shoulder.

He came closer and towered over me, gun in my face. "Well, Ben, it's been a pleasure working with you. But I'm afraid I have to let you go."

The back doors flew open with a metallic clang. "Freeze, sucker!" It was Duke Wellington and Weisnecki, finally come to join us.

Hal turned and fired on them. That gave him just the moment he needed to climb up into the machines. He reached the overhead catwalk and crouched there, using one of the support beams for cover.

He had nowhere to go, and I think he knew it. He stood up to shoot off a couple rounds at them, but all he did was open himself up. One of the cop's shots connected, and blood spouted from Hal's neck. He let loose a gargled cry of pain and fell back into the huge machine's inner workings.

I glanced over at my shoulder. To my surprise, Hal had only grazed me. But it was enough to get blood all down my sleeve and for it to hurt like hell.

I scuffled over to where Hal lay. His body was mangled, twisted wildly between the metal bars and wheels of the pinsetter machine. A wicked-looking piece of metal had pierced his belly. His eyes were twitching and he was losing a lot of blood. Duke Wellington strolled over, slid his big gun into its holster, and peered down at Hal.

As if Hal could sense us there, he managed, gritting his teeth against the pain, to lift his head and focus his eyes on me. "Damn you, Drake," he croaked. "You weren't supposed to figure this out. No one was." He coughed violently, spitting a mouthful of foamy blood all over the front of his shirt. "I should have given this case to Manetti."

His head fell back against a metal bar with a sickening thud, but he managed to keep his eyes fixed on me.

Duke Wellington and I just stood there and watched the life fade out of Hal's eyes. His wounds were far too severe for us to do anything else. Then in my mind, one last problem jumped out at me. Not so much a problem as it was an anomaly. "Wait a second! If you didn't know about Jack Walker and Suzi Biggs, why did you plant ball bearings at both crime scenes?"

Hal gasped for air. I could barely make out his last words: "What ball bearings?" Then he closed his eyes, and his body was still. Maybe I imagined it, but the faint trace of a smile seemed to flicker across his face.

"Well, Drake," Duke Wellington drawled, "looks like you were right . . . again." I thought I heard the tiniest bit of admiration slipping out from behind the gruffness in his voice.

One of the three calls I'd made that morning was to Wellington. When I laid out the whole scenario for him, he was skeptical. But despite his feelings toward me, he knew that I was good at solving convoluted cases, and he understood me well enough to know that I wouldn't be setting my boss up for a hard fall if I didn't have a damn good reason.

"So, are we finished here, then?" I asked.

He nodded his big head. "Yeah, we're finished. I think we've got everything we need. Don't go skipping town on us, though," he ordered. "Just in case we don't."

"Don't worry, I'm not going anywhere."

"Yeah? So now whatcha gonna do, hotshot?"

"First, I'm going to sleep for a few days. Then, it looks like I'm self-employed."

"Jesus!" Duke Wellington spouted. "That's all this town needs— a goddamn lone-wolf Ben Drake runnin' around stickin' his nose in all the places it don't belong!"

I couldn't let him have the last word. "Come on, DW, you didn't think I'd want to stop solving your cases just because my boss is dead, did you?"

He had more to say, but I wasn't hearing any of it. I walked outside and took a breath of late-night air.

I'd made two other calls that morning. One was to Elizabeth Biggs, letting her know that this mess was about to come to an end. She told me over and over how proud she was of me and that she knew I was the right man for the job.

Without going into detail, I told her that I knew of two little dogs that suddenly found themselves without a home. I figured they'd be good company for her. She seemed to agree, even though this made her start in with the questions. I promised I'd give her the whole story later. We made plans to have coffee together the following week.

As usual, talking to her made me feel good. Her words gave me the strength to see the night's events through to the bloody end.

Walking to my car, I realized I was shaking, the reality of the evening finally overriding the blur that comes with a rush of adrenaline. I paused, lit a cigar, and continued across the parking lot.

I was glad—and more than a little surprised—to find Rebecca Hortzbach leaning against my powder-blue Galaxie 500, smoldering cigarette between her lips. My third call had been to her, and I wasn't expecting to see her until later in the week. It'd been awhile since I'd seen her in street clothes. It didn't take me long to notice she looked great.

Rebecca took a long last draw on her cigarette, then flicked the butt across the dark lot. "Looks like you need to relax. Let's take care of that shoulder and get you some breakfast."

I tugged on the knot of my tie and unbuttoned my collar. "Sure. You got any ideas of where to go?"

"Ben, my dear, I've got plenty of ideas."

"Yeah, that's what I was hoping you'd say."

ACROSS THE LINE

(2013)

I leaned against a streetlight post, pulled the brim of my fedora down, and kept my eyes locked on the small figure limping away from the drugstore. In his grubby little hands, he held a brown paper sack about the size of a lunch bag. During the hour or so I'd been on his tail, I'd been waiting for him to slip up, get sloppy, or in some other way show his hand. All people have weaknesses. Crooks, cops, grifters, gift-givers, pimps, pushers, and priests—all the same. Watch someone long enough and you'll see hairline faults vein their way across the strongest of façades. Just a matter of waiting it out.

Or was that all a load of no-good nonsense, some feel-good, pulpy truism that I told myself while I battled the bad guys? They say some things, some people, *do* change. Certainly, I changed a lot in the days after I cracked the Gentleman Joe Biggs murder case. My office location had changed: up two floors in the William Kemmler Building, a more modest space than the open layout of the Always Reddy Detective Agency. My relationship with Rebecca had changed, and for the better.

One person I didn't expect to change was Detective Duke Wellington, which is why I was surprised to find him turn up as the first paying customer at my brand-new agency.

I pushed off the light post and eased into the thin foot traffic on Porras Street. My target walked at a good, steady pace until he reached the corner. He stopped next to a blue mailbox, craning his neck to see if the coast was clear. *Clear for what?* I wondered as I ducked into the closest alcove. It couldn't be anything good. The last time I saw Zef Ehrenreich, he was shouting threats and giving me a good time with his foot in my gut.

That's not why I was now following this diminutive loudmouth, though. I'd gotten a tip-off while doing some investigating at the Short Stop—a popular cop bar on the east side of town—that Ehrenreich would lead me to my real mark. The more suspiciously he behaved, the more I knew I had the right guy.

Ehrenreich put the paper bag down next to the mailbox and walked away.

My first thought was to wait for him to clear the corner and race over to the bag and check its contents. But I froze, realizing that it could easily be a trap. A bomb? A cache of toxic chemicals? How could I test the bag without putting myself or the folks on the street at risk? Every second I thought about it was more time that Zef Ehrenreich had to lose my tail.

Hell, I'd done a lot riskier things than pick up someone's drug-store throw-away. I went to grab it when a kid, only about eleven, ran in front of me, snatched the bag, and started shouting around the corner: "Hey, mister! You forgot your lunch!"

"No!" I yelled. "Put that sack down, kid!"

He eyed me with all the uncertainty of a preteen. "What's your deal? It's not your lunch."

"It's not yours either. Just put it down." I suddenly had a flash-back to an adult telling *me* not to do something. I never listened. I knew this kid wouldn't either.

A quick standoff. Me and the kid. Eyes locked. The kid broke it by opening the bag, shoving his hand inside like it was a Cracker Jack box.

"I said no!" I ran over to him.

He crumpled the bag in a loose ball, tossed it at my chest. "There's nothing in it."

He ran off. I picked up the brown ball, uncrumpled it, looked inside.

It was empty—almost, except for a white index card, with a type-written message on it: *Come and get me.*

So I guess the good news was I hadn't lost Ehrenreich. He was bound to be right around the corner, waiting.

"I'm tellin' you, Drake, this is unusual business, highly unusual. Duke Wellington doesn't make a habit of asking private heat for help." The big policeman paced in front of my metal desk. He was wearing a green sports coat over skinny black slacks. He looked more like a real estate agent than a cop.

"Believe it or not, DW, I want to help you." I had a hard time believing it myself. "When was the last time you saw him?"

"Over a week ago." He patted his sweaty bald head with a colorful handkerchief.

I opened the bottom desk drawer, pulled out a bottle of bourbon and two small juice glasses.

"Sit down. Have a drink with me."

"Can't do that, Drake. I'm a public servant, on duty. Wouldn't be right, just wouldn't be right."

I poured the hooch in both glasses. Pushed the one glass over toward him. Pointed at the glass, pointed at the chair.

He sat and took a drink.

"Mark's not the kind of guy to go missing. Not like this. I smell trouble. I got to get to the bottom of this."

I nodded my head. I took a deep breath before diving in. "Look, I don't know how to say this, but Mark strikes me as a cop whose sense of the law is a little more gray than pure black and white."

He clenched his white teeth. "You got something to say, why don't you spit it out and say it."

"Have you ever noticed Weisnecki doing something on the wrong side of right? Something that might get him in over his head?"

Duke Wellington paused long enough to give truth to my suspicions. I knew the cops in this town. Just like I knew the crooks. "Let me tell you somethin', Drake, I've seen things, okay, things that don't make me any too happy. I got my way of doin' things. Mark's got his way of doin' things." He stood up. "That don't mean he's gone rollin' to the other side! He's police."

I didn't say anything. I wanted to let him cool down. The last thing I needed was a fistfight with the fuzz. He sat back down.

I tried a different approach: "I know you're not going to tell me details of the cases you two were working. Can you tell me anything?"

"I'll give you details, Drake. Details like this: we're workin' an art heist. But that ain't it. That case is a piece of cake, even you could solve it . . . I mean, you could solve it even without gettin' your face kicked in a couple times."

I rolled my eyes. He continued: "Okay, we also got two homicides. A hit-and-run that took place on South 15, near the city line. A woman shot in the stomach with a tiny-caliber load—probably lovers' spat got out of hand. So what else? We're trackin' a money-laundering scheme run by a joker named Small-Tooth Kelley, and a few narco runs that're probably unrelated."

I knocked back my bourbon. "Wait, did you say Small-Tooth Kelley?"

Suddenly the mysterious disappearance of Detective Mark Weisnecki had me very interested.

I turned the corner and saw the smug little jerk a few blocks down the street, just standing there eyeing up the latest fashions in the haberdashery window. I adjusted my hat against the glare of the late-afternoon sun and started a slow stroll down Cherry Boulevard.

When I got about halfway to him, he checked his watch and started north. He walked for a few blocks, speeding up, before he turned down a side street. I picked up the pace myself, sprinting for a block and a half, before I slipped back into a brisk walk as I turned the corner.

Ehrenreich was up ahead of me a lot farther than I expected him to be. He was pretty fast for such a little guy—I'd have to put a little more hustle into my efforts if I wanted to catch him.

We did the cat-and-mouse thing for about half an hour, Ehrenreich leading me on some kind of manic chase right into Testacy City's warehouse district, a sprawling assemblage of stone and steel just across the freeway from downtown.

There was a time, not too long ago, when the warehouses were bustling with commerce, but these days many of the buildings were just husks, bleak reminders of a once-promising era.

Ahead of me, Ehrenreich disappeared down a narrow alley between two derelict buildings. I really wanted to get this over with. I dashed up the street, turned the corner, and bolted down the alley. I burst out into the cross street, looking left, then right, then skidding to a stop on a patch of loose gravel.

Nothing. I'd lost him. I bent over, breathing hard, thinking about a smoke. Over my ragged breaths and pounding heart, a noise caught my attention. I looked across the street and saw Buck Bixel, the muscle to Ehrenreich's mouth, casually tossing a baseball up and catching it, over and over. He stared right at me, grinned, and stepped through a small door on the side of an unmarked warehouse, chased by the day's growing shadows.

I sighed, checked my gun. I knew it was loaded but checking made me feel better, made me think I'd be ready for whatever was going to happen inside. Thinking back to the last time I followed a maniac into a building, I felt for the small flashlight in my suit pocket.

I crossed the street, searching for something—anything—that would give me a clue about just what the hell was going on. The whole place was deserted, except for the nose of a once-red, rusting-out late-model Ford pickup poking out from another alley just down the street.

The handle of the door Bixel went through wasn't locked. I didn't think it would be. The door opened silently. After one last glance around, I slipped inside, pistol up, ready for anything.

The cavernous warehouse, dimly lit from above by mercury vapor lights, housed rows of boxes and crates stacked to various heights on thick metal racks. The whole place looked like a maze. I hated mazes.

I heard the distant *ding* of an elevator arriving. I peered down a long aisle toward the back of the building. One of those big freight numbers where the doors closed up and down whirred to life.

I ran down the aisle, knowing I'd never make it in time, knowing I had to try. I glimpsed the outline of a short man inside the elevator before the doors clamped shut and a green arrow pointing up winked out.

Noticing a big steel door in the corner, I pulled it open and rushed up the steps, taking two at a time. The warehouse ceiling was at least thirty feet high, so I knew I had a good climb ahead of me. I rushed up six flights, footsteps clanging on the diamond-plate steel, before I burst through the door, gun leading the way.

Nothing. I stood in a dark room, elevator to my right, doors closing. I frantically slapped at the down button, hoping to stop it. I didn't.

This game was getting old, and I was tired of playing. Then the lights went out.

Even though there were a few hours of light left in the day, the inside of this place was as dark as a cave. Dark and silent. I was half-expecting something to hit me on the back of the head. Instead, I heard the click-and-slide of a door locking behind me.

I turned on my flashlight and tried the door to the stairs. It didn't budge. Even if I took the time to pick the lock, the heavy bar on the other side would make sure the door stayed shut. I couldn't see it, but knew it was there.

Going backward wasn't an option. I was being led somewhere, that much was obvious, so I decided to take a look around and see where I was headed.

I shined my light around the room. I couldn't see very far into the gloom, just far enough to spot two bodies lying motionless on the floor. The body closest to me, a big man in a dirty T-shirt and ripped jeans, lay facedown on the cold stone floor, arms splayed out to the sides. The back of his head had been cracked open by something heavy. A red halo of blood, shimmering in my light, surrounded his head.

Gun in one hand, flashlight in the other, I pushed him with my foot. He flopped over onto his back. Turned out I knew him—or at least *of* him. Beast Benton, face puffy from a recent beating, had taken his last fall.

Ehrenreich. Benton. Small-Tooth Kelley. This thing was starting to make some sense: That run-in I'd had with Small-Tooth Kelley— a little gambit with a big bag of oranges—when he was trying to fix one of Benton's fights, and I broke it. Now Benton was dead, and it was probably my fault. Damnit.

The other body groaned. I shined my light over in time to see a man start to sit up. I knew this one too, and a lot better than I'd known Benton. "Weisnecki!"

He rubbed an eye with one hand. "Drake? What the hell are you doing here?"

"Looking for you."

"Well, you've done a bang-up job." He reached under his coat and pulled out his big pistol. The barrel pointed right at me. "But it ends now."

"Mark, wait!"

He fired. His shot went wide.

I didn't want to shoot a cop. Even in Testacy City that would mean trouble. I dropped my gun and held my arms out. "Look, Mark, I have no idea what your beef is here. But let's talk it out."

Weisnecki struggled to his feet, chuckling softly. "Figures Kelley would bring you in on this." He leveled the gun at me again.

I tossed my flashlight off to the side. There was just enough light in the room to see Weisnecki's vague black-on-black outline. I ran at it, and tackled him low around the waist. He brought the butt of his gun down on my back once, twice, before we hit the ground. I heard the weapon skitter across the floor, disappearing deeper into the darkness.

Weisnecki brought his knee up hard, right into my stones. He fought dirty. I should have seen that coming. Pain lanced through my body and burrowed deep into my kidneys. My eyes watered, the back of my throat burned. I rolled onto my side, groaned, and caught Weisnecki's shoe straight in my gut.

"Nice try, Drake, but I ain't going out that easy."

I struggled to make my mouth form words. "Mark, what the hell are you talking about?"

"I—we—know you've been dealing with Kelley. That business with Benton? We know you were mixed up in that."

"Dealing with? Mixed up? Christ, Mark. I had a case. I closed it, plain and simple. It's what I do." I tried to sit up, but Weisnecki slammed his foot down on my shoulder. My senses were all haywire. I spit out a mouthful of bile, my eyes stung, my nostrils burned.

"Uh-huh. And then you tried to cover your tracks, but you got sloppy." He stood over me, an angry silhouette, hands balled into fists, daring me to make a move.

"Seriously, I have no idea what you're talking about." I tried to sit up again. This time I made it. My nostrils still burned, a gasoline smell, smoke and ash. I knew that smell—fire, and too close to where I was. "Look, we have to get out of here. Let's talk this out later."

"We ain't going anywhere, Drake." He pulled a pair of handcuffs from inside his coat. "You're not slipping away this time."

I held my hands up. "No time for the bracelets. This place is going to be cinders, and I don't want to be inside when it goes. We have to get out of here. Now."

Weisnecki hesitated, looked around. He could smell it now too. I dragged myself to my feet. We could both hear the crackling and popping from below as the fire ate through the warehouse.

"Mark, we don't have a lot of time. We can figure this out together—"

"Together? Like you and Brockman did? Think I forgot about that?"

A few years back, I'd had an accidental run-in with a tough-guy cop by the name of Bob Brockman. He'd set up a crazy murder-and-get-rich-quick scheme. I busted up his plan, we tussled, he didn't make it. Weisnecki knew how it ended, and, no, I didn't think he'd forgotten. I knew I hadn't. More often than I cared to admit, memories of that day—a twisted mess of a day that changed my life forever—sneaked up on me.

"No. Look. Brockman was—"

"—Dirty, yeah, I know. He was working a score. And someone cleaned up behind him."

"Yeah, you." When I left Brockman's body in the basement of a burned-out building, I left the cash behind too. Someone else took it. I always suspected a certain policeman.

Weisnecki snorted and pointed at my chest. "You think I took the cash? Hell, Drake, I think it was *you*."

Smoke came up from the first floor. The temperature rose steadily. I looked down, shaking my head. "None of this makes any sense. I'm leaving with or without you, but I could use your help."

Weisnecki coughed. He put the handcuffs back into his pocket. "All right. Let's go."

You see, tough guys try to break down a door by throwing themselves into it, leading with the shoulder. In my experience, all that's going to do is give you a sore shoulder. I've busted down more than a few doors in my day, and I've always had the best results with a well-placed kick, right at the lock. Sometimes it takes a few hits, but most doors can't stand up to that kind of punishment. This door's construction gave more fight than I'd hoped it would, but after a repeated assault from both of us, the lock popped, and we raced down to the first floor.

I put my hand against the door at the bottom of the stairs. Hot, and that meant danger. But I didn't see how I had a choice. We were either going to die in this building or we were going to make it out alive. I pulled the door open, wincing against the blast of heat that roared into the stairwell.

The first floor was nothing but flame. We had a long run ahead of us. I glanced over at Weisnecki. He was looking at me, scared. Hell, I was scared too. But I'd done this before. It was up to me to get us out. "Follow me. Stay close."

Weisnecki nodded. I nodded back, and moved out into the inferno. We dodged and danced our way through the flames, making good progress toward the door. We were almost clear when I heard Weisnecki's strangled cry. I looked back in time to see him falling, landing in a pile of flaming debris.

I ran back to him. Blood streamed from a gash on the side of his head. I grabbed him under his arms and started dragging.

He gasped. His eyes rolled up and back.

His weight slowed me down. My skin itched. I could feel it getting pink. I pulled the two of us across the threshold, but the fire chased us out of the building, trying to follow us into the alley. Fire snaked along Weisnecki's body, smoldering on his cheap suit.

I struggled to get out of my jacket. I jumped on top of him, padding the flames out with my coat. He started coughing, singed but alive.

I dragged him further into the alley, away from the building. I slumped down onto the cracked blacktop next to him and watched the flames twist and dance along the warehouse's bleak façade, the low wail of approaching sirens howling in the distance.

"Mark, I didn't take that money."

Weisnecki leaned back on his elbows, pulled out a crumpled pack of cigarettes, put one between his lips. He didn't light it.

"Yeah, okay," he grunted. "So who did?"

Getting a car wasn't easy. I had to call in my op Mike Manetti, who had a spare key to my Galaxie 500. I'd worked with Mike at the

Always Reddy Detective Agency, and he never disappointed me with his displays of sloppiness, impatience, ignorance, and general obtuseness. I thought having my own shingle would rid me of him, but his low salary worked well with my start-up bank account. Plus, I was determined to make a detective out of him.

Weisnecki insisted that we proceed alone. My original suggestion had us reuniting with Duke Wellington, who, in addition to being my paying client, was going to be none to happy to be cut out of the action. Going after Small-Tooth Kelley without police backup was a fool's game, especially with the condition we were in.

"Ben, I'm not going to lie to you: enough of my boys at the station are in the pocket; so, for something like this, I don't know who to turn to."

"That include DW?"

"No, of course not. That guy is straight as a razor. A little too straight. I'm thinking we might have to do things a little off the book if we want to set things right. I don't want to be the one to get his hands dirty."

"And you don't mind about my hands."

"I don't."

My amped-up adrenaline helped convince me of Mark's barn-burner plan. So when Manetti arrived with my ride, I kicked him to the curb and left him in a cloud of dirt and exhaust. He could walk back. He was young.

Small-Tooth Kelley's hideout sat sandwiched between a used tire shop and a Mexican seafood restaurant. The pink stucco storefront had bars on the windows and door. Hand-painted near the entrance in clashing red paint were the words: *Paca Party Rents & Sells*.

The front looked less than hospitable. We wandered around the back, a small alley framed by landscaped weeds and wildflowers. From behind this overgrowth, we spied a delivery truck pulling into the back loading dock.

A large metal roll-up door on the dock slowly yawned open. Out walked Buck Bixel. The baggy fabric of his oversized suit flapped loudly in the evening wind. He handed the driver—a grubby immigrant with a mean, grubby face—a bunch of cash. The driver weaseled away saying something about going to get some fish tacos.

A loud rumble echoed in the alley as Bixel threw open the truck's back. Weisnecki and I crept over. With our heads close to the big tires, we could see Bixel's feet as he began to unload the cargo.

I waited until he was walking away from the truck. I came up behind him and kicked at the back of his left knee as hard as I could. He dropped the large box he was carrying. I heard the crunch of broken glass under the howl of pain. While he was low, I wrapped an arm around his neck, put his head in a half-nelson. I squeezed real good. Even with the blown knee, he tried to toss me. Weisnecki came up around him and started the punching bag routine on his flabby abs.

"Go to sleep, big boy," I whispered in his ear. With the fight gone from him, Bixel succumbed to my sleep hold. He collapsed in my arms, so I dropped him, let him fall to the ground hard.

"That's quite the stash of party supplies," Weisnecki said as he delivered a parting kick to Bixel's midsection. I looked in the back of the truck. True enough, it was filled with new TVs, state-of-the-art stereos, and other hi-fi equipment. All hot.

We climbed the few stairs to the loading ramp. To the right was a long hallway. Next to that, a single door labeled: *Mail Room.*

I put an ear to the thin wood, heard Zef Ehrenreich's distinctive whine. I knocked.

"Yeah? It's open," Zef called out from behind the door.

Weisnecki smiled, knocked again.

"Bixie, ya overgrown galloop, it ain't locked or nothin'!"

We took a step back, waited for the door to open. When it did, I pistol-whipped Ehrenreich's cranium, sending his tiny bowler hat spinning to the ground.

Inside, the small room reeked of cheap tobacco, but held nothing of importance. No sense ransacking the sea of papers on the fold-out card table. We had a bigger fish to catch.

Back to the hallway. It narrowed down as we slowly made our way into the building. At the end it switched left for an even longer stretch. This throughway was filled with piñatas and streamers and half-inflated balloons. Up above, the giant cartoon characters swung from the ceiling, a gallows' party; below, the floor, junked up with yesterday's confetti. It gave the passage a dark, claustrophobic feel, despite all the bright, happy colors. Even more noticeable, the air stank of the heavy smell of balloon rubber.

Mark and I stepped slowly past a series of doors. I checked the ones on the left; he, the right. Each one filled the air with more tension. Listen at the door, turn the knob, listen again, toss the door open. One after another, jammed up with stacks of chairs and folded tables, but otherwise empty. As we went on, the hallway filled with more and more party stuff, so much so that it was hard to tell whether the end of the hall turned left or right.

A hollow metallic clang sounded out behind me. I swung around to look at Weisnecki. He'd bumped into a group of compressed air canisters. That set off some kind of clown automaton, its garish tinny recording echoed out: *HEE-HAR-HAR! HEE-HAR-HAR!*

Weisnecki's hands were on his knees. Seems the fight and the fire had knocked him down more notches than he was willing to admit. I shook my head at him. This was no time to have to rely on a grounded wingman.

"Gun up and man up," I said. "Let's get this job done."

Instead of a smart-aleck response, I was greeted with the shriek of a banshee. Out of the jungle of streamers jumped a topless vixen. She landed square on Weisnecki's back and wrapped her fingers around his throat.

"Party crashers! Party crashers!" she screamed with abandon. I couldn't tell if she was a professional or a lost soul hopped up on headbangers on the wrong way to a good time. What I knew for certain: she only wore purple ruffled panties and hot-pink nail polish—nothing else. And she had a voice box like a she-devil.

Weisnecki choked out a plea for help. He dropped his gun. As she throttled the police officer, her bazoomas bounced aggressively up and down, a Tweedledee/Tweedledum dance that would have hypnotized a lesser man. I was no lesser man. I holstered my gun and pounded at her back, the back of a strong monkey.

Her grip stayed locked like a vise. Pro or no, this girl was on something, something other than Detective Mark Weisnecki. He stumbled back, and I stepped away so that he could slam her once, twice, three times against the cracking drywall.

I was going to pull my gun, when I figured out how to best this bombshell. Honey instead of vinegar, they say. I was neither proud nor embarrassed when I reached up alongside her bare rib cage, found her armpit, and tickled her for all it was worth.

She flinched on command, retracted her left arm enough for me to grab it and spin it up around her back. More screaming. This time, real pain.

I heard a door slam behind us. I swore loud and hard. This go-girl was a full-stop setup. Small-Tooth Kelley was going to waltz right out of here.

"Heave-ho, man!" I yelled at Mark, as I twisted the girl's wrist with all I had. He bucked his bronco best. This crazy lady back-flipped off him and landed, motionless, in a belly flop right on the floor. Ouch.

Weisnecki was still gasping for air when I pulled him by the collar. "Come on! We're losing him."

"You ain't losing nothing, Drake. Except your life! You owe me!"

I knew the rat that went with that cheese. His small-tooth grin spread wide on his narrow face. He held a Thompson submachine gun.

Both Weisnecki and I raised our hands in the air. He had dropped his gun and I had holstered mine in the girl fight. That dame had done us good.

"And you, Weisnecki! I thought you were going to be a smart cop and let me run the show." Kelley bounced the barrel of the gun between Weisnecki's chest and mine.

"Listen to me, Kelley," Weisnecki said slowly. "There's a line. Everyone in this city knows it. Lots of people like to dance up close to it, peer over the edge." He lowered his hands.

"What kinda nonsense you goin' on about?"

Weisnecki ignored him. "You're going to kill us? Kill me? You're going to shoot a cop with an assault weapon?" He started walking forward.

"Hold it right there, copper!" Small-Tooth Kelley started to quiver ever so slightly.

Weisnecki continued: "If I'm dead, I won't be the one who gets you. But believe me, brother, someone's coming for you. And he's going to bring you down, down, down ..." He stopped talking and stopping walking. The three of us stood there. A triangle of silence.

I saw what Weisnecki's plan was, and I slowly moved toward the opposite edge of the hallway, trying to keep my eyes on Small-Tooth so I wouldn't give anything away. He wasn't even looking at me, he was too heated up on Weisnecki's hype.

"I don't like all this talk. I'm a man of action!" I could hear the doubt in Small-Tooth's voice. Especially when he was cut off by a tinny sound behind him.

HEE-HAR-HAR! HEE-HAR-HAR!

The gangster froze, uncertain whether to look back or keep his aim on us. His hesitation would be his downfall. I had learned long ago that it's the small things that matter, that determine what kind of man you are.

BLAM. A single shot sounded out. Kelley's small teeth would grin no more. His lifeless body thumped to the ground. Behind him stood Duke Wellington.

"You took your goddamn good time getting in that shot, partner," Weisnecki said as he stumbled down the hallway.

The big detective raced right up to his partner and wasted no time reading him the riot act: "Hail Mary, Mother of God, give me patience with this man! You disappear without one word, then still expect me to come racing in to save your scrawny hide at the very last second?" DW built his rant to a crescendo. "In what plane of reality are you existin' in which *you* are criticizin' *me* for this here rescue? If it wasn't for that Manetti yoohoo tippin' me off on you and lone wolf's crazy-man plan, you'd be a flesh bag fulla bullets."

The two cops began to bicker. I thought about butting in to tell DW how much he owed me, but better to toss him an invoice in the mail. Some things never change.

I made my way out toward my car. The Testacy City sun sat low in the sky, casting a burnt-orange glow all around. Twilight always got me thinking about the end of things. Silhouette heroes riding off into the horizon. Masked adventurers with capes billowing in the wind. Some stories end the way you want them to, and a bunch of others don't. There are stories that don't end at all, not really. These are the stories you have to walk out of, force the hand of fate, look that old girl right in the kisser and say good night, sweetheart.

KIND WORDS

*Reflections on Fifteen Years
of By the Balls and UglyTown*

During the fifteen years since Ugly Town first released *By the Balls*, we have been very fortunate to get to know—and even work with—a great group of writers, editors, and artists.

So instead of asking for simple blurbs from today's biggest names, we sent out a request for a contribution of any kind to this select group of raconteurs, and in return received quite an outpouring of stories, memories, hype, and new love—all very humbling.

If our introduction to this collection tells the secret history of how and why we did what we did, then this afterword is the war record of the result: what it was like on the street, at the stores, and in the bars during the heyday of UglyTown.

MARK HASKELL SMITH
Author of *Heart of Dankness*, *Baked*, and *Salty*

I first laid eyes on the UglyTown boys at some forgotten book event at a now-defunct bookstore. They were slouching by the door, looking like some kind of Weimar Republic punk rock cabaret act—the Sex Pistols drawn by David Mazzucchelli. They rocked cheap suits and cheaper beer. Fassbender looked like a pit boss from Reno and smelled like Aqua Velva. Pascoe had dyed his hair the color of a

ChemLawn golf course. They were troublemakers, pulp fiction maniacs who published cool-looking books by cool writers no one had heard of. (I was instantly desperate to be published by them.) They were writers too. They'd written a book called *By the Balls* that wasn't even about testicles or scrotums or anything that you'd normally associate with that title and crime fiction. It was a detective novel about bowling and they didn't give a fuck what you thought about it. The world needs more people like them.

GREGG HURWITZ

Author of twelve novels including *The Survivor*

The UglyBoys rolled into a dreary gray landscape jacked up on style and color and flare, steampunk rockstars with Underwoods. I remember those early books—not just how they looked, but how they *felt*, slick enough for slicksters and packed wall-to-wall with badass. I keep 'em on my shelves when they're not busy leaping off.

JAMES A. OWEN

Author of *Drawing Out the Dragons:*
A Meditation on Art, Destiny, and the Power of Choice

UglyTown was, and remains, one of the best examples I know of the perfect execution of a specific creative vision. For a couple of passionate, driven, ambitious guys like Jim and Tom to jump headfirst into a publishing venture designed around their own unique interests took, well, balls. Publishing books that could not be categorized—and if they could be were basically pulp crime noir, and thus difficult to market—took guts. And doing it well, producing works that were sparely elegant, beautifully direct, and absolutely true to their original intent . . . Well. That's simply brilliant.

MARK COGGINS
Author of the August Riordan Series and the memoir
Prom Night and Other Man-Made Disasters

Welcome to Testacy City: diamond of the desert. Only UglyTown boys Jim Pascoe and Tom Fassbender could have created the town and the private eye in it: cigar-smoking, Kant-reading, bourbon-drinking, Galaxie 500-driving Benjamin Drake.

With their ear for snappy dialogue, ability to conjure arch characters like ball bearing bigwig Jack Walker, and their well-developed neo-noir sensibilities—reflected in everything from the plot built around a murder in a bowling alley, to the design and illustration of the first edition, to the fashion sense they displayed at book signings—they made *By the Balls* a pulp fiction classic in the *Black Mask* tradition.

DENISE HAMILTON
Author of *Damage Control*, five novels in the Eve Diamond series, and editor of
Los Angeles Noir and *Los Angeles Noir 2: The Classics*

I met Jim and Tom at a Bouchercon World Mystery convention eleven years ago and immediately gravitated toward these snappy dressers with the punky demeanor and old-school noir aesthetic. Oh, and the green hair. Jim was sporting a kelly-green mop that month. Tom wore a skinny tie. When they told me they were indie publishers and the name of their outfit was UglyTown, well, I was hooked. I also knew a good yarn when I heard it, so I promptly wrote their story up for the *Los Angeles Times*.

In doing so, I also read three or four of their books, marveling at the retro-pulpy covers, the humor, intelligence, and design chops that went into making books like *By the Balls* and *Five Shots and a Funeral* artifacts at every level. And it hit me that UglyTown was filling an important publishing niche, both for authors and the reading public. They were bringing out edgy, noiry guttersnipe crime fiction that the big publishers, with their more conservative, establishment tastes, would probably have run away from screaming because they Just Didn't Get It.

UglyTown was a breath of fresh air for me, an electric jolt that reminded me what simple, balls-out fun crime writing and reading could be. The entire enterprise filled me with glee and delight with its seat-of-the-pants, outlandish, bawdy, blackly humorous, and seriously twisted plots. Being on the periphery of the UglyTown world was the literary equivalent of hanging out backstage with the Talking Heads or The Clash. Jim and Tom and their stable were serious comic book/art/design nerds who gathered like minds around them.

These guys also had an ear for finding good writing from the slush pile. Who can forget the great Victor Gischler's opening line in one of UglyTown's first books, *Gun Monkeys*: "I turn the Chrysler onto the Florida Turnpike with Rollo Kramer's headless body in the trunk, and all the time I'm thinking I should have put some plastic down."

Judges felt the exuberance too and rewarded it accordingly—*Gun Monkeys* was a finalist for an Edgar Award. It would be the first of many coups for UglyTown over the years. So I'm delighted to see that UglyTown is back courtesy of another rocking indie publisher, Akashic Books. A shotgun wedding made in pulpy noir heaven.

SCOTT MORSE
Graphic novel author and Pixar filmmaker

Unless you've picked up a seven-ten split, you're not likely to feel a sense of wonder as palpable as this beauty of noir. Pascoe and Fassbender deliver a punch of nostalgic flair as strong as three fingers of Old Grand-Dad, as Pope drips his periodic atmosphere to punctuate the madness. Make your other books jealous they've got to share the spotlight on their shelf with this monster of mayhem.

BILL FITZHUGH
Author of *Pest Control* and *Cross Dressing*

Fassbender? You're talking about the actor guy in *Inglourious Basterds*? Oh, wait, no, you mean the guy who hooked up with Pascoe, did the whole UglyTown thing. Sure, yeah, I remember them. Something a little off about that pair. Can't put a finger on it sitting here but yeah, I remember them. Hustlers, but in a good way. Publishers, also in a good way. Had that logo, like a half-Chinese Sherlock Holmes with Will Smith's ears, big pipe and a derby, standing in front of some buildings with the rays of the sun, I guess it was, fanned out in the background. Never knew what that was supposed to be but I liked it. Way I heard it, they got fucked by the distribution end of things, that old story. Of course, for all I know, that could have been all horse shit to cover for embezzlement or god knows what, a ten-thousand-dollar-a-day coke habit, or maybe they were doling out hundred-thousand-dollar advances. I'm kidding, nobody does that. Anyway, Fassbender and Pascoe were a stylish pair of jacks. Inglourious Basterds too, as far as that goes. So, anyway, yeah, I remember them, why you bringing them up? They in trouble for something? Wouldn't surprise me a bit. Give 'em my regards. Tell 'em I said, Good luck.

LAUREN HENDERSON

Author of *Flirting In Italian*, *Kiss Me, Kill Me*, and *The Black Rubber Dress*
(and better known as the bonkbuster author Rebecca Chance)

It wasn't the sight of Tom Fassbender and Jim Pascoe that made me spit out my drink all over the big, horseshoe-shaped bar of the Adam's Mark Hotel in Denver: that was a barman who thought you made a white wine spritzer with lemonade instead of soda. I remember John Connolly and Dennis Lehane laughing like drains as the poor barman grabbed my glass back, utterly embarrassed, and then had to clean out all of the little olive and maraschino cherry containers, into which my mouthful of white wine and lemonade had landed. Thank goodness, then, that just as a new drink was set in front of me, the UglyBoys walked into the bar, all dapper suits and brightly dyed hair, and immediately everyone forgot about my high-trajectory spit and focused on them instead.

Nothing like them had ever been seen at a crime convention before. Male crime writers and publishers aren't the nattiest of dressers, and I distinctly remember hearing an older male bookseller bitch jealously about "upstart young guys with blue hair." But the UglyBoys were the opposite of upstarts. They were there, I think, to publicize *By the Balls*, and to look for new authors, but they were utterly, charmingly unpushy. My abiding memory of their comportment at the convention—during the day, at any rate—was of them standing or sitting beside each other, entirely composed, calm and focused, their hands folded in front of them or in their laps. I'm sure it was I who went up to them and introduced myself: I was dying to meet them. They were the soul of politeness and affability. I think Jim had green hair then, and Tom blue streaks, the perfect contrast to their sharply tailored suits. I saw them as the incarnation of a certain LA style, nouveau dandies who, Beau Brummell-like, let their clothes speak for them. They were certainly not strutting peacocks.

It was my favorite Bouchercon ever, and the UglyBoys were an essential part of that. We hung out one evening—Thursday?—drinking in the bar. I remember them ordering Ketel One martinis, the first time I had ever heard someone specifying the brand of vodka they wanted: LA-style again, ahead of the rest of the country, perhaps even the world. The next morning I had a panel. To my great pleasure, as the panelists all trooped in, I saw the UglyBoys had not only turned up, despite the late night we'd all had, but were sitting right in the front row, bless them, smart-suited and self-possessed as ever. No friends, before or since, have ever sat in the front row at a panel of mine; I cannot say how much I appreciated the gesture, how lovely it was to see sympathetic faces laughing at your jokes and nodding gravely as they agreed with the points I was making. (Even if they didn't, it was hugely appreciated.)

That evening we all went out—I think it was that evening, but it may have been Saturday. We found an Irish pub in Denver, which had never seen anything like us: Jim and Tom in their sartorial splendor, me in a black silk fringed dress with Chinese embroidery, and Gary Phillips, who I'm sure was the only black guy in the bar. Some man came over to ask us if we were part of a circus. I told him that Gary and I had just eloped and that the UglyBoys had been our witnesses. This made Gary smile widely and edge as far away from me as he could get, just in case I threw myself upon him to prove the point. John Connolly turned up, having just won a Shamus, and

I was sure that the bar would keep serving us even though it technically closed at twelve—after all, John was an authentic Irishman flourishing an award with an Irish name.

But no. We were chucked out on the street at 12:10, roaming the empty wastes of Denver by night, looking for somewhere which would take us in, but all we found, after what seemed like a very long walk to me in my high-heeled sandals, was a brightly lit diner. It didn't serve alcohol, but Gary was insisting loudly that he needed to eat something, *now*, so in we went, only to discover that it was the gathering place for all the disaffected youth of Denver. Pretty little girls and boys with carefully placed piercings and equally carefully ripped clothes stared at our group, their mouths open in shock. Two girls in the toilet asked where I was visiting from, and when I said London and New York, one started to cry, saying how much she wanted to visit those cities. Gary proceeded to put away a double stack of pancakes smothered in maple syrup, which made John—I think it was John—proclaim incipient nausea and hold his laminated menu over his face. On the way back to the hotel, seeing that my heels were killing me, Jim chivalrously carried me the last two blocks. It was one of those random, hilarious nights that so rarely happen, when a group finds itself in utter humorous harmony; John and I loudly bantering, Gary dropping in dry observations between pancakes, Jim and Tom expertly feeding the flames. We never stopped laughing. They were simply perfect company.

I fell in love with the UglyBoys that night, but then I think we all did; I remember so many people talking about how funny, how nice, how unpretentious, and how clever they were. If I had known then that they would barely be back to future Bouchercons, that we wouldn't hang out like that for years to come, a group of metropolitan sophisticates roaming strangely shuttered American cities that, for the hours they kept, might as well have been small towns, making our own entertainment, finding amusement in the eccentricities of every new locale, I would have been heartbroken.

They were the first Los Angelenos that I met, and they turned out to have given me a rather over-elevated idea of their city's populace: when I eventually visited to pitch a movie, I was very disappointed that LA's denizens weren't more—well, Ugly. But I had a lovely meal out with Jim and Gabrielle, his gorgeous wife, who took me and my agent to an old-school cocktail bar where they got the pianist to sing "New York, New York" in my honor, and later Tom and Jim visited New York and stayed in my apartment. I went to sleep at my boyfriend's place, to give the men a bed each, and Tom rang me there the first full day they were visiting to ask me where my iron was. I told him I didn't have one, but that there was a dry cleaners round the corner that would iron anything he needed. There was a sharp intake of breath at the first part of the sentence; I don't think he even heard the second half.

When I returned to the apartment, I found that Tom had bought me an iron "as a house present." Clearly, he had been unable to bear the thought of not being able to iron his shirts to his own precise specifications. They'll be dandies to the last, the UglyBoys. Buried in tailor-made suits that fit them perfectly. And despite their lack of peacocking, they do know how good they look. They wouldn't have called their company UglyTown otherwise, after all . . .

SCOTT ALLIE

Editor in chief, Dark Horse Comics

Reading *By the Balls* marked the beginning of one of my ongoing policies, which serves me well to this day: if someone has written one thing that blew me away, I will move heaven and earth to work with that writer. I don't have to read everything from a writer, because it's pretty hard to make that big an impression on me, and if lightning struck once, I'm willing to gamble it'll strike again for me. For the UglyTown boys, it struck for a second time with *Five Shots and a Funeral*. Why did I think their ability to create a fresh take on pulpy crime prose would translate to *Buffy the Vampire Slayer* comics? The UglyTown work showed their ability to get inside an idea, to put their colorful, loud personalities aside and commit to the work. We spent a couple years doing those *Buffy* comics, before they decided to move on to other things, and those colorful, loud personalities made for a lot of good times.

Sean Doolittle
Author of *Lake Country*, *Safer*, *The Cleanup*, *Burn*, and *Dirt*

Awhile back I took a spin by the UglyTown.com website, my former home base. I wanted to see what the old stomping ground looked like after all these years. What I found was a bare-bones photostream hosted by agents unknown. Ironically—or maybe fittingly, depending your view—the first image I plucked from that stream depicted a dreary gray office building on a dreary gray street, in a dreary gray city, somewhere in the overcast West Country of England, all tagged with the following brief caption: *A town destroyed by modern architects.*

Instantly my nostalgia tripled for the vivid yellow streets of the UglyTown I remembered: its quirky swagger, its high-style juxtapositions, its energetic boomtown vibe. I wasn't the only young prospector to stumble out of the desert and set up a stake there, but I was one of the lucky first, and I'll never forget my initial trip out to the ore seams that started the place: one book called *By the Balls*, and another called *Five Shots and a Funeral*, both written by Dashiell Loveless, the shared alter-ego of town fathers Tom Fassbender and Jim Pascoe. I remember thinking, gratefully, *Here's the place I've been looking for.*

So what the hell happened? Where did it all go? What damned fool modern architects came along and turned the rootinest, tootinest indie burg this side of Testacy City into a stripped-down online slideshow from a collection of strangers?

Nothing happened. Nobody went anywhere. Nobody touched a thing. Because UglyTown wasn't a location, it was an idea—the vision of two guys with an inspiring, invigorating, sometimes alarming combined sense of fashion and manifest destiny. And nowhere is that idea more clearly preserved than right here, in these two books, presented together, the way they belong.

It's *so* nice to see the place again.

Victor Gischler
Author of *The Deputy*, *Go-Go Girls of the Apocalypse*, *Pistol Poets*, and *Gun Monkeys*

The Internet is amazing. You can explore the whole world in your boxer shorts. This is exactly what I was doing nearly fifteen years ago. I had a manuscript, wanted a publisher, and knew next to nothing about the publishing industry.

At the time of writing this reflection, I am an agented author who writes for a living. It's how I pay the mortgage and feed my family. These considerations were the furthest thoughts from my mind as I was trying to find a publisher for my first novel. I mean, yes, the dream clunked around somewhere in the back of my brain, the distant idea that I could actually be a professional writer, but my sincere goal at the time was just to get my name on the cover of a book. The notion that I could walk into a bookstore and pull a paperback off the shelf with my name on it literally made me giddy.

But I felt strongly that not just any publisher would do. I needed a publisher with *attitude*. Some guys who shared the same irreverent streak for violent, crazy pulp fiction. When I saw the words *By the Balls* accompanied by Paul Pope's great pulp cover, I felt sure I'd located kindred spirits. These were guys, I imagined, who were serious about putting out kick-ass books while not wallowing in literary self-importance. In short, they seemed to be the publishers with the attitude I was looking for. I wrapped up my first manuscript—a collection of linked short stories about a detective who took supernatural cases—and sent it off to Los Angeles. And then something great happened.

They rejected me.

Okay, that's not the great part. But in an atmosphere where new, unagented authors were being swatted away like annoying mosquitoes, UglyTown took me seriously. They didn't accept my manuscript, but neither did they ignore me, and for a rookie author trying to break in, that's no small thing. When I immediately sent them the manuscript for my first novel, *Gun Monkeys*, we made a connection, and I was on my way to seeing my name on the cover of a book.

What you're holding in your hands is the reprint of *By the Balls*, and I'm here to tell you it was more than just a great fun pulp read when it first came out. It was a beacon for writers and readers like me who were looking for a publisher with that certain attitude. The original paperback, reminiscent of an old pulp mapback, signaled clearly to the world just what they were getting into when they read an UglyTown publication. Publishers large and small have risen and fallen since those original days of *By the Balls,* but none have been quite like UglyTown—although at least one publisher has admitted to me at a convention that he looked to UglyTown as an inspiration.

Now you, lucky reader, have a chance to glimpse what those heady days must have been like. Read. Enjoy.

CURT COLBERT

Author of *Queer Street, Sayonaraville, Rat City*; editor of *Seattle Noir;* and coauthor of the new Barking Detective mystery series

My introduction to the publisher UglyTown was anything but ugly. I'd just parted ways with my agent after my first private detective novel was turned down by most of the major publishers. So I started looking for a publisher on my own—a publisher that might appreciate a 1940s-style private detective novel.

Raymond Chandler gave this advice about writing a hard-boiled thriller: "When in doubt, have a man come through a door with a gun in his hand." Well, I was in doubt about ever getting published when *Publishers Weekly* came through my door with an article about UglyTown and the two-fisted, hard-boiled books that its founders had coauthored: *By the Balls* and *Five Shots and a Funeral.* Written in a 1940s style, they featured a hard-charging private dick named Benjamin Drake. Fassbender and Pascoe were kindred spirits and I had to get their books!

By the Balls had me by the short hairs as soon as I started to read it—same-same for *Five Shots and a Funeral.* The books really lived up to the great reviews they received. They could be read as a straight homage to the noir era PIs, as wickedly playful satire, or both.

In a nutshell, I sent my novel *Rat City* off to UglyTown and it was accepted for publication. Tom and Jim gave me the opportunity to be published and also produced my next two novels over a three-year period. They were, and are, great editors and authors.

And now their Ben Drake stories (and two new ones) are being combined in a single volume from Akashic Books, itself a terrific press led by the talented Johnny Temple whom I had the good fortune to work with when I edited *Seattle Noir* in 2009.

Pascoe, Fassbender, and Temple will make a fantastic team. Lovers of hard-boiled derring-do are in for a real treat. I can't wait to get this edition in my hands!

JON JORDAN

Copublisher and coeditor of *CrimeSpree Magazine*

In the summer of 2001 I went away for the weekend with my wife, and as a result we missed a book signing with a new author named Sean Doolittle. When we returned home, my pal at the bookstore informed me that he'd arranged for me to interview Sean. I was a little put out as I had not read the novel and didn't even know if I would like it. I took home my first book from a publisher called UglyTown and fell in love. Not only was *Dirt* a great book, but it was a great-looking book. I did the interview and became friends with Sean. Fast forward to October, Washington DC, Bouchercon.

The first night of the convention I ran into Sean, a tall guy with a deep voice. He asked if I wanted to meet the publishers, and so I followed Sean to the bar. He introduced me to Jim Pascoe and Tom Fassbender, along with fellow UglyTown author Victor Gischler, who had a book coming out soon. Jim and Tom were both dressed up in great shoes, wonderful smoking jackets, and had dyed hair. They talked fast and I liked them immediately. What really struck me was that these guys had such a great attitude.

Obvious fans of crime fiction, Jim and Tom had an idea of how publishing worked, and they promptly decided that they didn't care. They were going to publish their way. Their way meant damn good-looking books, books you want to own and read and show off. Books that they loved. Over the next year it became obvious that if it said *UglyTown* on it, I would love the book. Everything they did was unique and wonderful.

Without even knowing it, they inspired a whole generation of writers; people saw what they were doing and realized there is more to books than huge office buildings in New York. UglyTown was more than books, it was an attitude, a look, a way of seeing the world. If you've read a small press book in the last ten years, its existence might just be due in part to what UglyTown did.

Tom and Jim wrote a wonderful book themselves, *By the Balls,* under the moniker Dashiell Loveless. A PI novel like something right out of the '40s and set in our time. Funny, fast paced, and wonderfully pulpy. They followed this up with *Five Shots and a Funeral*, a collection of five short stories. People claim to be fans of noir and pulp, but if they haven't read these books they are just pretending. There should be a class that centers on these books and what UglyTown is.

Tom and Jim have gone on to new things, leaving their mark wherever they go. Two cool guys who are just cool—they don't try to be, they just are. To be perfectly honest, reading these two books will make you a bit cooler.

GARY PHILLIPS

Author of *Warlord of Willow Ridge* and editor of *Orange County Noir*

Before I met Jim and Tom I'd bought a copy of *By the Balls*. This would have been at the Mysterious Bookshop on Beverly Boulevard in Los Angeles. Fact, seems to me Shelly McArthur, who ran the place, must have steered me to it among the new books as I wandered about the overstocked shop checking out recent titles one afternoon.

Now I'll admit it wasn't the idea that one Dashiell Loveless was the supposed author, though I found that wordplay intriguing. What really drew me to the book was the cover by Paul Pope, a guy whose style I recognized from his comics work. I figured this UglyTown publisher must be cool if they had the savvy to hire Pope—who it turned out did some interior illustrations for the book as well. How much sweeter was it that I dug the first-person tale Jim and Tom's private eye Ben Drake got immersed in when some nefarious type began bumping off bowlers. Nice.

Lost in my memory bank is how the three of us eventually met, but I distinctly recall how our paths crossed professionally. A few years down the line I'd written an action-adventure novella called *The Perpetrators*. This was for a publisher tapping into the zeitgeist of hip-hopism and had several writers doing books as a kind of homage to Holloway House of the '70s. This was the white outfit here in LA that published the black experience, as they would term it: novels by the men who would become the Godfathers of Ghetto Lit, Donald Goines and Robert Beck a.k.a. Iceberg Slim.

But I was at odds with the publisher over the book. Put simply, the publisher didn't dig the way I'd told the story and I did. Okay, I'm the writer, so of course I'm biased, but I didn't think it was as bad as the publisher did. I made some changes per his suggestions and neither of us were happy with the results.

Somehow or other—and I believe Tom and I had been commiserating the way writers do—the offer was made to give my then orphaned manuscript a read. The UglyTown gentlemen offered me some sound edits that tightened and honed *The Perps*. Post those changes, we were off to the races. How sweet was it that they got Paul Pope to do the eye-catching pop art–style cover and interior illos.

But the best were the bus bench ads UglyTown put up for the book. Fuckin' great. See, that's what can happen when you have publishers who are also talented writers and think with both hats when it comes to promoting their line. While those of us who were published by them and readers alike mourned the passing of the press, we can celebrate the issuance of this definitive volume by Akashic: *By the Balls: The Complete Collection*.

Most excellent all around.

Eddie Muller
Author of *Dark City Dames*, *Dark City: The Lost World of Film Noir*, and *The Distance*

The UglyTown boys were ahead of the curve before anybody knew there was a curve. That was the great glory Tom and Jim shared. It was also, unfortunately, an aspect of their premature demise as publishers. They could sense where the publishing business was headed before there was a route to get there. They had the vision before the new tools existed to properly build it. They mapped the brave new world, but still had to cope with broken and outmoded distribution channels.

My novel, *The Distance*, was the first "reprint" UglyTown ever pub-

lished. Known for their original taste in crime fiction and icono-
clastic approach to its packaging, Tom and Jim had developed their
own stable of authors, like Victor Gischler, Nathan Walpow, Curt
Colbert, Mike Lester. But after we'd drank and caroused together,
developing a terrific rapport and a genuine trust, I wanted the
paperback edition of my first novel—originally published by the esteemed New York house Charles Scribner's Sons—to be produced by
UglyTown.

A lot of people thought I was stupid, opting to go with a tiny
boutique publisher instead of a big New York house. But the writing
was already on the wall for the big boys too. The ship was sinking,
and I preferred to be in a smaller, lighter craft—one with a full bar
and good conversation.

UglyTown compensated for an unsatisfying experience at Scribner's. These guys worked off gut instinct and uncommon clever-
ness. We came up with terrific, fresh ideas for repackaging the book.
Where it took months of painfully slow "communication" with the
various departments at Scribner's to accept or reject an idea, things
happened with Tom and Jim in inspiring bursts of creativity. Working with Jim on the cover design for *The Distance,* we scanned photo
options, e-mailed, designed, reworked, typeset—all in a single phone
call. What would have taken a month or more with Scribner's took
less than an hour with Jim.

We were living in the future, before it had actually arrived.

Okay, boys, let's do something new.

NATHAN WALPOW
Author of *The Manipulated, One Last Hit, Death of an Orchid Lover,*
and *The Cactus Club Killings*

I met the UglyTown boys at the yearly paperback show in the San
Fernando Valley. There, tucked in among the bald and/or gray dealers in the side room, I found two youngsters pitching a couple of
books they'd written: *By the Balls* and *Five Shots and a Funeral.* The kids
were charming and enthusiastic and I bought their books, which
were good and fun and different.

Shortly thereafter they published a Sisters in Crime anthology I had a story in, and it was gorgeously produced, and people started noticing them. Tom and Jim built a reputation as "the future of crime fiction." They found new authors and revitalized old ones, and they got an Edgar Award nomination for *Gun Monkeys*, and when my Joe Portugal series got dropped by a New York monolith, they gave Joe a new home and a chance to appear in two more beautifully realized adventures.

The boys were excellent editors; I got far more useful notes from them, sitting there dodging the noise at Swingers on Beverly Boulevard in Los Angeles, than I ever did from the monolith. And we became friends. My wife and I were around when Tom's first child was born (Frankie!) and when Jim got married. They introduced us to *Iron Chef*. And still each book was more beautiful than the last, and the "mystery community" marveled, and Jim's hair became legend.

That time ended way too soon, victim of a bankrupt distributor and a capricious universe. But I'll always treasure it, and I'll always have my shelf full of elegant, french-flapped prizes to remind me of the UglyTown Days.

BRETT BATTLES
Author of *The Destroyed, No Return, The Silenced,* and *The Cleaner*

For me, it was all about timing.

My UglyTown adventure started at the very end of the company's reign, though I don't think any of us knew it at the time. It started off on the highest of high notes: me sitting at a coffee shop, doing edits on what I thought would be the next novel I sent out on submission; my phone on the table in front of me suddenly ringing with a number I didn't know; and on the other end? Jim Pascoe telling me he wanted to buy the rights to my book. And it seemed to end on the lowest of lows: Jim and Tom coming to the difficult conclusion that UglyTown had to go on what turned out to be a permanent hiatus about four months before my scheduled publication date.

But it didn't actually end on the lowest of lows. What could have been a horrible, gut-wrenching experience, wasn't. Not even close.

Jim and Tom could have abandoned me and concentrated on their own concerns. They had every right to do that. They didn't owe me anything more. In fact, they had already given me a lot by working with me to make my book so much better.

But they didn't abandon me. They did something I will forever be grateful to them for: they passed my book on to an editor at a much larger house, and they sent their highest recommendations with it.

Without their assistance, my publishing career could have very well ended with the closing of the UglyTown doors. It did not. Not by a long shot. So where I am today is due in no small part to Jim and Tom. It's this kindness and advocacy that symbolizes what UglyTown was and remains to me, and I will be thanking the two of them for the rest of my life.

NAOMI HIRAHARA
Author of *Summer of the Big Bachi*, *Gasa-Gasa Girl*, and *Snakeskin Shamisen*

"My friend's husband is starting a publishing house," Martie, a former newspaper coworker, told me one day in the late 1990s. "Something about mysteries."

Say what? We were in Los Angeles, the home of celluloid with little interest in print publication, aside from *Hustler*, *Tiger Beat*, and *Motor Trend* magazines. An actual mystery book publisher? Here in my little hometown?

Working on the same novel since the mid-1980s, I submerged myself in writing communities in hidden margins of the city. A beat-up houseboat in Marina del Rey. A photo gallery with hardwood floors a stone's throw from MacArthur Park. An expansive residence in the Hollywood Hills next door to the director of the Freddy Krueger horror movie franchise. But an honest-to-goodness book publisher? A publisher anchors a writing community. While everything else seems to float by, a publisher has weight.

So when this publishing house had an event at a local crime bookstore in Pasadena, I was there. The name of the house: UglyTown.

The logo: absurd but strong and memorable. The two publishers, cowriters of UglyTown's first two books: Tom Fassbender, a handsome Abe Lincoln-like figure, tall, willowy, and more introverted; and Jim Pascoe, a naughty leprechaun with eyes that danced—I can't remember exactly what color his hair was that day—green, blue?

I bought those two books, *By the Balls* and *Five Shots and a Funeral*. They were paperbacks, small and compact, that felt good in my hands. Collectors would immediately think of the pulps in the 1940s and '50s, but I saw them more in the fashion of Japanese paperbacks. Beautifully designed with fabulous ink drawings by Paul Pope, they were immaculately produced—seams that held together, terse but interesting front matter, vibrant prose that moved the stories of Dashiell Loveless forward.

Was it a send-up to pulp? An homage to Los Angeles? I don't actually think it was either. For one thing, there's the fictional town, Testacy City. There are elements that are familiar—the dame in trouble, the rundown bars—yet there's also something that feels like a parallel universe, almost of another world. The publishers have said it best: "[Dashiell Loveless] exists solely in fiction time . . . the true creator and innovator of the pulp artifact—a novel out of place in time."

At the turn of the twenty-first century, the UglyTown boys were pretty much a fixture of the mystery scene in Southern California. They created fine, beautiful books by other authors as well, with the same consistent attention to detail. My favorites: Sean Doolittle's *Dirt*, Victor Gischler's *Gun Monkeys*, Gary Phillips's *The Perpetrators*, the paperback edition of Eddie Muller's *The Distance*, Nathan Walpow's two Joe Portugal novels, and Curt Colbert's *Sayonaraville*, a mystery which told the story of Japanese Americans in Seattle in the 1940s. What I appreciated, too, was that both Fassbender and Pascoe seemed to really care about their writers, even helping to broker deals with an editor (also my editor!) at Random House for a wider release.

I had always imagined that one of the large New York City publishers would buy the UglyTown brand and whisk these two men to the Big Apple to oversee its operation. That didn't happen. But now we have Akashic Books here breathing new life into UglyTown.

I don't see this reprint as nostalgia. I view it as more of a kick in the pants. You see, as we have been distracted with whatever for the past several years, Testacy City has continued on. *By the Balls: The Complete Collection* will give us a clue of what we have been missing.

ROBERT S. LEVINSON

Author of *Phony Tinsel*, *A Rhumba in Waltz Time*, and *Ask a Dead Man*

The UglyGuys, Jim Pascoe and Tom Fassbender.

Met 'em and learned about their UglyTown publishing operation about a dozen years ago, at one of those Bouchercon conventions designed for mystery authors and fans, not necessarily for the likes of an UglyJim or an UglyTom, who looked as if they'd made a wrong turn heading for a convention where delegates dress up like their favorite comic book or movie characters.

They were impossible not to notice in their retro suits and ties, Runyonesque Warner Bros. movie mobsters on a break from their next bank heist or rub-out or—no, wait a minute—that wouldn't explain UglyJim's punk green hair and loop earrings.

Anyway, you get the idea, right?

So now, while sharing a cocktail-reception wall with them, they're telling me about this UglyTown publishing partnership they've created on a foundation of the mystery novels and short stories they're selling from a card table they've set up in a hotel corridor outside the legit book sales room that costs more than they can afford, hawking their relatively new and rising UglyTalents—names like Victor Gischler, Eddie Muller, Gary Phillips, Nathan Walpow, and Dashiell Loveless.

With the passage of time, those spotlighted author dudes all rose to genre prominence beyond UglyTown, except for Loveless, credited as the author of the imprint's first two titles, *By the Balls* and *Five Shots and a Funeral*, who never existed.

Loveless was the nom de plume UglyTom and UglyJim used on novels and short stories of their own outlandish invention. He went underground about the same time as the economy dove south, pushing UglyTown six feet under and the two publishing Uglies off to other creative pursuits, but—

Whaddaya know?

The great thing about forever is that it doesn't necessarily last forever.

The boys are back in all their pulp glory, along with Dashiell's books and some old and new Loveless short stories, wisely resurrected by publisher Johnny Temple's equally adventurous Akashic Books and hopefully for a longer stay than last time.

KEVIN BURTON SMITH

Founder and editor of the *Thrilling Detective* website

The first UglyTown book I ever saw grabbed me, appropriately enough, by the eyeballs.

There, among all the neat, genteel rows of shiny new mysteries was a rude little paperback that looked like it belonged on a spinner rack in a downtown bus station—fifty years ago.

If ever there was a cover that had been whupped by an ugly stick, this was it. It looked like an ill-conceived Dell Mapback; a phlegm-clearing cascade of pulpy, over-the-top graphic elements and grungy mismatched typefaces that bumped against each other like surly rush hour passengers on a crowded subway car. Even the ink-heavy illustration of a hairy arm gripping a bowling ball—with a skull emblazoned on it—seemed somehow not quite ready for prime time.

By the Balls, the title read, in loud red hand lettering. By Dashiell Loveless.

Hah. Good one. Dashiell Loveless. Was this for real?

Off in the top corner, it proclaimed itself *A Bowling Alley Murder Mystery*. Then down along the right, it said the illustration was by indie comic hotshot Paul Pope, no stranger to ugly himself.

And then, almost as an afterthought, we were told it was written by Jim Pascoe and Tom Fassbender.

Finally, just to make sure nobody could possibly take this seriously, an oversized logo, itself heavy on the cheese, and the proud announcement that it was *An UglyTown Mystery*. Oh, and that there was a "Crime Map" on the back cover.

Of course.

I scanned the first few pages. *What this Mystery is about. List of Exciting Chapters. List of Thrilling Illustrations.*

Was this for real? What were these guys smoking? Benjamin Drake was the hero, one of the *Persons this Mystery is about*. A private dick with "a passion for small cigars and Old Grand-Dad, and a weakness for women in trouble."

No way was I letting this sucker escape. I plunked down my $8.95 (Canadian) and chuckled all the way home.

By the Balls proved to be every bit as audacious and fun as promised, full of mysterious women, gangsters, murder, and . . . um . . . bowling; a two-fisted riff on classic pulp fiction that was as much love letter as lampoon. Evidently Jim and Tom, the evil masterminds behind UglyTown, took this stuff every bit as seriously as I did.

Even better? *By the Balls* was no one-shot effort, but a first spit in the eye of the prim, cloistered world of crime fiction. UglyTown was a real publisher, albeit a selective one, bringing out only a few books a year, but each one a killer. Smart, hard, proud stuff that didn't pull punches, and never took cheap shots, either. Transgressive, I'd call it, if I knew what that meant. They published some great crime books—by Sean Doolittle, Curt Colbert, Eddie Muller, and others.

Tom and Jim kept the overheated pulp look for their own stuff, but all the UglyTown books had great covers—clever and classy designs that set them apart from the mainstream. Endpapers even. Like I said, classy.

And for a few glorious years, UglyTown rode the buzz. Tom and Jim, he of the ever-changing hair hues, were the Belles of the Bouchercon Balls, the Abbott and Costello of Crime Publishing, the Clown Princes of Pulpitude. The future looked bright.

Sadly, distribution was a real bitch. Or maybe they were simply too hip for the room. Whatever. Like Puff, UglyTown simply slipped into its cave.

And now Akashic has gone spelunking, and has dragged *By the Balls: The Complete Collection* up into the light . . .

What can I tell you? Like Tars Tarkas once said, "You are ugly, but you are beautiful."

Welcome back, boys . . .

Benjamin LeRoy

Publisher of Tyrus Books, former publisher of Bleak House Books

Back when things were starting to get off the ground at Bleak House Books, the publishing world felt vast and isolating. My business partner and I were two kids in the middle of flyover country. For a guy who had grown up on a steady diet of punk rock and middle fingers, the big-office, white-gloved approach to literature that I assumed was the domain of folks in NYC was not exactly what I wanted to do. It was my parents. I was an unruly kid.

Metaphorically speaking, salvation would ultimately come in the form of a bus ride west to Los Angeles, like it had for so many aspiring actors and musicians in the past.

It wasn't until I met with Jon and Ruth Jordan of *CrimeSpree Magazine* at an event in my hometown of Madison, Wisconsin that somebody introduced me to the work of UglyTown, an independent press with a home in LA.

Jon told me stories of these two brash but brilliant characters cutting a larger-than-life swath through the crime fiction community. Outrageous suits. Theatrics. Jon told these stories with a gleam in his eye, a clear indication that whatever magic the UglyTown folks were conjuring was contagious in its aftereffects. It was enough to make me go back to the office and hop on the dial-up to see what all the fuss was about.

Let's be honest—American pop culture is littered with gimmicky marketing angles, often enough as a sleight of hand to hide the fact that the end product isn't actually *good*. Any trip to Book Expo America, complete with its collection of people dressed up in gorilla costumes or pacing the show floor with toilet seats around their necks, will show you that the publishing industry is not immune from this, no matter how literate it hopes to be. It was possible Jim and Tom's antics were merely cheap parlor tricks to attract a reading crowd that would ultimately end up disappointed by the books they purchased.

But a quick glance at their website then, and a scan of the authors they published who are still working in today's crime fiction world, would let you know they were on to something and had a genuine eye for talent. Sean Doolittle, Gary Phillips, Victor Gischler (who I would later have the good fortune of publishing at Tyrus), and the list goes on and on. The books published by UglyTown are a lasting testament to their genius.

Without the long distance and, to Tom and Jim, unknowing guidance of UglyTown, I'm not sure that I'd be here today. I needed to know that it was okay to be different in the business world, to carry over a love and appreciation for fringe culture with confidence. In the end, what ultimately mattered was producing books that resonate with others. Jim and Tom set the model for me, and for that, I am forever grateful.

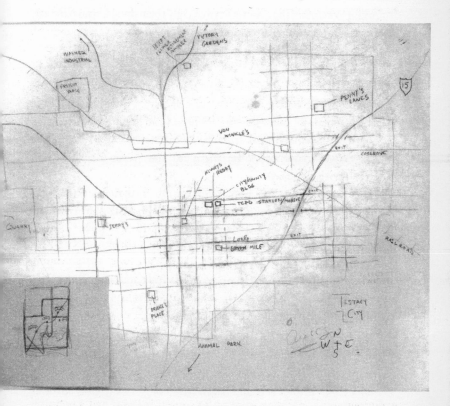

ACKNOWLEDGMENTS

In no particular order, we humbly give our heartfelt thanks to:

Our families, for standing by us through the years and tolerating our eccentricities: Gabrielle, Samantha, Poppy, Frankie, Blaise, and Jackie—you are all very precious to us.

Paul Pope, our blood brother.

The gang at Akashic: Johnny, Johanna, Ibrahim, and Aaron. Great partners, collaborators, and friends.

Chad Hermann, original editor of our first two novels. And the many folks who proofread those works, especially Jackie Estrada and Liesel Schulz.

Adam Waldman, the unsung hero of UglyTown design, who patiently oversaw—and sometimes completely redid—almost all of our book covers, teaching us invaluable lessons along the way.

Leisa Mock, Ryn Speich, Judy Wheeler, and Jeff Scott of Words, our first distributor. They brought us in from the cold, hard world of the wholesaler shuffle to the warm embrace of direct distribution. Words was a family, one we were very proud and honored to be part of.

Our favorite ink-slingers from *Publishers Weekly*: Calvin Reid (who was, is, and will continue to be, the man) and Steven Zeitchik (now with the *Los Angeles Times*).

Heather Harrison, who, upon bumping into us in the elevator of the Westin Bonaventure, gave us our first-ever publishing industry drink tickets. How can you not love that?

Kristin Keith, the first sales rep who really got us.

Dawn Bestafka, our very first printer rep.

Comrades-in-arms Adam Parfrey (Feral House/Process Media), Jodi Wille (Dilettante Press/Process Media), James Walsh (Silver Lake Press), and Mark Anderson (Ten Speed Press).

The three Sarahs (it was a very confusing time around the office): Sarah Ciston, our beleaguered editorial intern (and the best intern two guys could have asked for); Sara Frank, our dedicated and creative Phoenix Color printer rep; and Sarah Rosenberg, our tireless advocate at PGW.

UglyTown was fortunate to have a lot of support from booksellers all over the world. Independent bookstores, especially mystery stores, kept us going and inspired us to tell great stories and make great books. There is a small group of booksellers who backed us from day one, and each has our eternal thanks: Malcolm and Christine Bell of Mystery and Imagination; Barry Martin of Book'Em; Sheldon McArthur of the Mystery Bookstore; Kerry Slattery of Skylight Books; J.B. Dickey of the Seattle Mystery Bookshop, who we never met face-to-face but rallied behind us anyway; Linda Bivens of Crime Time Books, now closed, but it's where we held our first signing; Maryelizabeth Hart of Mysterious Galaxy; and Ed Kaufman of M is for Mystery.

And finally, we thank all of the people who took the time to write some kind words about us. If you haven't read them, please do.

UGLYTOWN